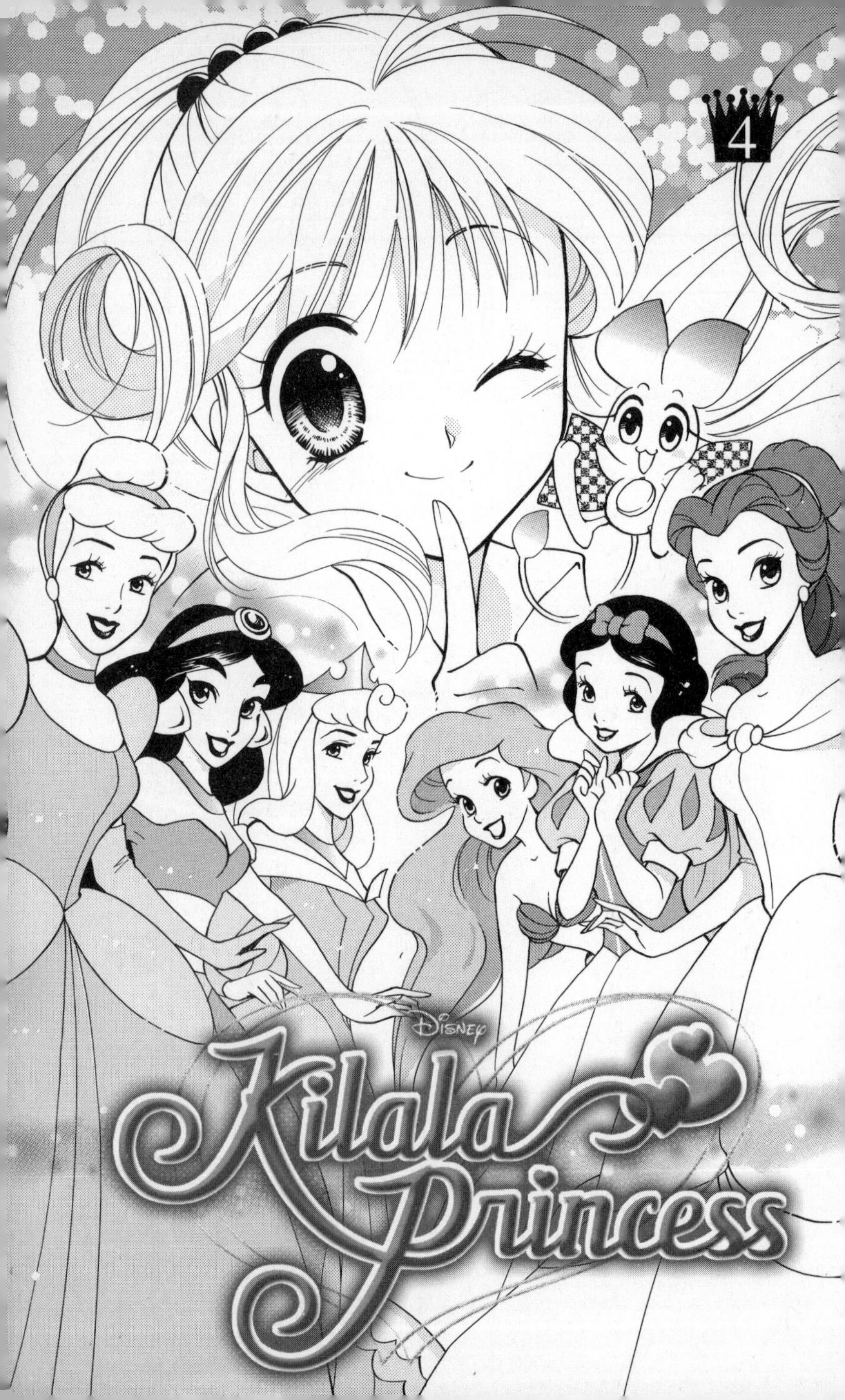
4
Disney
Kilala Princess

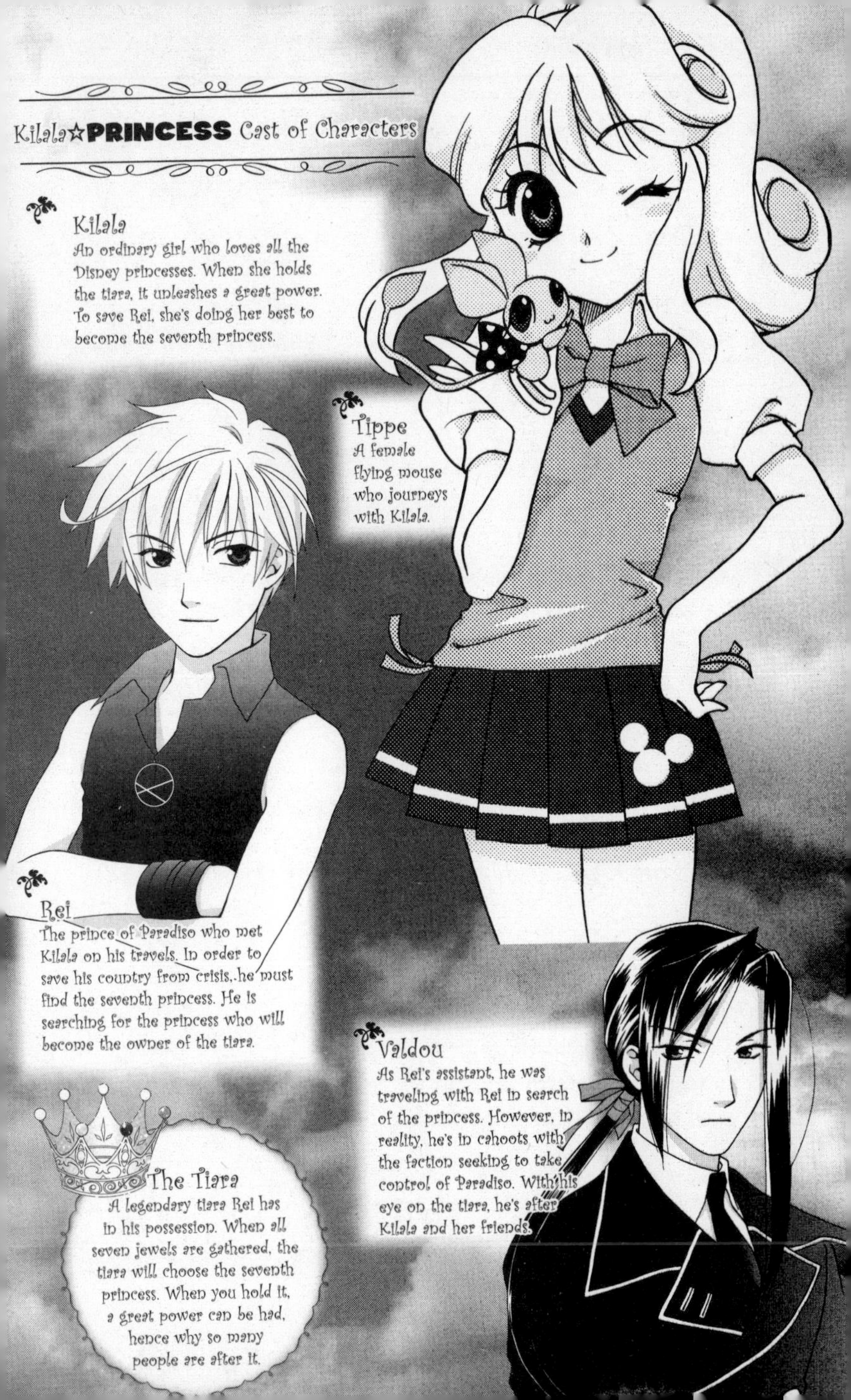

Kilala☆PRINCESS Cast of Characters

Kilala
An ordinary girl who loves all the Disney princesses. When she holds the tiara, it unleashes a great power. To save Rei, she's doing her best to become the seventh princess.

Tippe
A female flying mouse who journeys with Kilala.

Rei
The prince of Paradiso who met Kilala on his travels. In order to save his country from crisis, he must find the seventh princess. He is searching for the princess who will become the owner of the tiara.

Valdou
As Rei's assistant, he was traveling with Rei in search of the princess. However, in reality, he's in cahoots with the faction seeking to take control of Paradiso. With his eye on the tiara, he's after Kilala and her friends.

The Tiara
A legendary tiara Rei has in his possession. When all seven jewels are gathered, the tiara will choose the seventh princess. When you hold it, a great power can be had, hence why so many people are after it.

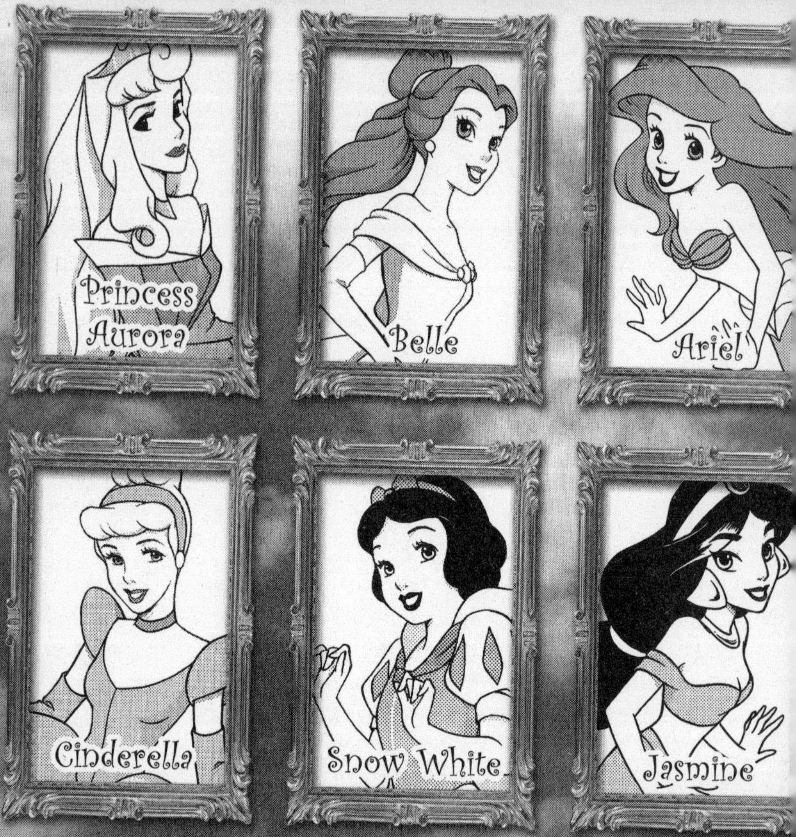
Princess Aurora
Belle
Ariel
Cinderella
Snow White
Jasmine

Story so far:

♦Kilala, a young girl who idolizes princesses, meets Rei and instantly her destiny awakens in a big way. Led by the mysterious tiara Rei possesses, Kilala finds herself in the worlds of the Disney princesses!

♦When Kilala gets lost in the world of Snow White, she defeats the evil queen and gains a jewel for the tiara: ruby. At the bottom of the ocean with Ariel, she battles the sea witch and receives the second jewel: aquamarine. In Cinderella's world, she saves Cinderella from her wicked stepmother and is given a diamond.

♦But there are other villains who have their eye on the mysterious powers the tiara possesses. Kilala resolves to become the seventh princess and save the world and departs on a journey to track down the fourth jewel. But who will the fourth princess be...?

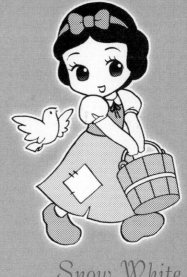

Snow White

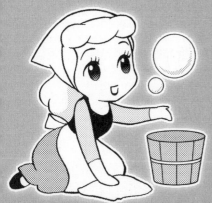

Cinderella

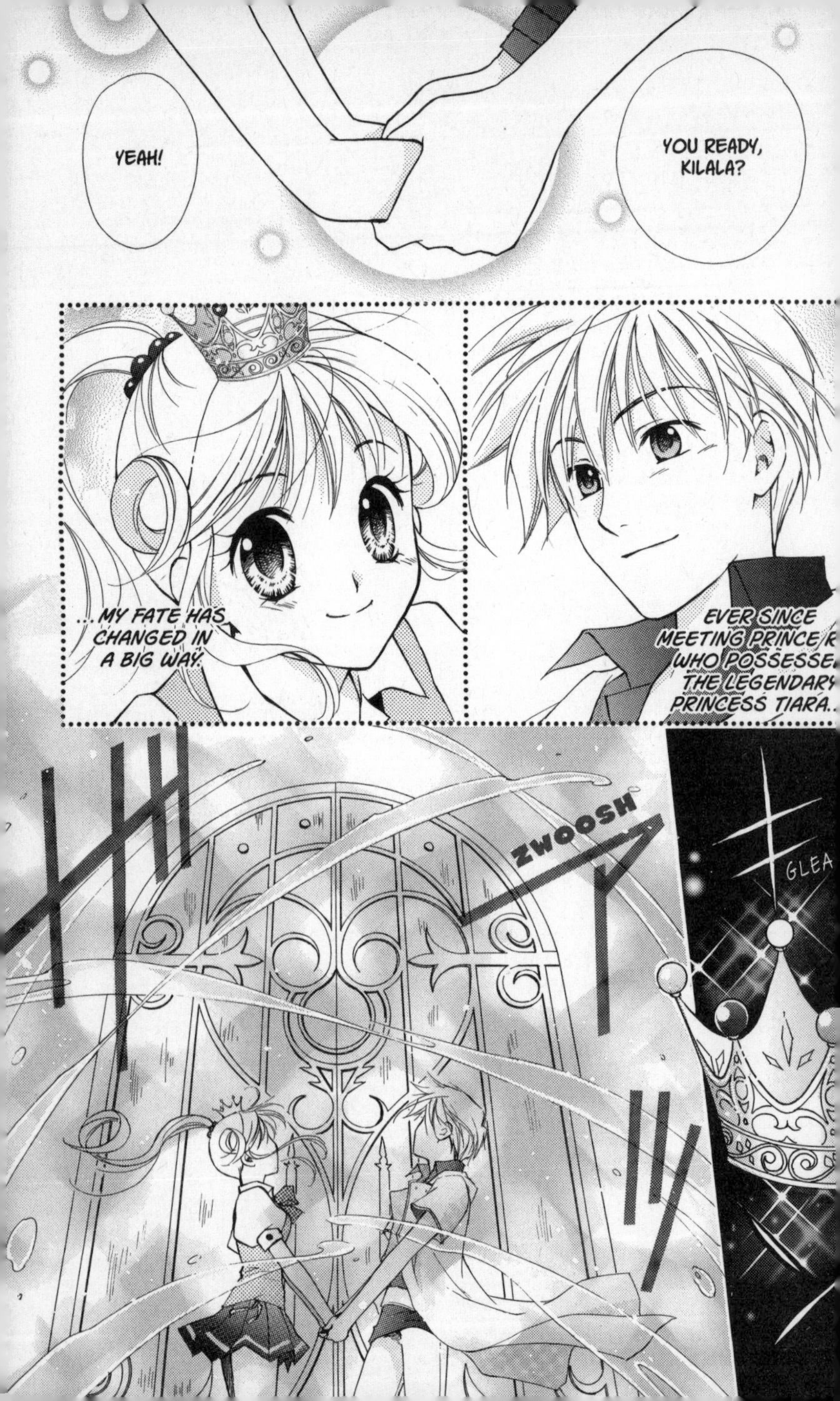
YOU READY, KILALA?
YEAH!
EVER SINCE MEETING PRINCE R WHO POSSESSE THE LEGENDARY PRINCESS TIARA...
...MY FATE HAS CHANGED IN A BIG WAY.
GLEA
ZWOOSH

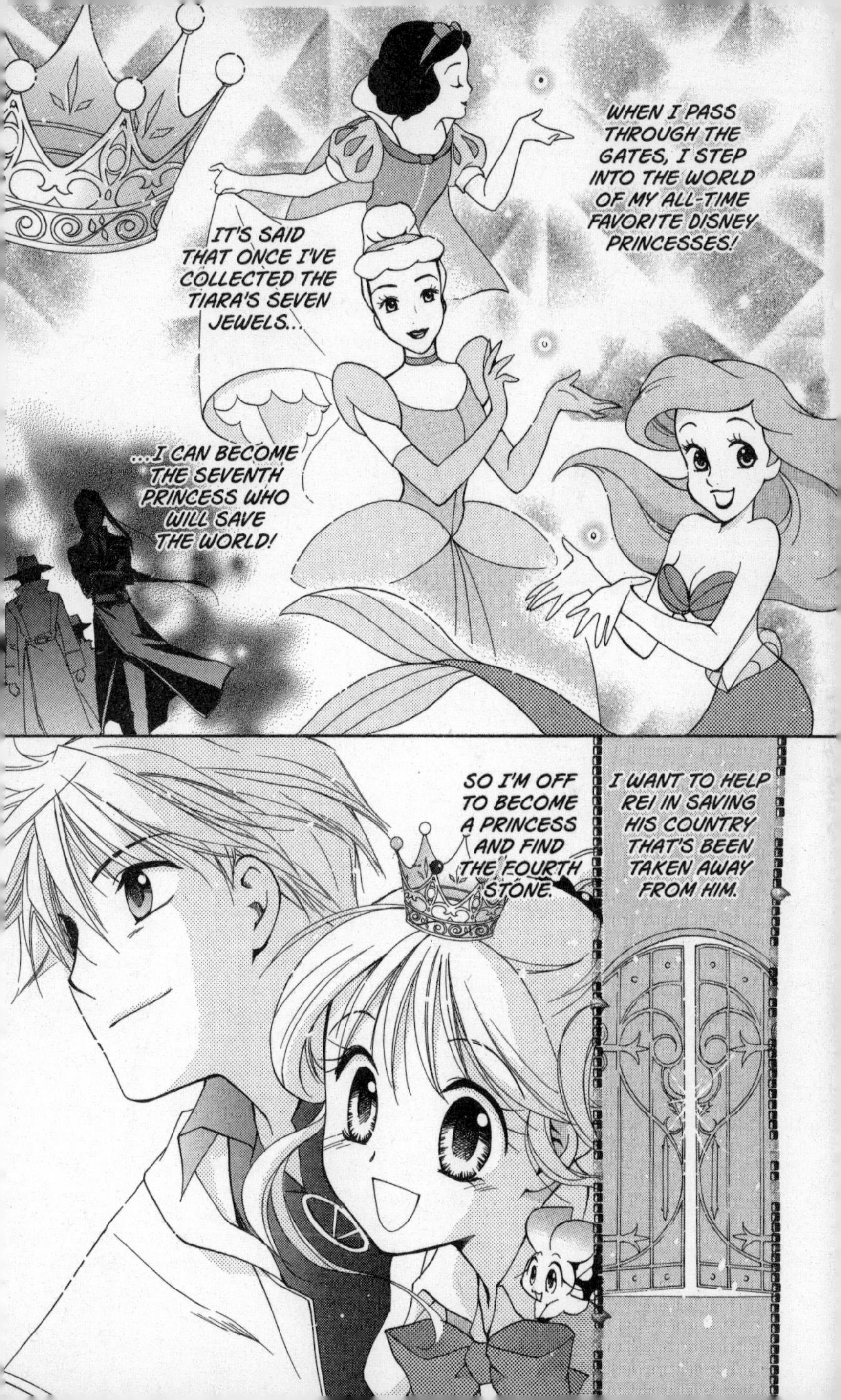
WHEN I PASS THROUGH THE GATES, I STEP INTO THE WORLD OF MY ALL-TIME FAVORITE DISNEY PRINCESSES!
IT'S SAID THAT ONCE I'VE COLLECTED THE TIARA'S SEVEN JEWELS...
...I CAN BECOME THE SEVENTH PRINCESS WHO WILL SAVE THE WORLD!
I WANT TO HELP REI IN SAVING HIS COUNTRY THAT'S BEEN TAKEN AWAY FROM HIM.
SO I'M OFF TO BECOME A PRINCESS AND FIND THE FOURTH STONE.

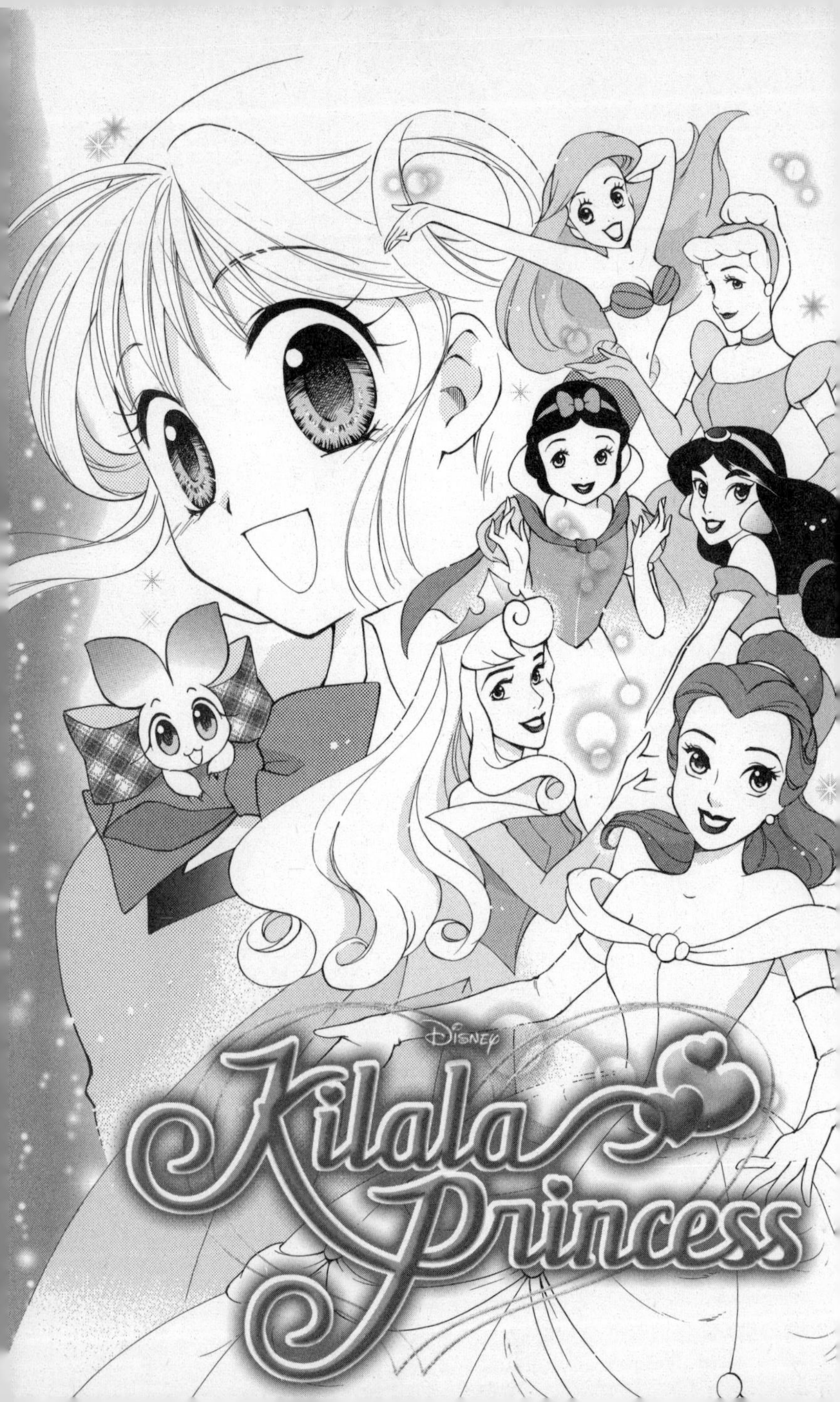
Disney
Kilala Princess

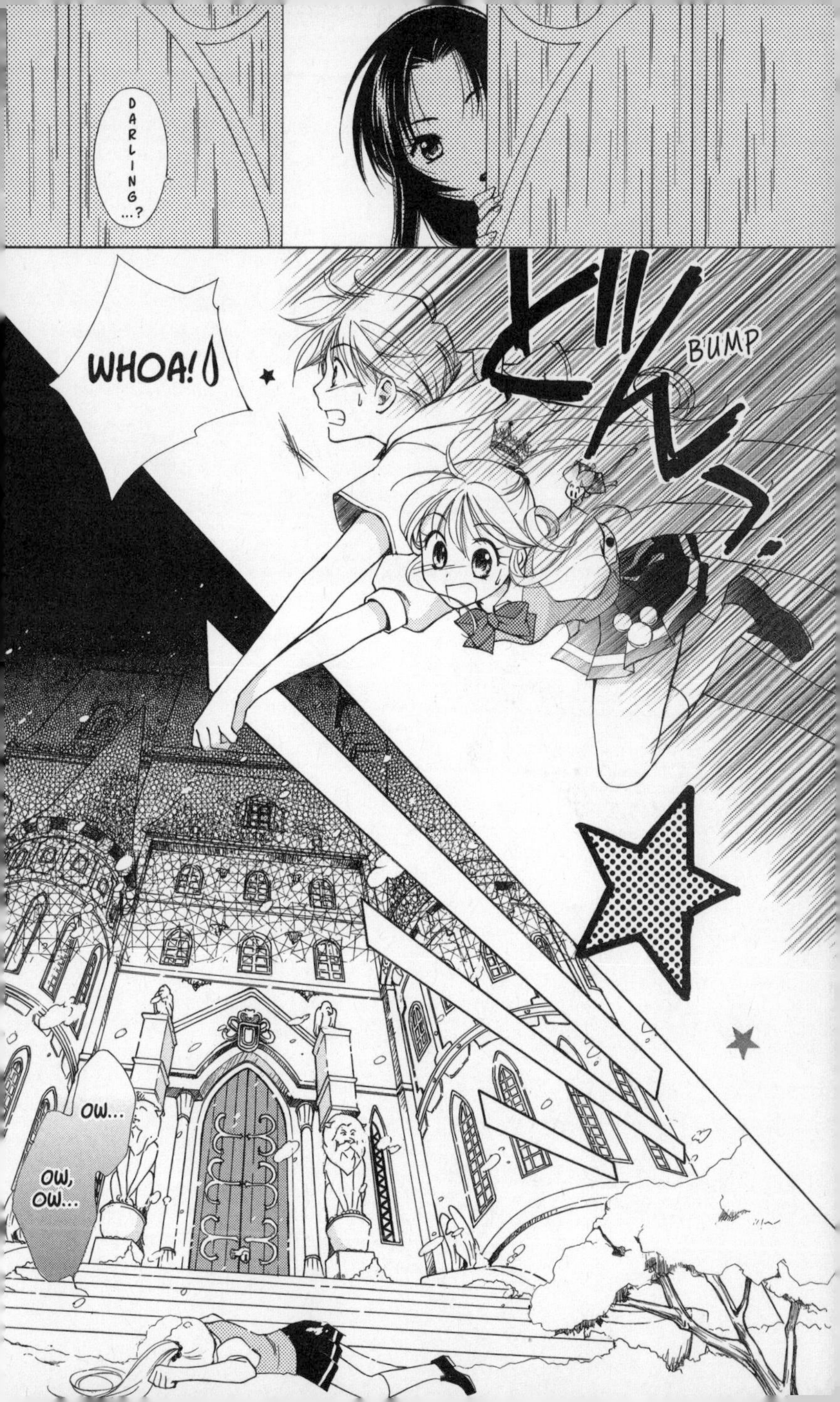

DARLING...?
WHOA!
どんっ
BUMP
OW...
OW, OW...

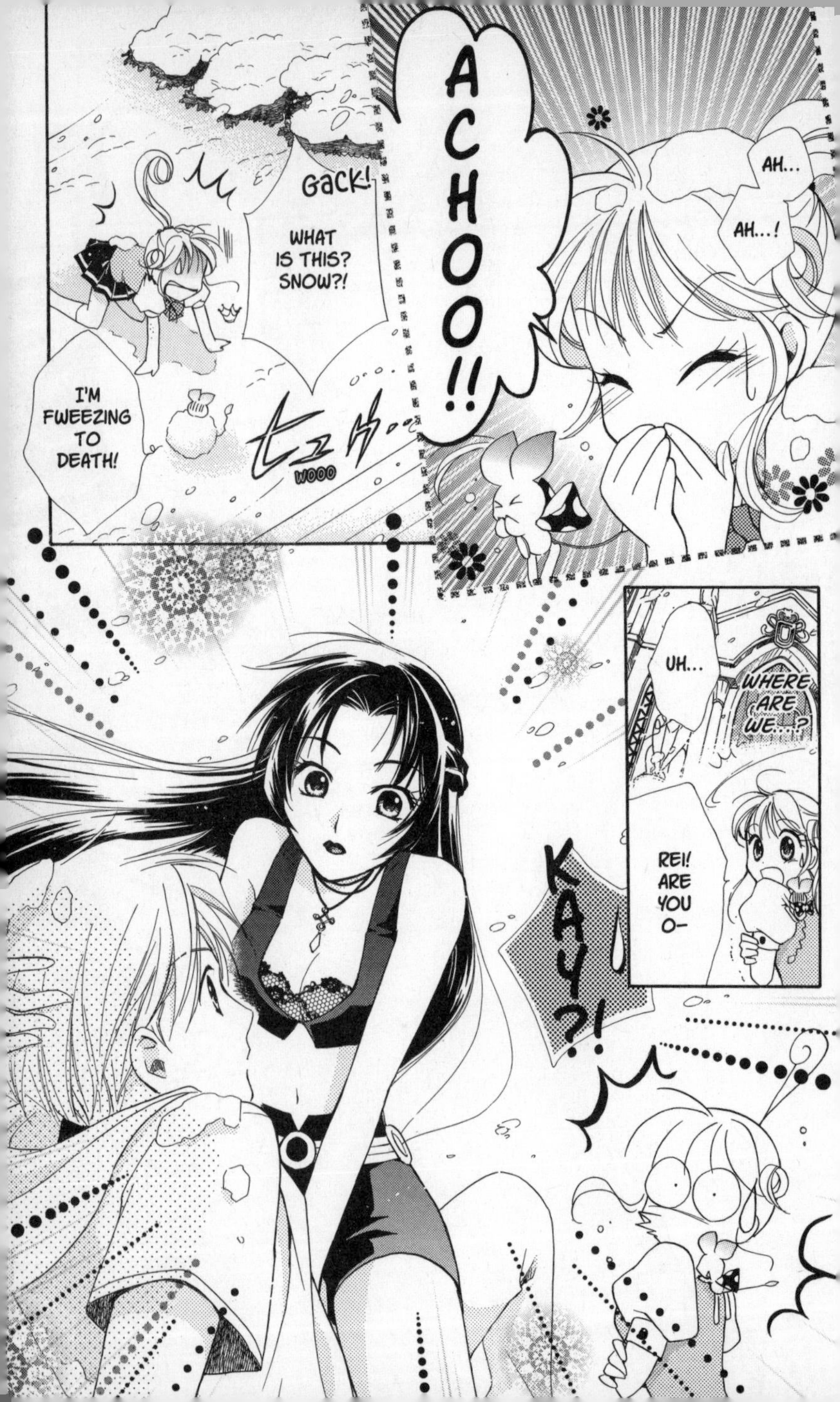
AH...
AH...!
ACHOO!!
GACK!
WHAT IS THIS? SNOW?!
I'M FWEEZING TO DEATH!
WOOO
UH...
WHERE ARE WE...?
REI! ARE YOU O-
KAY?!

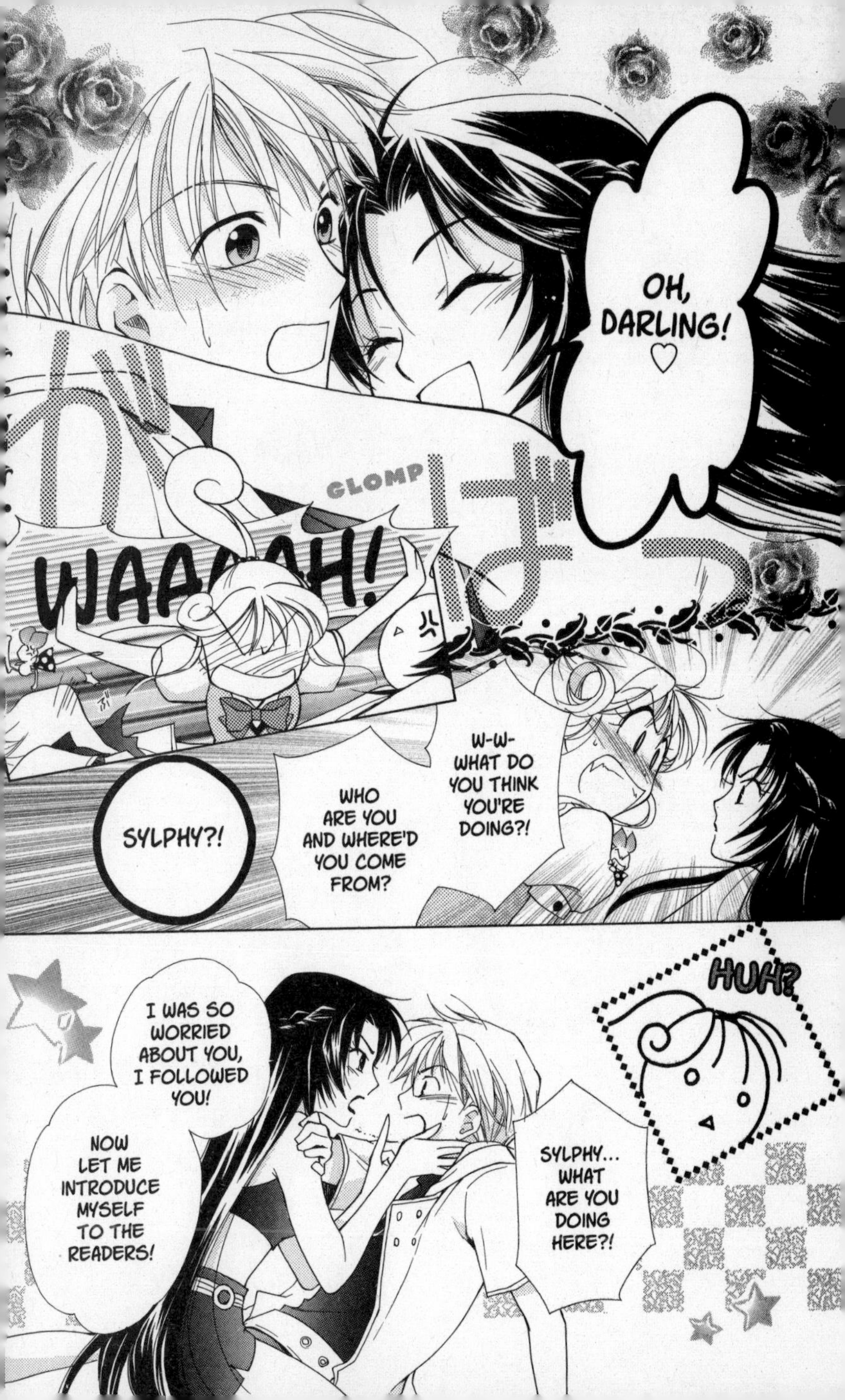
OH, DARLING! ♡
がばっ
GLOMP
WAAAAH!
W-W-WHAT DO YOU THINK YOU'RE DOING?!
WHO ARE YOU AND WHERE'D YOU COME FROM?
SYLPHY?!
HUH?
SYLPHY... WHAT ARE YOU DOING HERE?!
I WAS SO WORRIED ABOUT YOU, I FOLLOWED YOU!
NOW LET ME INTRODUCE MYSELF TO THE READERS!

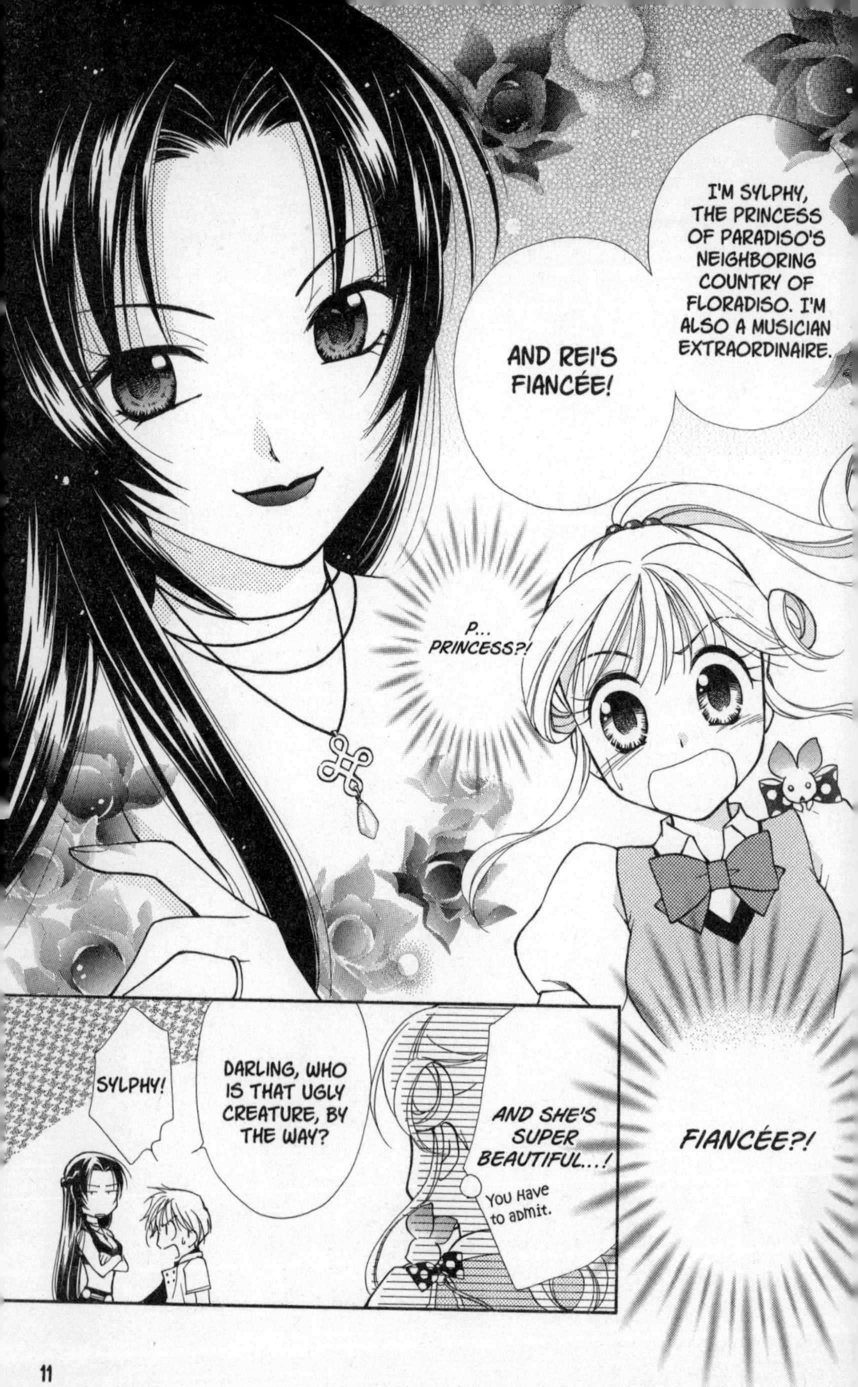
I'M SYLPHY, THE PRINCESS OF PARADISO'S NEIGHBORING COUNTRY OF FLORADISO. I'M ALSO A MUSICIAN EXTRAORDINAIRE.
AND REI'S FIANCÉE!
P... PRINCESS?!
FIANCÉE?!
AND SHE'S SUPER BEAUTIFUL...!
You have to admit.
DARLING, WHO IS THAT UGLY CREATURE, BY THE WAY?
SYLPHY!

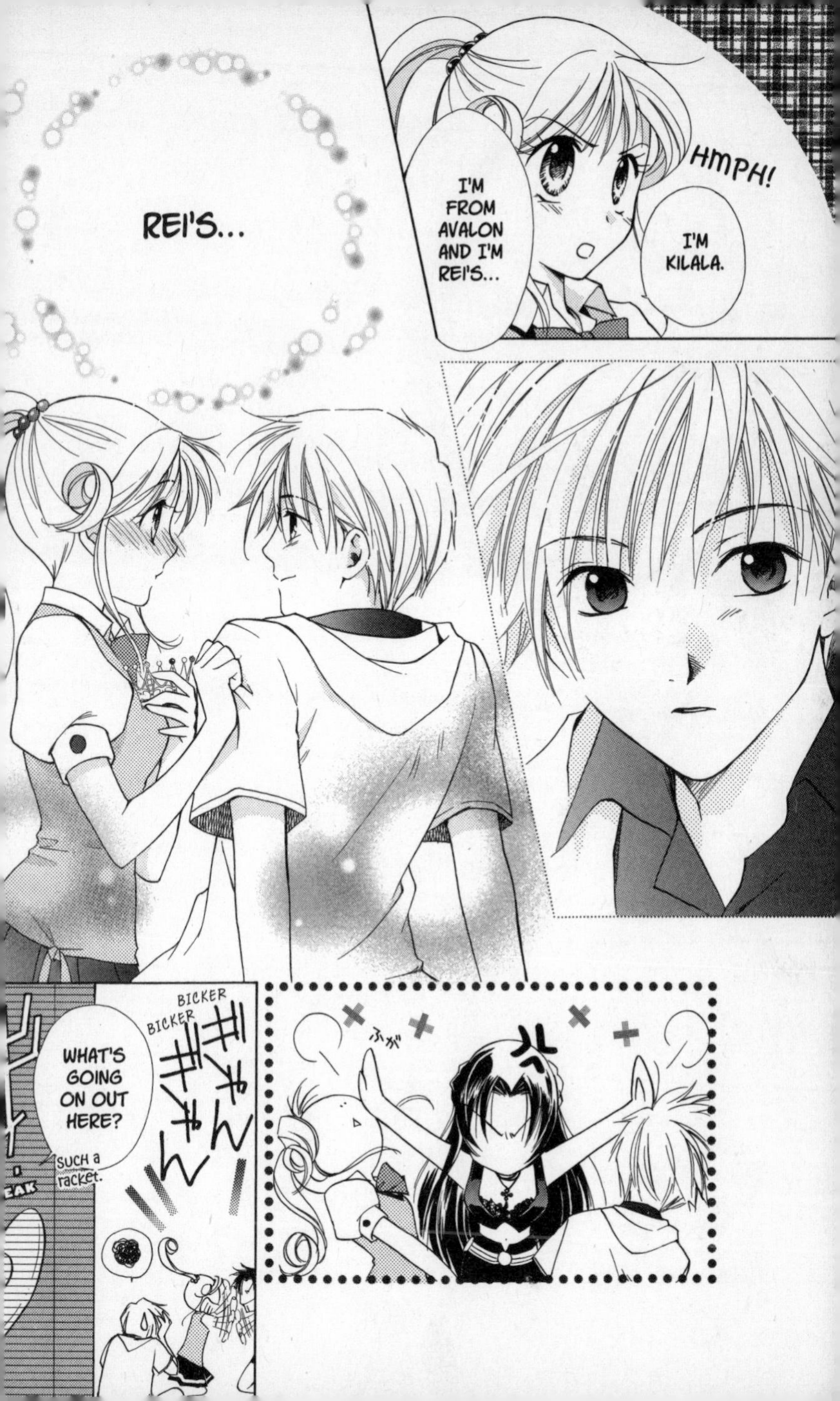
HMPH!
I'M KILALA.
I'M FROM AVALON AND I'M REI'S...
REI'S...
ふが
BICKER BICKER
WHAT'S GOING ON OUT HERE?
SUCH a racket.

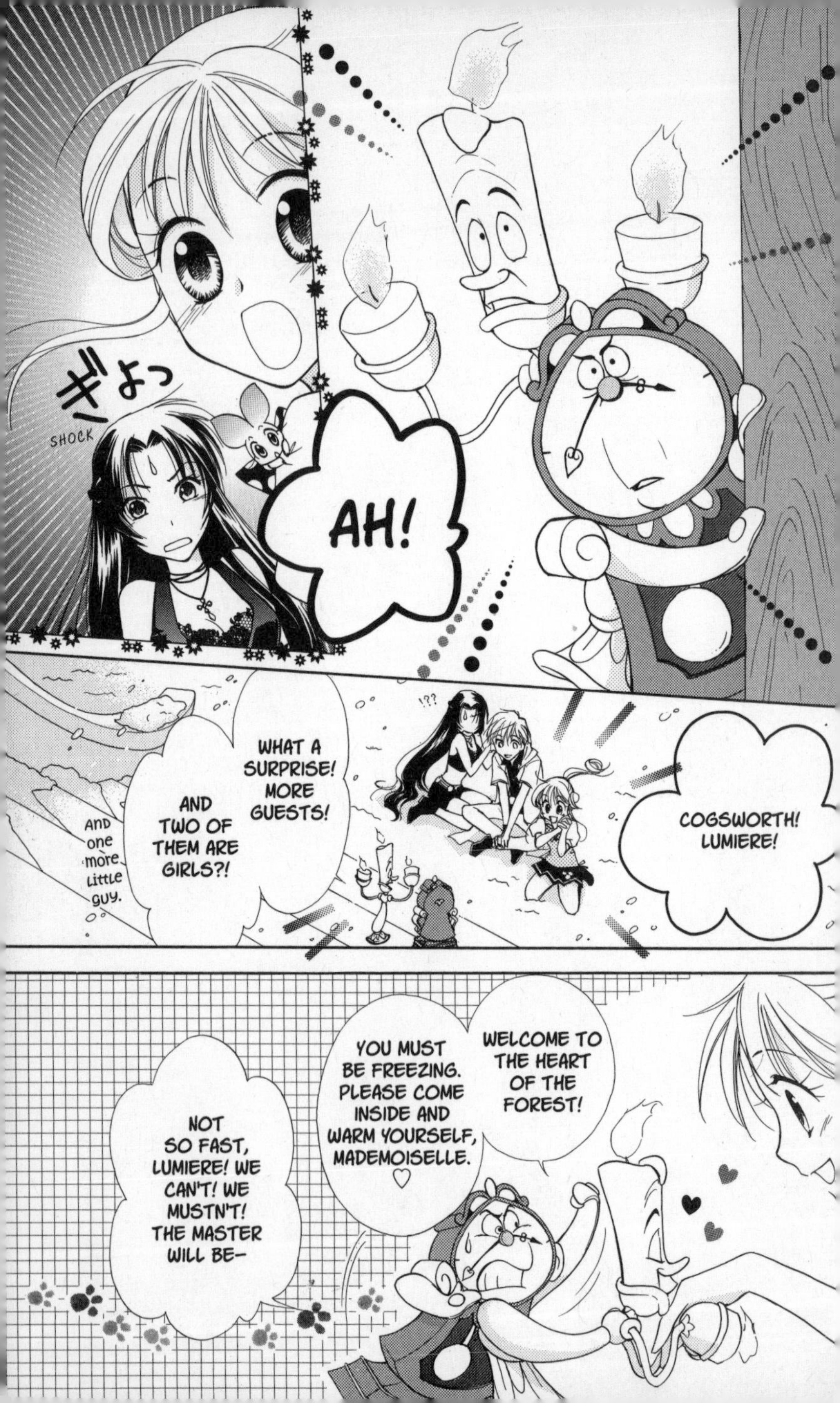
AH!
ぎょっ
SHOCK
COGSWORTH! LUMIERE!
!??
WHAT A SURPRISE! MORE GUESTS!
AND TWO OF THEM ARE GIRLS?!
And one more little guy.
WELCOME TO THE HEART OF THE FOREST!
YOU MUST BE FREEZING. PLEASE COME INSIDE AND WARM YOURSELF, MADEMOISELLE. ♡
NOT SO FAST, LUMIERE! WE CAN'T! WE MUSTN'T! THE MASTER WILL BE-

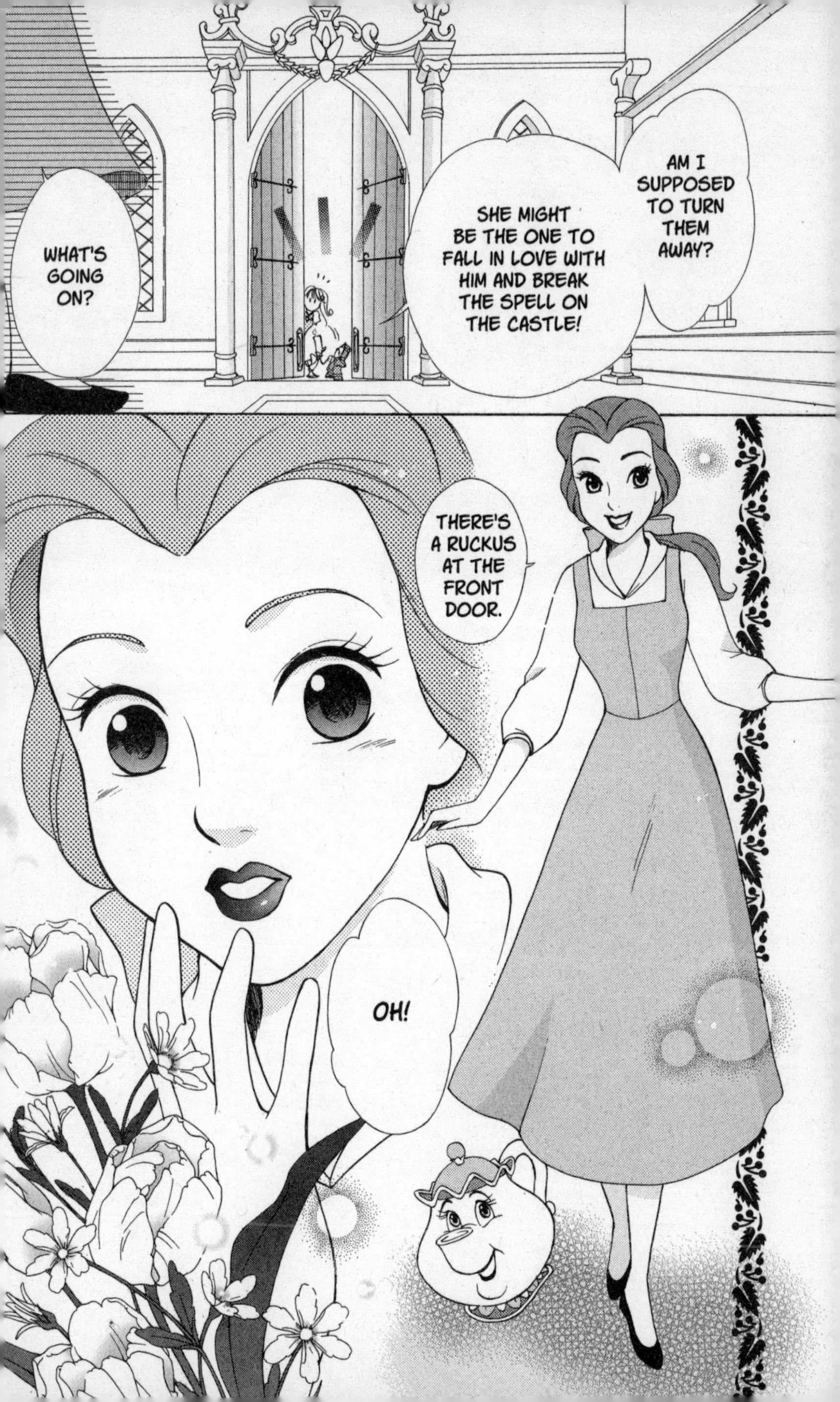
AM I SUPPOSED TO TURN THEM AWAY?
SHE MIGHT BE THE ONE TO FALL IN LOVE WITH HIM AND BREAK THE SPELL ON THE CASTLE!
WHAT'S GOING ON?
THERE'S A RUCKUS AT THE FRONT DOOR.
OH!

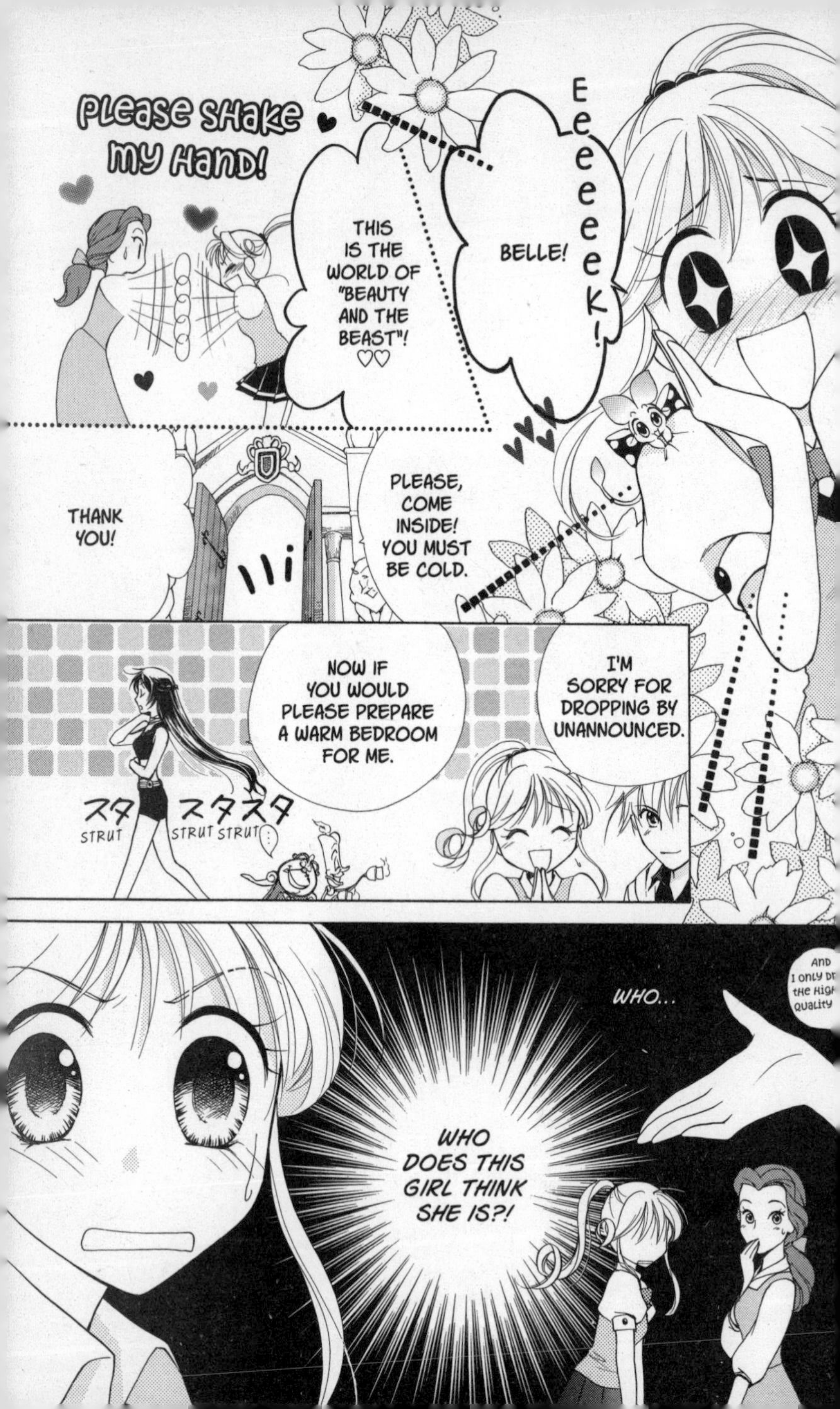
Eeeeek!
BELLE!
THIS IS THE WORLD OF "BEAUTY AND THE BEAST"! ♡♡
PLEASE SHAKE MY HAND!
PLEASE, COME INSIDE! YOU MUST BE COLD.
THANK YOU!
I'M SORRY FOR DROPPING BY UNANNOUNCED.
NOW IF YOU WOULD PLEASE PREPARE A WARM BEDROOM FOR ME.
スタスタ STRUT STRUT
スタ STRUT
AND I ONLY DR THE HIGH QUALITY
WHO...
WHO DOES THIS GIRL THINK SHE IS?!

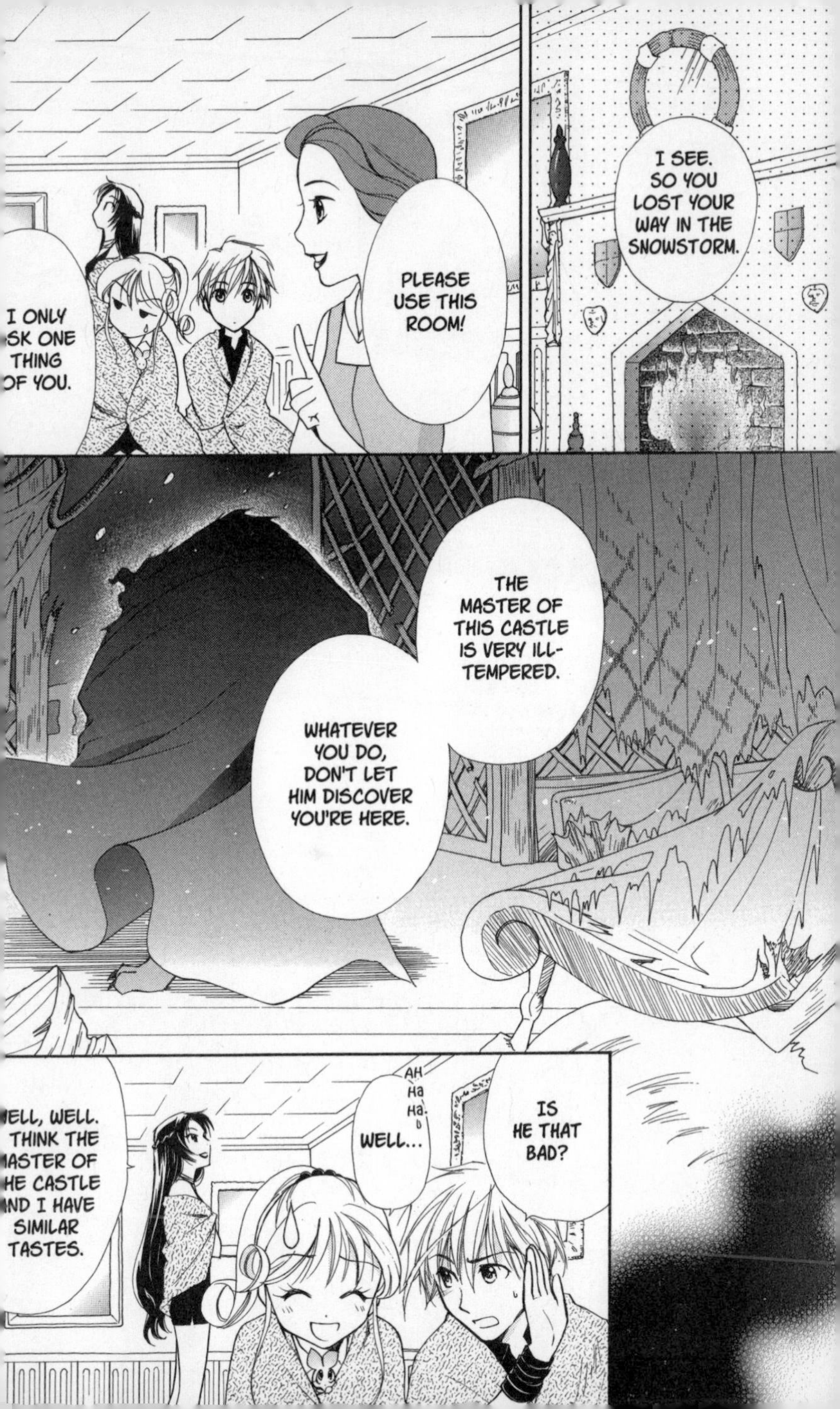
I SEE. SO YOU LOST YOUR WAY IN THE SNOWSTORM.
PLEASE USE THIS ROOM!
I ONLY SK ONE THING OF YOU.
THE MASTER OF THIS CASTLE IS VERY ILL-TEMPERED.
WHATEVER YOU DO, DON'T LET HIM DISCOVER YOU'RE HERE.
IS HE THAT BAD?
AH HA HA.
WELL...
ELL, WELL. THINK THE ASTER OF HE CASTLE ND I HAVE SIMILAR TASTES.

READ THIS WAY

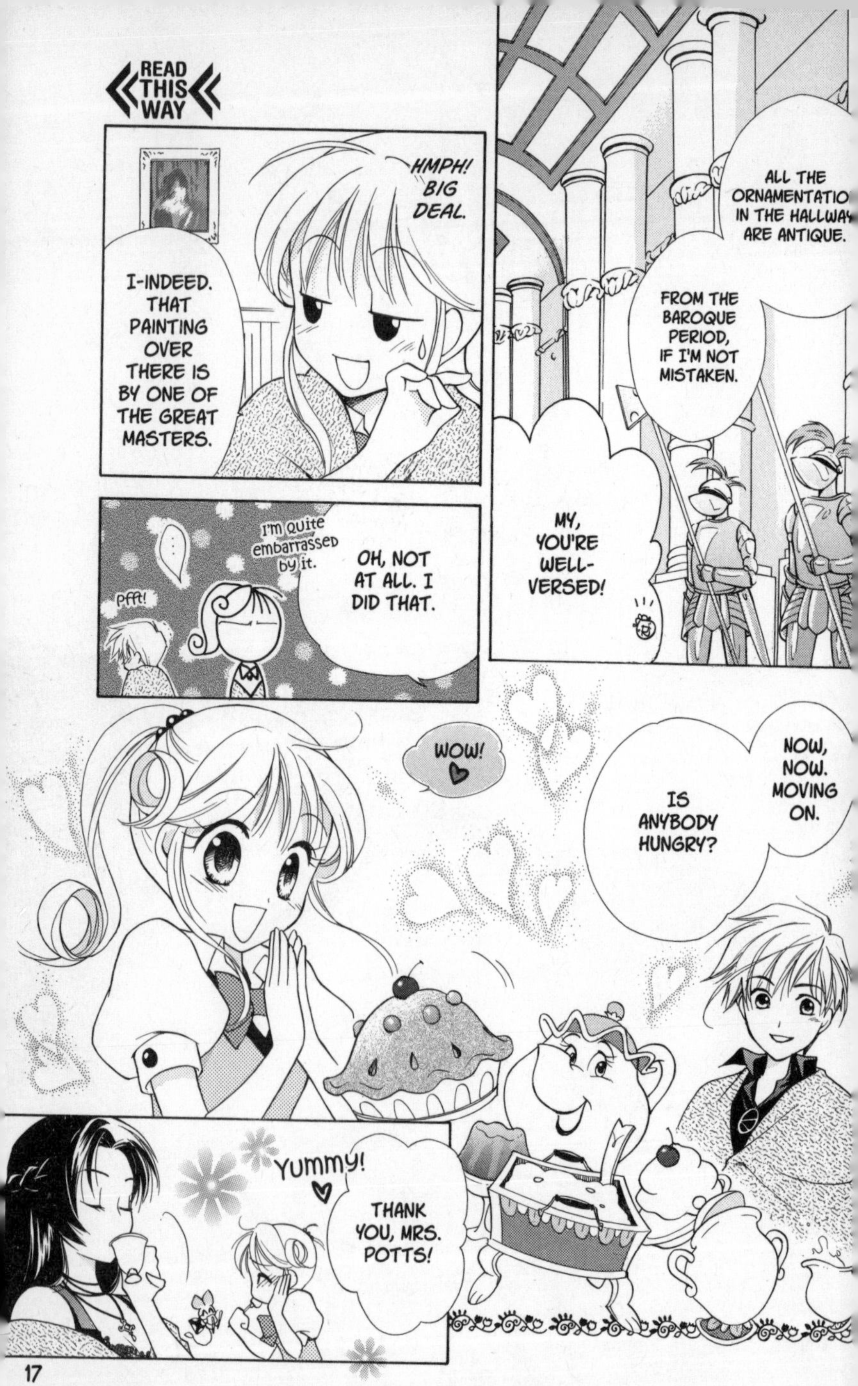

ALL THE ORNAMENTATIO IN THE HALLWA ARE ANTIQUE.
FROM THE BAROQUE PERIOD, IF I'M NOT MISTAKEN.
MY, YOU'RE WELL-VERSED!
HMPH! BIG DEAL.
I-INDEED. THAT PAINTING OVER THERE IS BY ONE OF THE GREAT MASTERS.
OH, NOT AT ALL. I DID THAT.
I'm quite embarrassed by it.
Pfft!
NOW, NOW. MOVING ON.
IS ANYBODY HUNGRY?
WOW!
Yummy!
THANK YOU, MRS. POTTS!

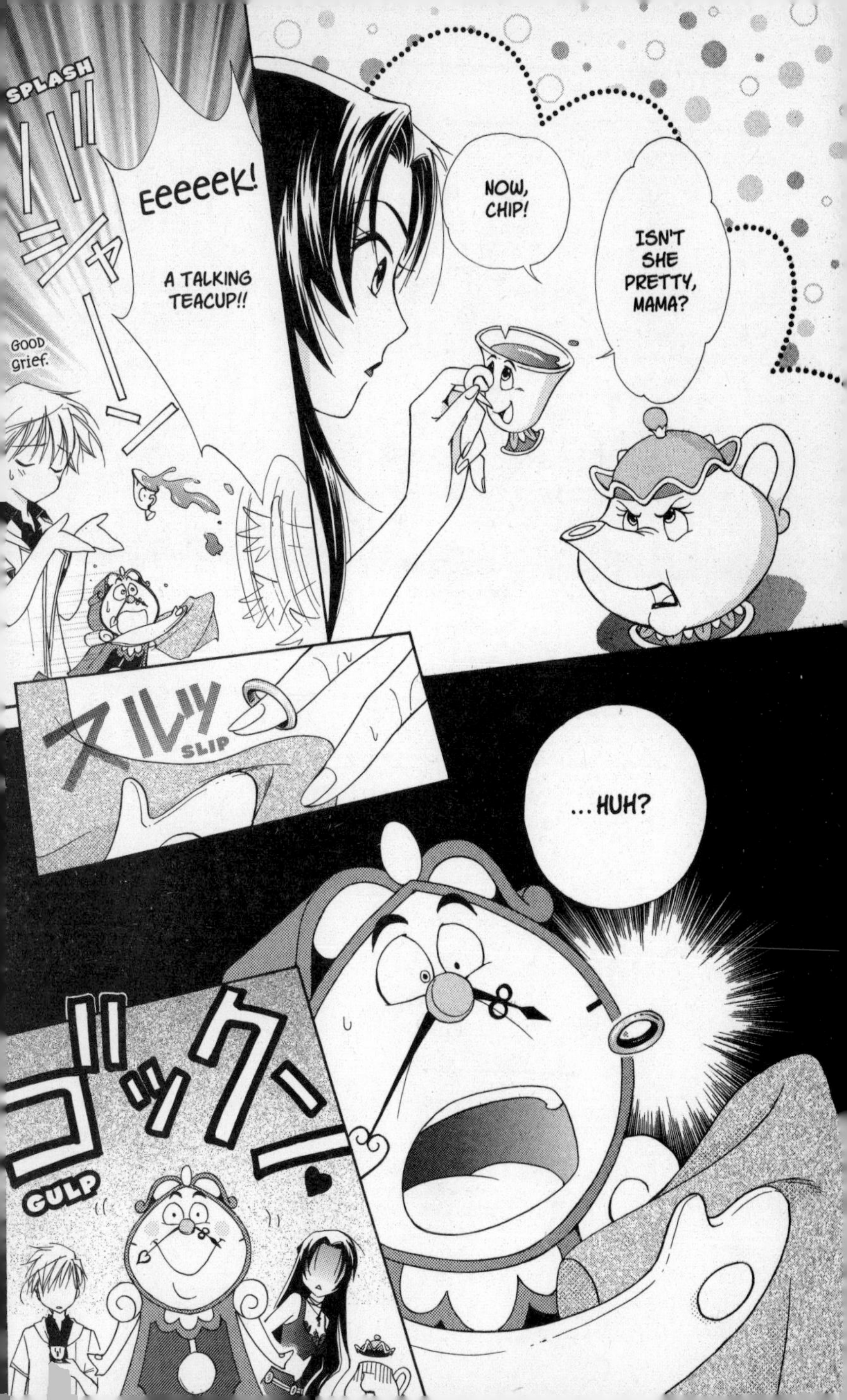
ISN'T SHE PRETTY, MAMA?
NOW, CHIP!
EEEEEK!
A TALKING TEACUP!!
SPLASH
GOOD grief.
SLIP
...HUH?
GULP

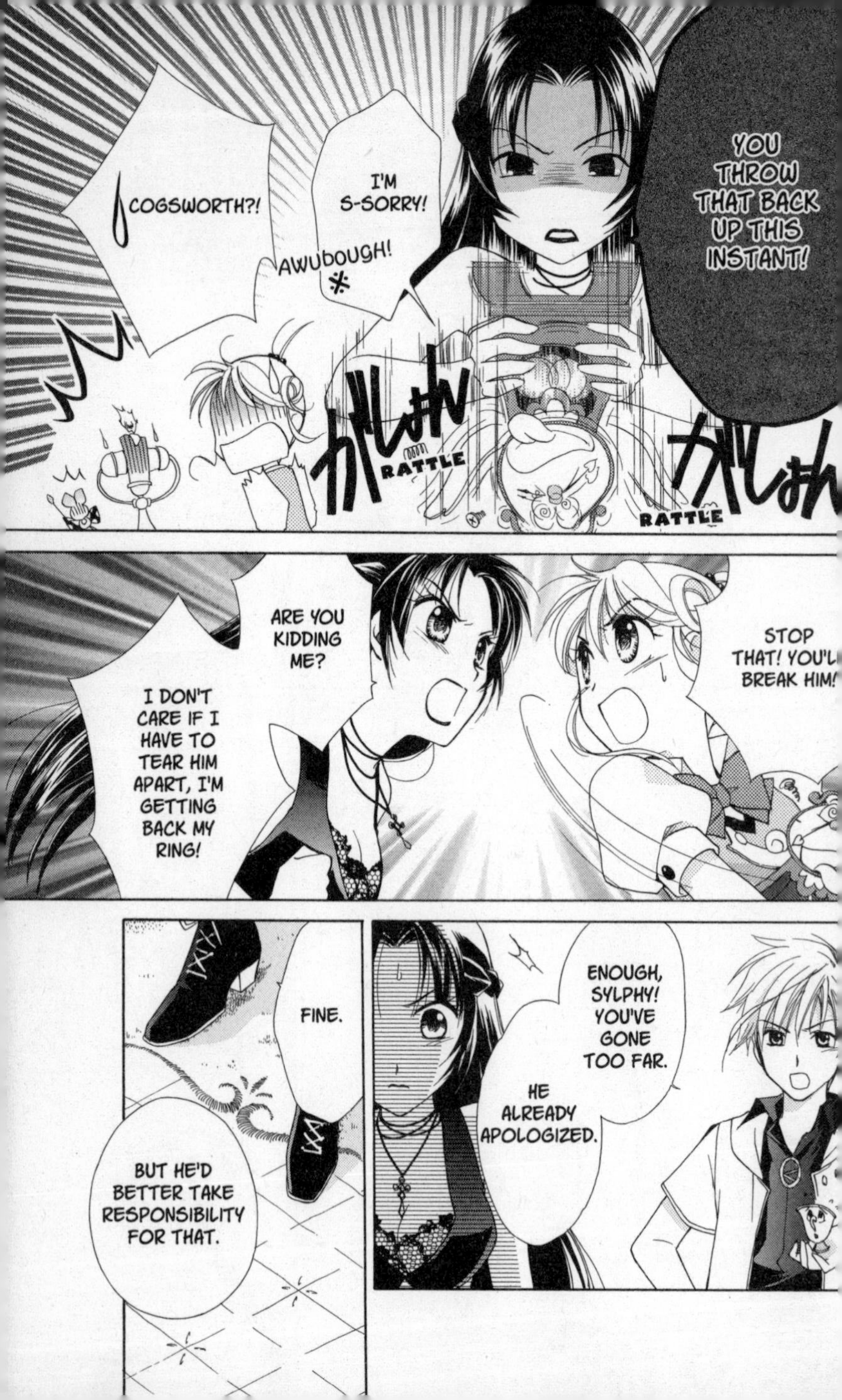
YOU THROW THAT BACK UP THIS INSTANT!
がしゃん
RATTLE
I'M S-SORRY!
AWUBOUGH!
がしゃん
RATTLE
COGSWORTH?!
STOP THAT! YOU'L BREAK HIM!
ARE YOU KIDDING ME?
I DON'T CARE IF I HAVE TO TEAR HIM APART, I'M GETTING BACK MY RING!
ENOUGH, SYLPHY! YOU'VE GONE TOO FAR.
HE ALREADY APOLOGIZED.
FINE.
BUT HE'D BETTER TAKE RESPONSIBILITY FOR THAT.

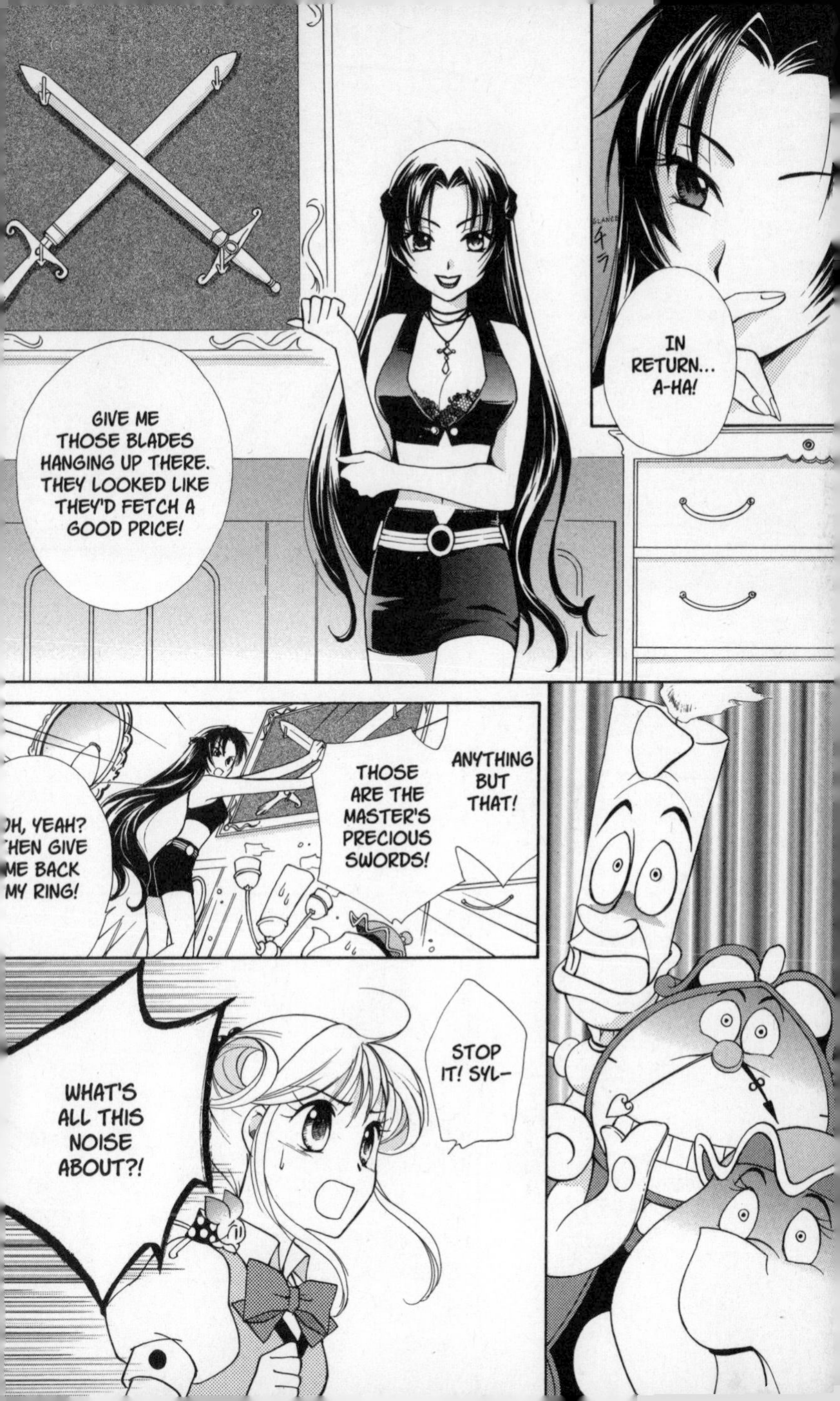

GLANCE
チラ
IN RETURN... A-HA!
GIVE ME THOSE BLADES HANGING UP THERE. THEY LOOKED LIKE THEY'D FETCH A GOOD PRICE!
ANYTHING BUT THAT!
THOSE ARE THE MASTER'S PRECIOUS SWORDS!
OH, YEAH? THEN GIVE ME BACK MY RING!
STOP IT! SYL–
WHAT'S ALL THIS NOISE ABOUT?!

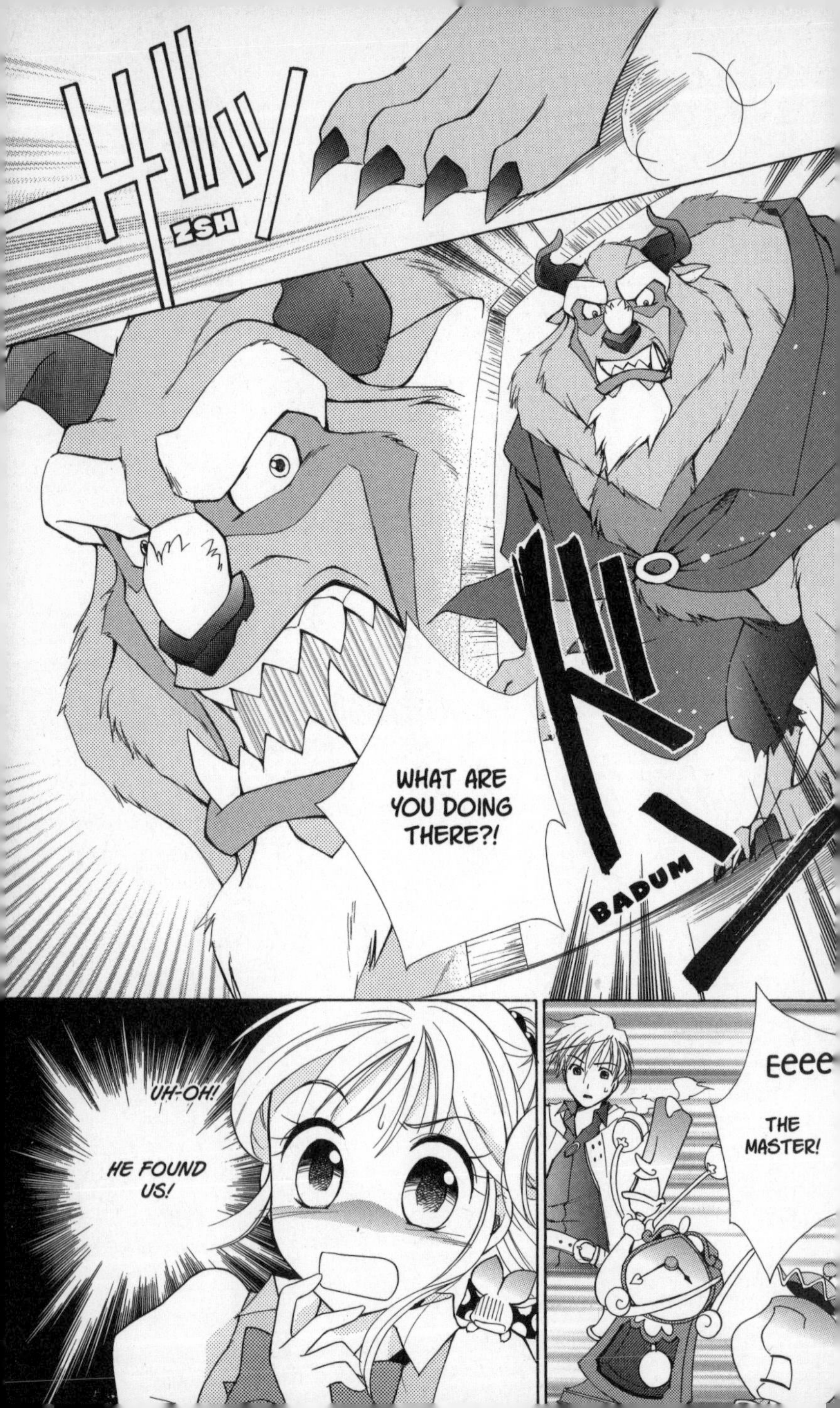
ZSH
WHAT ARE YOU DOING THERE?!
BADUM
Eeee
THE MASTER!
UH-OH!
HE FOUND US!

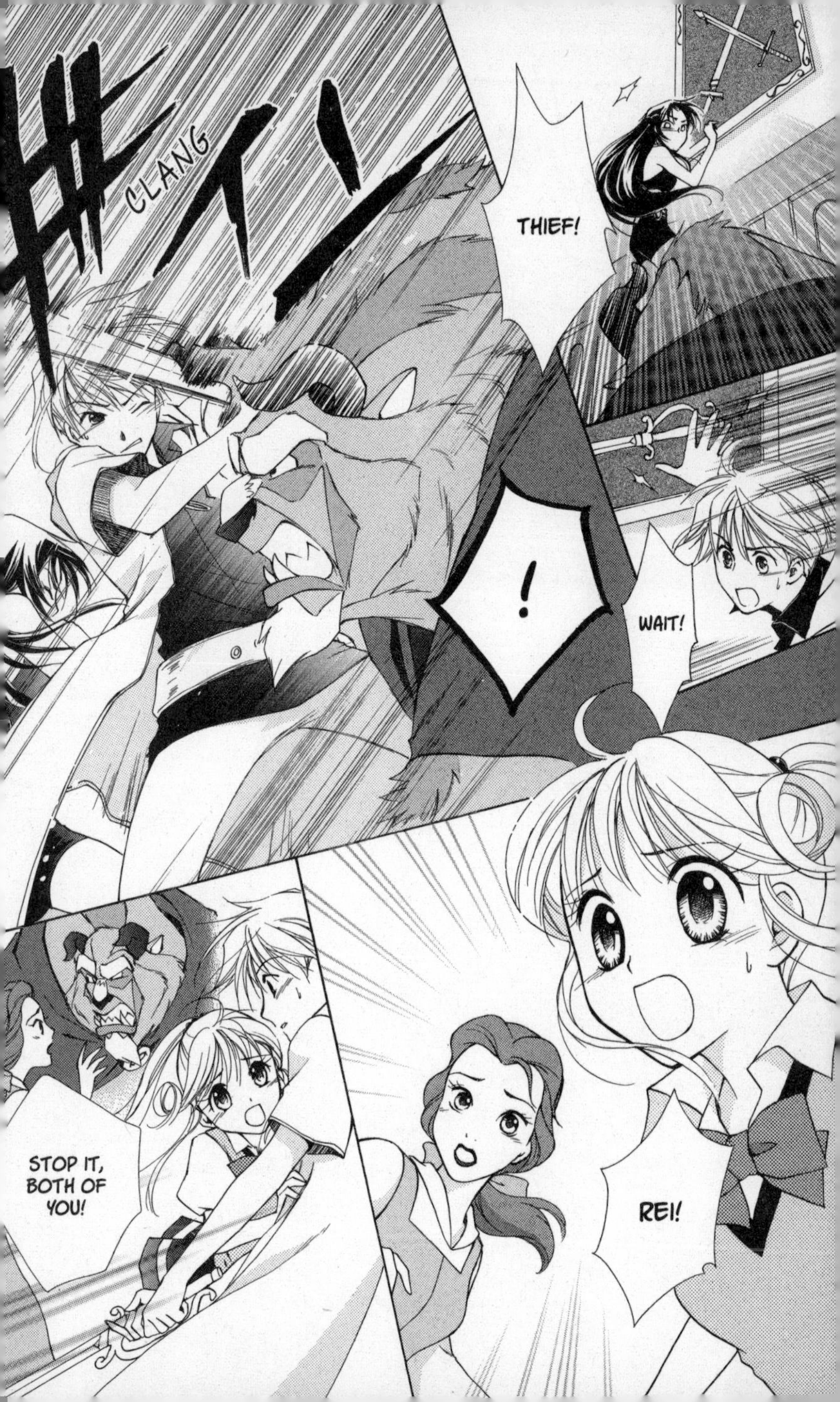
THIEF!
WAIT!
CLANG
!
REI!
STOP IT, BOTH OF YOU!

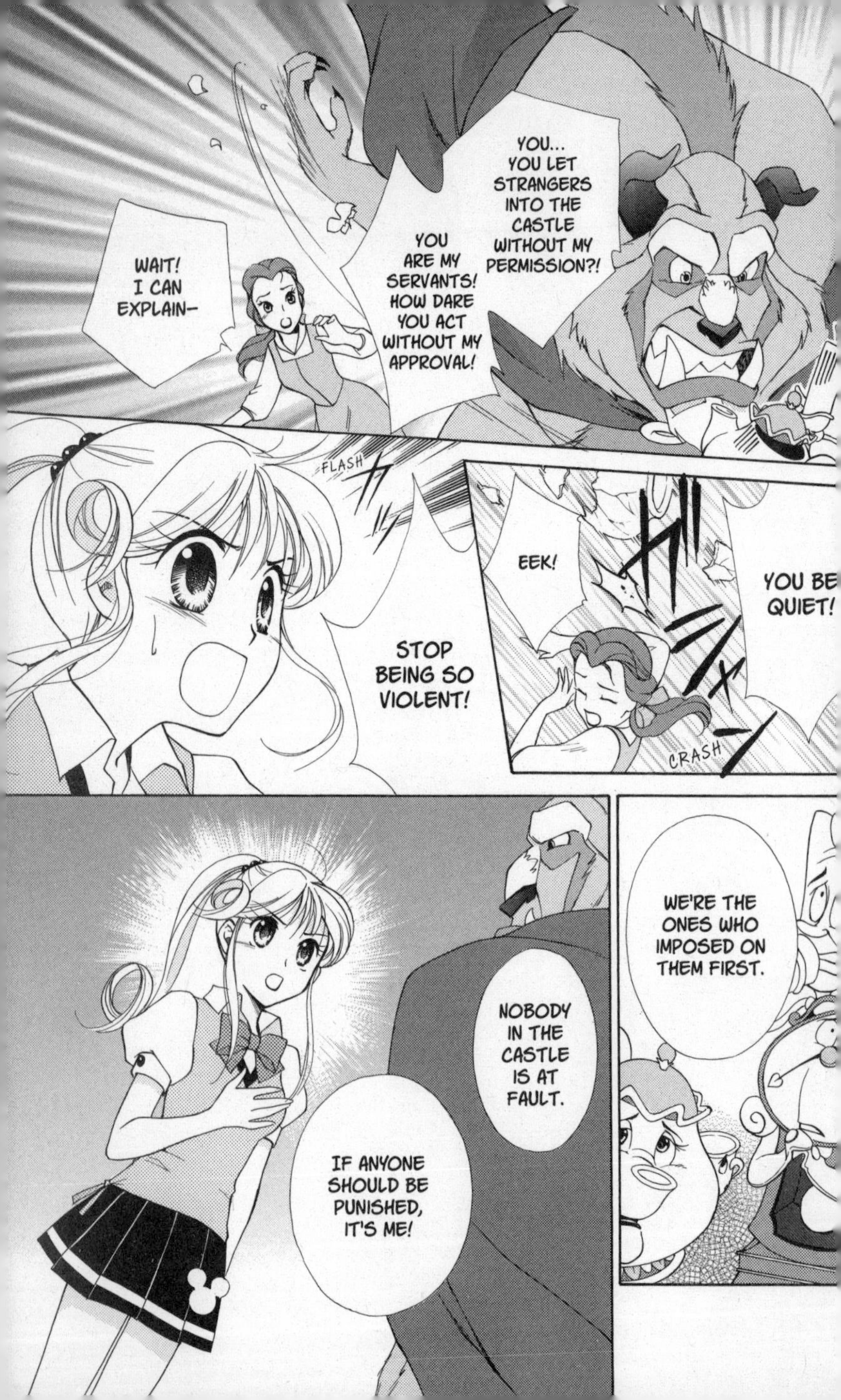
YOU... YOU LET STRANGERS INTO THE CASTLE WITHOUT MY PERMISSION?!
YOU ARE MY SERVANTS! HOW DARE YOU ACT WITHOUT MY APPROVAL!
WAIT! I CAN EXPLAIN–
YOU BE QUIET!
EEK!
CRASH
FLASH
STOP BEING SO VIOLENT!
WE'RE THE ONES WHO IMPOSED ON THEM FIRST.
NOBODY IN THE CASTLE IS AT FAULT.
IF ANYONE SHOULD BE PUNISHED, IT'S ME!

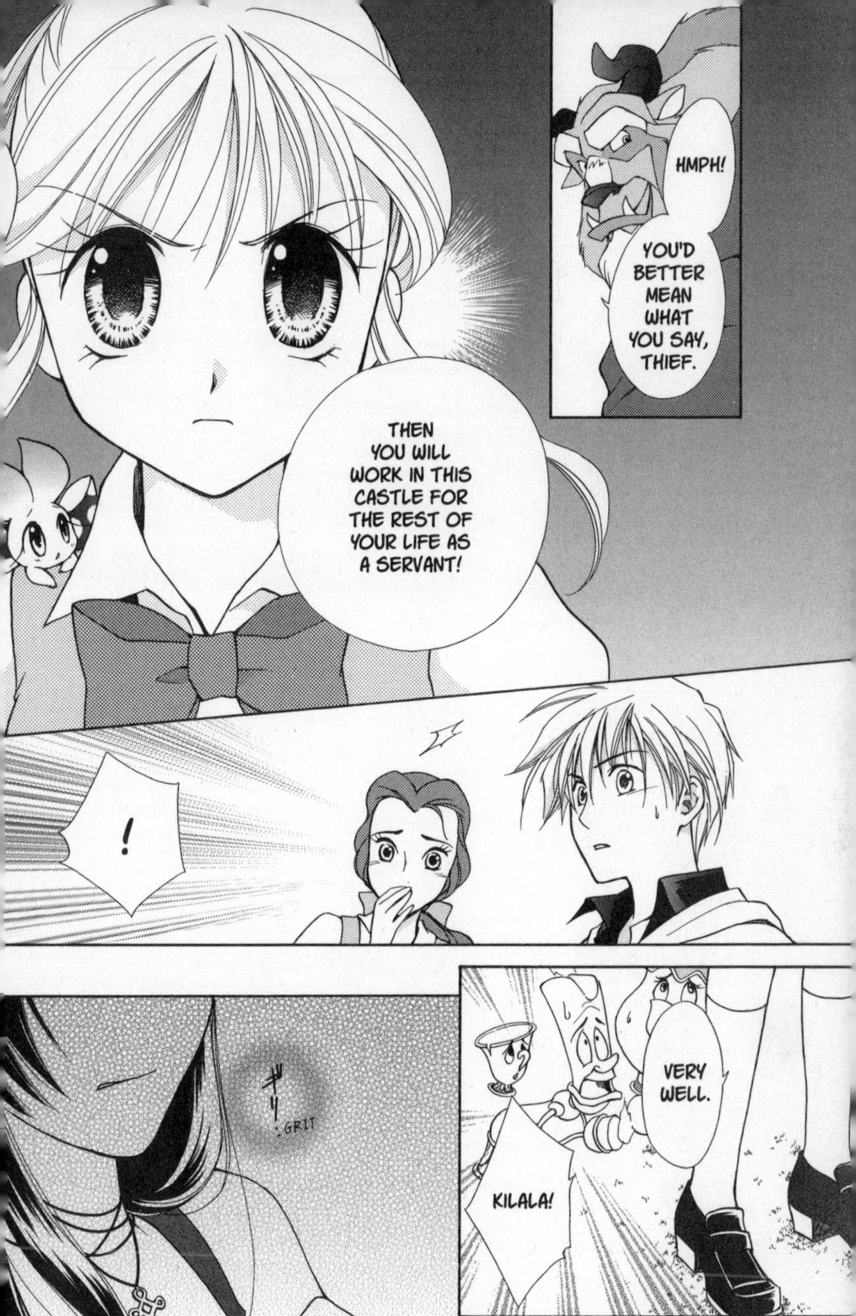
HMPH!
YOU'D BETTER MEAN WHAT YOU SAY, THIEF.
THEN YOU WILL WORK IN THIS CASTLE FOR THE REST OF YOUR LIFE AS A SERVANT!
!
VERY WELL.
KILALA!
GRIT

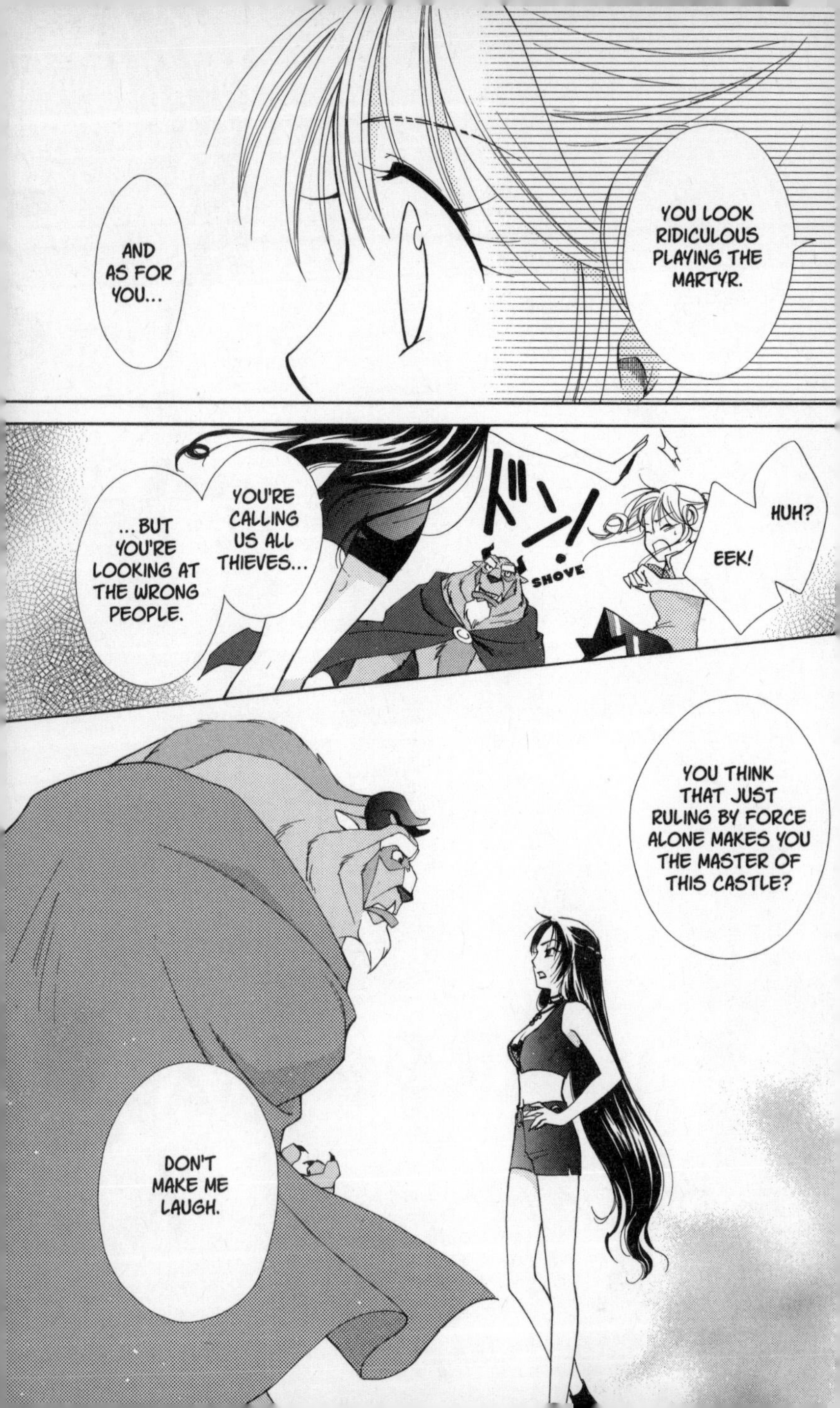
YOU LOOK RIDICULOUS PLAYING THE MARTYR.
AND AS FOR YOU...
HUH?
EEK!
ドン!
SHOVE
YOU'RE CALLING US ALL THIEVES...
...BUT YOU'RE LOOKING AT THE WRONG PEOPLE.
YOU THINK THAT JUST RULING BY FORCE ALONE MAKES YOU THE MASTER OF THIS CASTLE?
DON'T MAKE ME LAUGH.

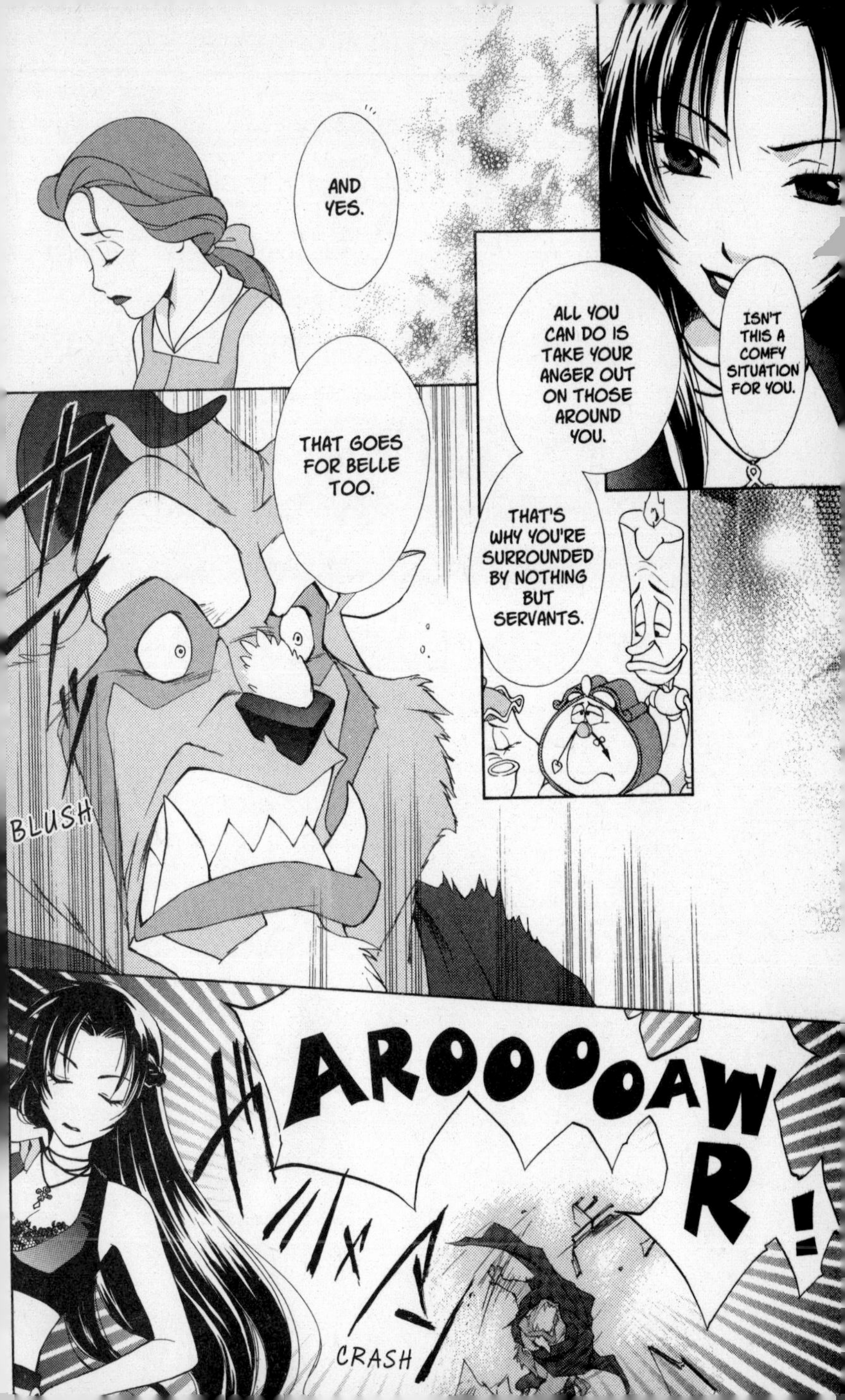
ISN'T THIS A COMFY SITUATION FOR YOU.
ALL YOU CAN DO IS TAKE YOUR ANGER OUT ON THOSE AROUND YOU.
THAT'S WHY YOU'RE SURROUNDED BY NOTHING BUT SERVANTS.
AND YES.
THAT GOES FOR BELLE TOO.
BLUSH
AROOOOAWR!
CRASH

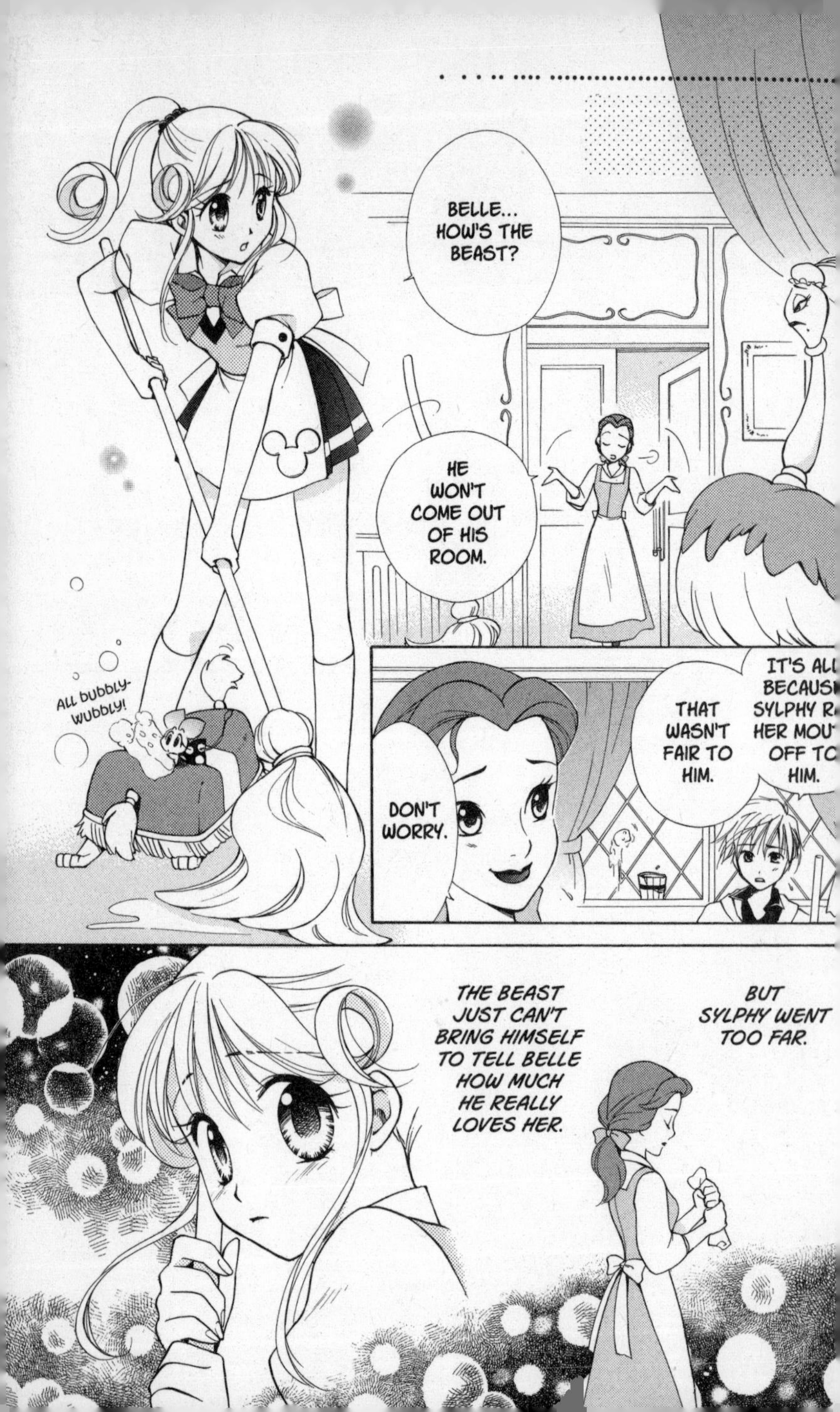
BELLE... HOW'S THE BEAST?
HE WON'T COME OUT OF HIS ROOM.
ALL bubbly-wubbly!
IT'S ALL BECAUS SYLPHY R HER MOU OFF TO HIM.
THAT WASN'T FAIR TO HIM.
DON'T WORRY.
BUT SYLPHY WENT TOO FAR.
THE BEAST JUST CAN'T BRING HIMSELF TO TELL BELLE HOW MUCH HE REALLY LOVES HER.

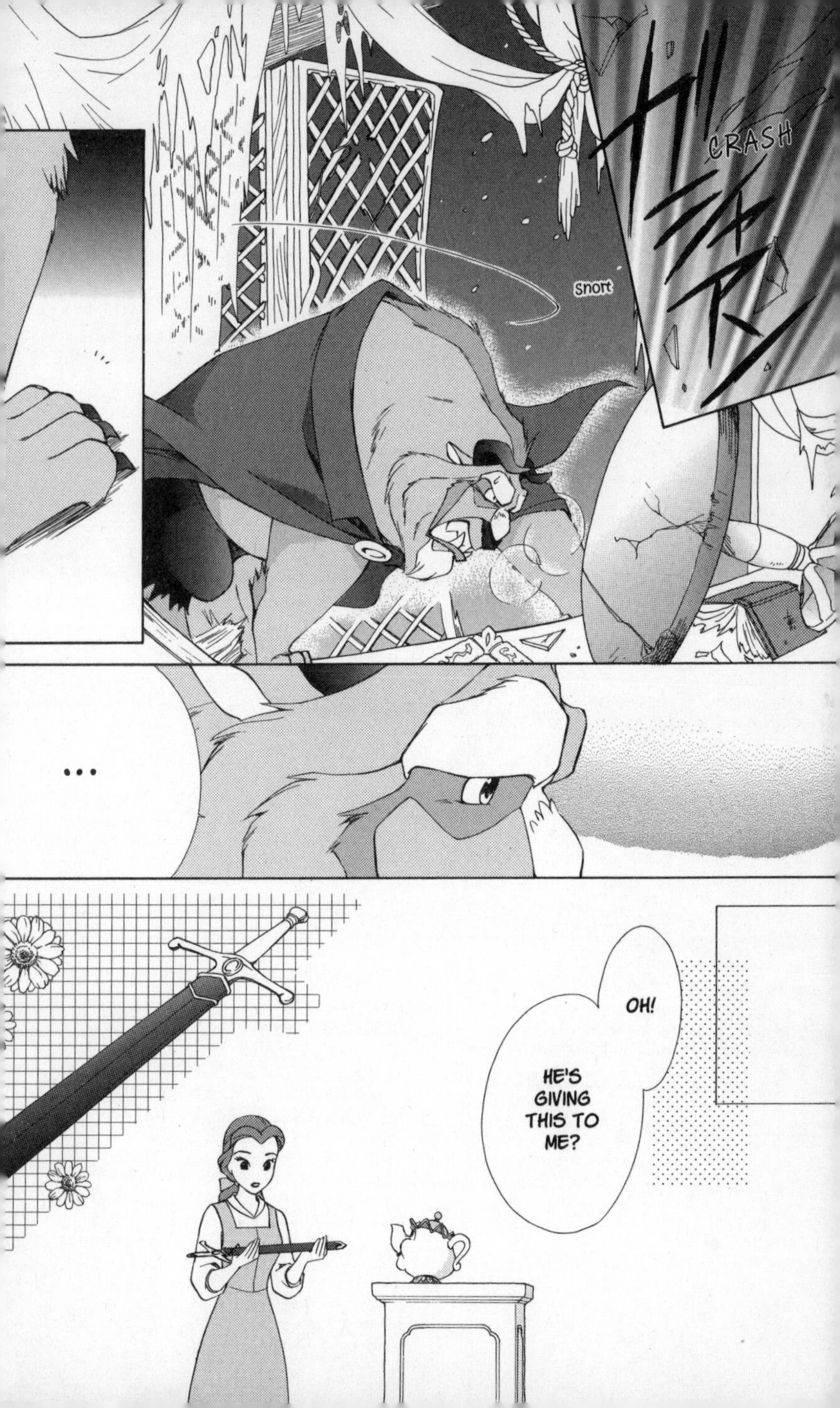
CRASH
snort
...
OH!
HE'S GIVING THIS TO ME?

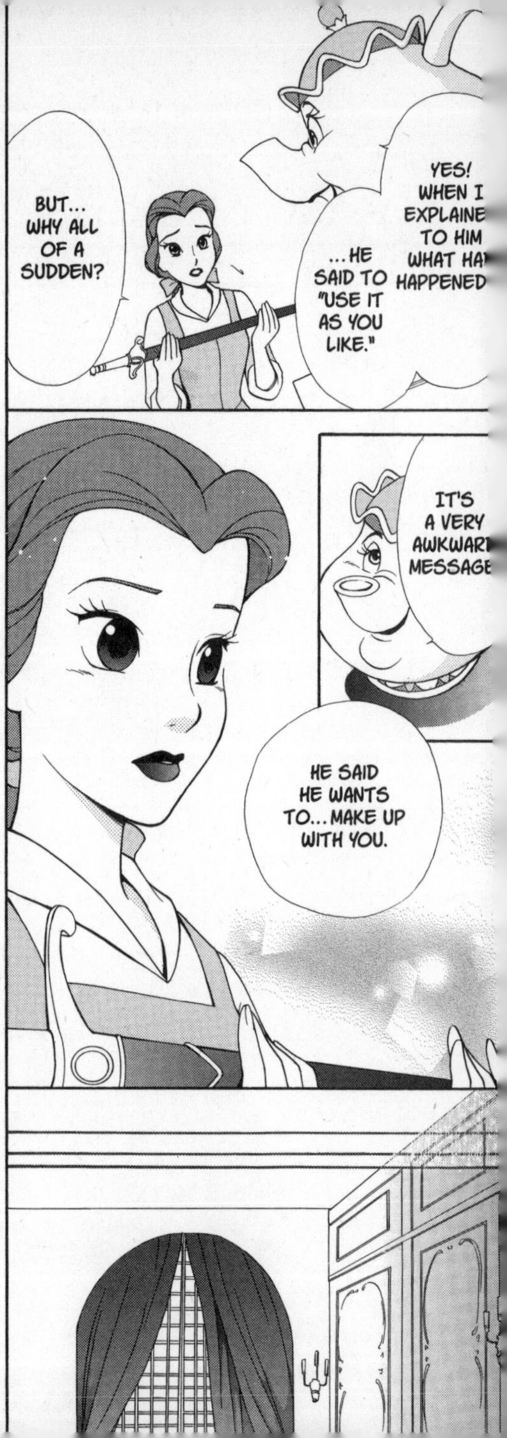
YES! WHEN I EXPLAINE TO HIM WHAT HA HAPPENED
...HE SAID TO "USE IT AS YOU LIKE."
BUT... WHY ALL OF A SUDDEN?
IT'S A VERY AWKWAR MESSAGE
HE SAID HE WANTS TO... MAKE UP WITH YOU.

Nao Kodaka 1

HELLO! KODAKA HERE. THE FOURTH VOLUME OF "KILALA PRINCESS" IS ALL COMPILED AND DONE. I'M SO HAPPY! AND THANKFUL!

ABOUT THE TIME THAT THIS VOLUME IS GOING TO THE PRINTER, THE MAGAZINE SERIALIZATION WILL HAVE MOVED TO THE SPECIAL RELEASE PUBLICATION, "NAKAYOSHI LOVELY." THAT MEANS THE SCHEDULE FOR THE RELEASE OF THE CHAPTERS WILL SLOW DOWN, EVEN THOUGH THE STORY ITSELF HAS INTRODUCED SOME NEW MAJOR DEVELOPMENTS. THERE'S THE OBJECT OF KILALA'S AFFECTION, AND EVEN AFTER SHE BECOMES A PRINCESS, THERE'S THE INTRODUCTION OF HER RIVAL, PRINCESS SYLPHY, WHO'S JOINED THEIR PARTY.

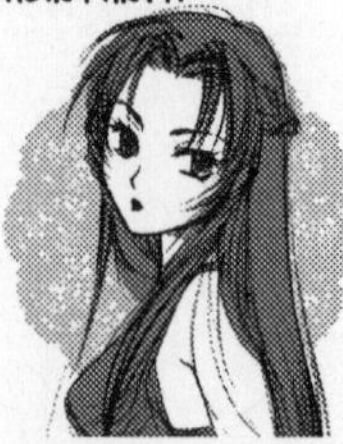

THIS GIRL IS DRAWN TO BE THE EXACT OPPOSITE OF KILALA. SHE'S SHARP-ANGLED, COOL-HEADED, WEARS REVEALING CLOTHES (LOL) AND HAS A MORE MATURE BEAUTY. AS USUAL, KILALA'S FUTURE WILL BE A DIFFICULT ONE, BUT YOU CAN DO IT, OUR BELOVED HEROINE!

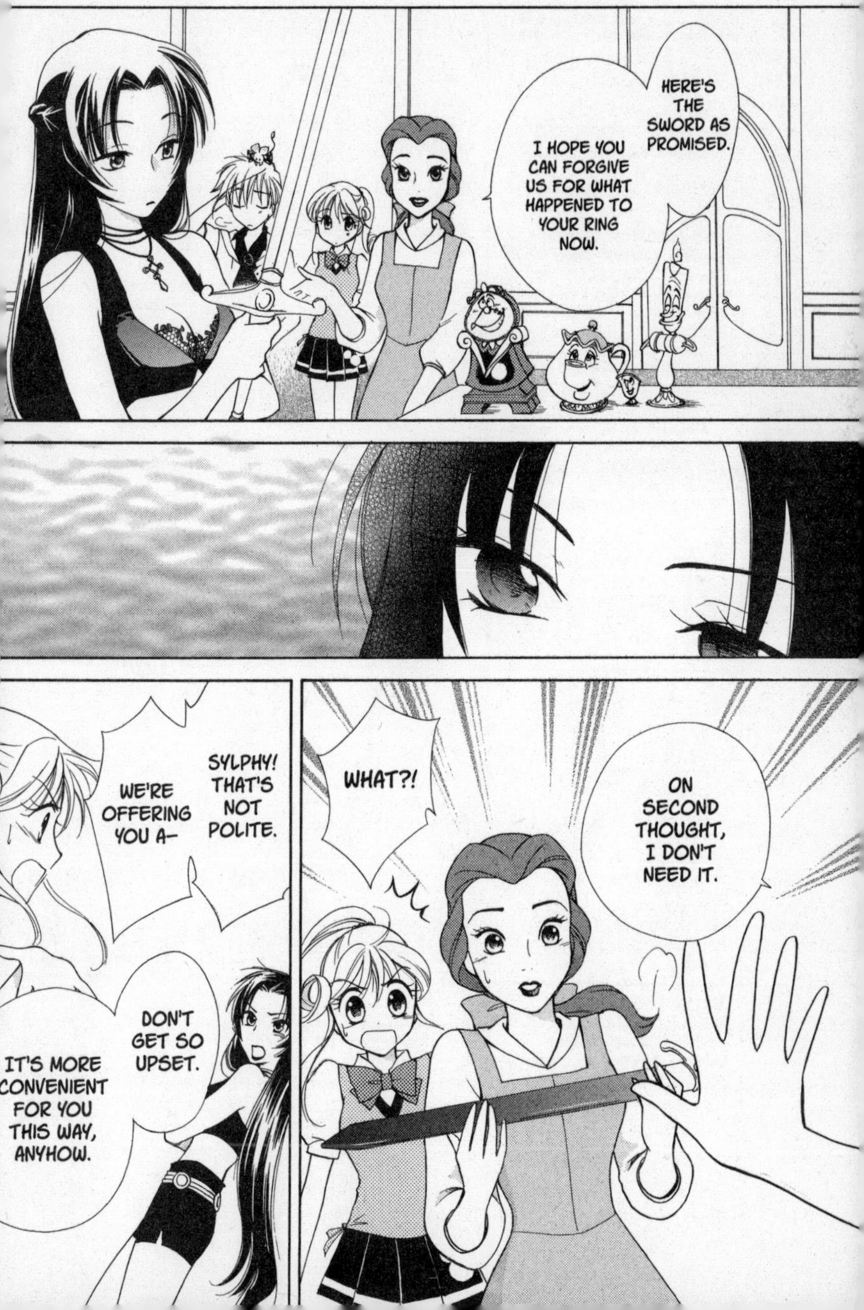
HERE'S THE SWORD AS PROMISED.
I HOPE YOU CAN FORGIVE US FOR WHAT HAPPENED TO YOUR RING NOW.
ON SECOND THOUGHT, I DON'T NEED IT.
WHAT?!
SYLPHY! THAT'S NOT POLITE.
WE'RE OFFERING YOU A—
DON'T GET SO UPSET.
IT'S MORE CONVENIENT FOR YOU THIS WAY, ANYHOW.

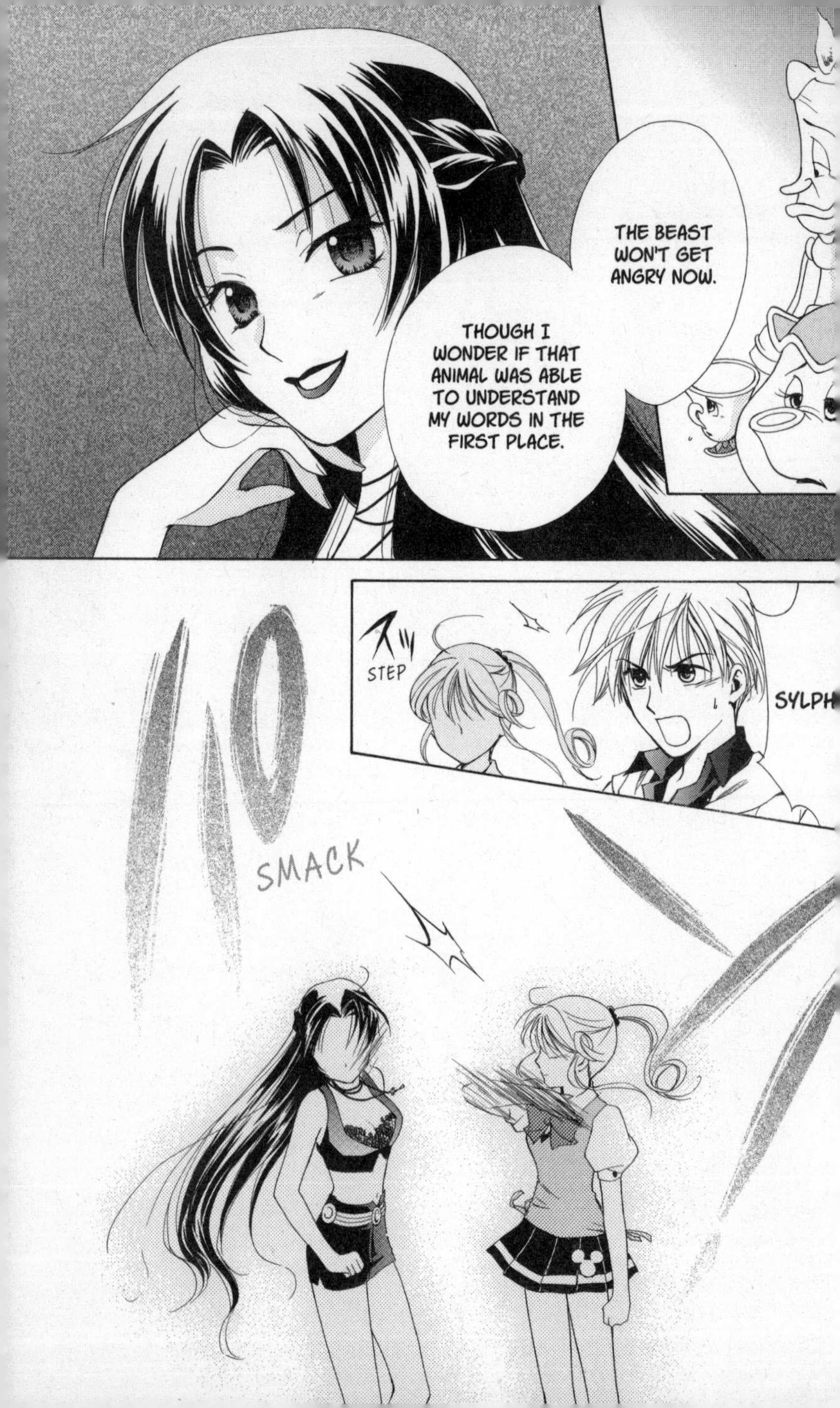
THE BEAST WON'T GET ANGRY NOW.
THOUGH I WONDER IF THAT ANIMAL WAS ABLE TO UNDERSTAND MY WORDS IN THE FIRST PLACE.
SYLPH
スッ
STEP
SMACK

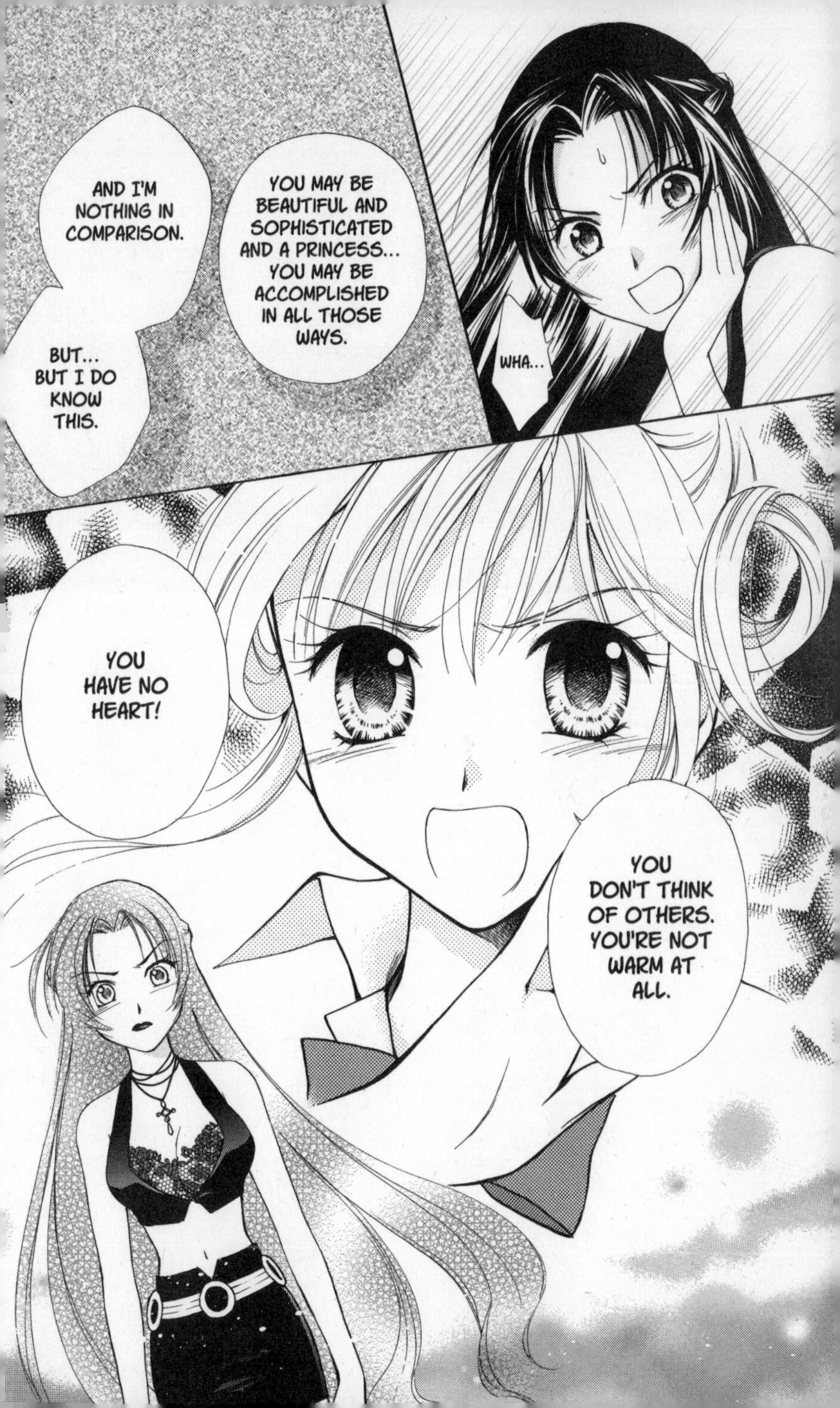
WHA...
YOU MAY BE BEAUTIFUL AND SOPHISTICATED AND A PRINCESS... YOU MAY BE ACCOMPLISHED IN ALL THOSE WAYS.
AND I'M NOTHING IN COMPARISON.
BUT... BUT I DO KNOW THIS.
YOU HAVE NO HEART!
YOU DON'T THINK OF OTHERS. YOU'RE NOT WARM AT ALL.

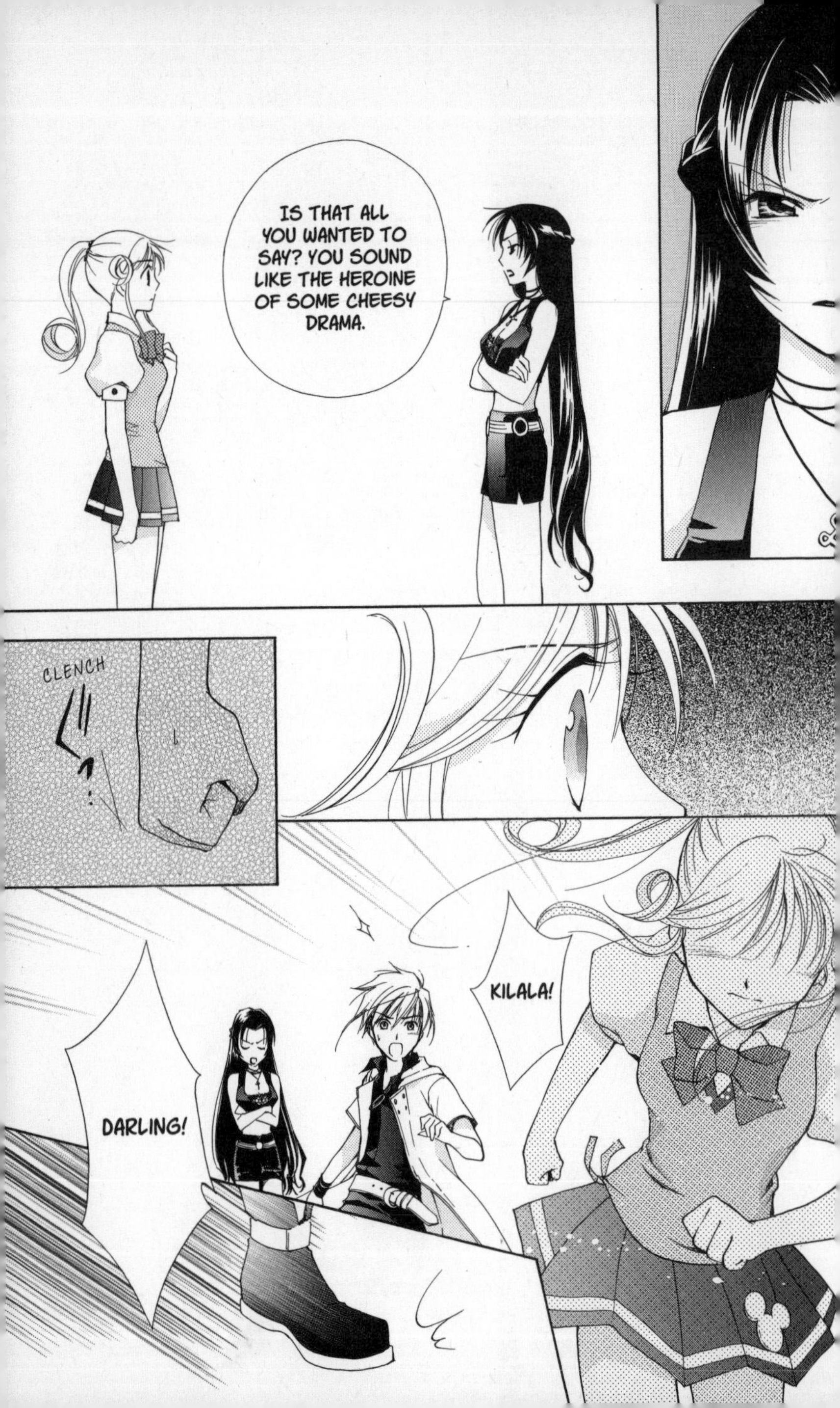

IS THAT ALL YOU WANTED TO SAY? YOU SOUND LIKE THE HEROINE OF SOME CHEESY DRAMA.
CLENCH
KILALA!
DARLING!

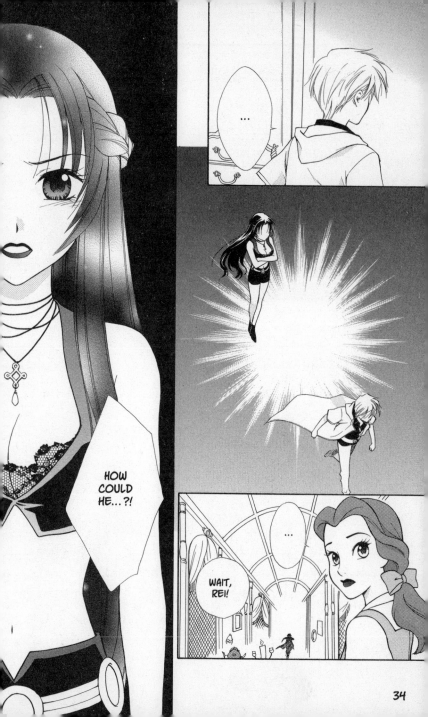

...

HOW COULD HE...?!

...

WAIT, REI!

34

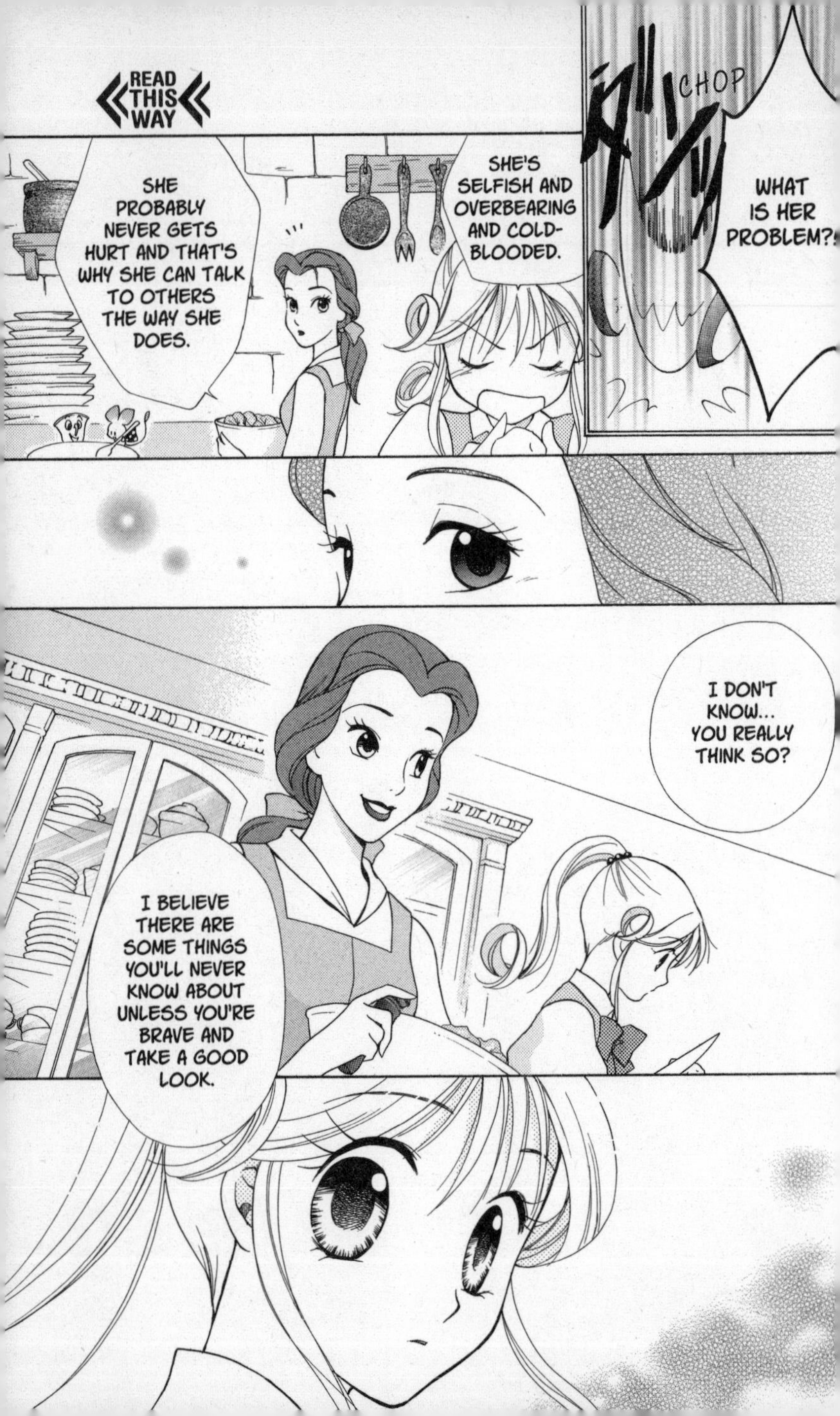
READ THIS WAY
CHOP
WHAT IS HER PROBLEM?!
SHE'S SELFISH AND OVERBEARING AND COLD-BLOODED.
SHE PROBABLY NEVER GETS HURT AND THAT'S WHY SHE CAN TALK TO OTHERS THE WAY SHE DOES.
I DON'T KNOW... YOU REALLY THINK SO?
I BELIEVE THERE ARE SOME THINGS YOU'LL NEVER KNOW ABOUT UNLESS YOU'RE BRAVE AND TAKE A GOOD LOOK.

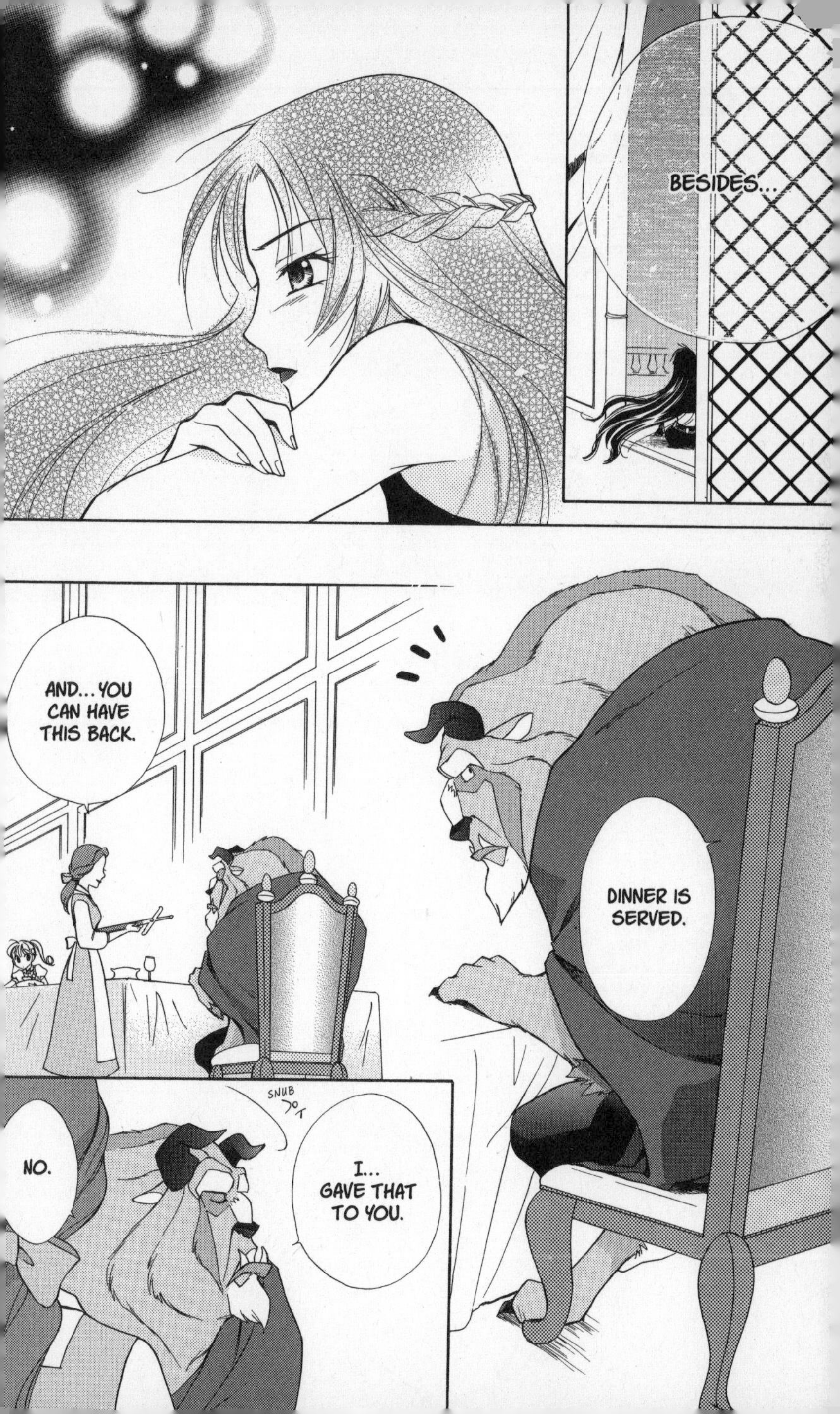
BESIDES...
DINNER IS SERVED.
AND... YOU CAN HAVE THIS BACK.
SNUB
I... GAVE THAT TO YOU.
NO.

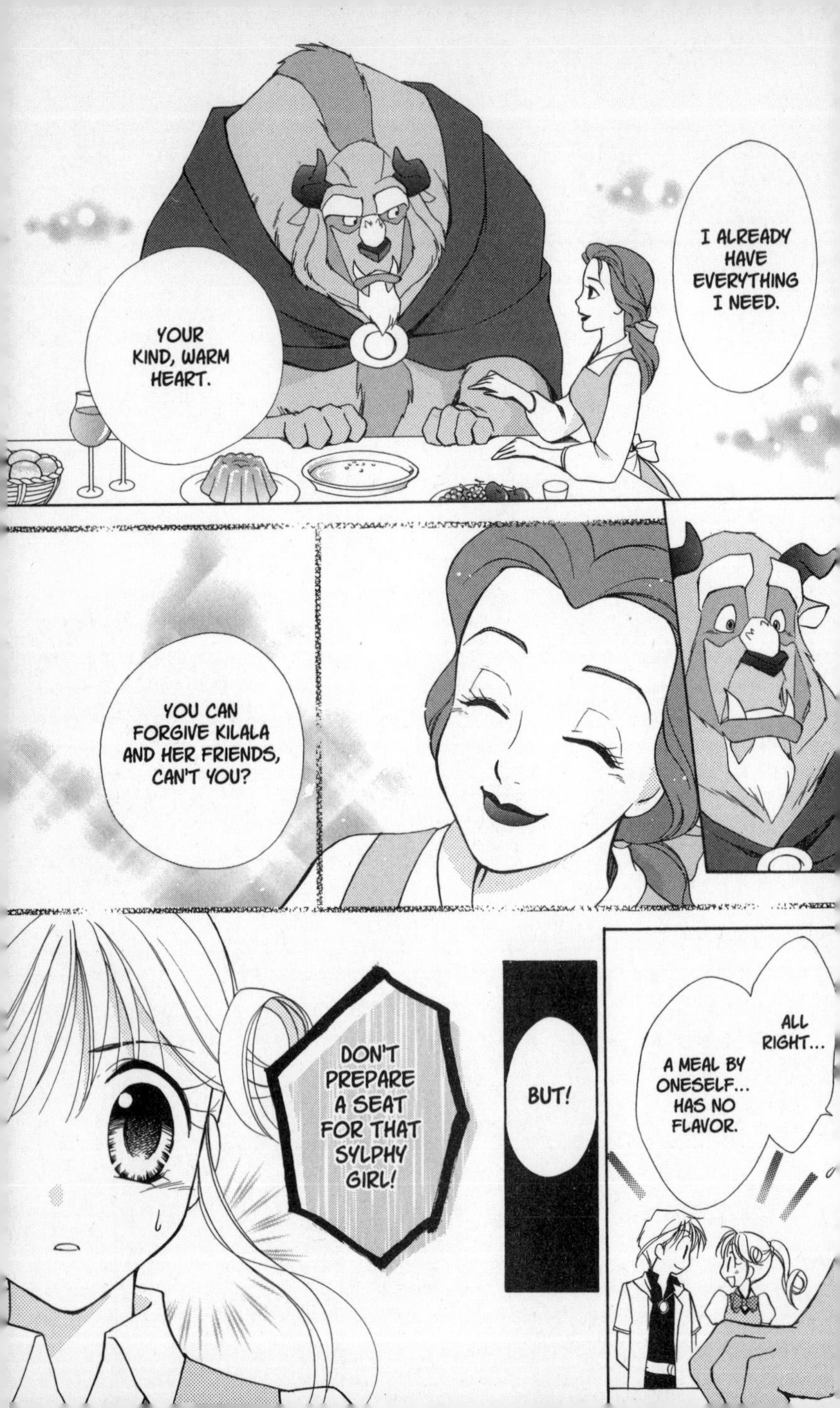

I ALREADY HAVE EVERYTHING I NEED.
YOUR KIND, WARM HEART.
YOU CAN FORGIVE KILALA AND HER FRIENDS, CAN'T YOU?
ALL RIGHT...
A MEAL BY ONESELF... HAS NO FLAVOR.
BUT!
DON'T PREPARE A SEAT FOR THAT SYLPHY GIRL!

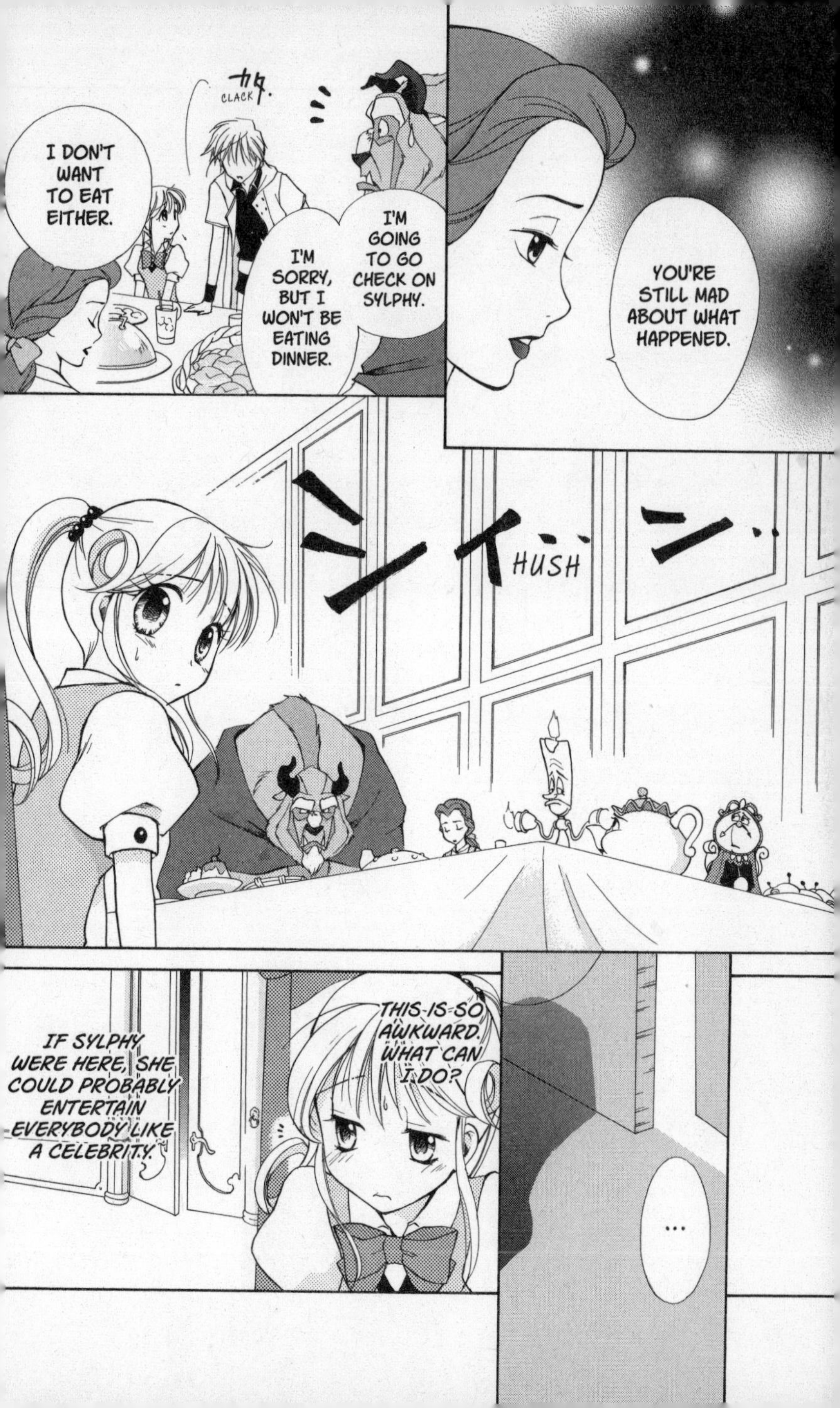
YOU'RE STILL MAD ABOUT WHAT HAPPENED.
I'M GOING TO GO CHECK ON SYLPHY.
I'M SORRY, BUT I WON'T BE EATING DINNER.
CLACK
I DON'T WANT TO EAT EITHER.
HUSH
...
THIS IS SO AWKWARD. WHAT CAN I DO?
IF SYLPHY WERE HERE, SHE COULD PROBABLY ENTERTAIN EVERYBODY LIKE A CELEBRITY.

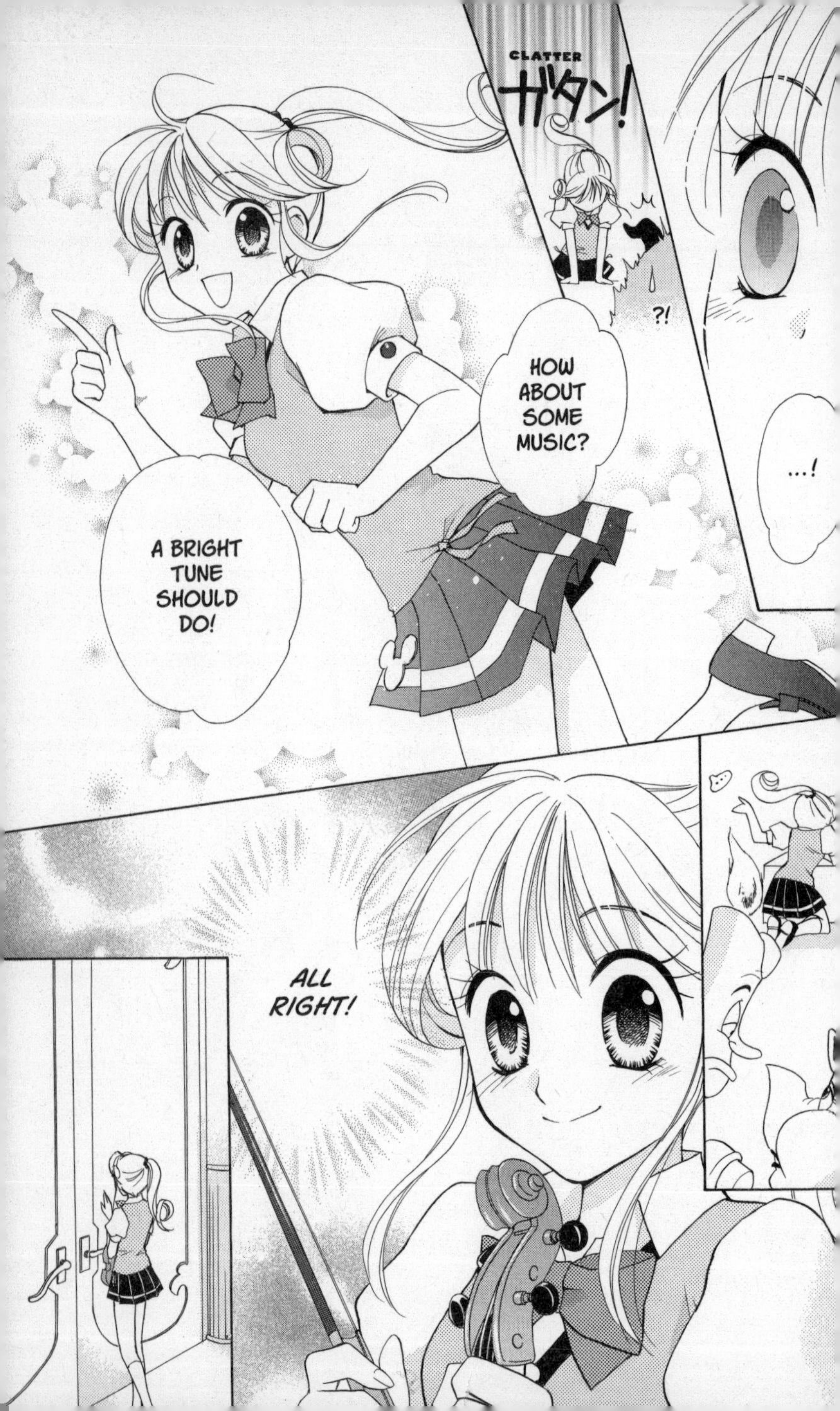
...!
CLATTER
ガタン!
?!
HOW ABOUT SOME MUSIC?
A BRIGHT TUNE SHOULD DO!
ALL RIGHT!

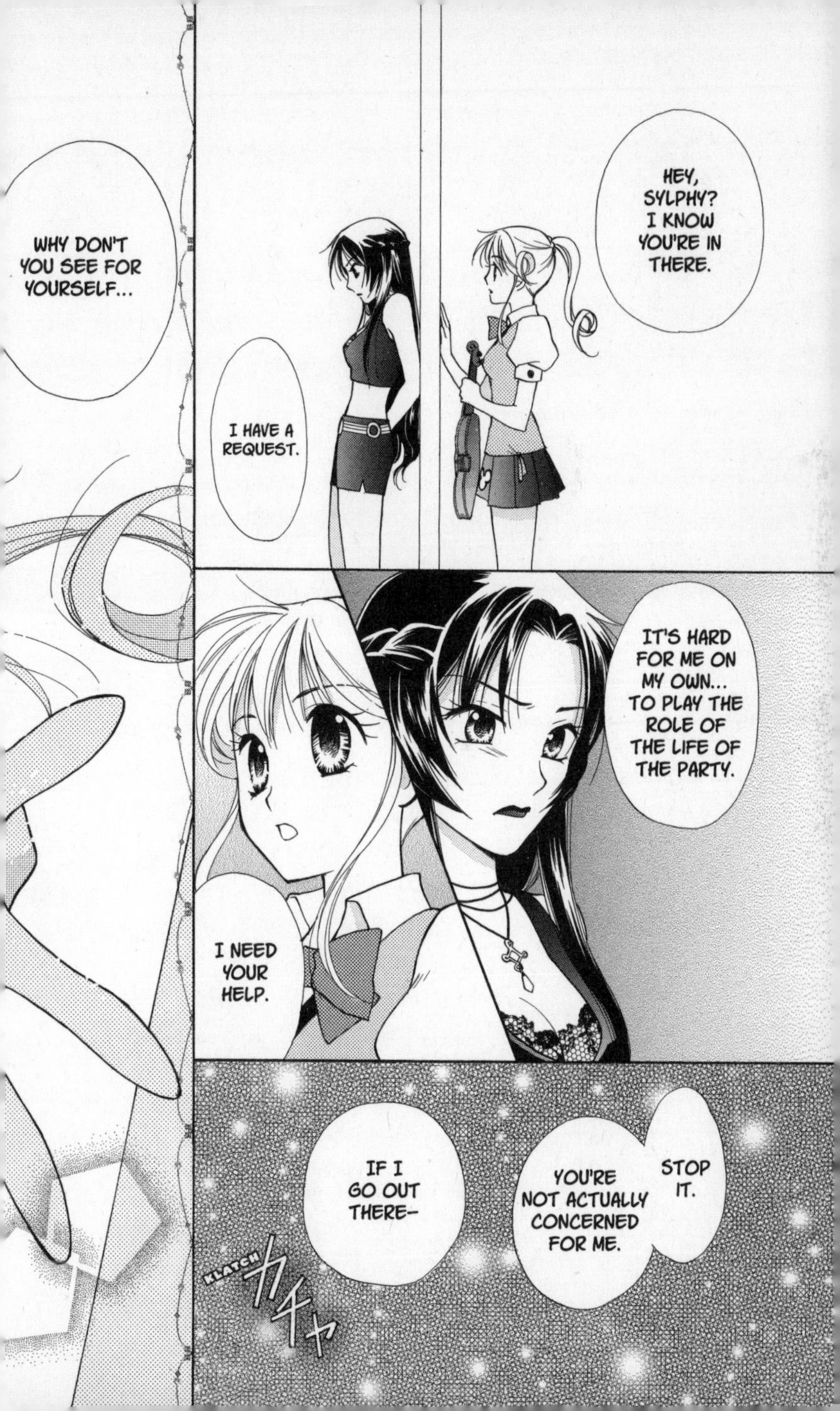
HEY, SYLPHY? I KNOW YOU'RE IN THERE.
I HAVE A REQUEST.
IT'S HARD FOR ME ON MY OWN... TO PLAY THE ROLE OF THE LIFE OF THE PARTY.
I NEED YOUR HELP.
STOP IT.
YOU'RE NOT ACTUALLY CONCERNED FOR ME.
IF I GO OUT THERE-
KLATCH
WHY DON'T YOU SEE FOR YOURSELF...

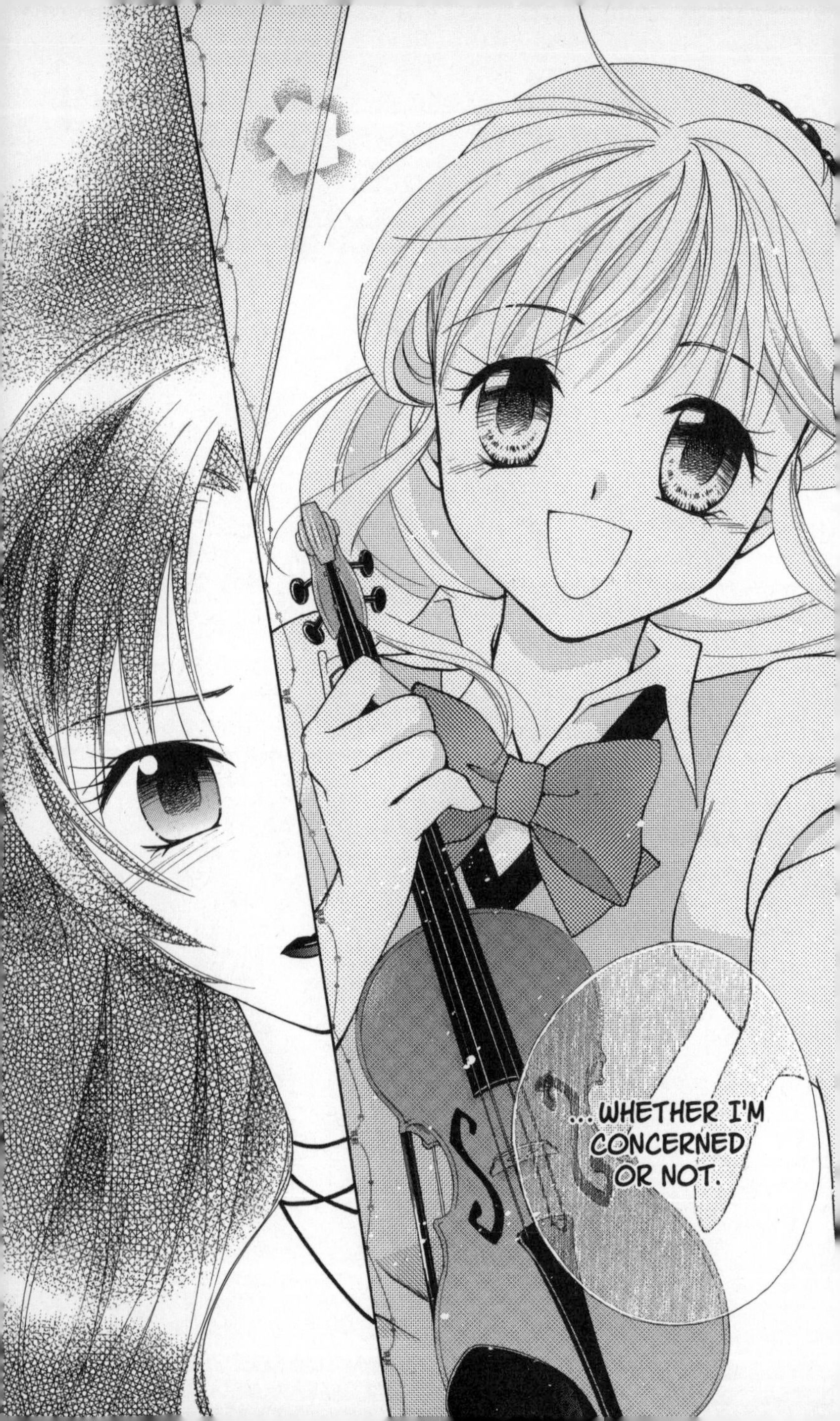
...WHETHER I'M CONCERNED OR NOT.

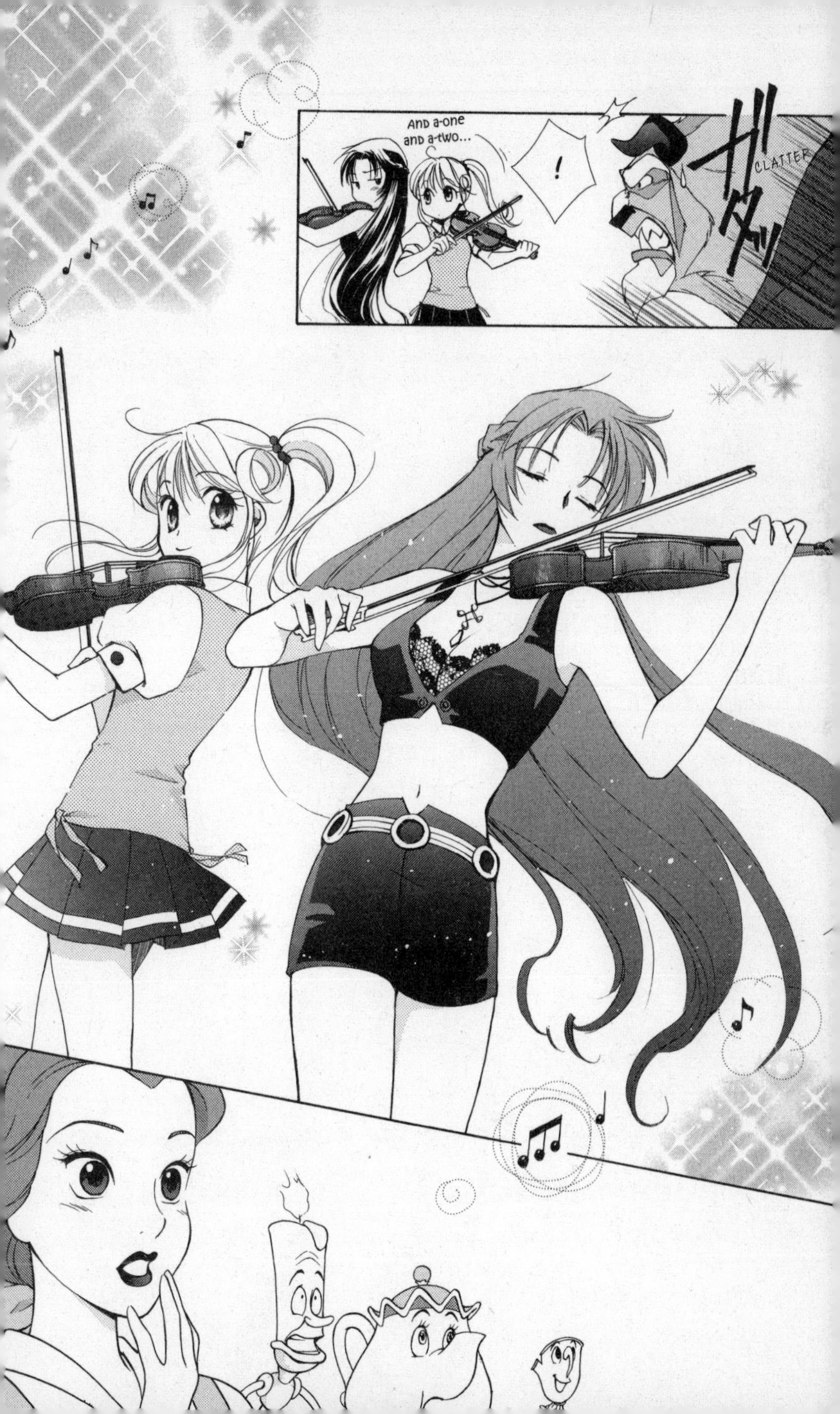
CLATTER
!
And a-one and a-two...

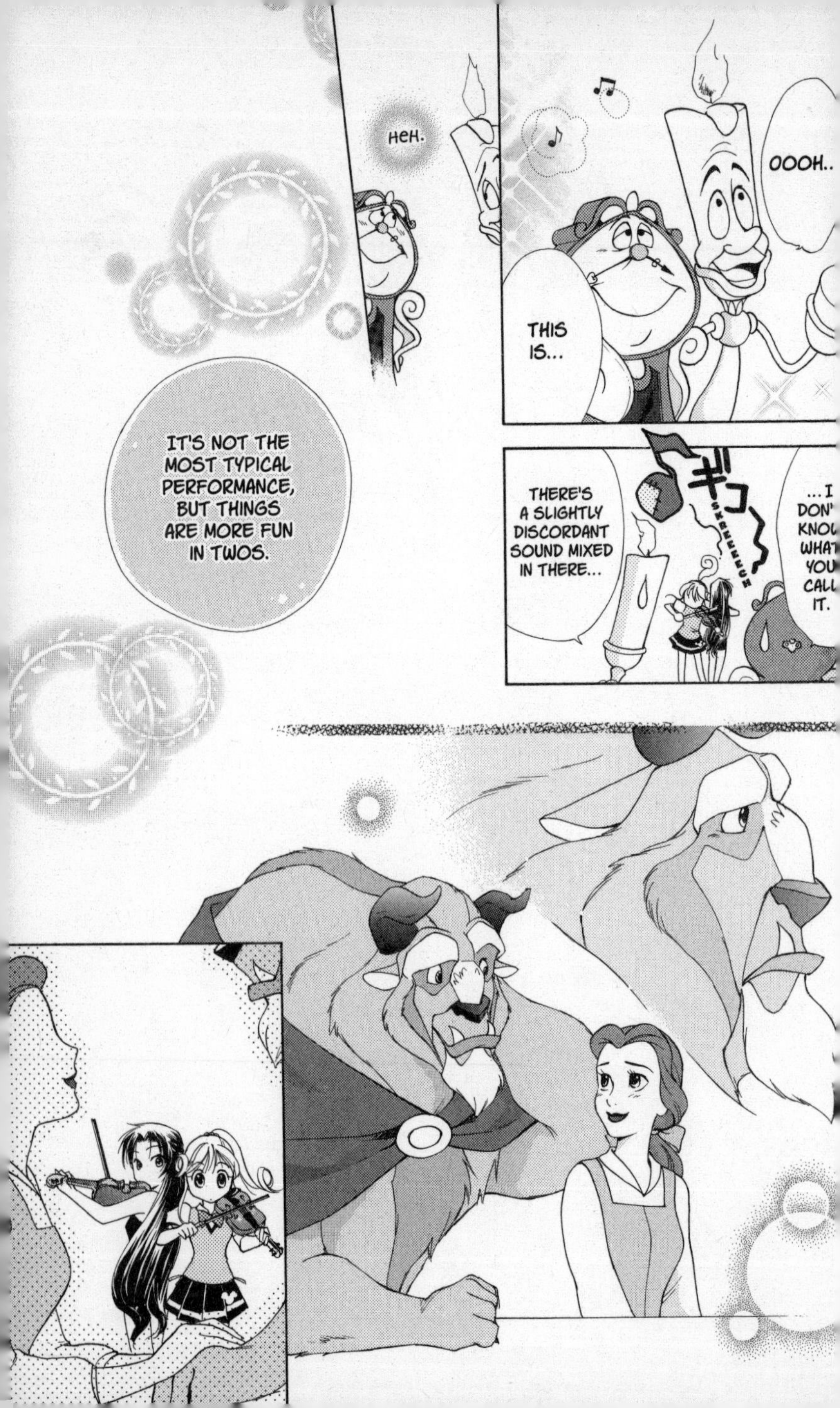
OOOH..
THIS IS...
HEH.
...I DON' KNO WHA YOU CALL IT.
ギコ
SKREEEECH
THERE'S A SLIGHTLY DISCORDANT SOUND MIXED IN THERE...
IT'S NOT THE MOST TYPICAL PERFORMANCE, BUT THINGS ARE MORE FUN IN TWOS.

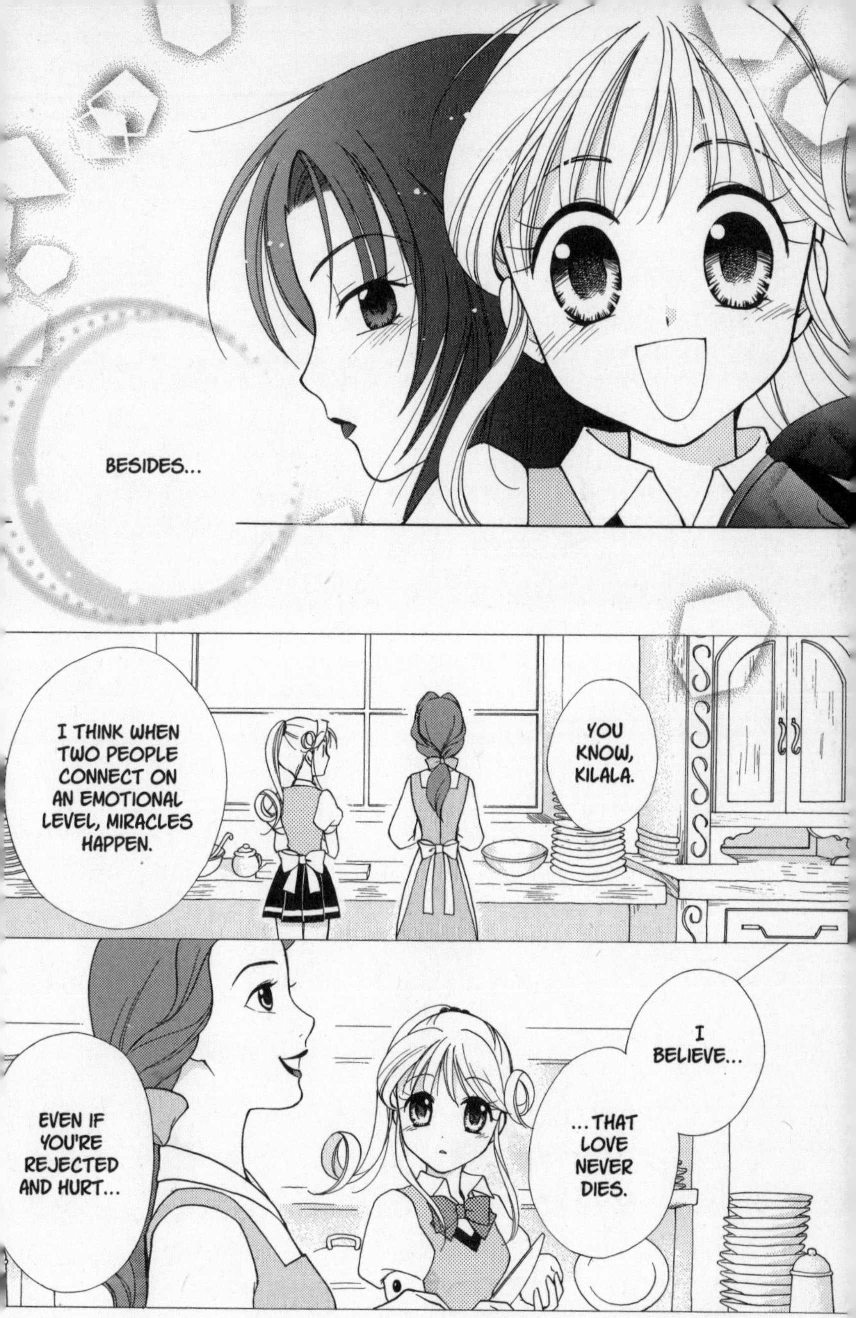
BESIDES...
YOU KNOW, KILALA.
I THINK WHEN TWO PEOPLE CONNECT ON AN EMOTIONAL LEVEL, MIRACLES HAPPEN.
I BELIEVE...
...THAT LOVE NEVER DIES.
EVEN IF YOU'RE REJECTED AND HURT...

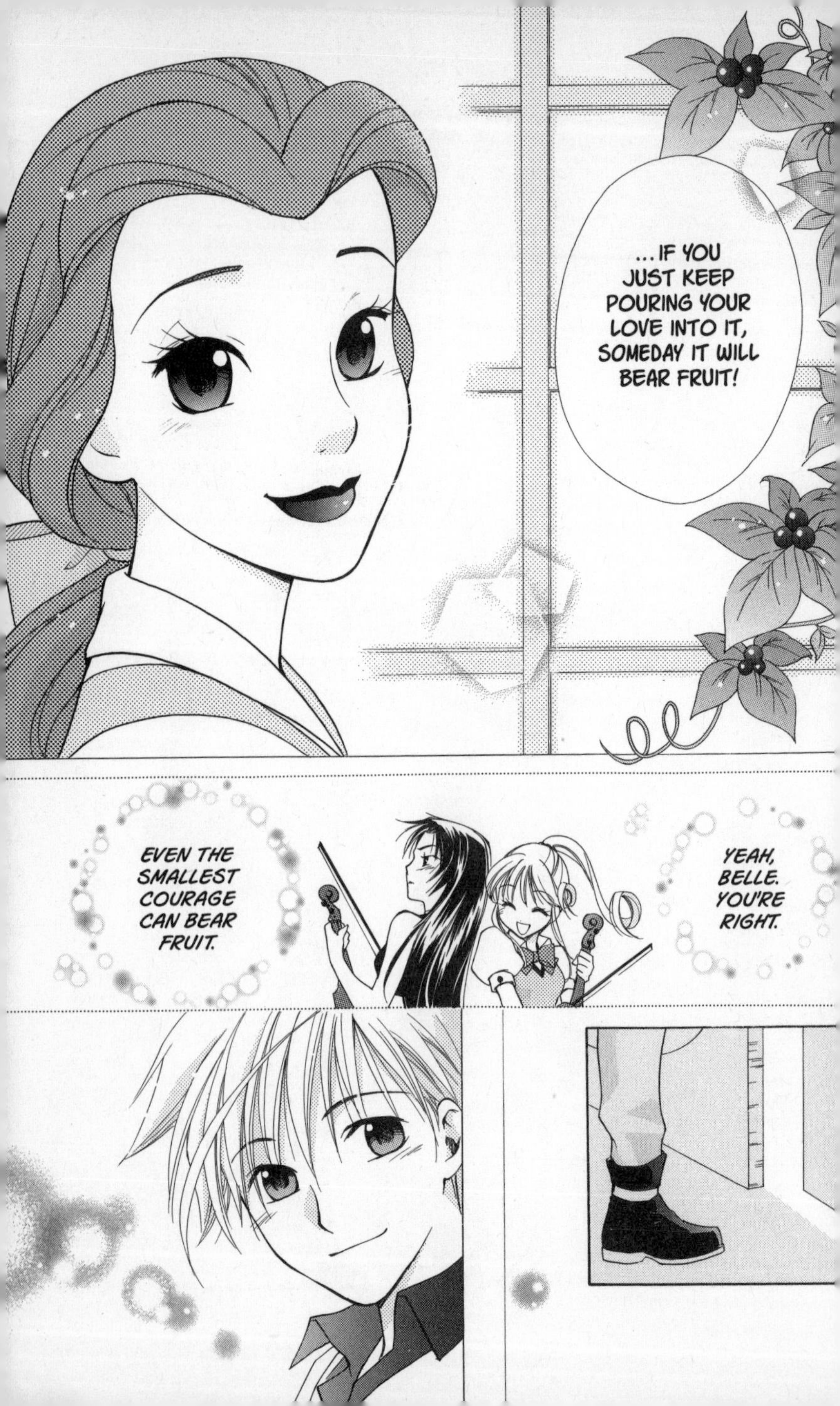
...IF YOU JUST KEEP POURING YOUR LOVE INTO IT, SOMEDAY IT WILL BEAR FRUIT!
YEAH, BELLE. YOU'RE RIGHT.
EVEN THE SMALLEST COURAGE CAN BEAR FRUIT.

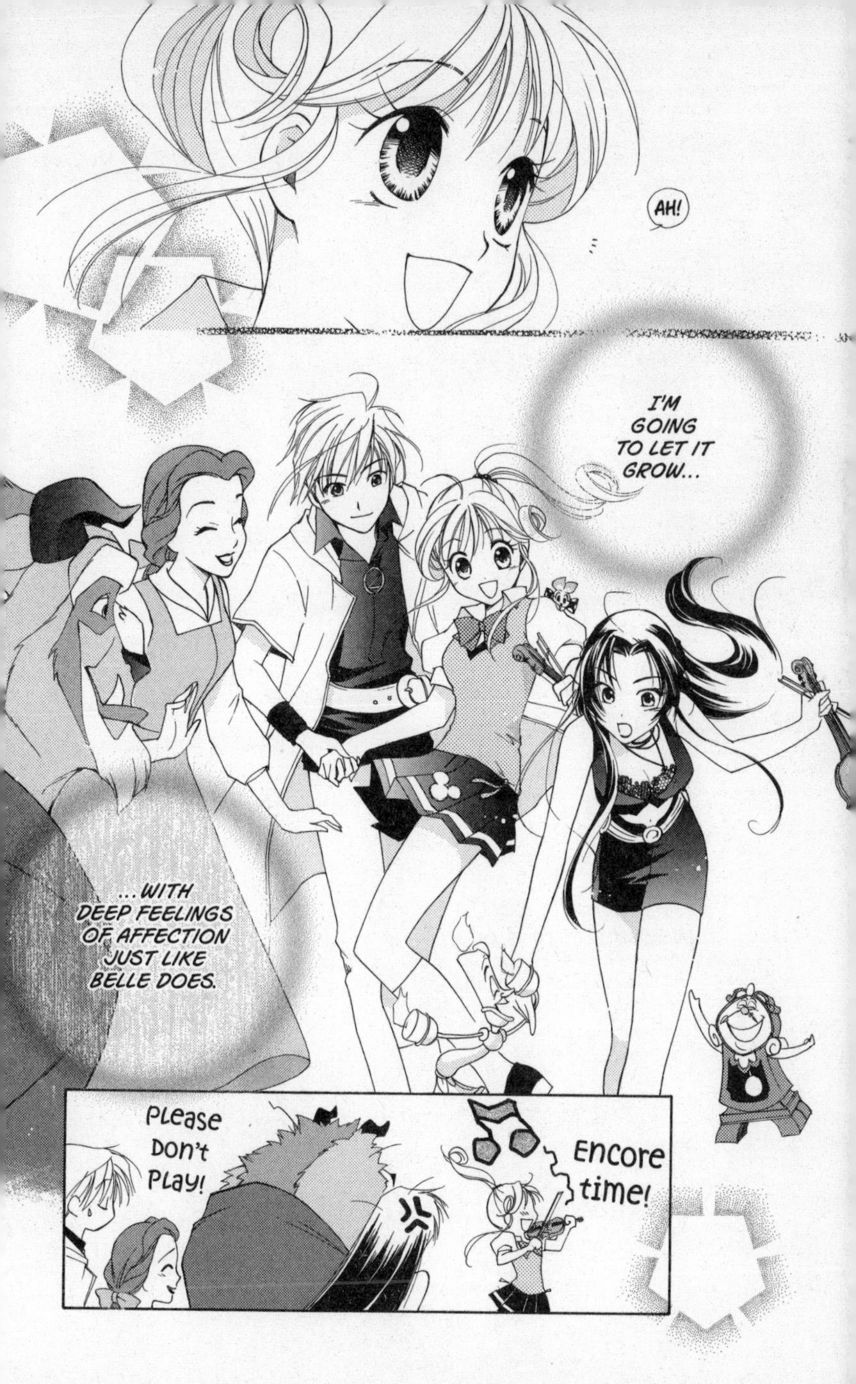
AH!
I'M GOING TO LET IT GROW...
...WITH DEEP FEELINGS OF AFFECTION JUST LIKE BELLE DOES.
Encore time!
Please Don't Play!

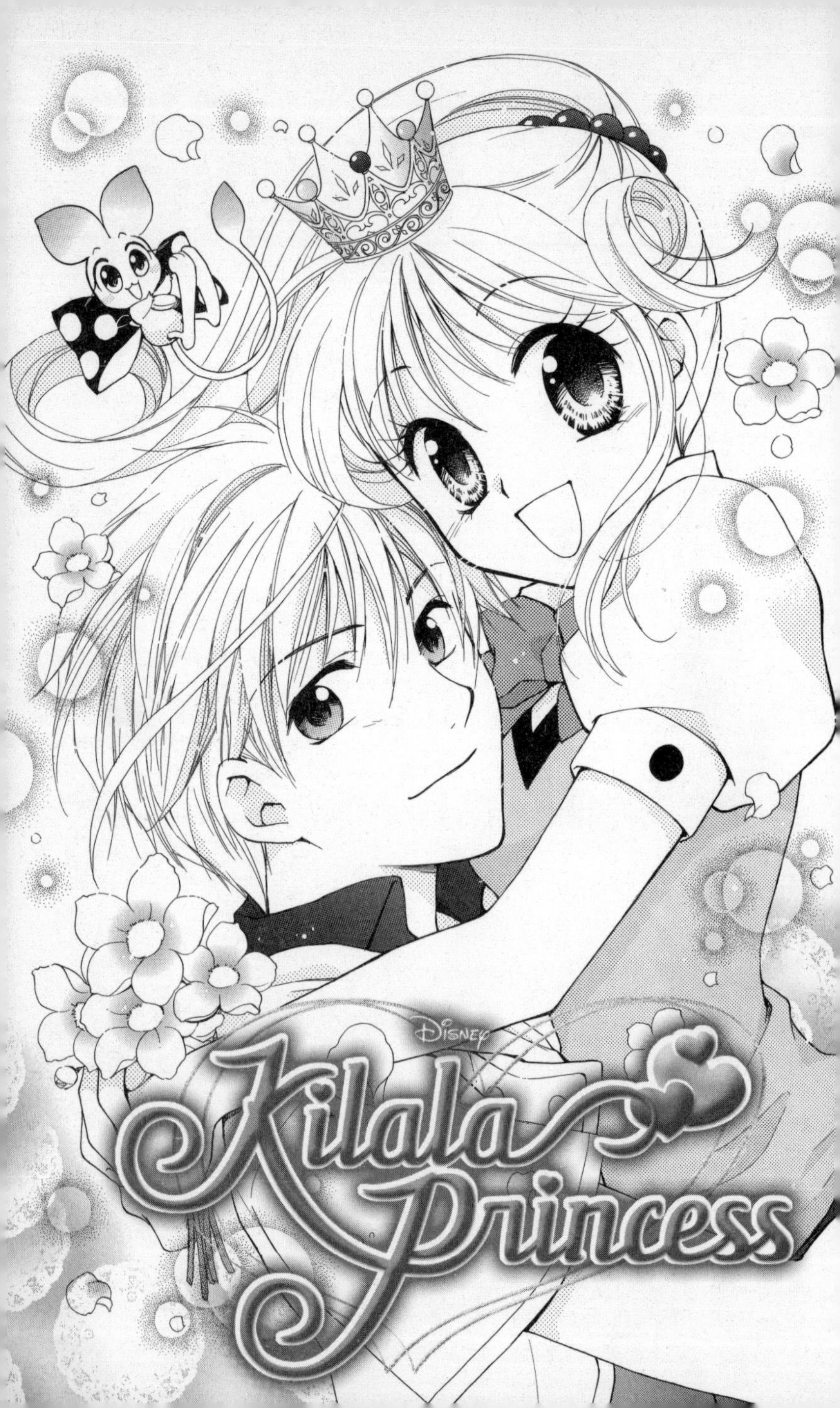
DISNEY
Kilala Princess

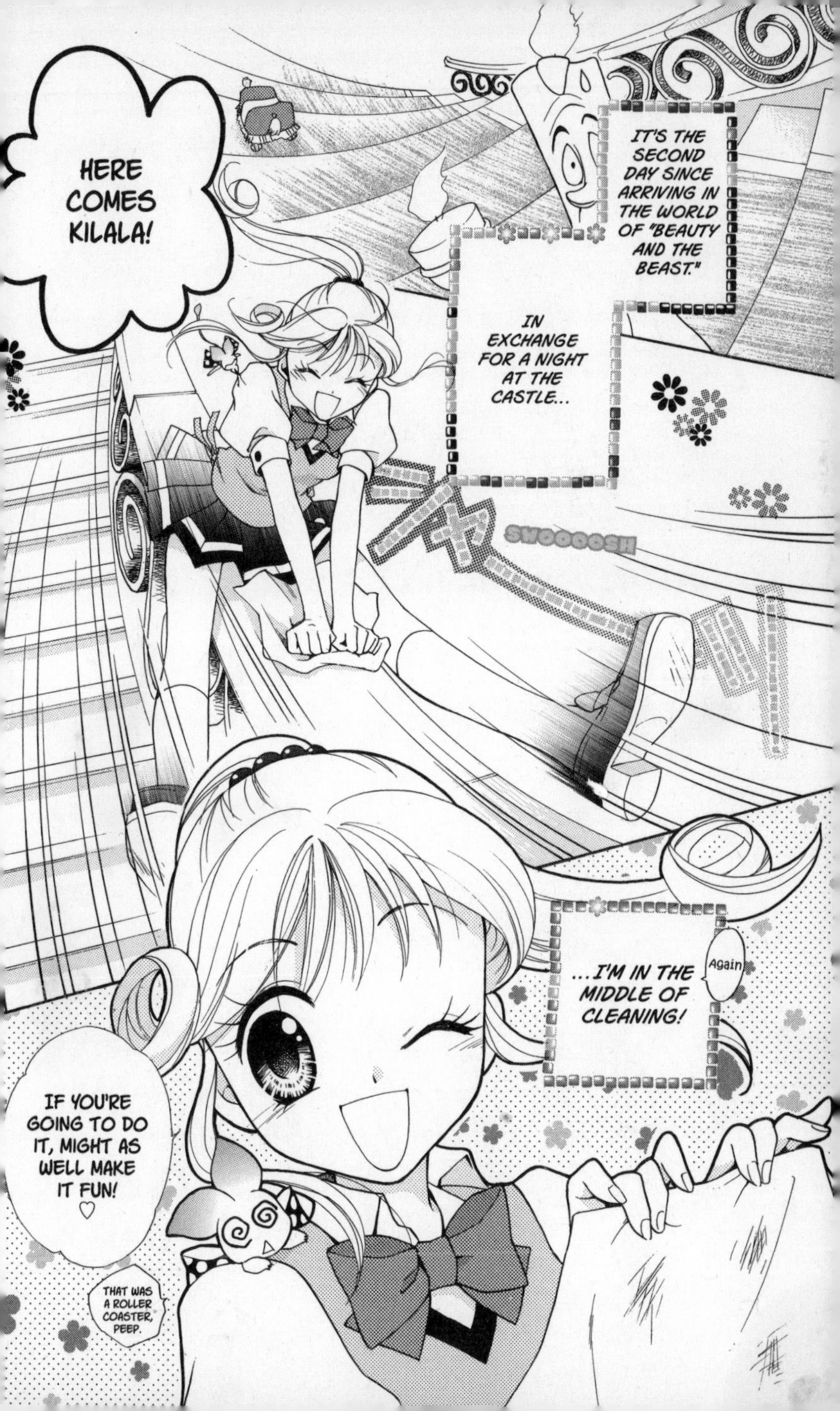
IT'S THE SECOND DAY SINCE ARRIVING IN THE WORLD OF "BEAUTY AND THE BEAST."
HERE COMES KILALA!
IN EXCHANGE FOR A NIGHT AT THE CASTLE...
SWOOOOSH!!
...I'M IN THE MIDDLE OF CLEANING!
Again
IF YOU'RE GOING TO DO IT, MIGHT AS WELL MAKE IT FUN! ♡
THAT WAS A ROLLER COASTER, PEEP.

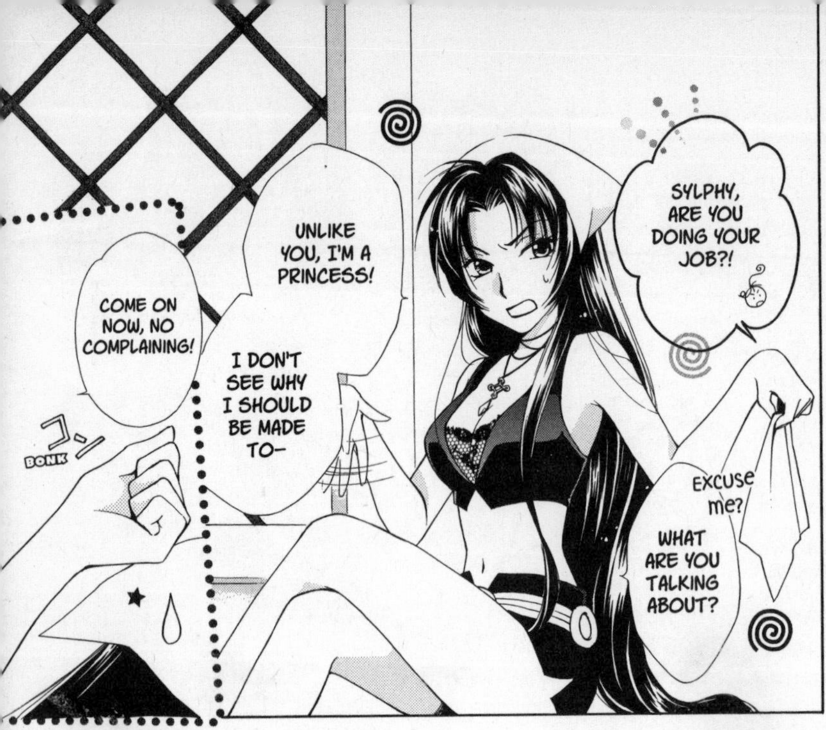
SYLPHY, ARE YOU DOING YOUR JOB?!
EXCUSE me?
WHAT ARE YOU TALKING ABOUT?
UNLIKE YOU, I'M A PRINCESS!
I DON'T SEE WHY I SHOULD BE MADE TO-
COME ON NOW, NO COMPLAINING!
コン
BONK

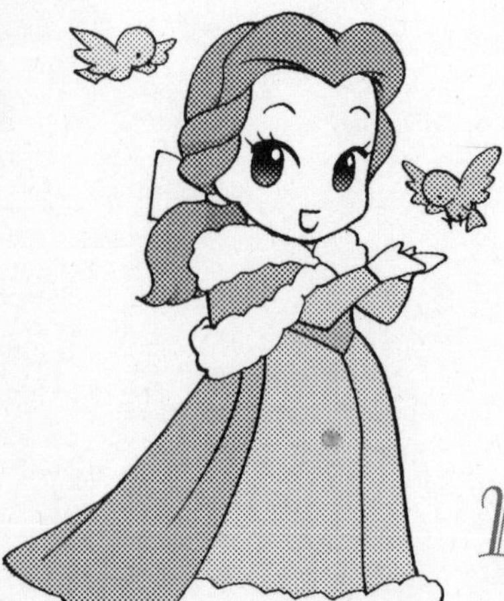

Belle

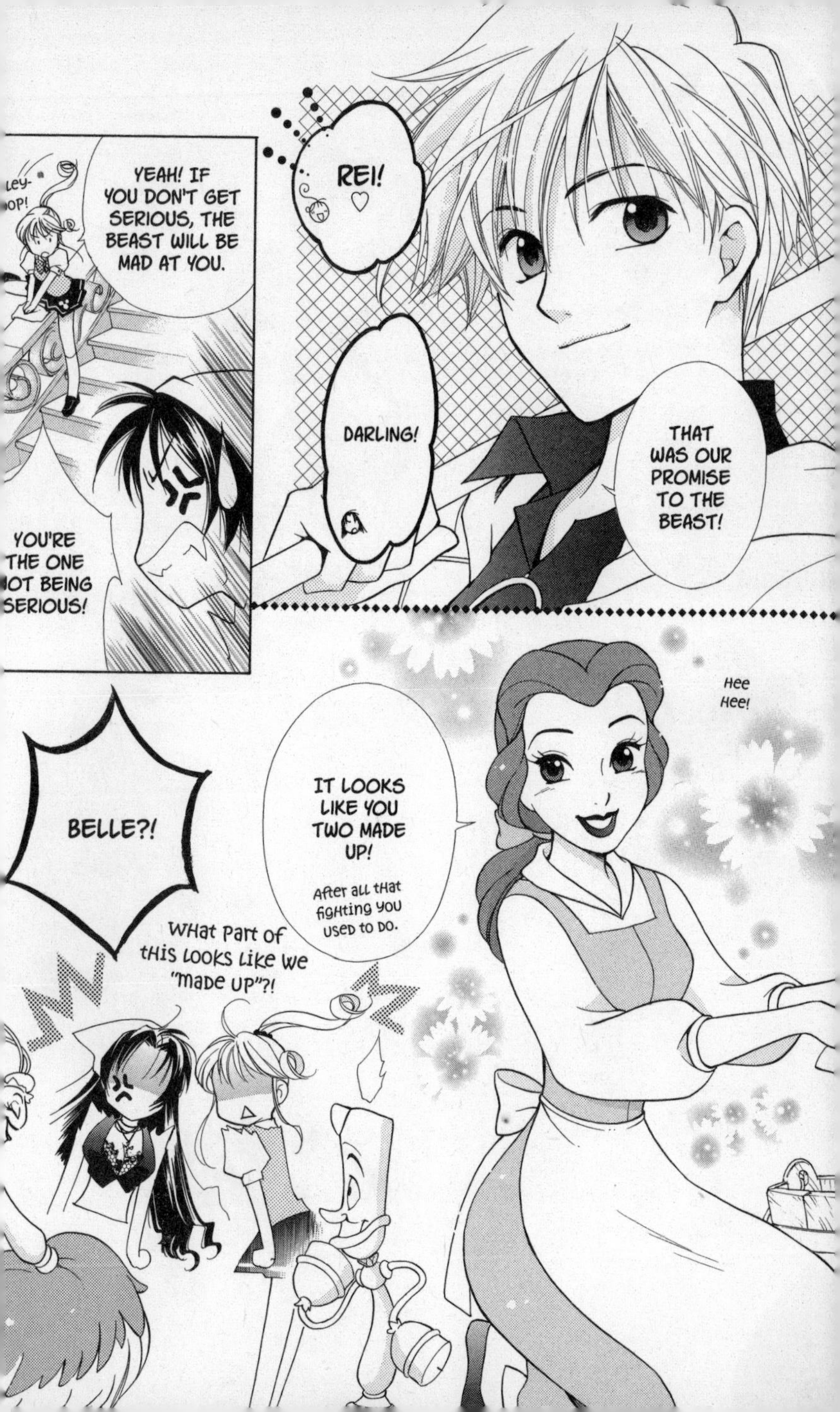
REI! ♡
THAT WAS OUR PROMISE TO THE BEAST!
DARLING!
YEAH! IF YOU DON'T GET SERIOUS, THE BEAST WILL BE MAD AT YOU.
Ley- OP!
YOU'RE THE ONE OT BEING SERIOUS!
Hee Hee!
IT LOOKS LIKE YOU TWO MADE UP!
After all that fighting you used to do.
BELLE?!
What part of this looks like we "made up"?!

READ THIS WAY

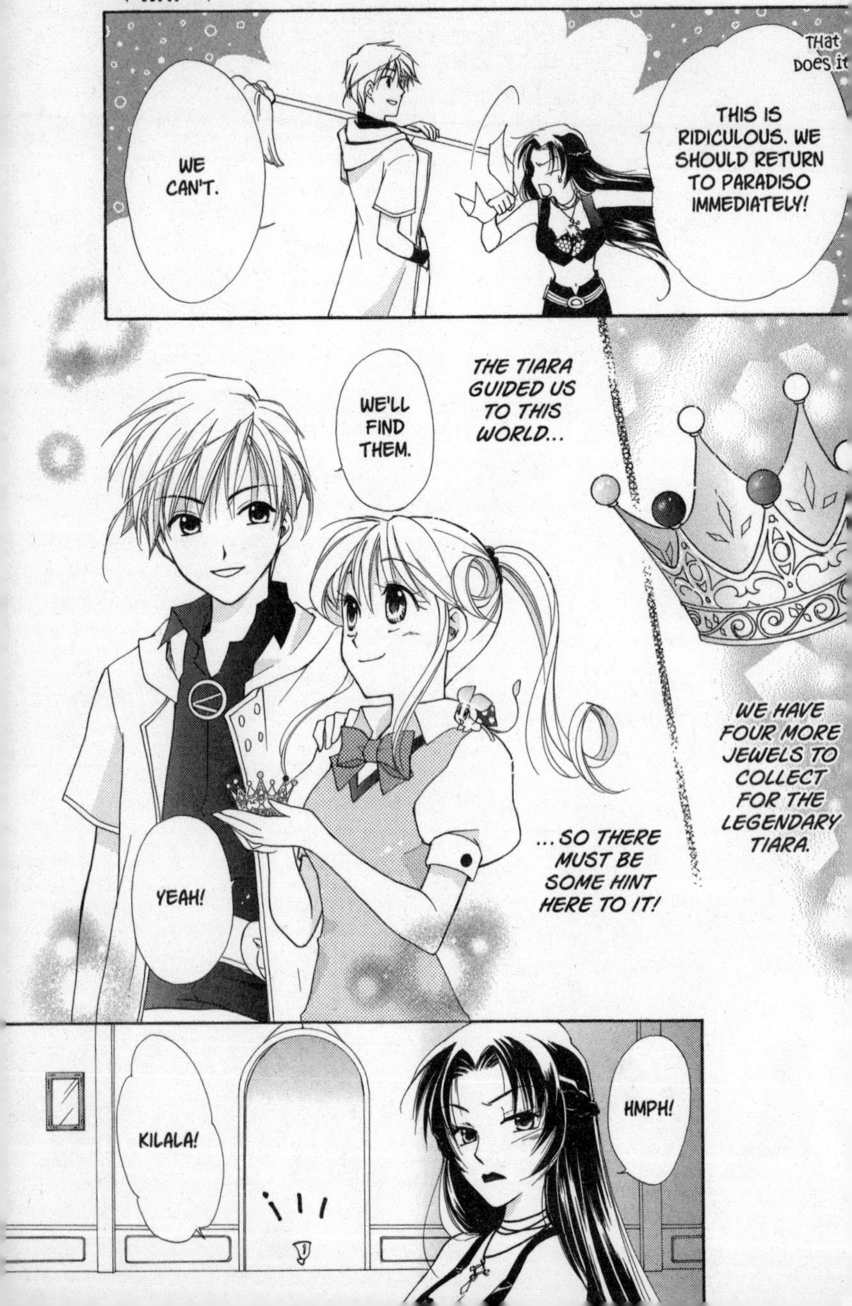
THAT DOES IT
THIS IS RIDICULOUS. WE SHOULD RETURN TO PARADISO IMMEDIATELY!
WE CAN'T.
WE HAVE FOUR MORE JEWELS TO COLLECT FOR THE LEGENDARY TIARA.
THE TIARA GUIDED US TO THIS WORLD...
...SO THERE MUST BE SOME HINT HERE TO IT!
WE'LL FIND THEM.
YEAH!
HMPH!
KILALA!

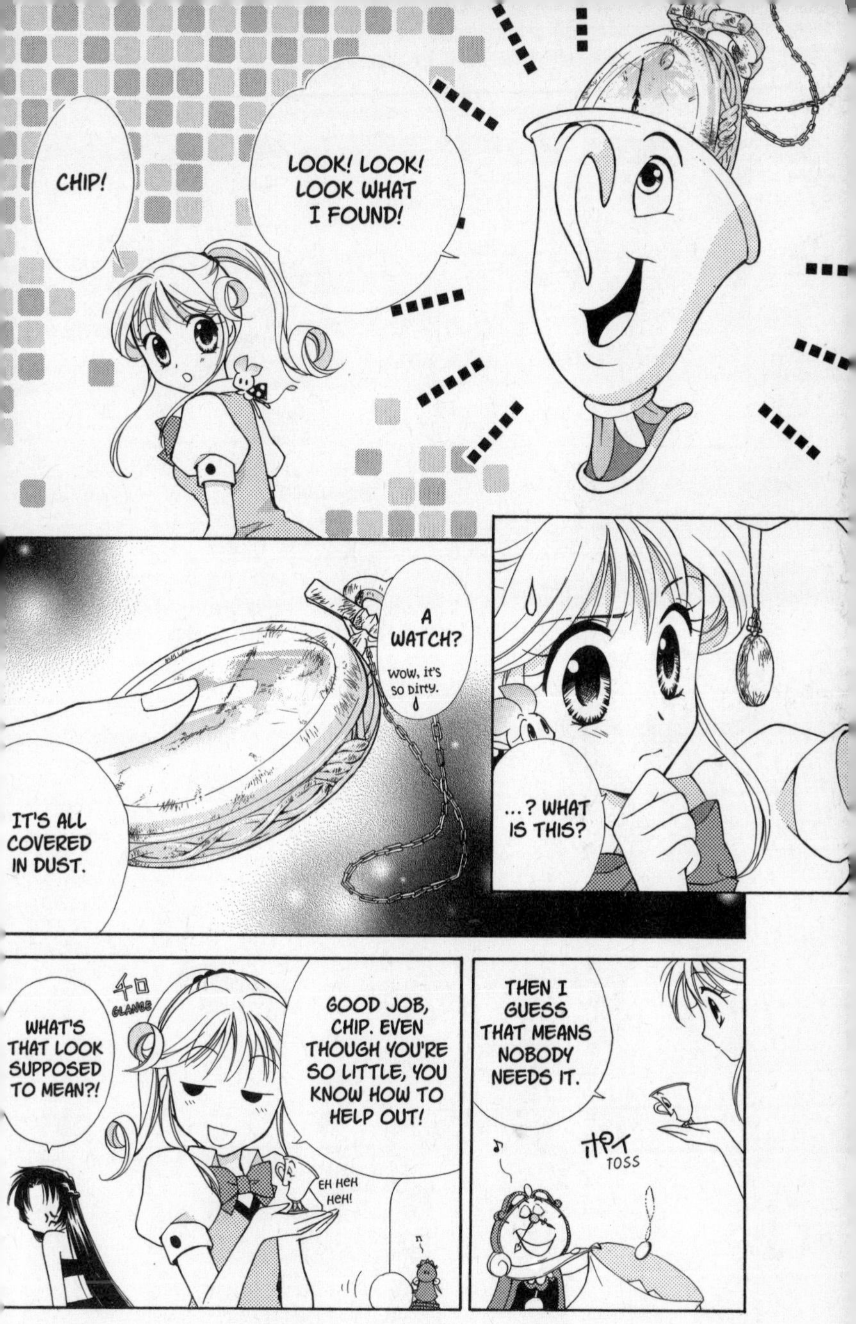
LOOK! LOOK! LOOK WHAT I FOUND!
CHIP!
...? WHAT IS THIS?
A WATCH?
WOW, it's so Dirty.
IT'S ALL COVERED IN DUST.
THEN I GUESS THAT MEANS NOBODY NEEDS IT.
ポイ TOSS
GOOD JOB, CHIP. EVEN THOUGH YOU'RE SO LITTLE, YOU KNOW HOW TO HELP OUT!
EH HEH HEH!
チロ GLANCE
WHAT'S THAT LOOK SUPPOSED TO MEAN?!

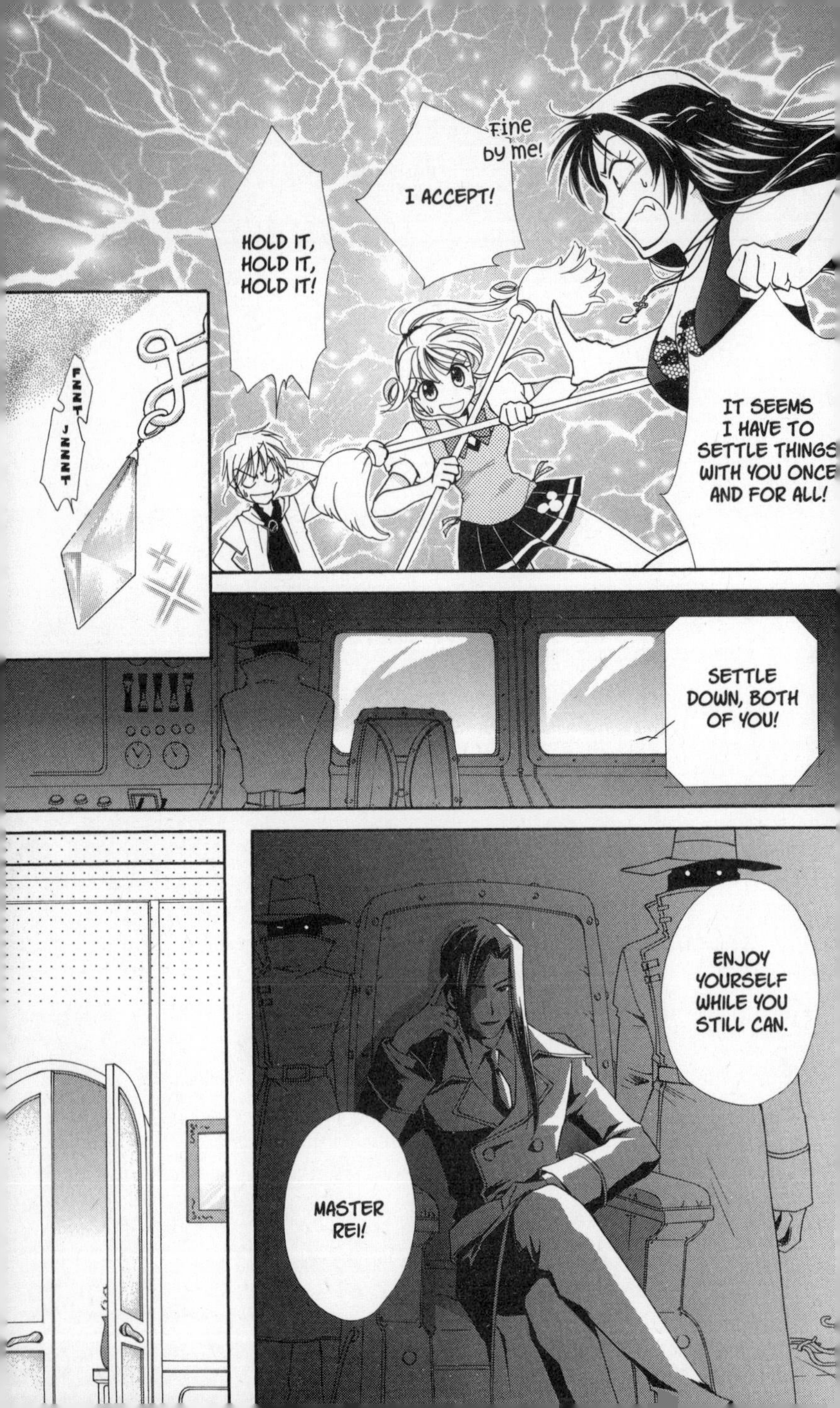
IT SEEMS I HAVE TO SETTLE THINGS WITH YOU ONCE AND FOR ALL!
Fine by me!
I ACCEPT!
HOLD IT, HOLD IT, HOLD IT!
FZZT
JZZZT
SETTLE DOWN, BOTH OF YOU!
ENJOY YOURSELF WHILE YOU STILL CAN.
MASTER REI!

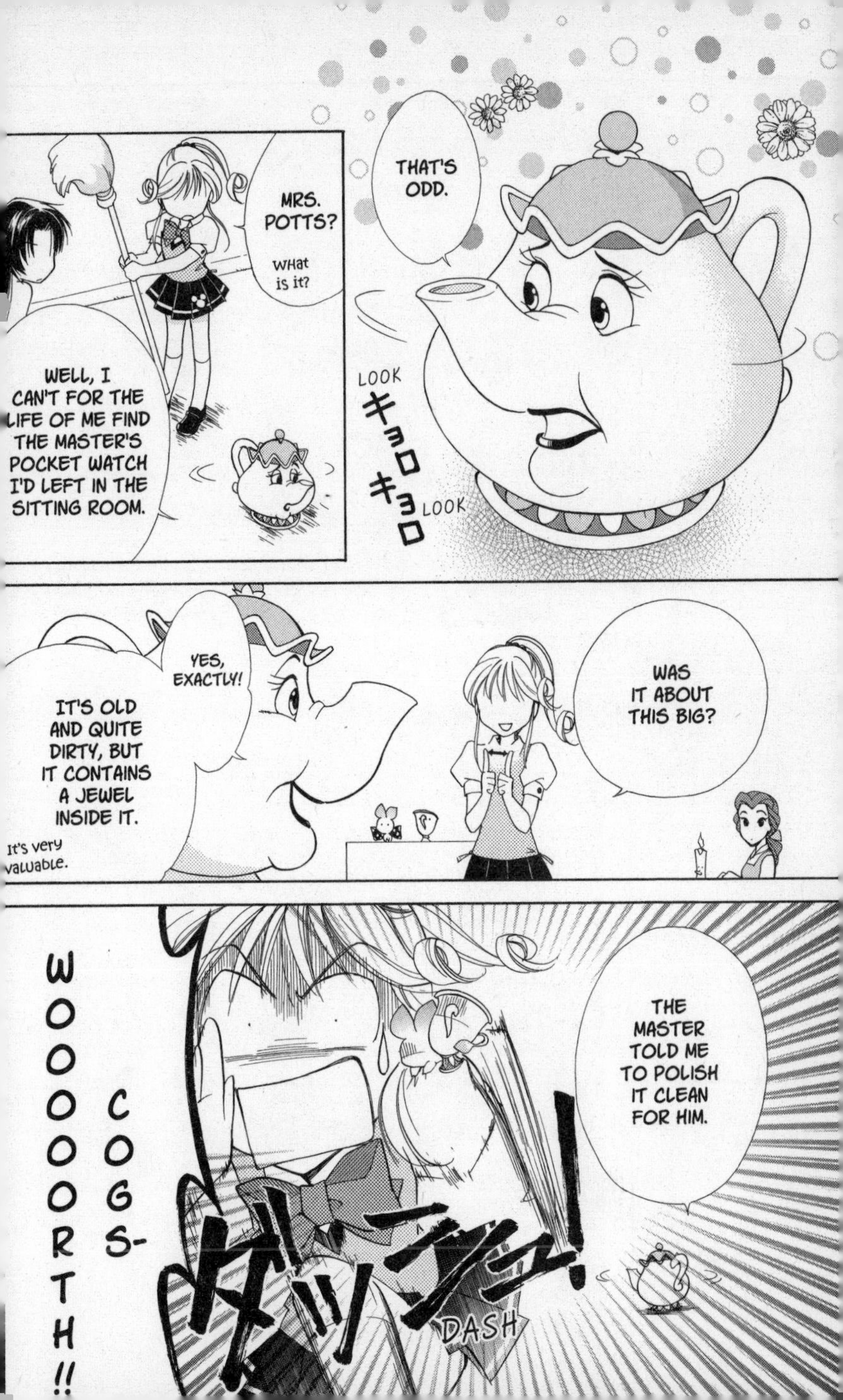
THAT'S ODD.
LOOK
キョロキョロ
LOOK
MRS. POTTS?
What is it?
WELL, I CAN'T FOR THE LIFE OF ME FIND THE MASTER'S POCKET WATCH I'D LEFT IN THE SITTING ROOM.
WAS IT ABOUT THIS BIG?
YES, EXACTLY!
IT'S OLD AND QUITE DIRTY, BUT IT CONTAINS A JEWEL INSIDE IT.
It's very valuable.
THE MASTER TOLD ME TO POLISH IT CLEAN FOR HIM.
DASH
COGS-
WOOOOORTH!!

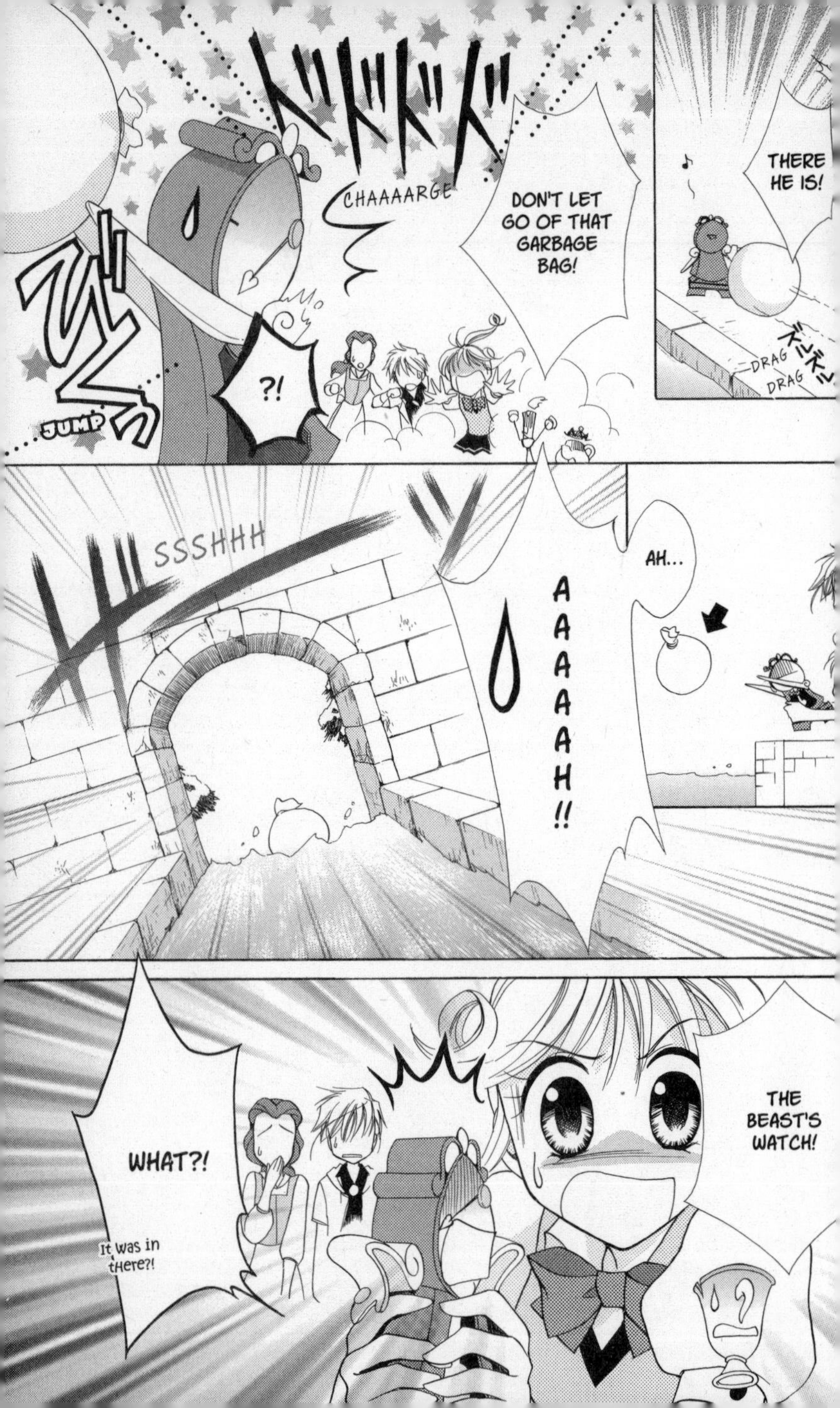
THERE HE IS!
DRAG DRAG
DON'T LET GO OF THAT GARBAGE BAG!
CHAAAARGE
?!
JUMP
AH...
AAAAAAH!!
SSSHHH
THE BEAST'S WATCH!
WHAT?!
It was in there?!

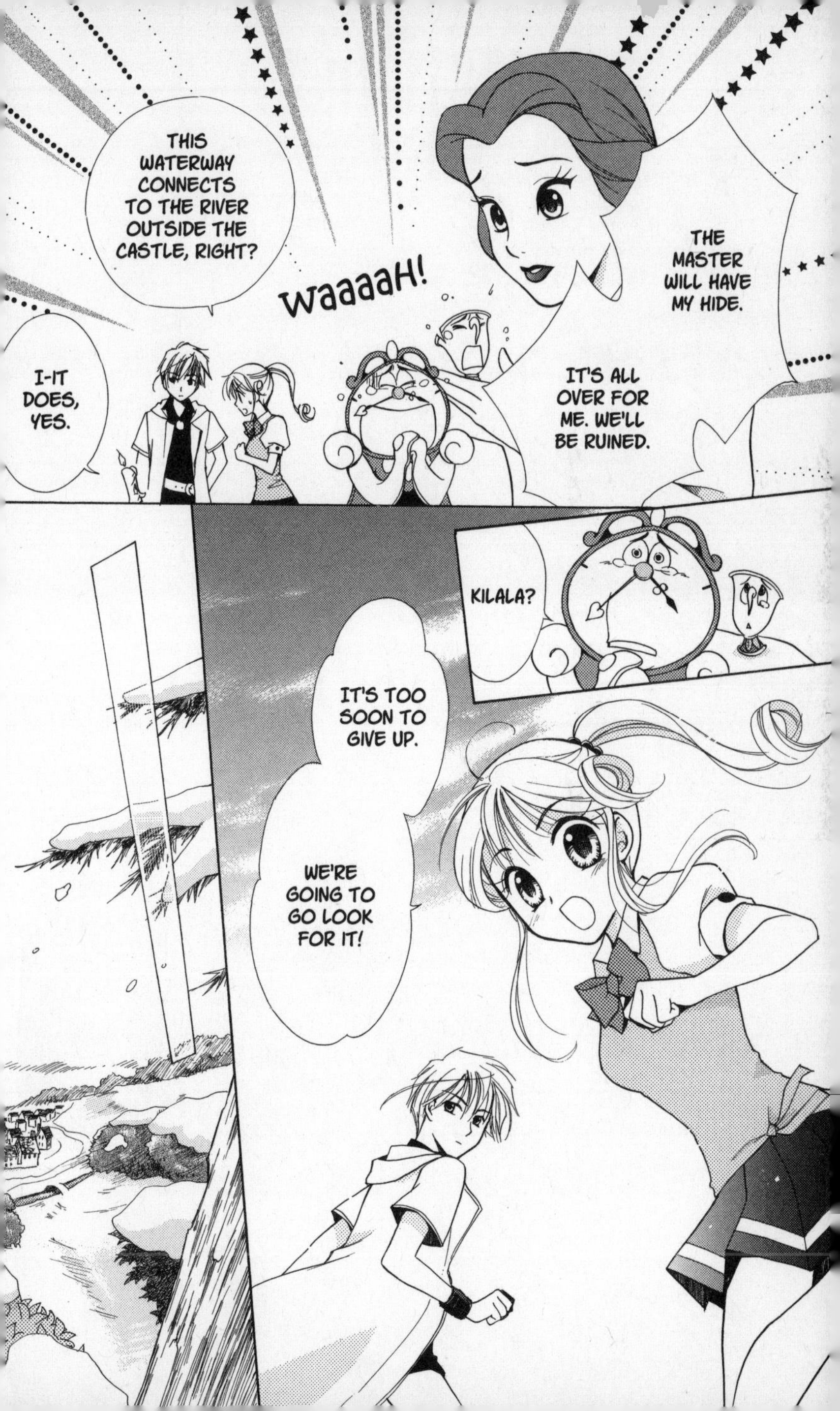
THE MASTER WILL HAVE MY HIDE.
IT'S ALL OVER FOR ME. WE'LL BE RUINED.
WAAAAH!
THIS WATERWAY CONNECTS TO THE RIVER OUTSIDE THE CASTLE, RIGHT?
I-IT DOES, YES.
KILALA?
IT'S TOO SOON TO GIVE UP.
WE'RE GOING TO GO LOOK FOR IT!

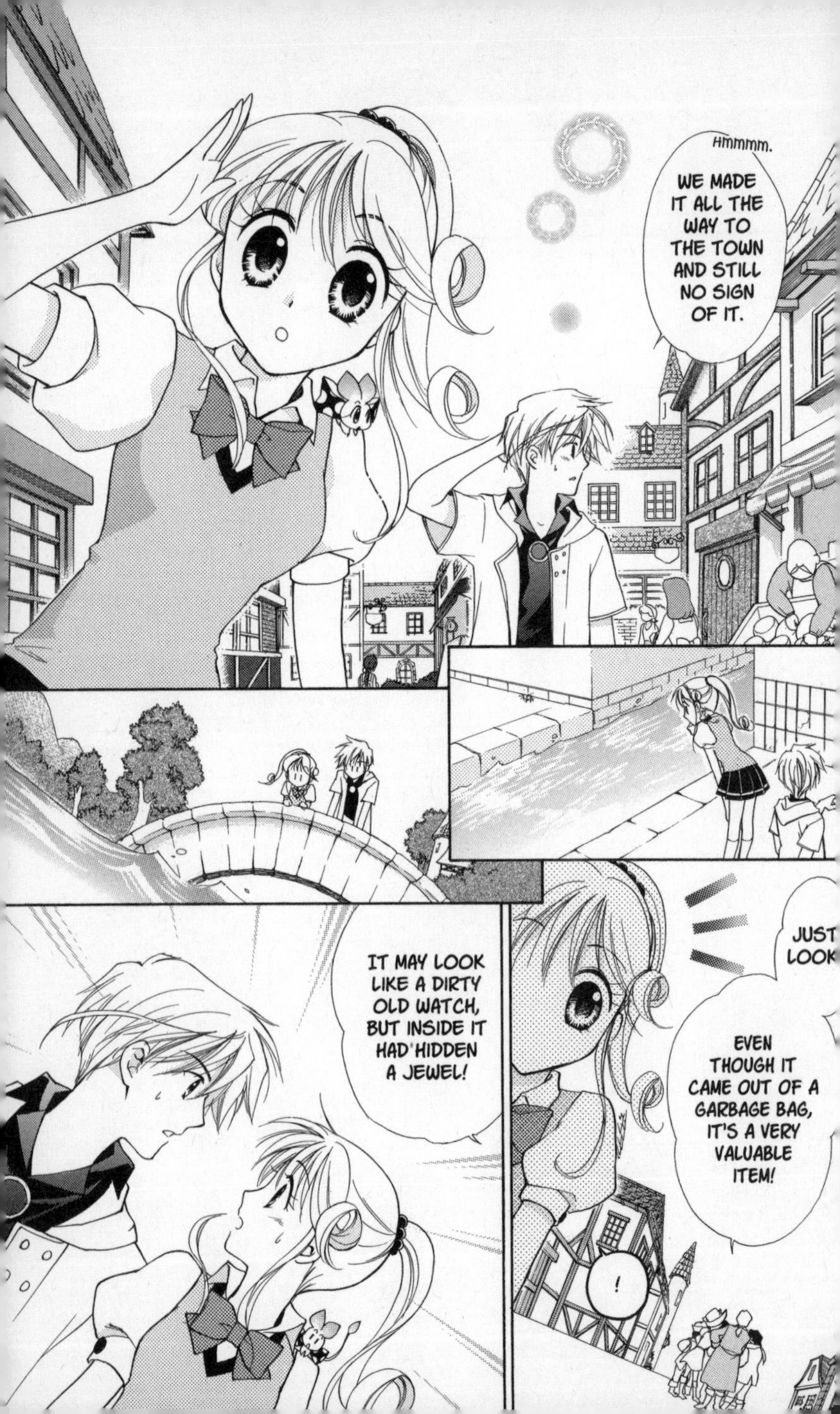
Hmmmm.
WE MADE IT ALL THE WAY TO THE TOWN AND STILL NO SIGN OF IT.
JUST LOOK
EVEN THOUGH IT CAME OUT OF A GARBAGE BAG, IT'S A VERY VALUABLE ITEM!
!
IT MAY LOOK LIKE A DIRTY OLD WATCH, BUT INSIDE IT HAD HIDDEN A JEWEL!

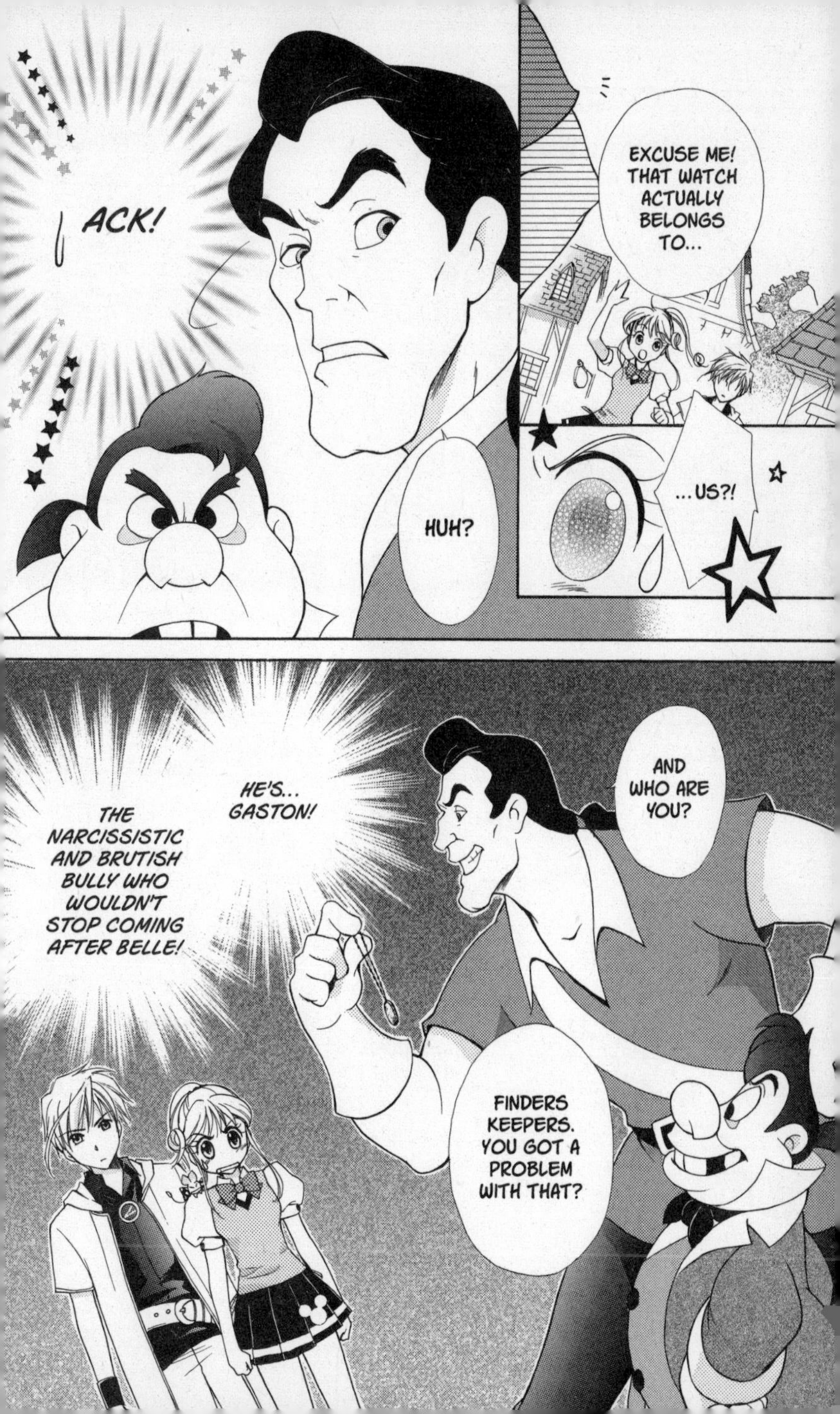
EXCUSE ME! THAT WATCH ACTUALLY BELONGS TO...
...US?!
ACK!
HUH?
AND WHO ARE YOU?
HE'S... GASTON!
THE NARCISSISTIC AND BRUTISH BULLY WHO WOULDN'T STOP COMING AFTER BELLE!
FINDERS KEEPERS. YOU GOT A PROBLEM WITH THAT?

READ THIS WAY

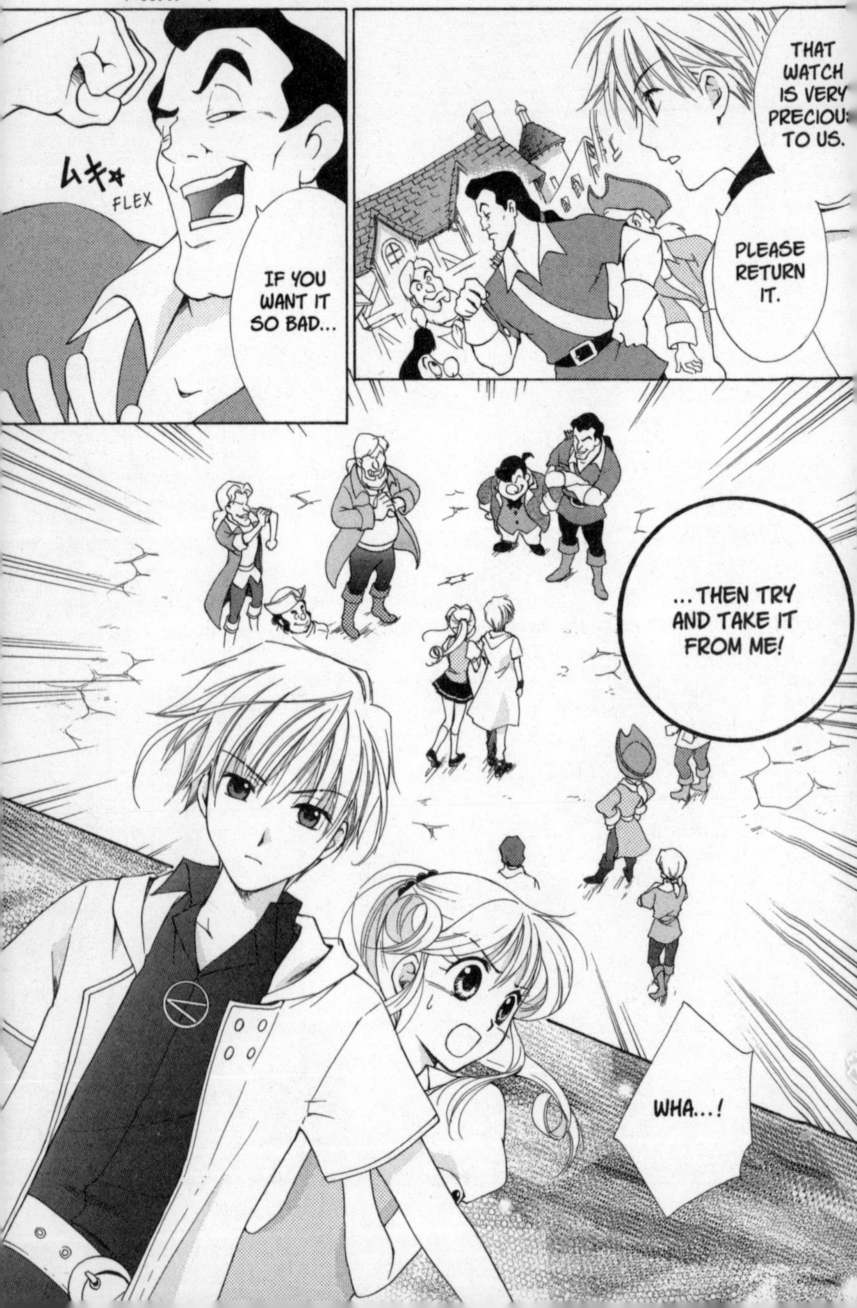

THAT WATCH IS VERY PRECIOU TO US.
PLEASE RETURN IT.
ムキ☆
FLEX
IF YOU WANT IT SO BAD...
...THEN TRY AND TAKE IT FROM ME!
WHA...!

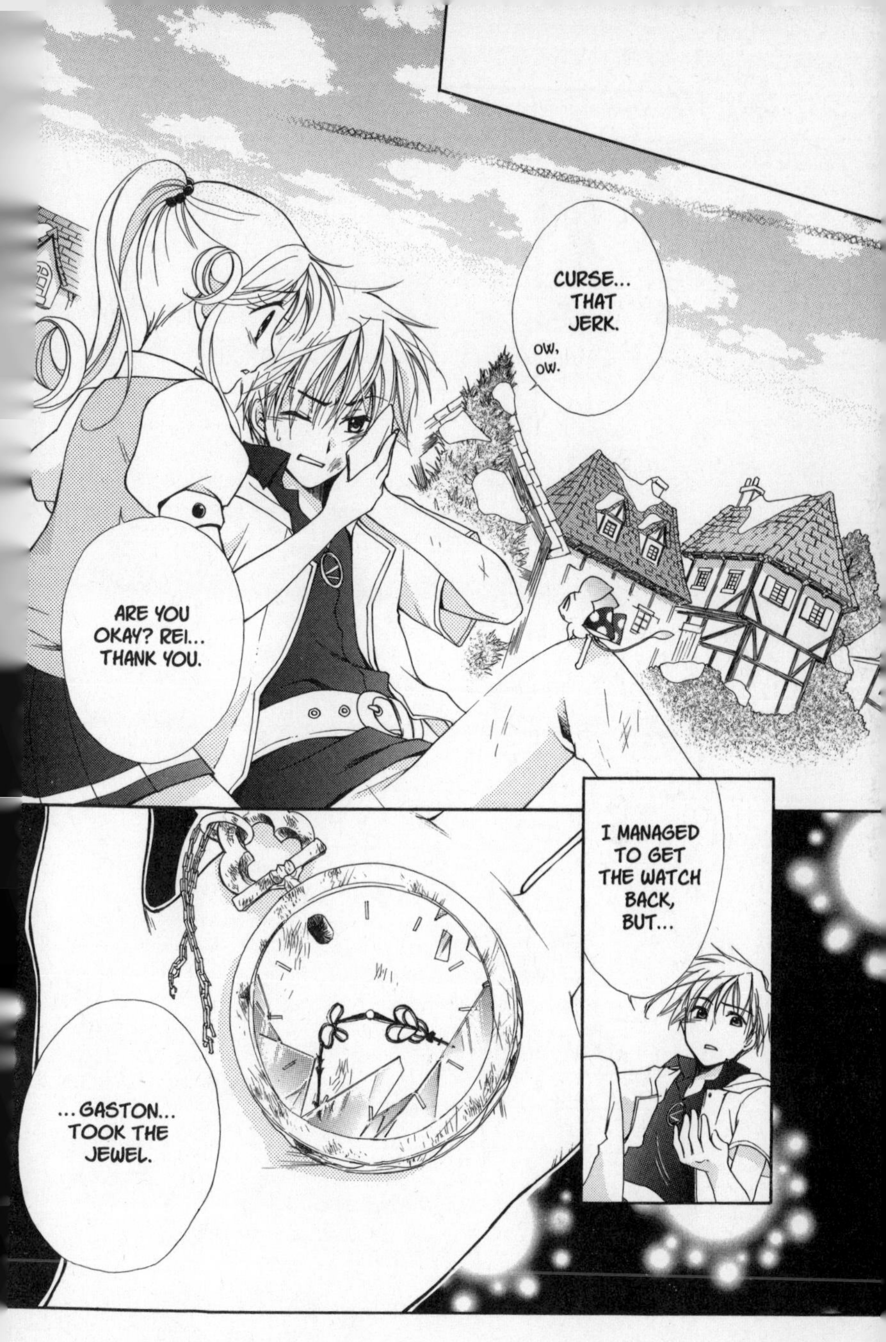
CURSE... THAT JERK.
OW, OW.
ARE YOU OKAY? REI... THANK YOU.
I MANAGED TO GET THE WATCH BACK, BUT...
...GASTON... TOOK THE JEWEL.

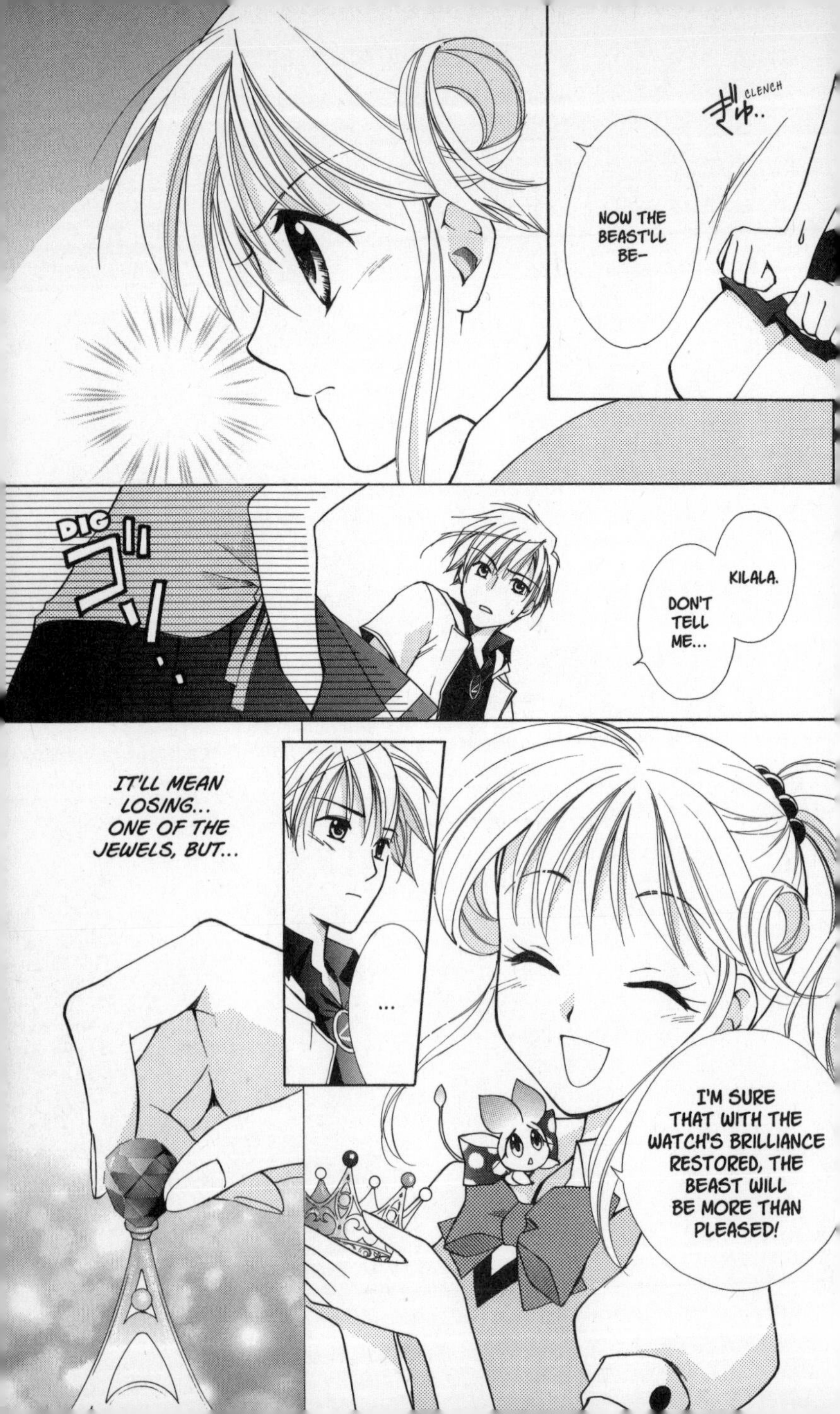
ぎゅ..
CLENCH
NOW THE BEAST'LL BE-
KILALA. DON'T TELL ME...
DIG
IT'LL MEAN LOSING... ONE OF THE JEWELS, BUT...
I'M SURE THAT WITH THE WATCH'S BRILLIANCE RESTORED, THE BEAST WILL BE MORE THAN PLEASED!
...

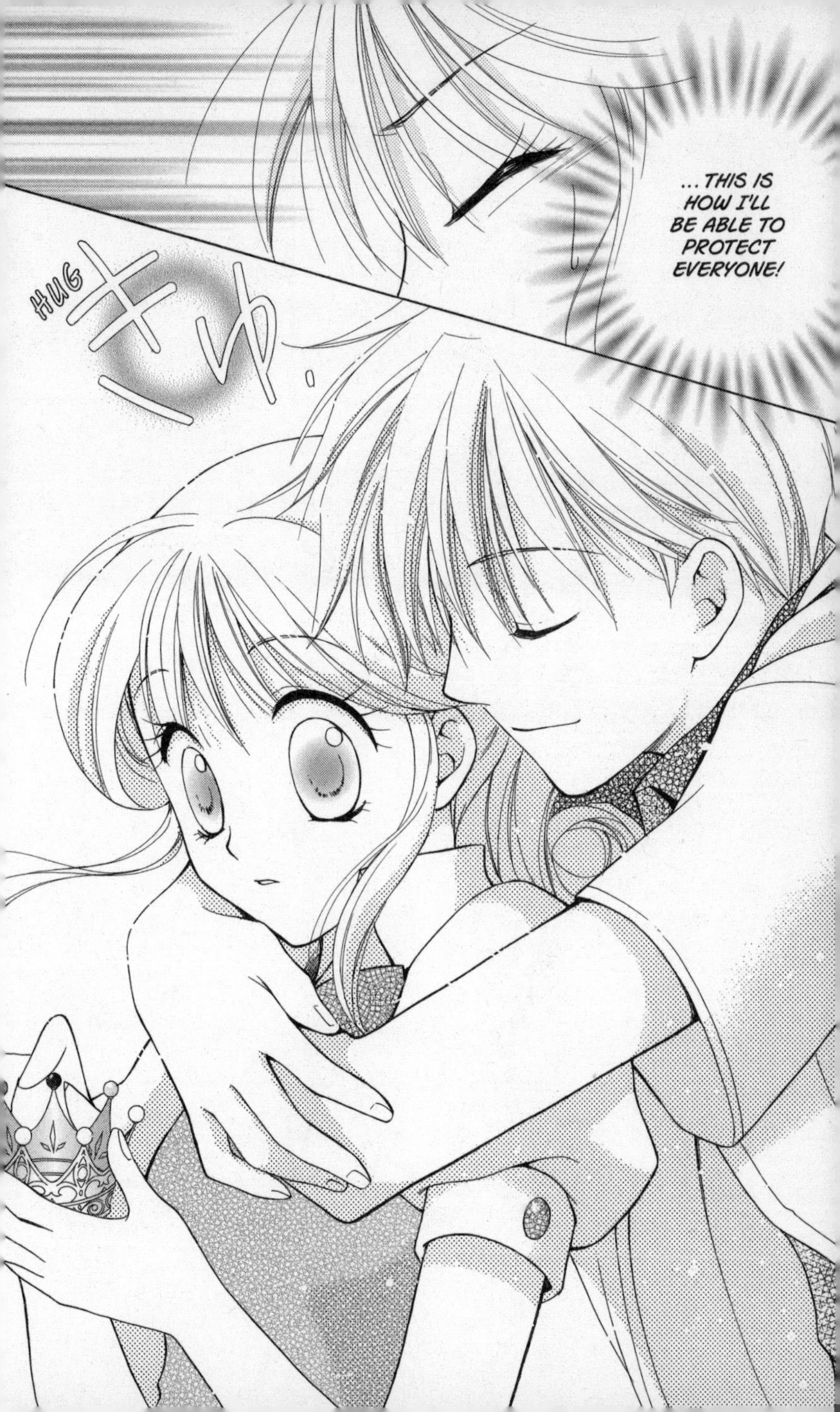
...THIS IS HOW I'LL BE ABLE TO PROTECT EVERYONE!
HUG
キュ

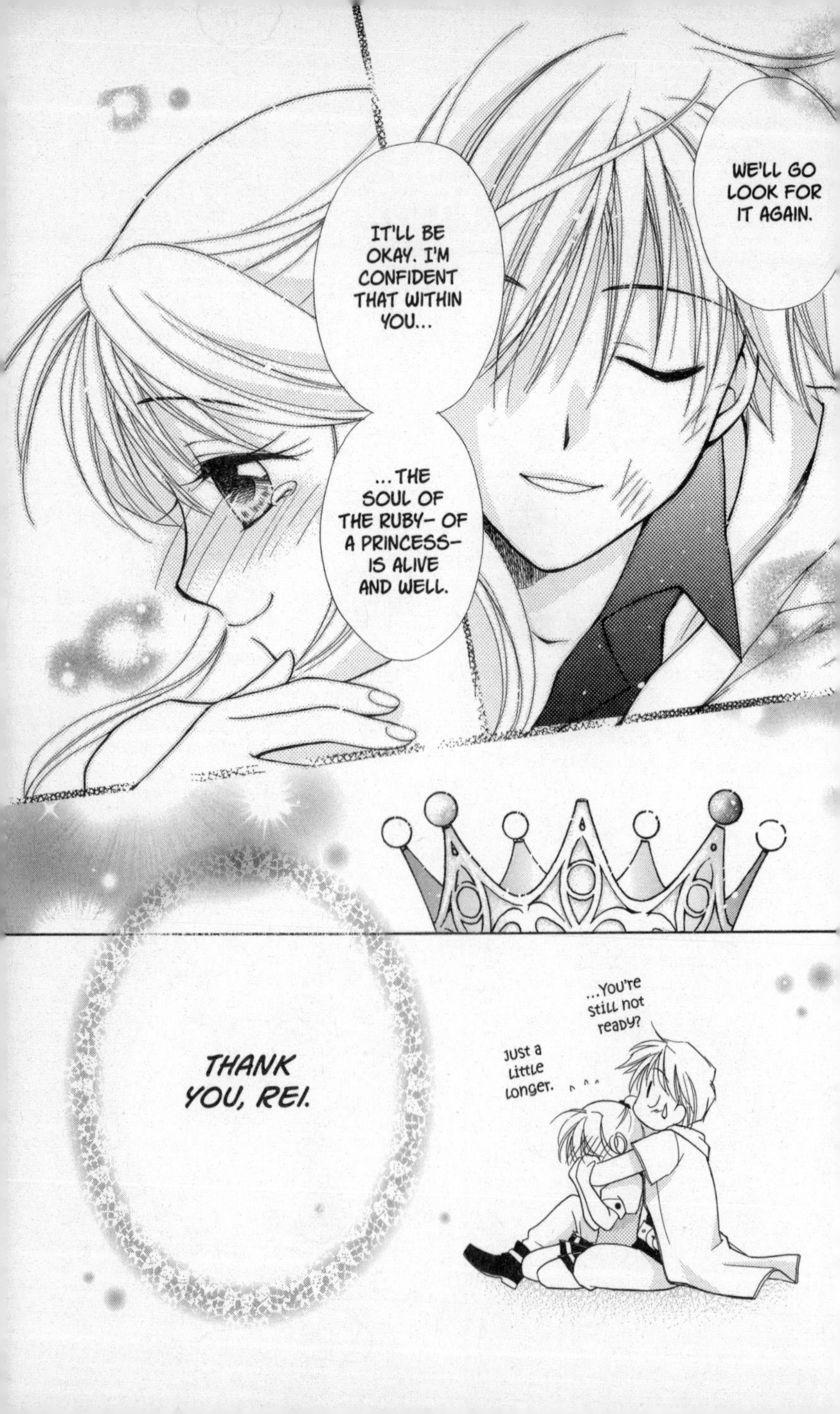
WE'LL GO LOOK FOR IT AGAIN.
IT'LL BE OKAY. I'M CONFIDENT THAT WITHIN YOU...
...THE SOUL OF THE RUBY- OF A PRINCESS- IS ALIVE AND WELL.
...You're still not ready?
Just a little longer.
THANK YOU, REI.

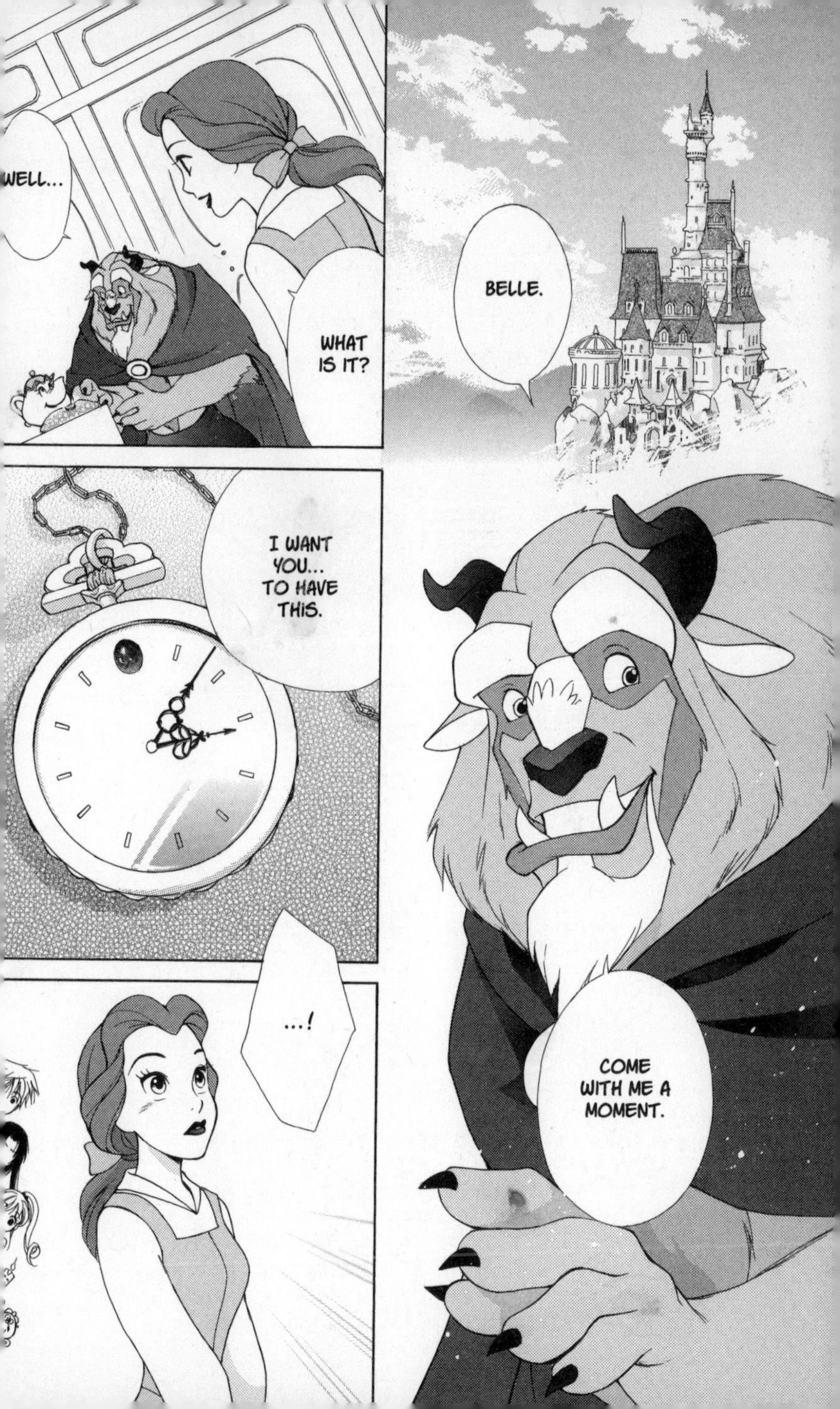
BELLE.
COME WITH ME A MOMENT.
WHAT IS IT?
WELL...
I WANT YOU... TO HAVE THIS.
...!

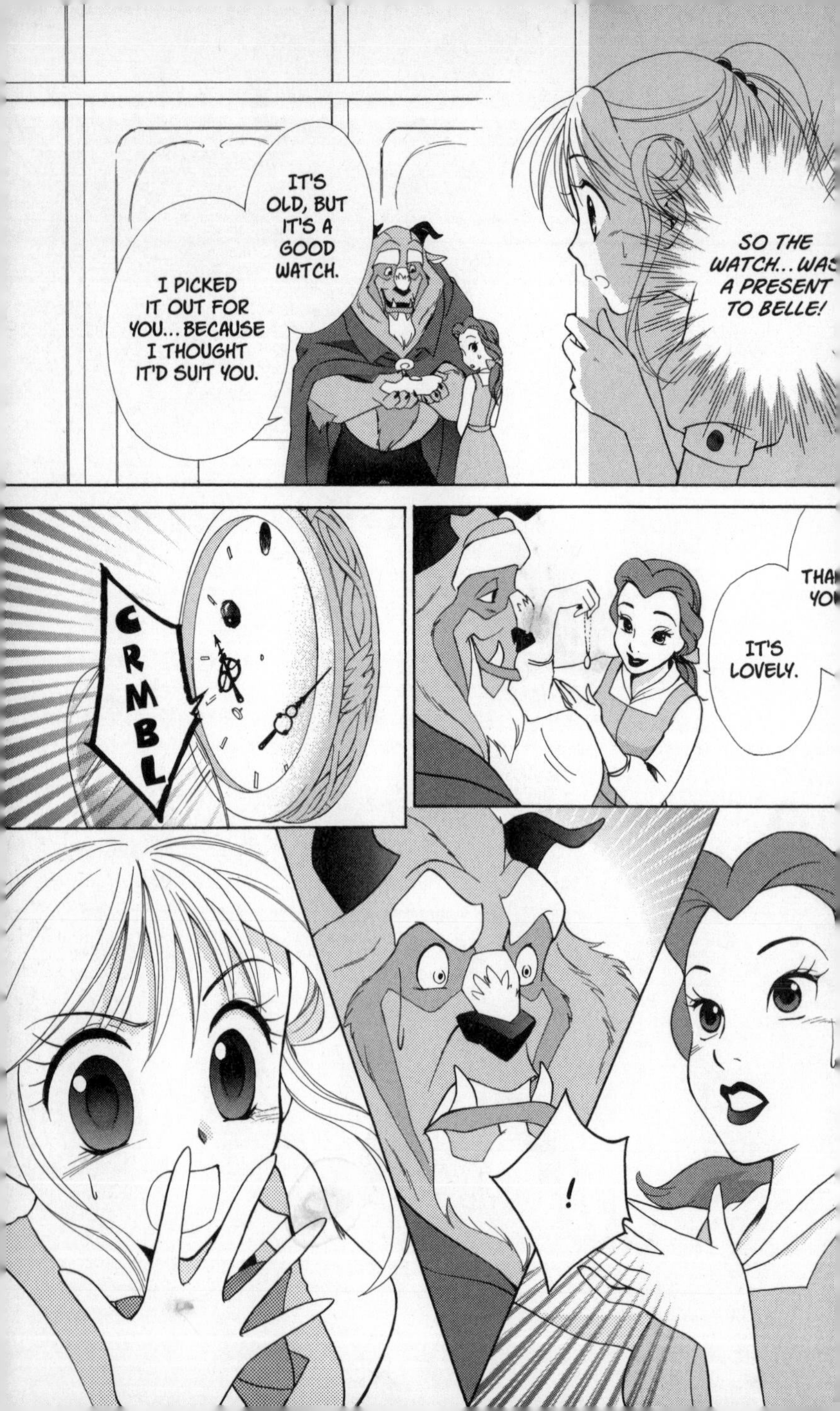
IT'S OLD, BUT IT'S A GOOD WATCH.
I PICKED IT OUT FOR YOU... BECAUSE I THOUGHT IT'D SUIT YOU.
SO THE WATCH... WAS A PRESENT TO BELLE!
THA YO
IT'S LOVELY.
CRMBL
!

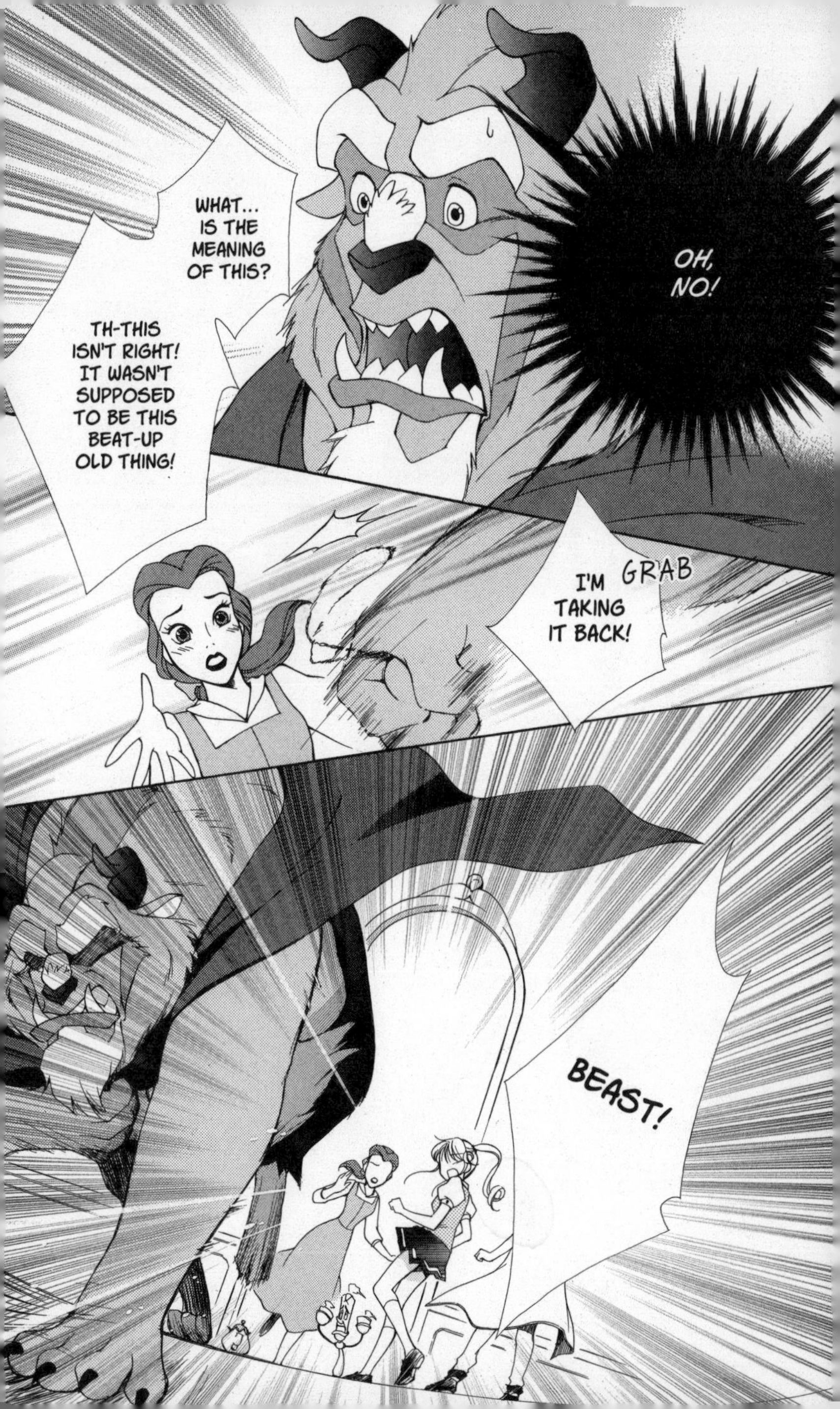
OH, NO!
WHAT... IS THE MEANING OF THIS?
TH-THIS ISN'T RIGHT! IT WASN'T SUPPOSED TO BE THIS BEAT-UP OLD THING!
GRAB
I'M TAKING IT BACK!
BEAST!

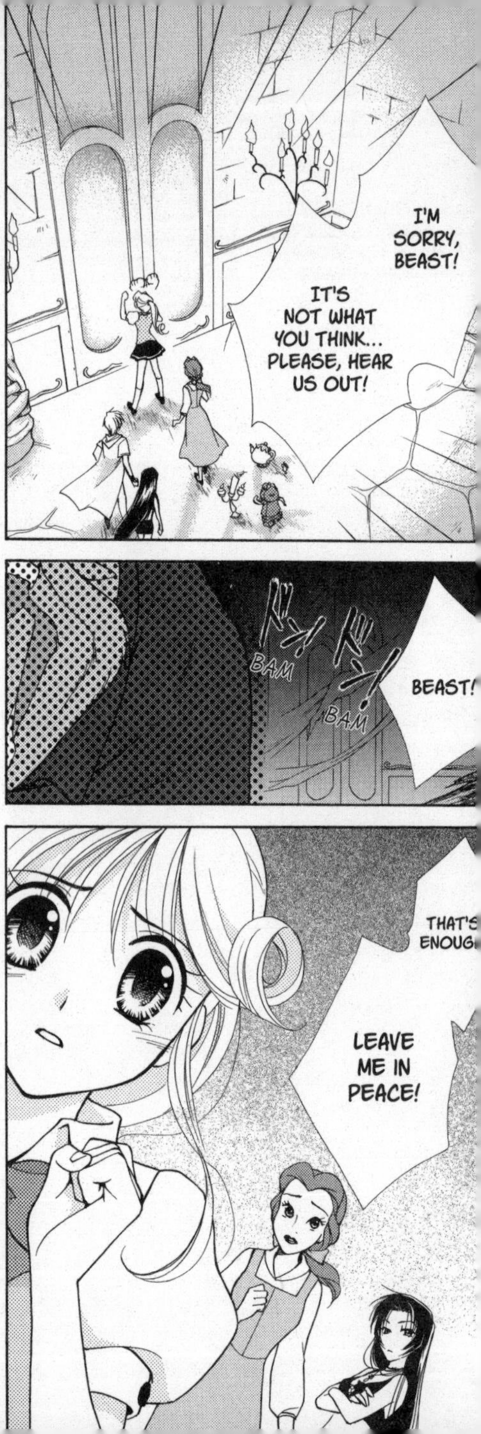
I'M SORRY, BEAST!
IT'S NOT WHAT YOU THINK... PLEASE, HEAR US OUT!
ドン! BAM
ドン! BAM
BEAST!
THAT'S ENOUG
LEAVE ME IN PEACE!

Nao Kodaka 2

THIS TIME AROUND, KILALA MEETS TWO BEAUTIFUL LADIES. BELLE FROM "BEAUTY AND THE BEAST" IS VERY POPULAR AMONG MY FRIENDS, TO SAY NOTHING OF ALL THE FAN LETTERS I'VE RECEIVED. DRAWING THIS ARC WAS BRUTAL... BUT IT WAS ALSO FUN SINCE THERE WERE SO MANY LIVELY CHARACTERS IN IT. AURORA FROM "SLEEPING BEAUTY" IS ALSO GRACEFUL, INNOCENT, AND INCREDIBLY BEAUTIFUL! THAT MADE HER VERY MUCH WORTH DRAWING (LOL). IT WAS FUN.

HAVING COLLECTED THE MAJORITY OF THE TIARA'S JEWELS, THERE'S ONLY ONE PRINCESS LEFT. LOOK FORWARD TO IT! AND I HOPE TO SEE YOU AGAIN IN VOLUME 5.

◆ Thank you ◆

YUKI-CHAN / MEG-TAN
HINO-CHAN / JUN-JUN
YURI-CHAN
KODANSHA + DISNEY
OUR EDITORS
TANAKA-SENSEI
MY SISTER

AND TO MY PARENTS AND LITTLE BROTHER WHO ALWAY SUPPORTED ME EVEN DURING THIS HARROWING WORK SCHEDULE, THANK YOU ALWAYS!

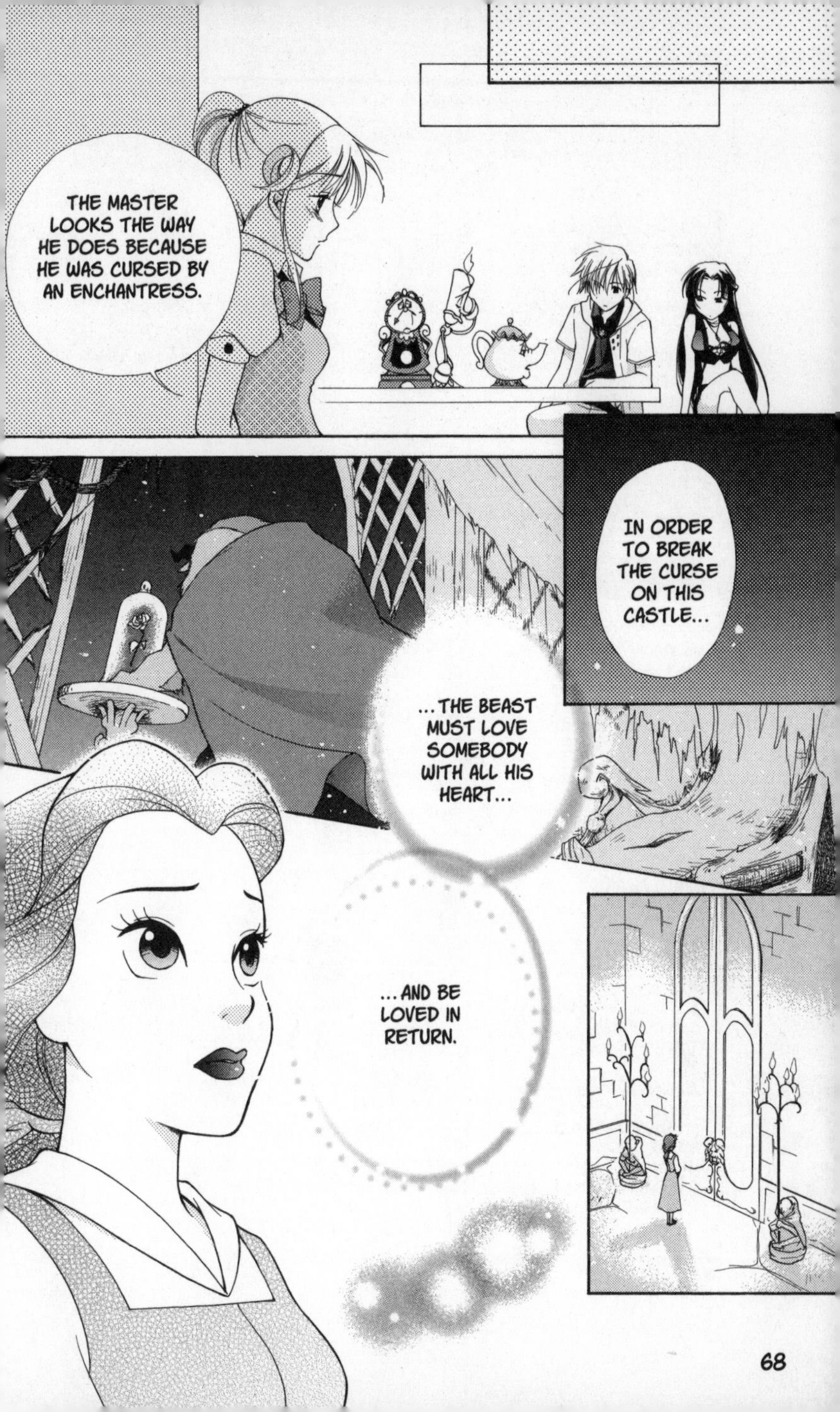
THE MASTER LOOKS THE WAY HE DOES BECAUSE HE WAS CURSED BY AN ENCHANTRESS.
IN ORDER TO BREAK THE CURSE ON THIS CASTLE...
...THE BEAST MUST LOVE SOMEBODY WITH ALL HIS HEART...
...AND BE LOVED IN RETURN.

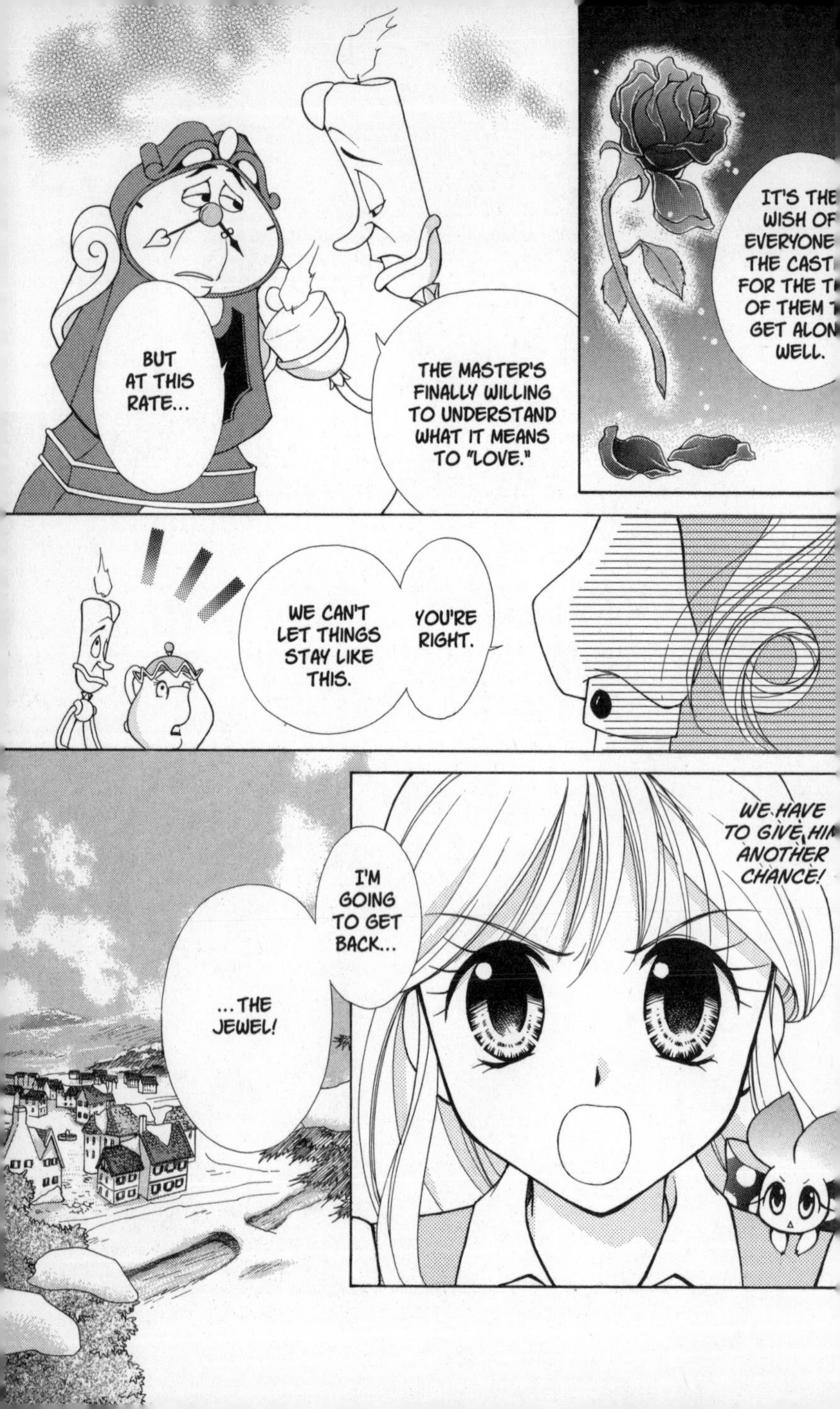

IT'S THE WISH OF EVERYONE THE CAST FOR THE T OF THEM T GET ALON WELL.
THE MASTER'S FINALLY WILLING TO UNDERSTAND WHAT IT MEANS TO "LOVE."
BUT AT THIS RATE...
YOU'RE RIGHT.
WE CAN'T LET THINGS STAY LIKE THIS.
WE HAVE TO GIVE HI ANOTHER CHANCE!
I'M GOING TO GET BACK...
...THE JEWEL!

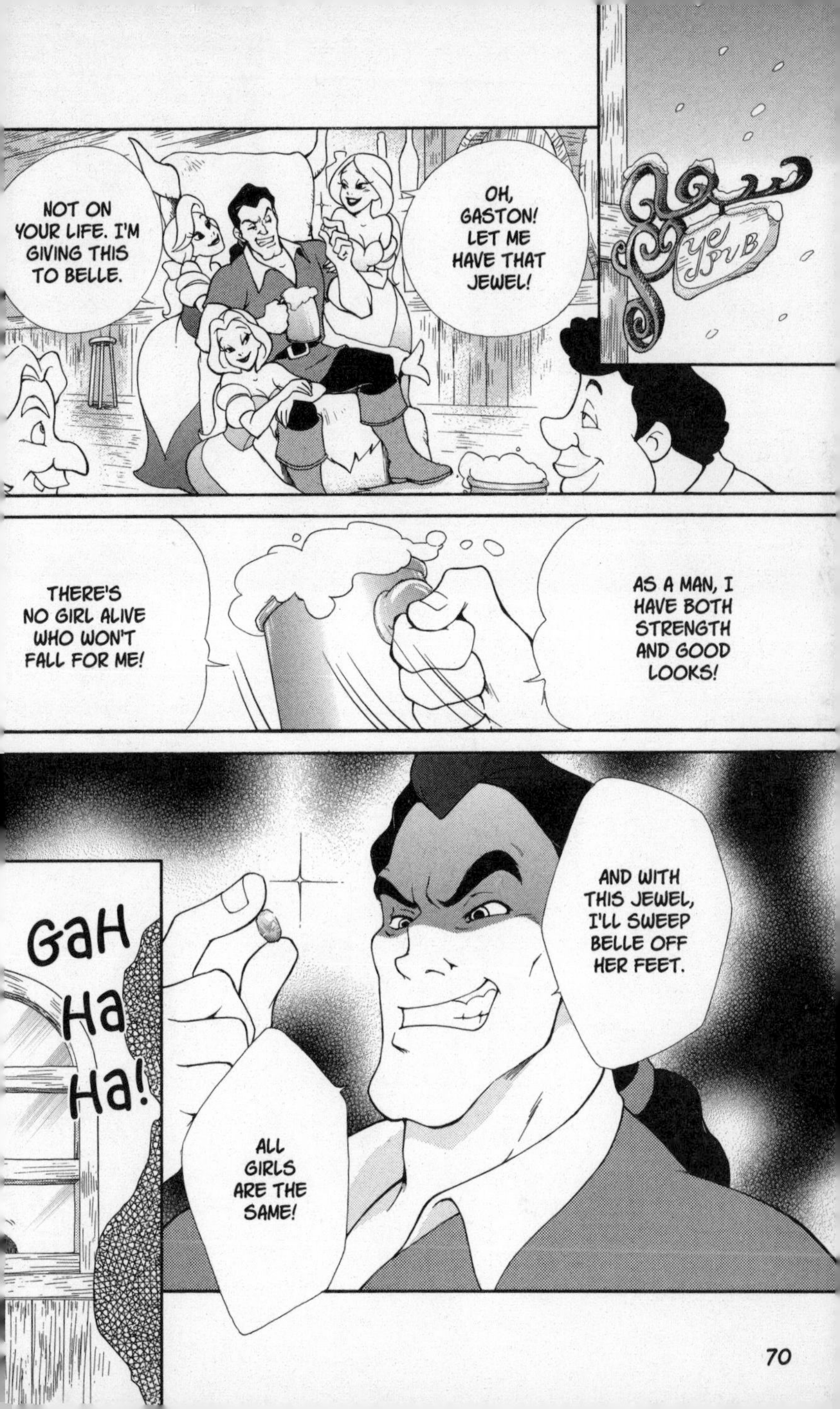
ye PUB
OH, GASTON! LET ME HAVE THAT JEWEL!
NOT ON YOUR LIFE. I'M GIVING THIS TO BELLE.
AS A MAN, I HAVE BOTH STRENGTH AND GOOD LOOKS!
THERE'S NO GIRL ALIVE WHO WON'T FALL FOR ME!
AND WITH THIS JEWEL, I'LL SWEEP BELLE OFF HER FEET.
GaH Ha Ha!
ALL GIRLS ARE THE SAME!

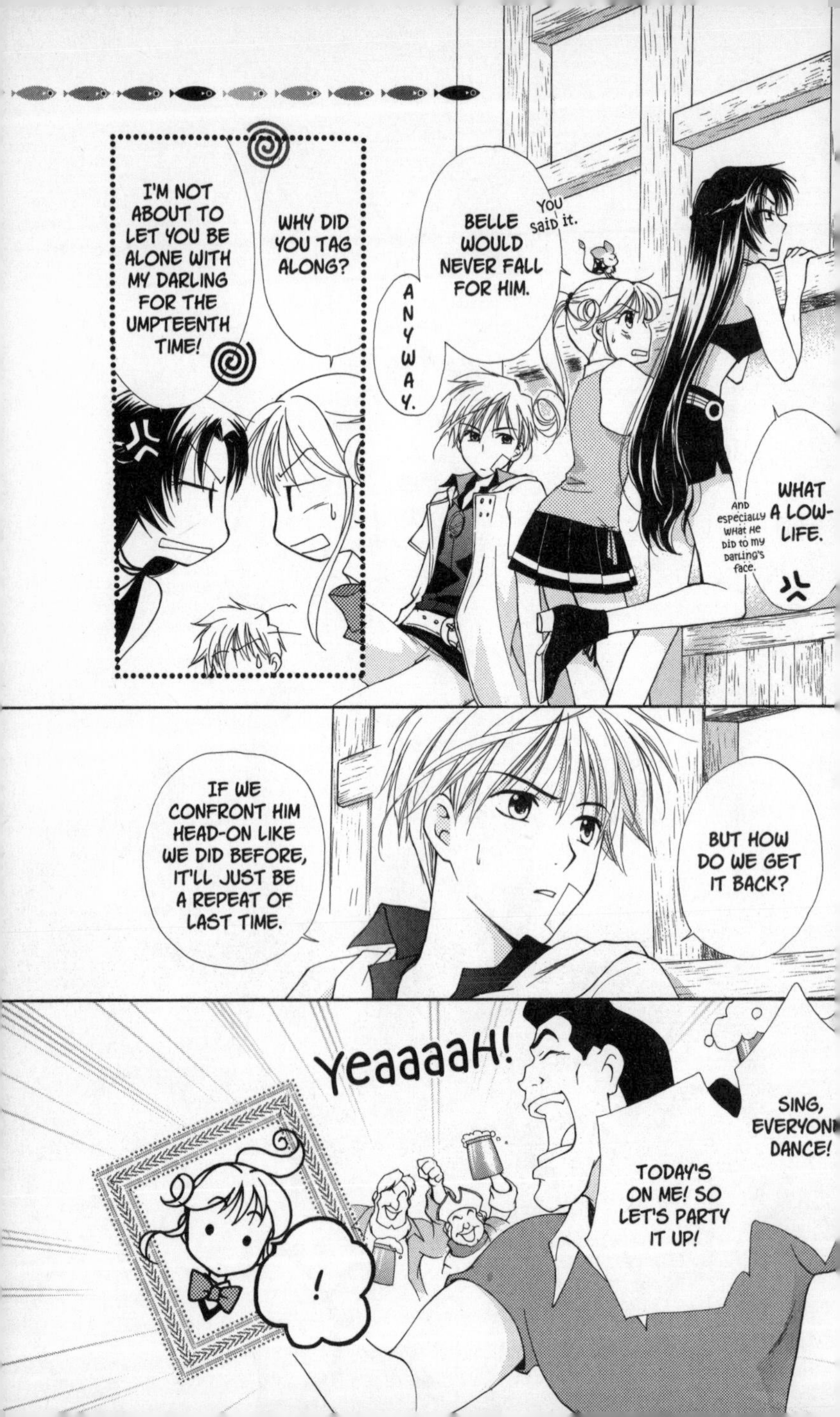
WHAT A LOW-LIFE.
And especially what he did to my darling's face.
BELLE WOULD NEVER FALL FOR HIM.
You said it.
ANYWAY.
WHY DID YOU TAG ALONG?
I'M NOT ABOUT TO LET YOU BE ALONE WITH MY DARLING FOR THE UMPTEENTH TIME!
BUT HOW DO WE GET IT BACK?
IF WE CONFRONT HIM HEAD-ON LIKE WE DID BEFORE, IT'LL JUST BE A REPEAT OF LAST TIME.
SING, EVERYON DANCE!
TODAY'S ON ME! SO LET'S PARTY IT UP!
YeaaaaH!
!

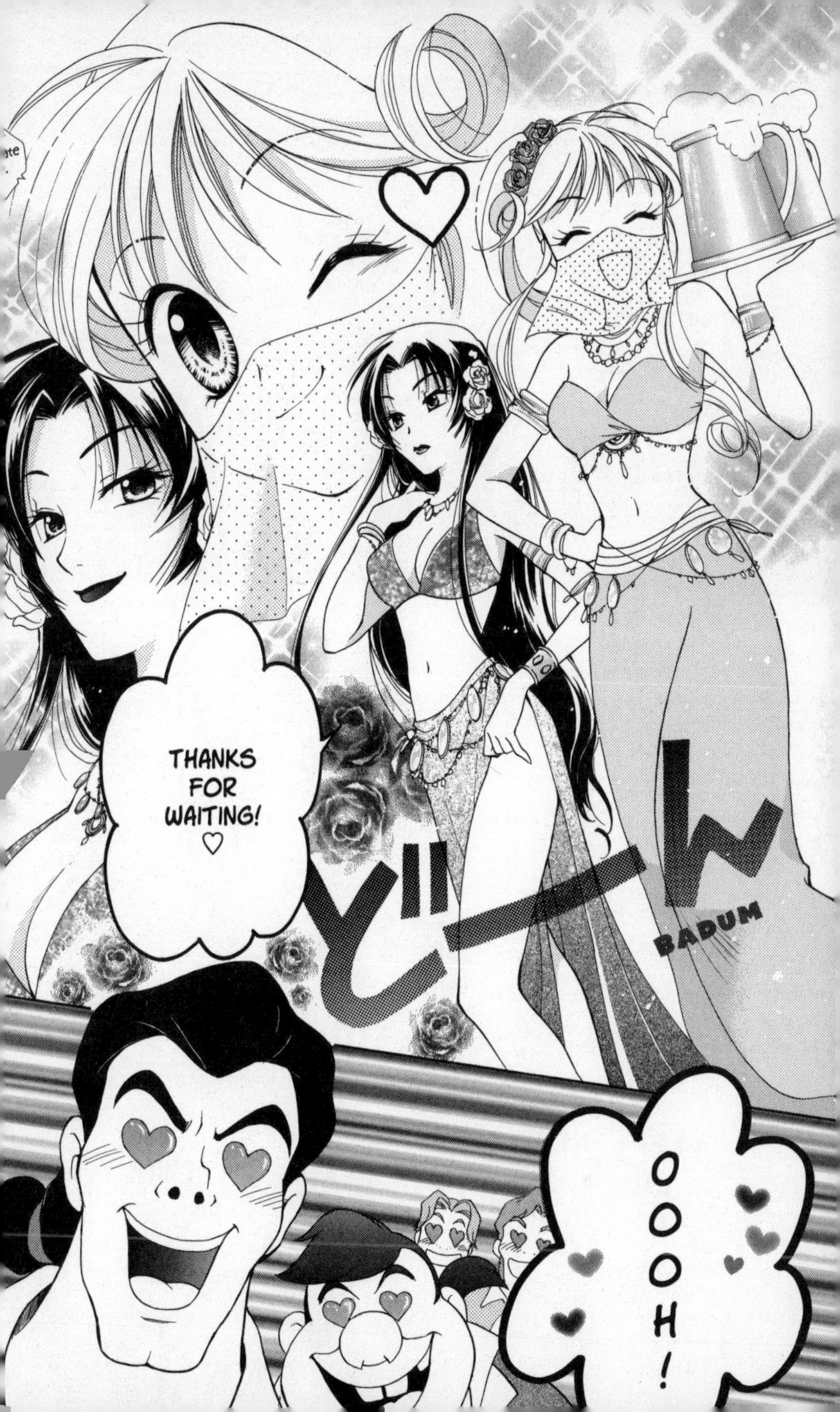
THANKS FOR WAITING! ♡
どーん
BADUM
OOOOH!

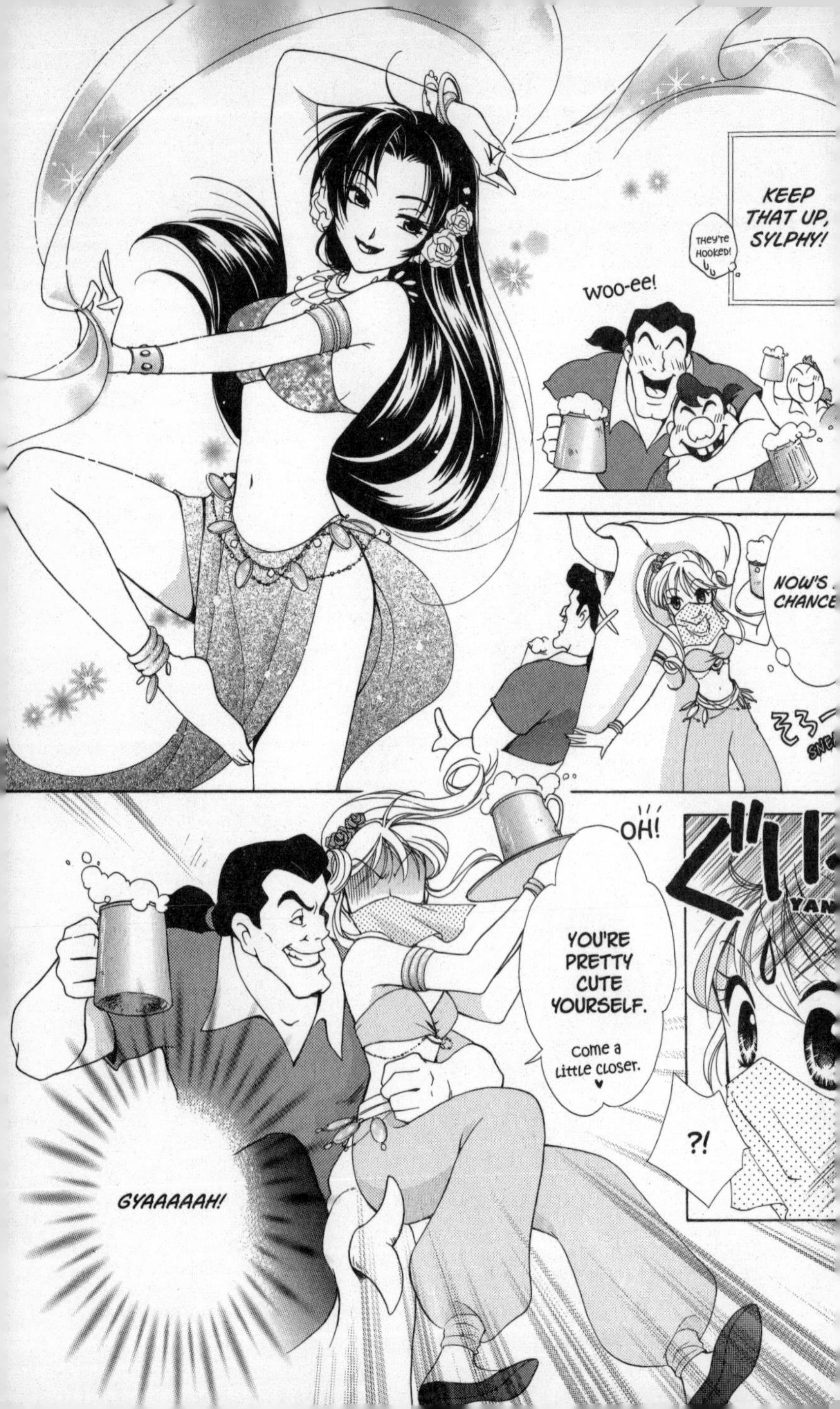

KEEP THAT UP, SYLPHY!
THEY'RE HOOKED!
WOO-EE!
NOW'S
CHANCE
?!
OH!
YOU'RE PRETTY CUTE YOURSELF.
Come a little closer. ♥
GYAAAAAH!

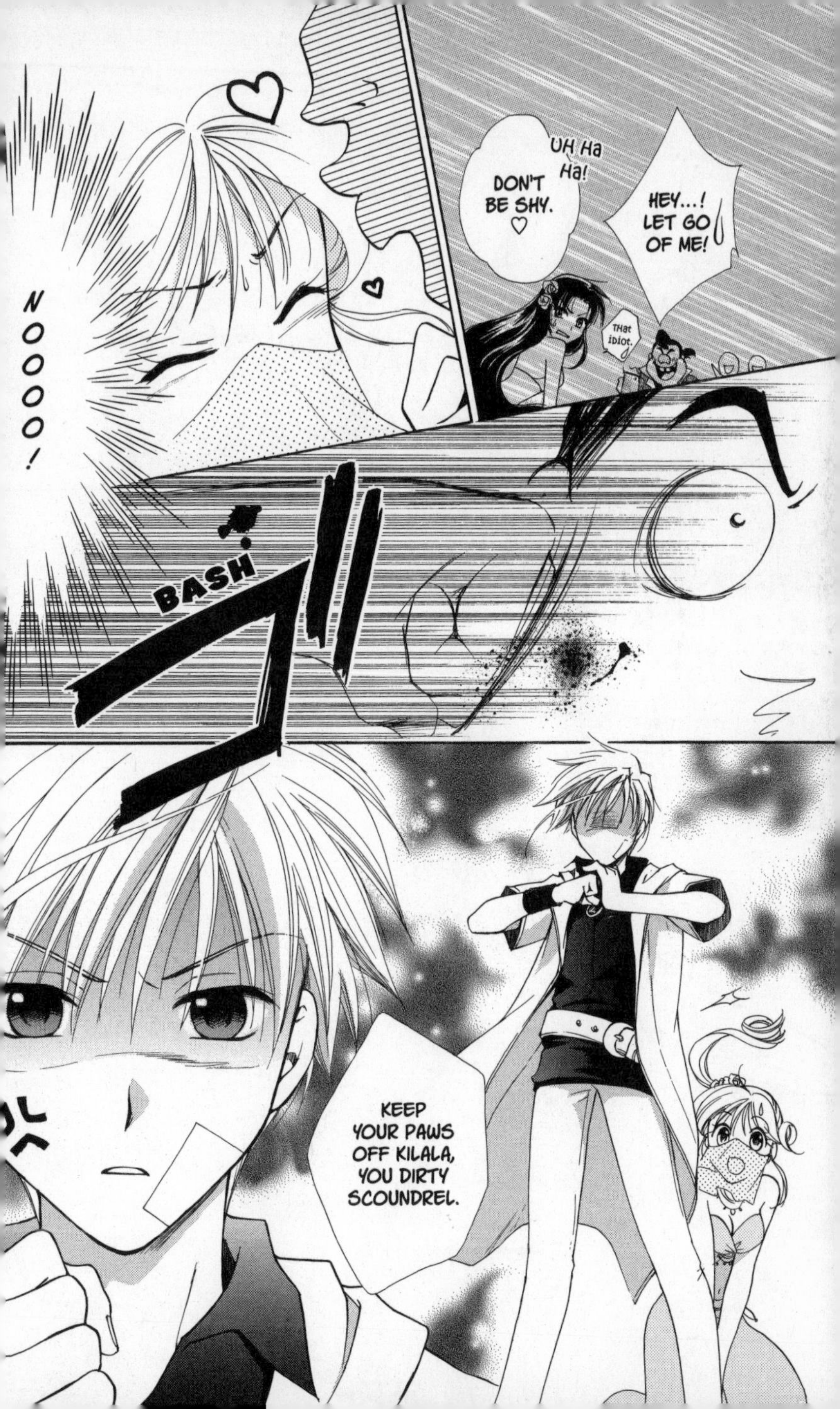

HEY...! LET GO OF ME!
UH Ha Ha!
DON'T BE SHY. ♡
THat idiot.
NOOOOO!
BASH
KEEP YOUR PAWS OFF KILALA, YOU DIRTY SCOUNDREL.

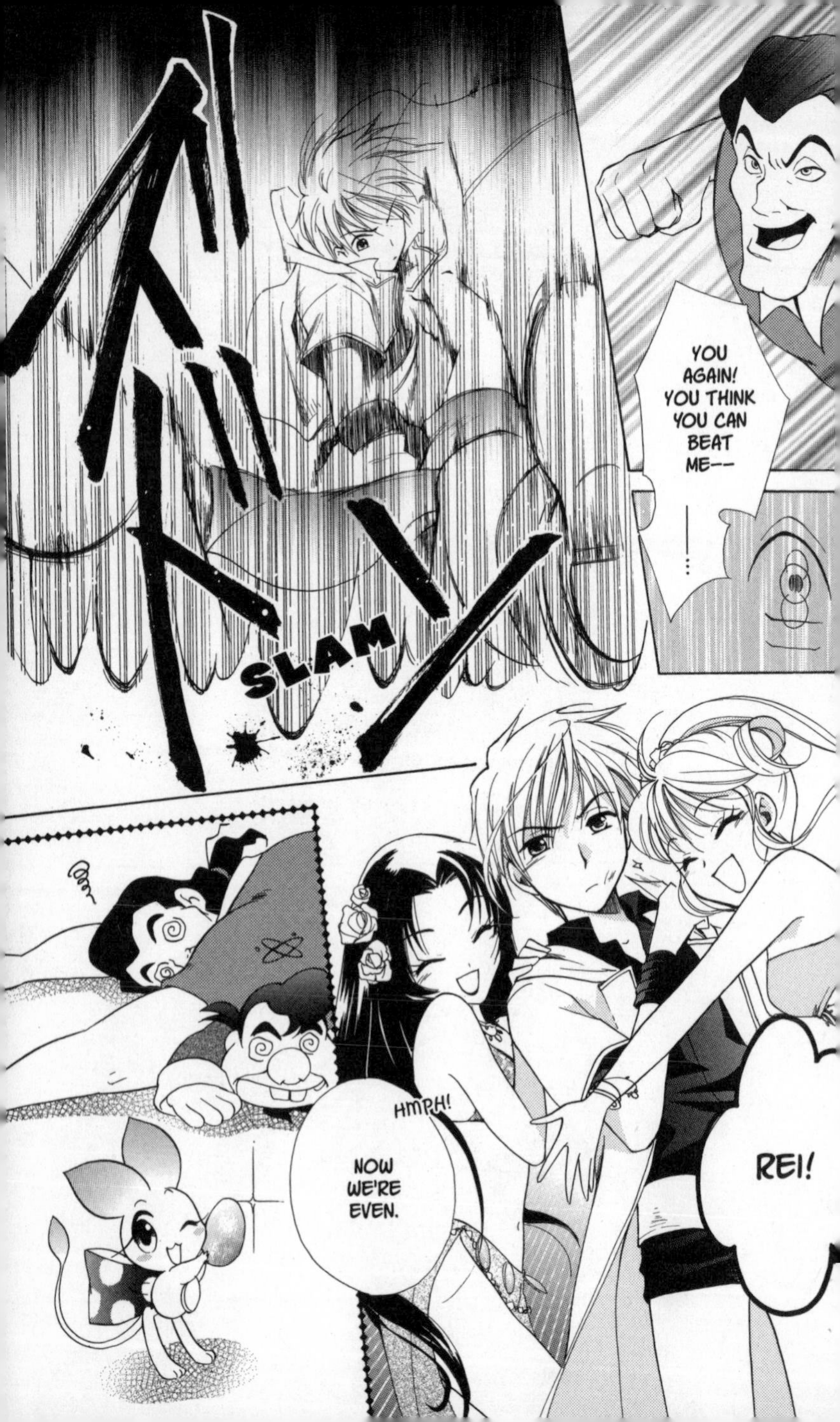
YOU AGAIN! YOU THINK YOU CAN BEAT ME--
......
SLAM
REI!
HMPH!
NOW WE'RE EVEN.

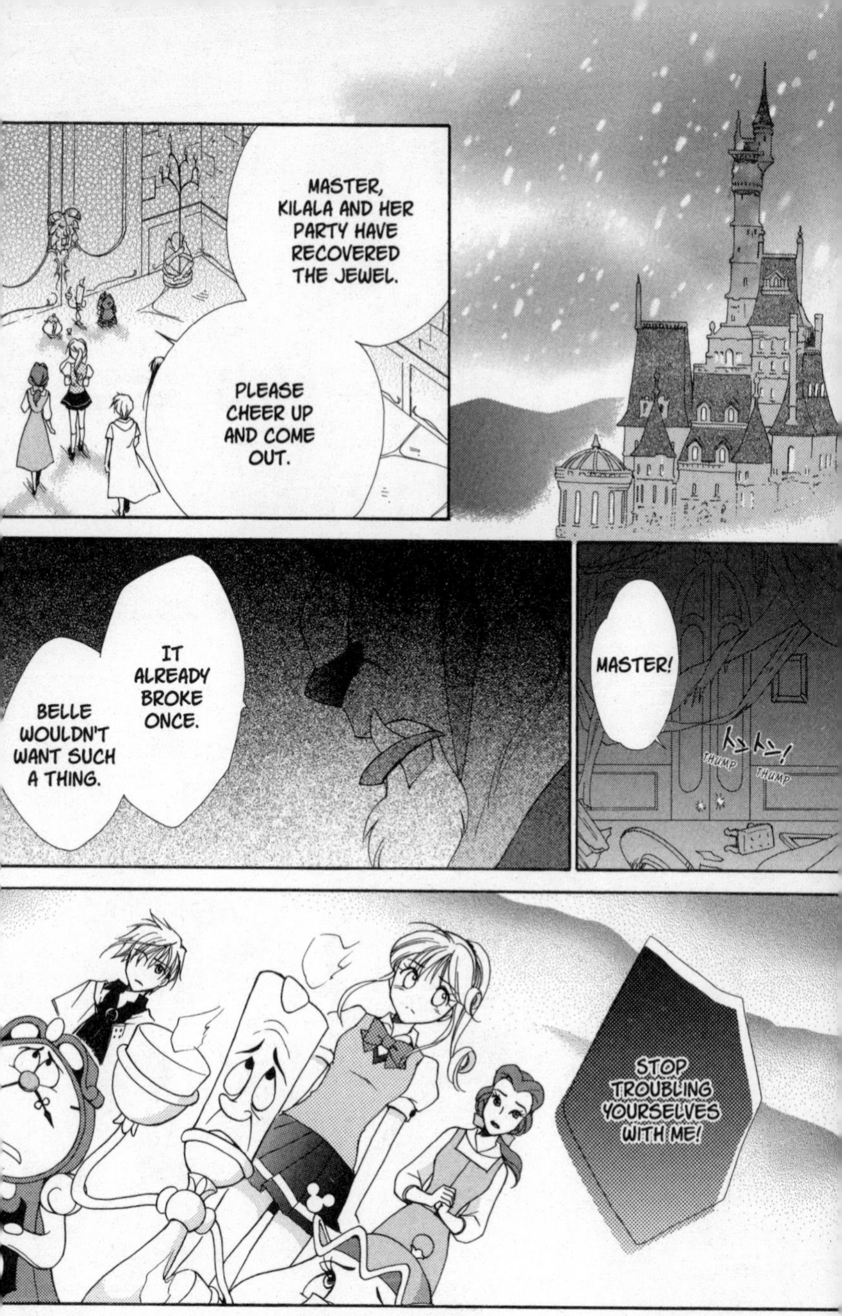
MASTER, KILALA AND HER PARTY HAVE RECOVERED THE JEWEL.
PLEASE CHEER UP AND COME OUT.
MASTER!
トントン!
THUMP THUMP
IT ALREADY BROKE ONCE.
BELLE WOULDN'T WANT SUCH A THING.
STOP TROUBLING YOURSELVES WITH ME!

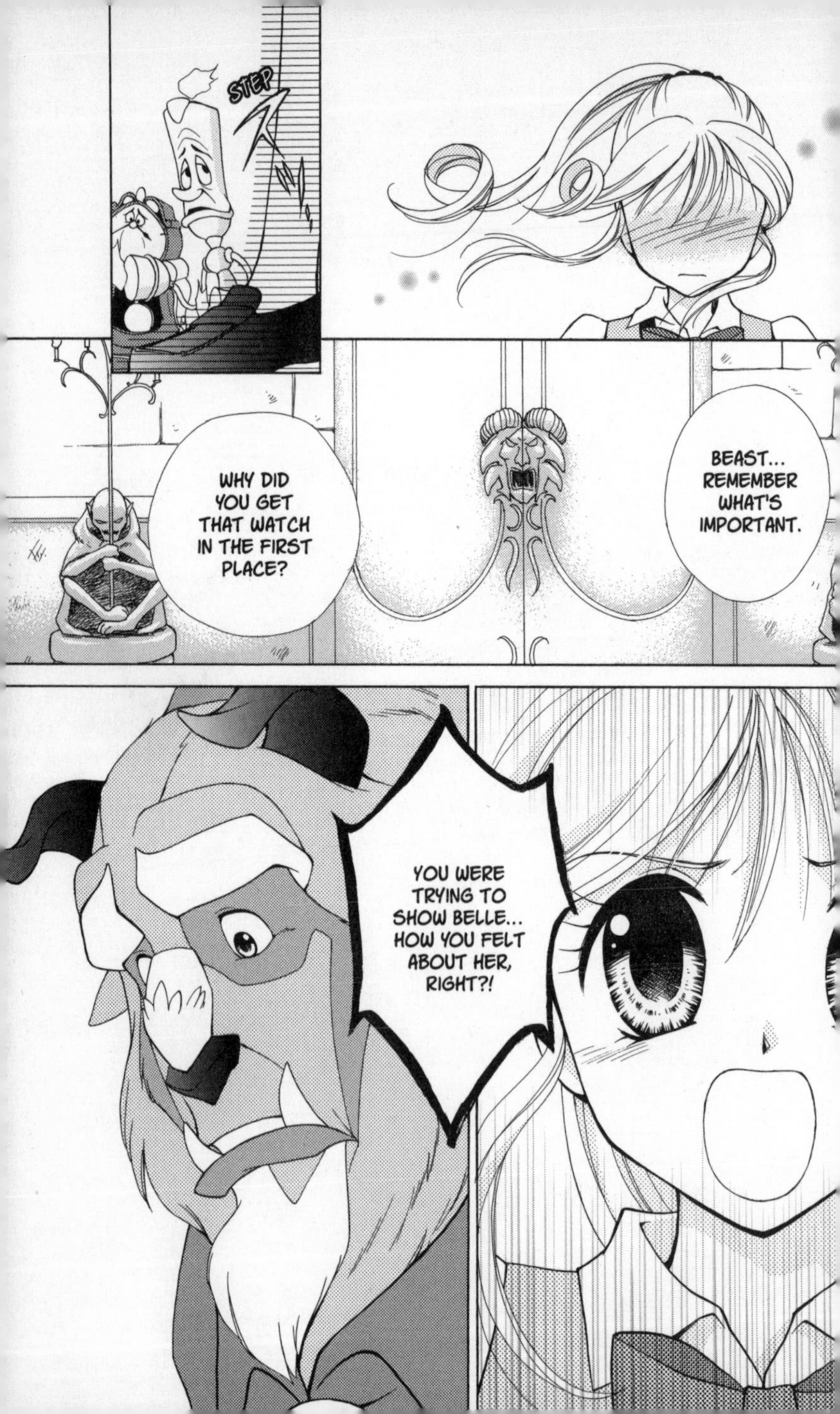
STEP
BEAST... REMEMBER WHAT'S IMPORTANT.
WHY DID YOU GET THAT WATCH IN THE FIRST PLACE?
YOU WERE TRYING TO SHOW BELLE... HOW YOU FELT ABOUT HER, RIGHT?!

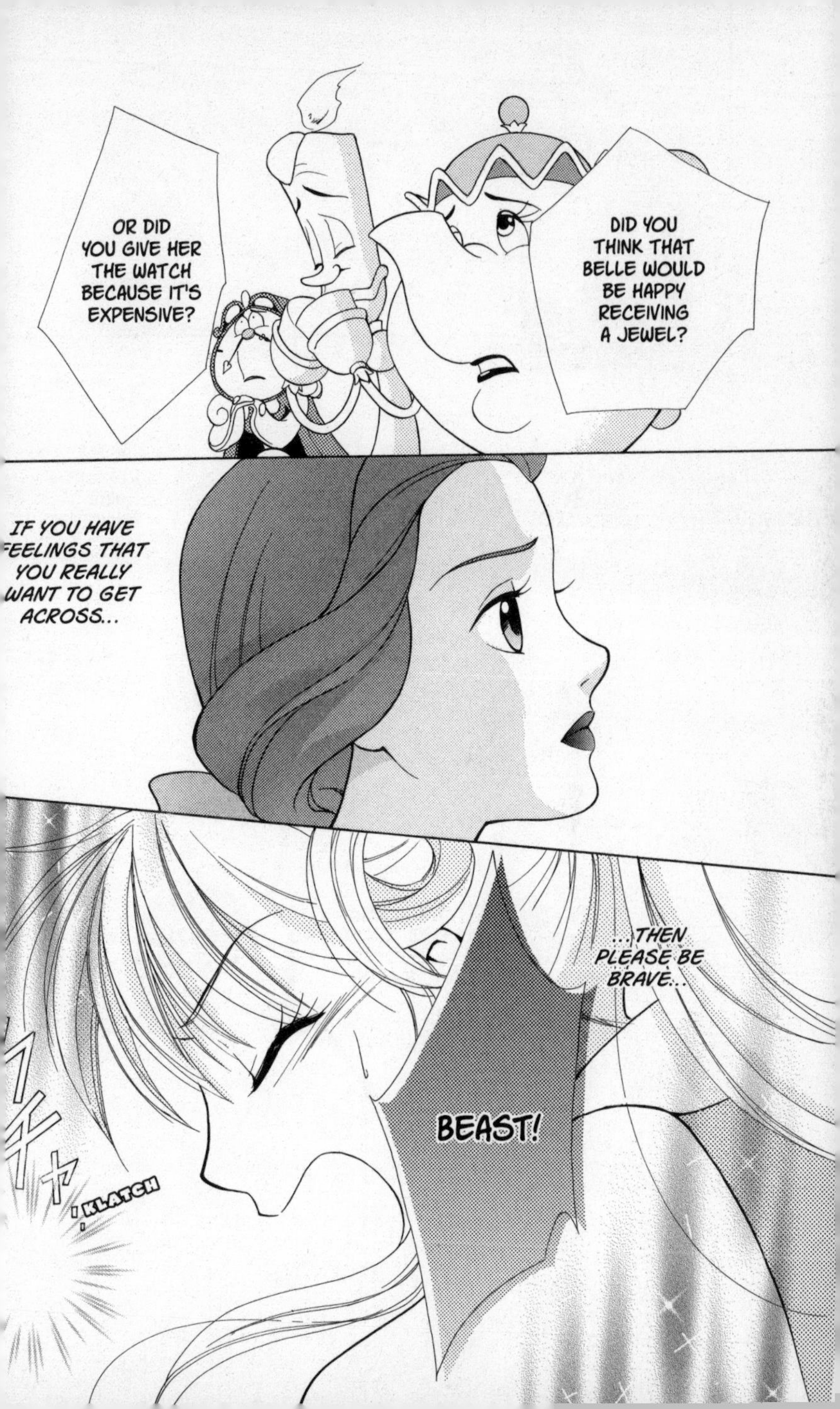
DID YOU THINK THAT BELLE WOULD BE HAPPY RECEIVING A JEWEL?
OR DID YOU GIVE HER THE WATCH BECAUSE IT'S EXPENSIVE?
IF YOU HAVE FEELINGS THAT YOU REALLY WANT TO GET ACROSS...
...THEN PLEASE BE BRAVE...
BEAST!
KLATCH

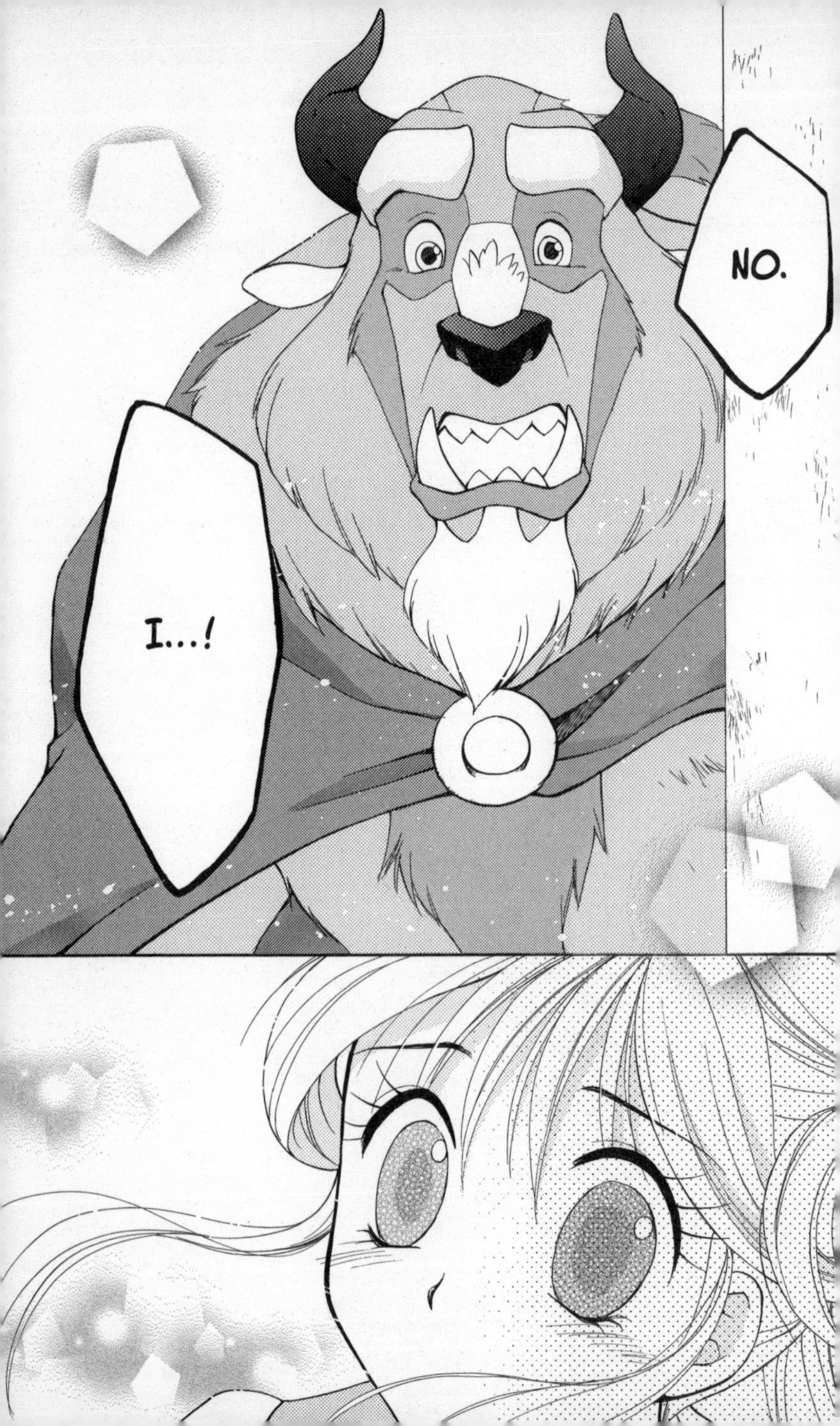
NO.
I...!

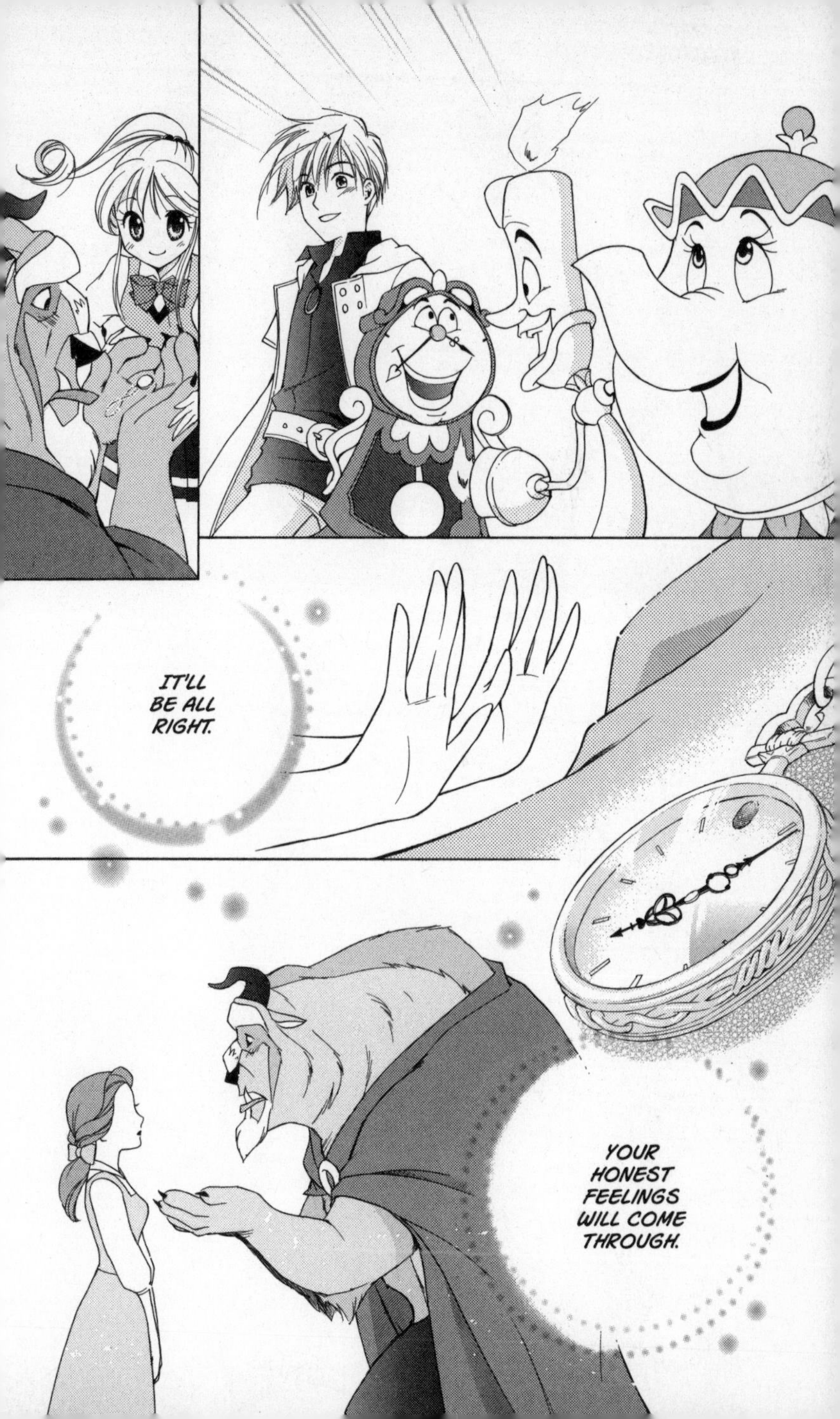
IT'LL BE ALL RIGHT.
YOUR HONEST FEELINGS WILL COME THROUGH.

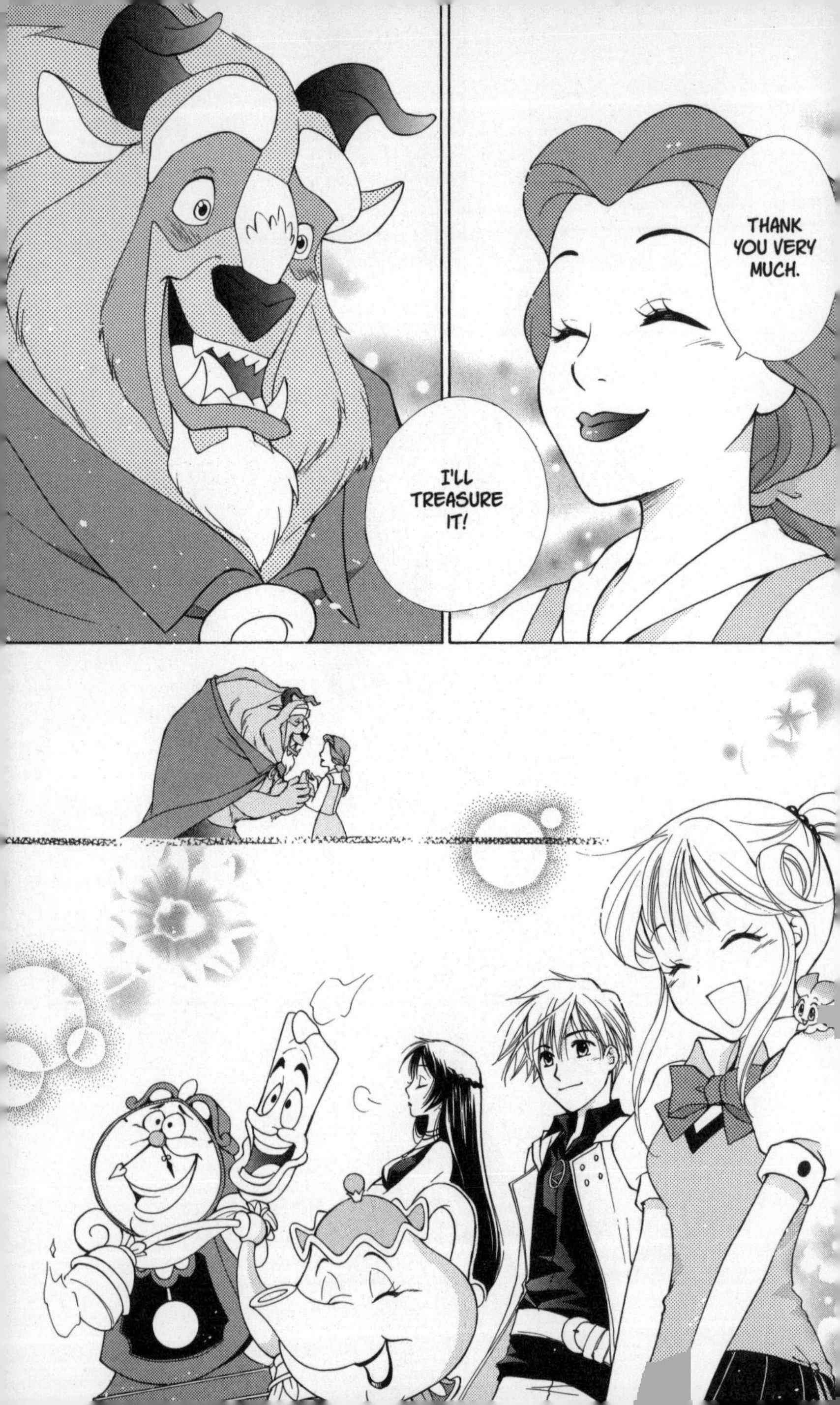
THANK YOU VERY MUCH.
I'LL TREASURE IT!

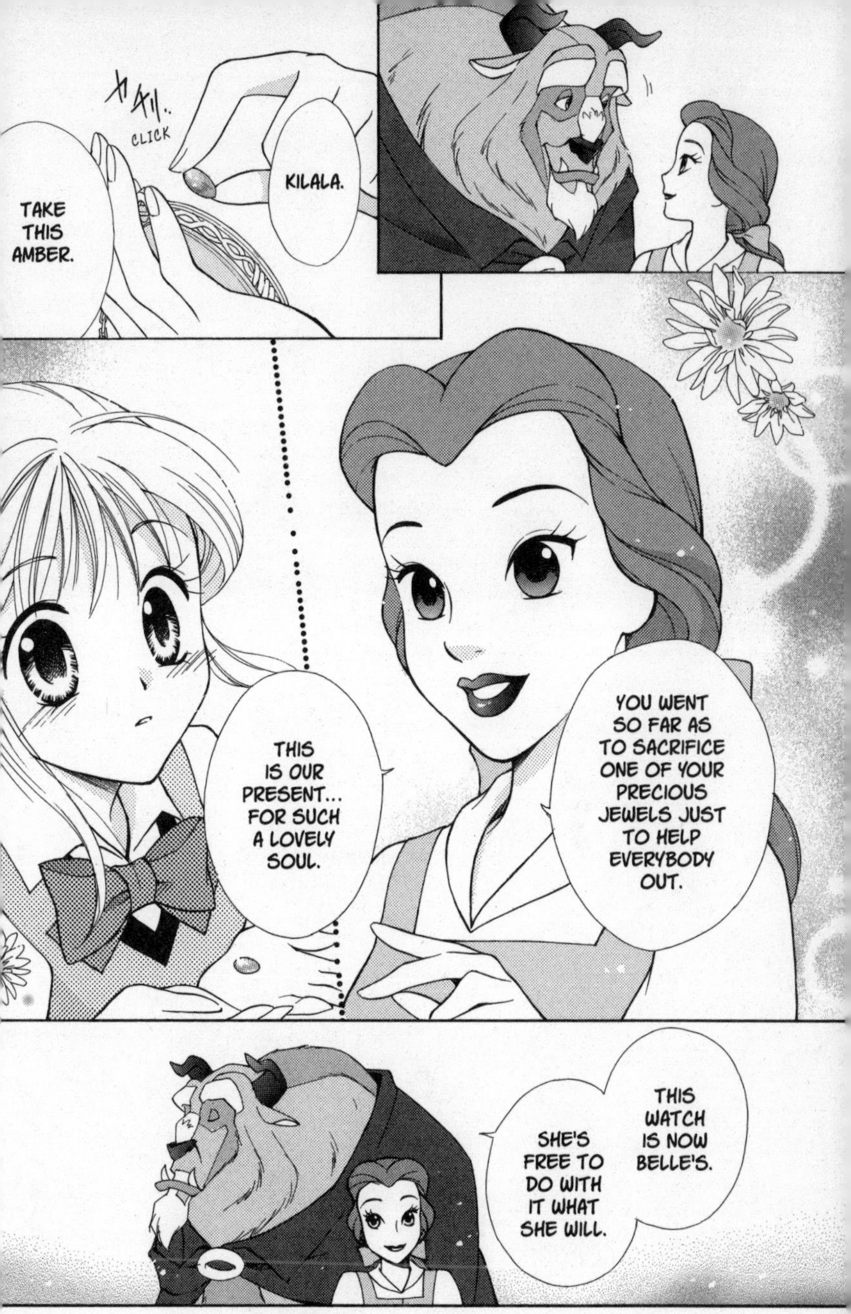
カチリ..
CLICK
KILALA.
TAKE THIS AMBER.
YOU WENT SO FAR AS TO SACRIFICE ONE OF YOUR PRECIOUS JEWELS JUST TO HELP EVERYBODY OUT.
THIS IS OUR PRESENT... FOR SUCH A LOVELY SOUL.
THIS WATCH IS NOW BELLE'S.
SHE'S FREE TO DO WITH IT WHAT SHE WILL.

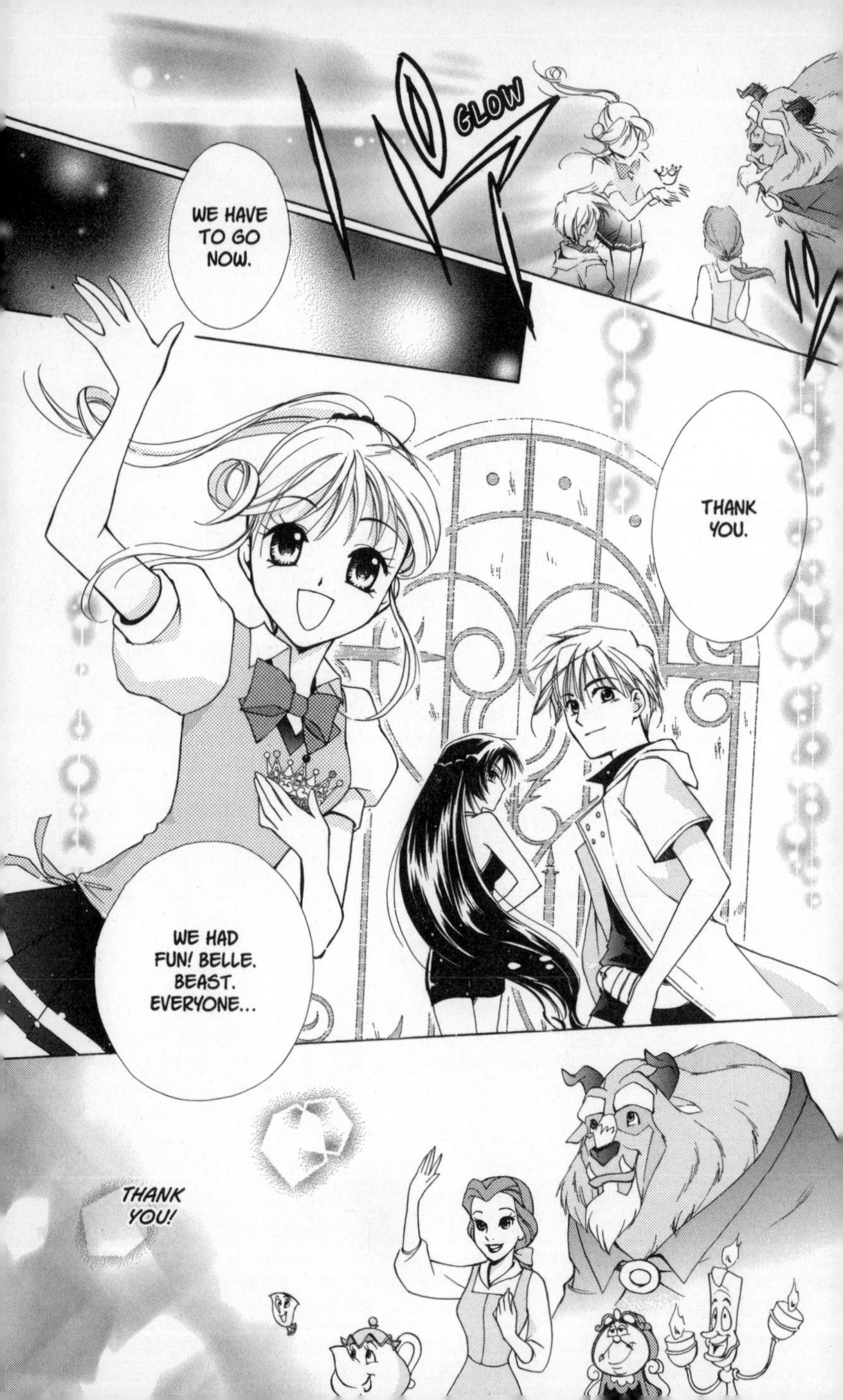
GLOW
WE HAVE TO GO NOW.
THANK YOU.
WE HAD FUN! BELLE. BEAST. EVERYONE...
THANK YOU!

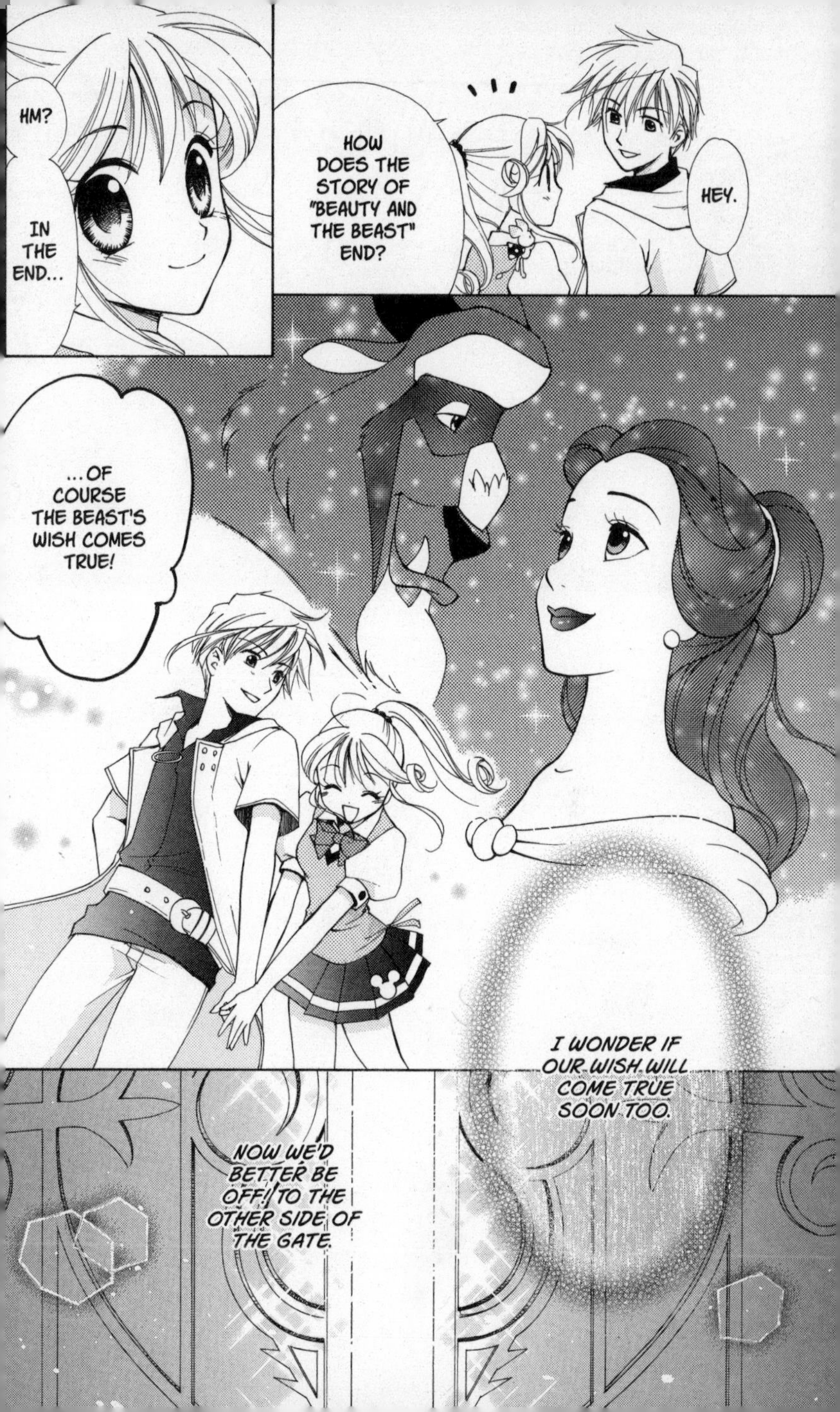
HEY.
HOW DOES THE STORY OF "BEAUTY AND THE BEAST" END?
HM?
IN THE END...
...OF COURSE THE BEAST'S WISH COMES TRUE!
I WONDER IF OUR WISH WILL COME TRUE SOON TOO.
NOW WE'D BETTER BE OFF! TO THE OTHER SIDE OF THE GATE.

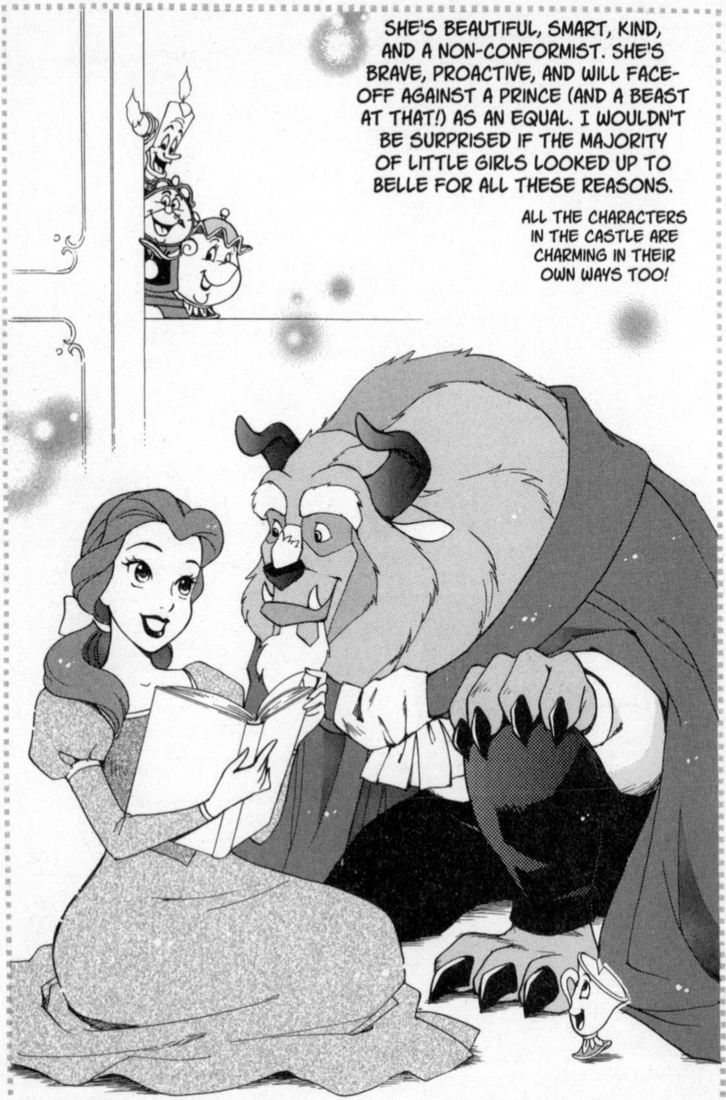
SHE'S BEAUTIFUL, SMART, KIND, AND A NON-CONFORMIST. SHE'S BRAVE, PROACTIVE, AND WILL FACE-OFF AGAINST A PRINCE (AND A BEAST AT THAT!) AS AN EQUAL. I WOULDN'T BE SURPRISED IF THE MAJORITY OF LITTLE GIRLS LOOKED UP TO BELLE FOR ALL THESE REASONS.
ALL THE CHARACTERS IN THE CASTLE ARE CHARMING IN THEIR OWN WAYS TOO!

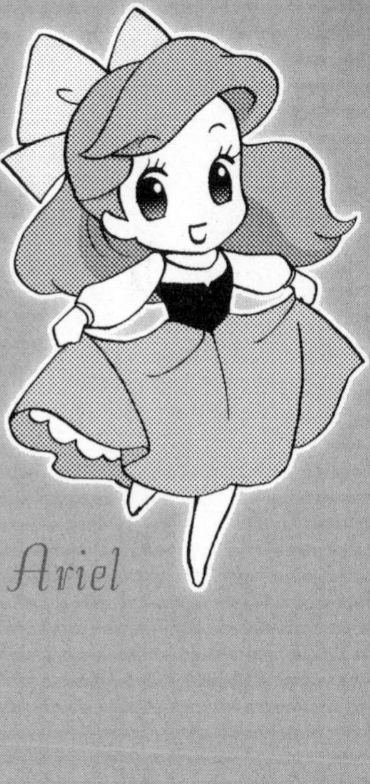

Ariel

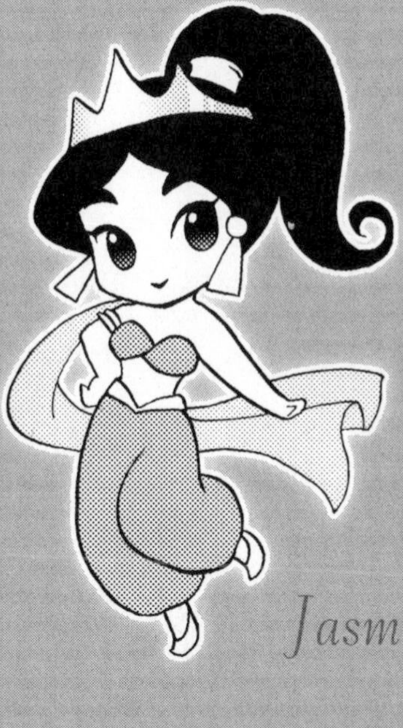

Jasmine

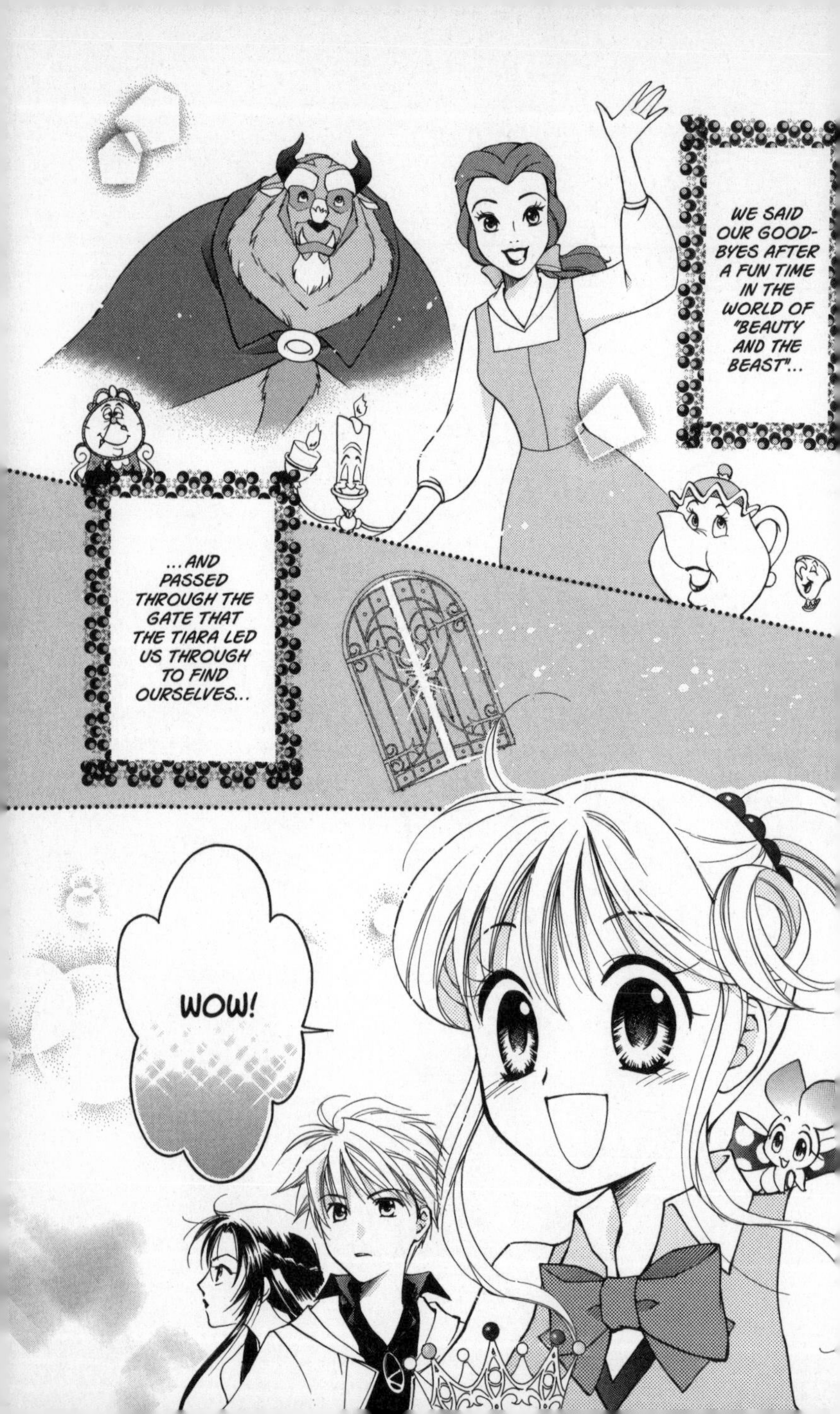
WE SAID OUR GOOD-BYES AFTER A FUN TIME IN THE WORLD OF "BEAUTY AND THE BEAST"...
...AND PASSED THROUGH THE GATE THAT THE TIARA LED US THROUGH TO FIND OURSELVES...
WOW!

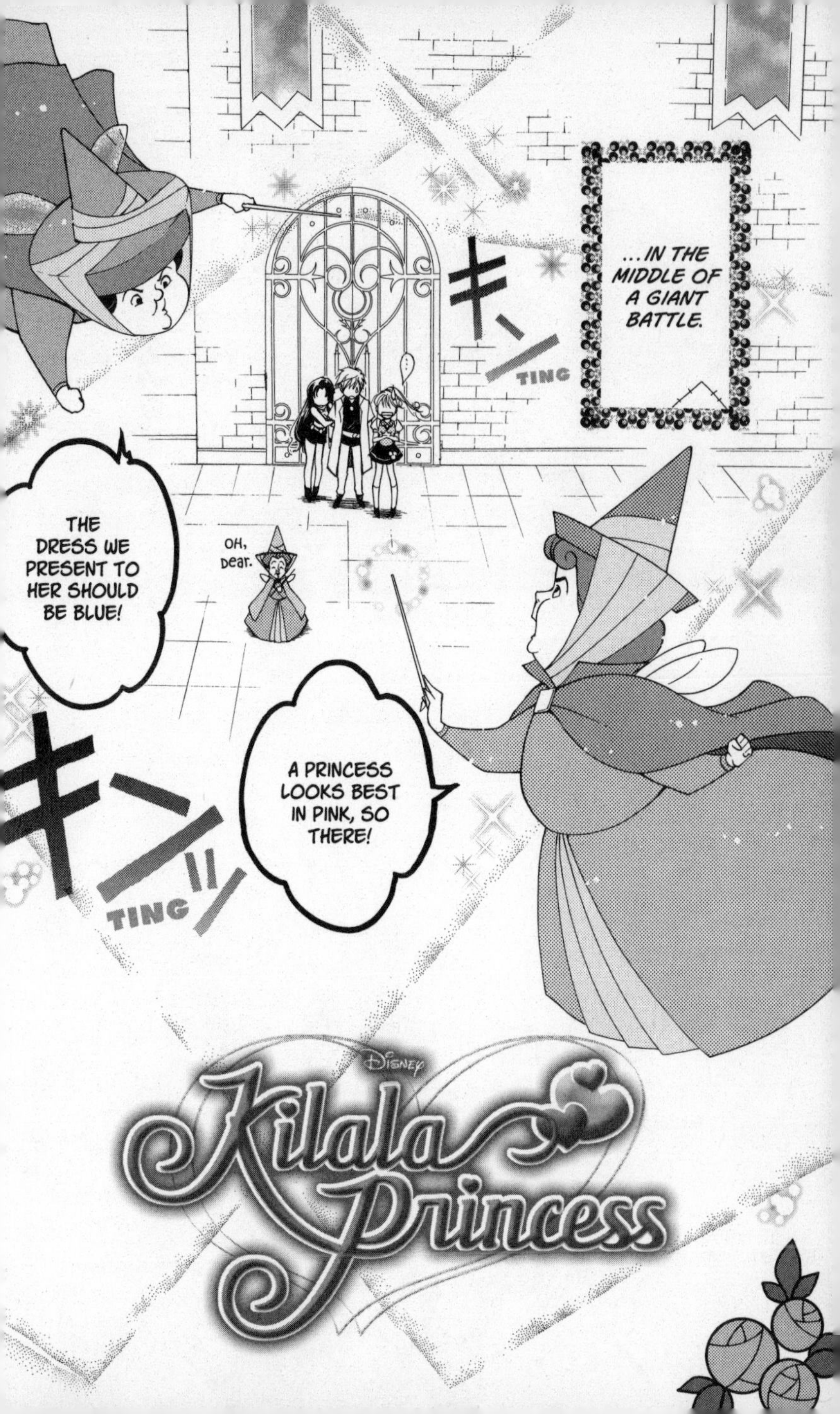

...IN THE MIDDLE OF A GIANT BATTLE.
キン
TING
OH, dear.
THE DRESS WE PRESENT TO HER SHOULD BE BLUE!
A PRINCESS LOOKS BEST IN PINK, SO THERE!
キン!!
TING
DISNEY
Kilala Princess

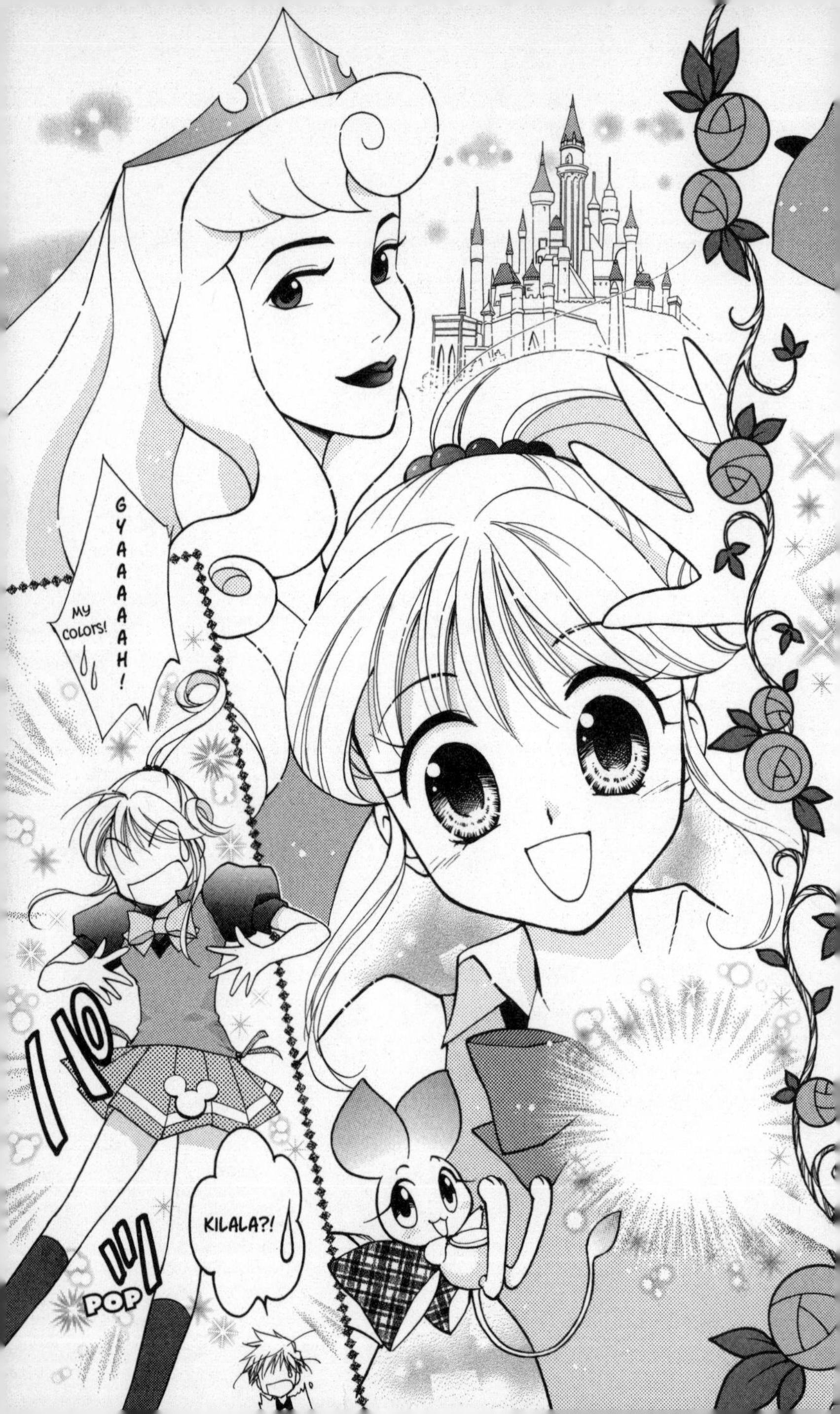
GYAAAAAAH!
MY COLORS!
KILALA?!
POP

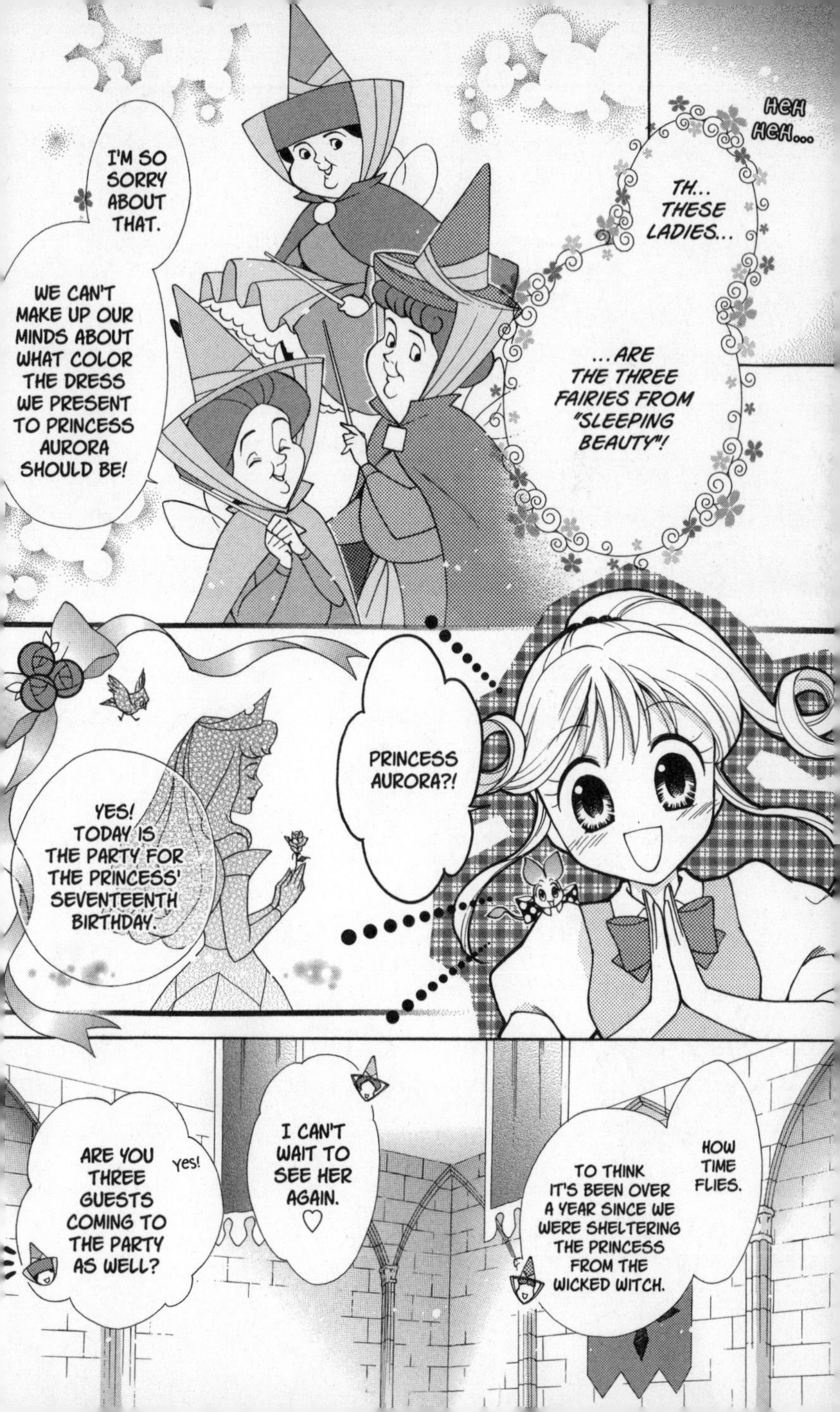
HEH HEH...
TH... THESE LADIES...
...ARE THE THREE FAIRIES FROM "SLEEPING BEAUTY"!
I'M SO SORRY ABOUT THAT.
WE CAN'T MAKE UP OUR MINDS ABOUT WHAT COLOR THE DRESS WE PRESENT TO PRINCESS AURORA SHOULD BE!
PRINCESS AURORA?!
YES! TODAY IS THE PARTY FOR THE PRINCESS' SEVENTEENTH BIRTHDAY.
HOW TIME FLIES.
TO THINK IT'S BEEN OVER A YEAR SINCE WE WERE SHELTERING THE PRINCESS FROM THE WICKED WITCH.
I CAN'T WAIT TO SEE HER AGAIN. ♡
Yes!
ARE YOU THREE GUESTS COMING TO THE PARTY AS WELL?

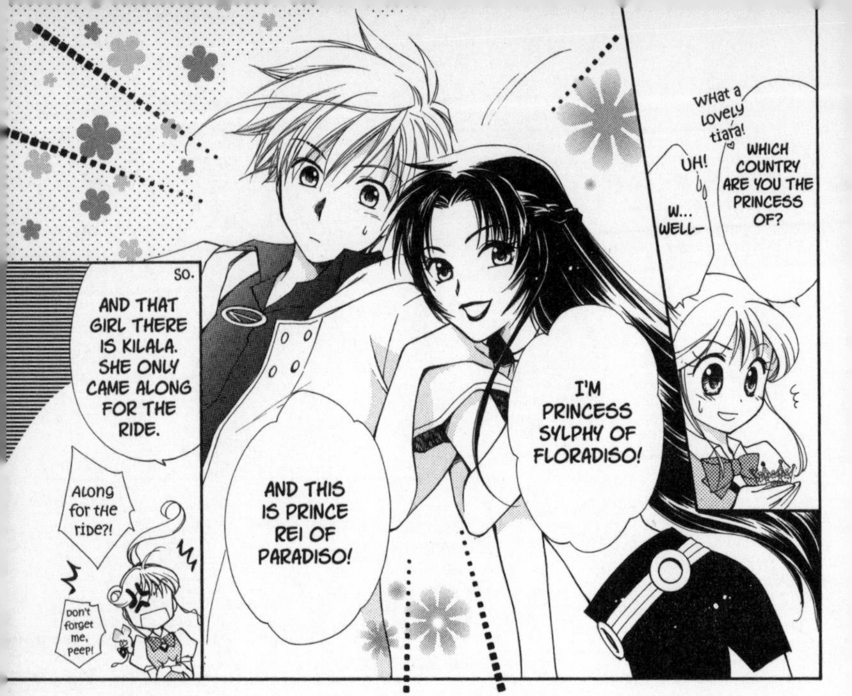
What a lovely tiara!
Which country are you the princess of?
Uh!
W... well—
I'm Princess Sylphy of Floradiso!
And this is Prince Rei of Paradiso!
So.
And that girl there is Kilala. She only came along for the ride.
Along for the ride?!
Don't forget me, peep!

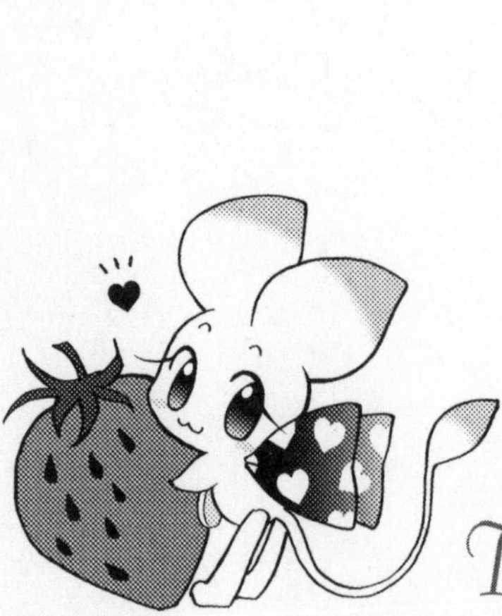

Tippe

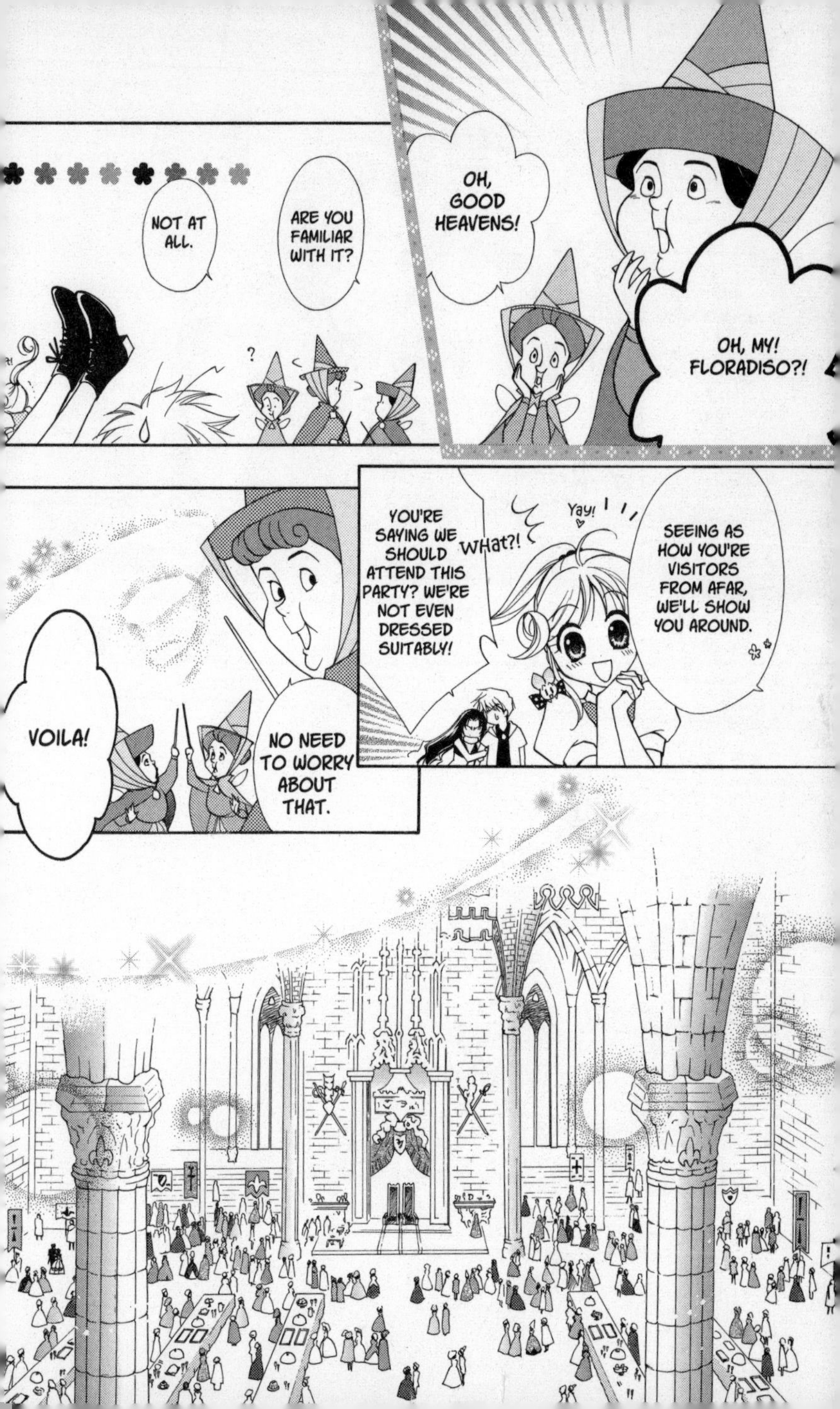
OH, MY! FLORADISO?!
OH, GOOD HEAVENS!
ARE YOU FAMILIAR WITH IT?
NOT AT ALL.
SEEING AS HOW YOU'RE VISITORS FROM AFAR, WE'LL SHOW YOU AROUND.
Yay!
What?!
YOU'RE SAYING WE SHOULD ATTEND THIS PARTY? WE'RE NOT EVEN DRESSED SUITABLY!
NO NEED TO WORRY ABOUT THAT.
VOILA!

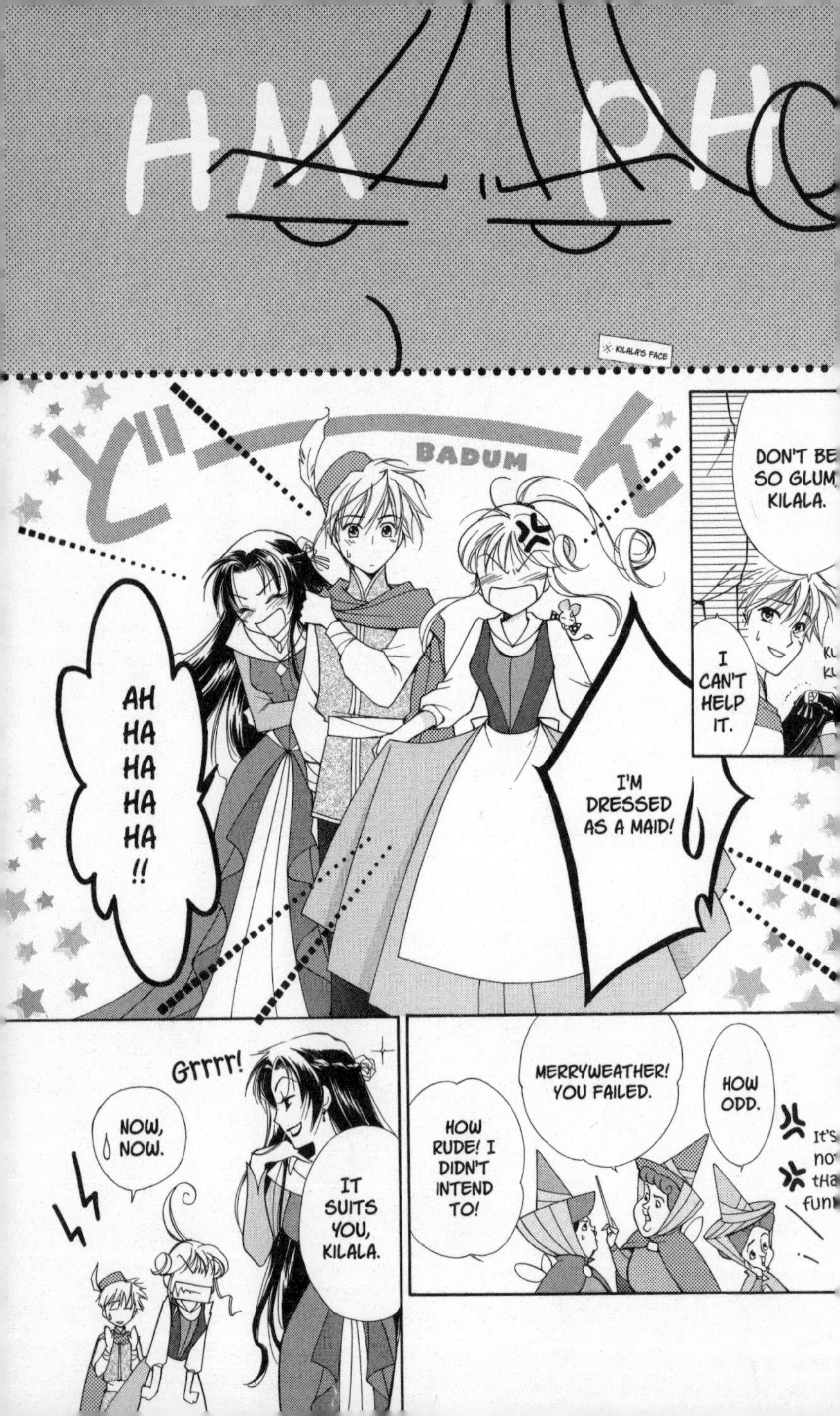
HMPH
※ KILALA'S FACE
DON'T BE SO GLUM, KILALA.
I CAN'T HELP IT.
どーん
BADUM
I'M DRESSED AS A MAID!
AH HA HA HA HA!!
HOW ODD.
MERRYWEATHER! YOU FAILED.
HOW RUDE! I DIDN'T INTEND TO!
Grrrr!
IT SUITS YOU, KILALA.
NOW, NOW.

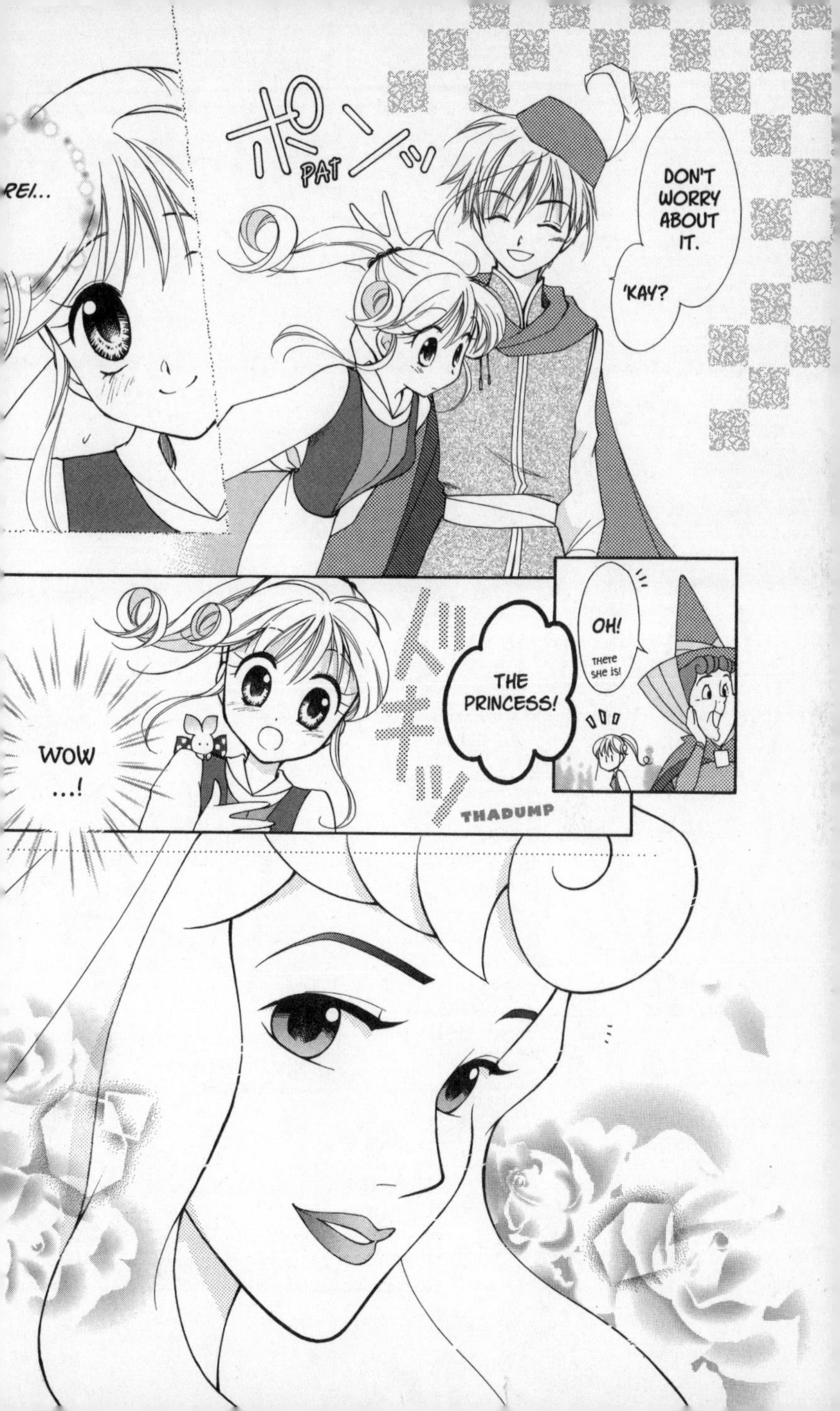
DON'T WORRY ABOUT IT.
'KAY?
PAT
REI...
OH!
There she is!
THE PRINCESS!
THADUMP
WOW ...!

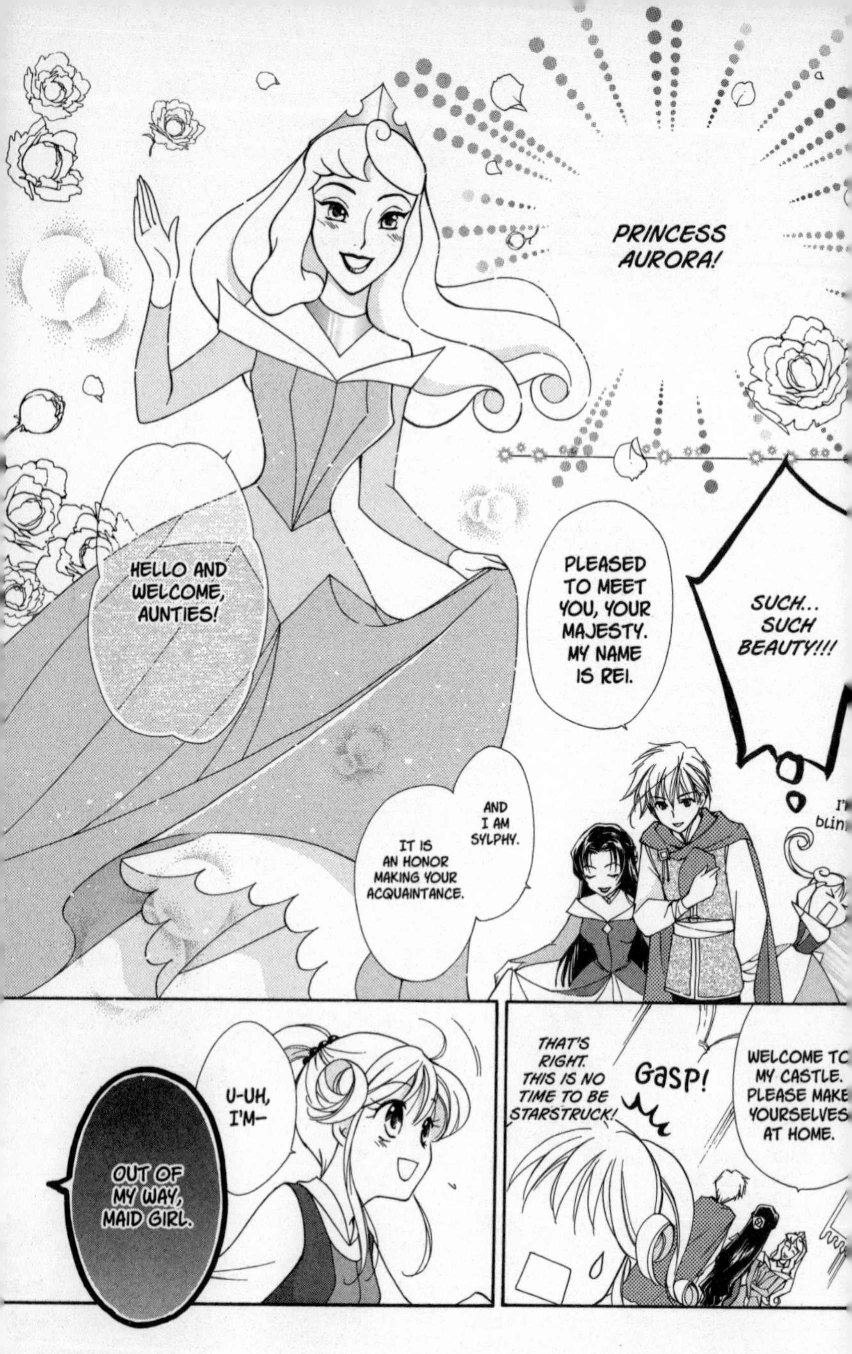
PRINCESS AURORA!
SUCH... SUCH BEAUTY!!!
PLEASED TO MEET YOU, YOUR MAJESTY. MY NAME IS REI.
AND I AM SYLPHY.
IT IS AN HONOR MAKING YOUR ACQUAINTANCE.
HELLO AND WELCOME, AUNTIES!
WELCOME TO MY CASTLE. PLEASE MAKE YOURSELVES AT HOME.
Gasp!
THAT'S RIGHT. THIS IS NO TIME TO BE STARSTRUCK!
U-UH, I'M—
OUT OF MY WAY, MAID GIRL.

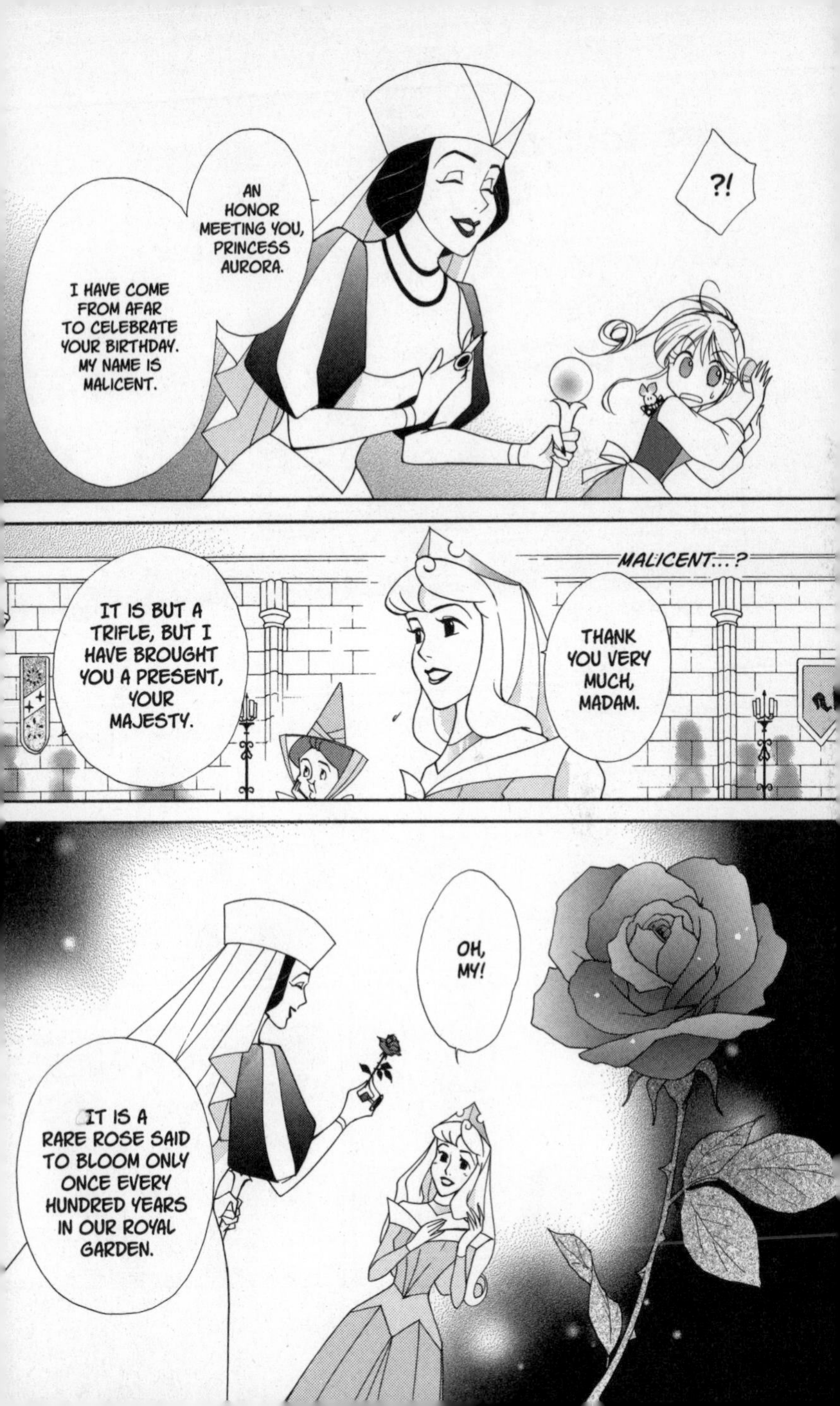
?!
AN HONOR MEETING YOU, PRINCESS AURORA.
I HAVE COME FROM AFAR TO CELEBRATE YOUR BIRTHDAY. MY NAME IS MALICENT.
MALICENT...?
THANK YOU VERY MUCH, MADAM.
IT IS BUT A TRIFLE, BUT I HAVE BROUGHT YOU A PRESENT, YOUR MAJESTY.
OH, MY!
IT IS A RARE ROSE SAID TO BLOOM ONLY ONCE EVERY HUNDRED YEARS IN OUR ROYAL GARDEN.

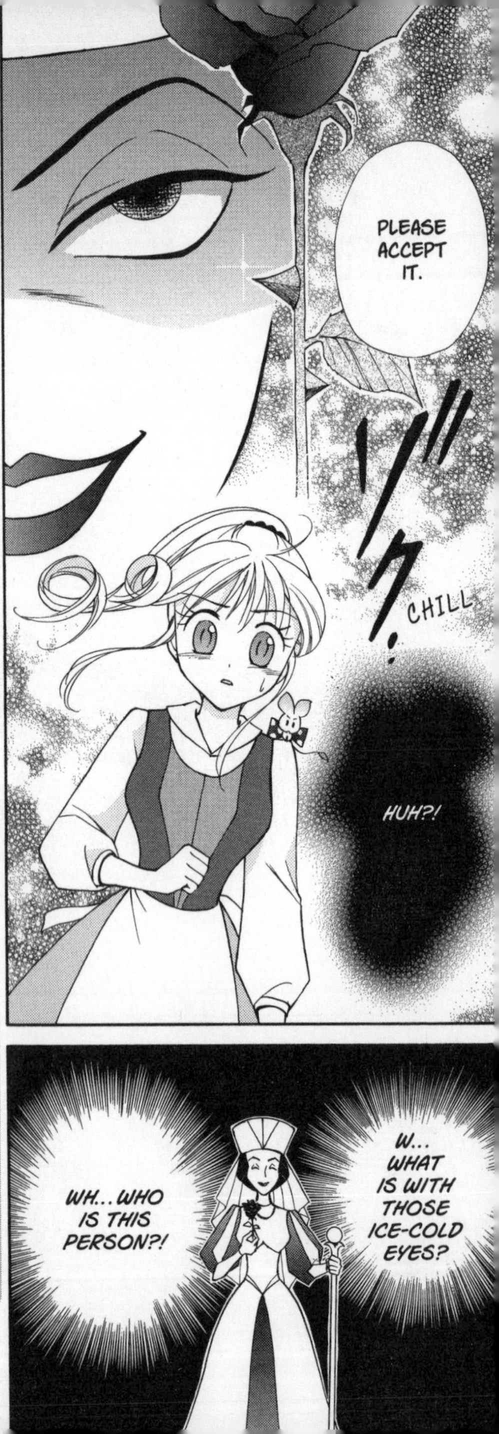
PLEASE ACCEPT IT.
CHILL
HUH?!
W... WHAT IS WITH THOSE ICE-COLD EYES?
WH...WHO IS THIS PERSON?!

Rika Tanaka

HELLO! THIS IS THE WRITER OF THE STORY, RIKA TANAKA. IN THIS VOLUME, KILALA AND FRIENDS TRAVEL TO THE WORLDS OF "BEAUTY AND THE BEAST" AND "SLEEPING BEAUTY"! THE TWO PRINCESSES WHO SHOW UP HERE, BELLE AND AURORA, ARE MORE MATURE PRINCESSES.☆ ESPECIALLY AURORA. EVEN THOUGH SHE'S ONLY SIXTEEN YEARS OLD, SHE HAS SUCH AN ELEGANCE TO HER! REMEMBERING HOW I WAS AT THAT AGE MYSELF, MAKES ME PALE WITH EMBARRASSMENT (LOL). I ALSO ADMIRE BELLE'S UNWAVERING STRENGTH AND DETERMINATION. ☆
I GUESS IT'S BECAUSE I'M AN ADULT NOW (LOL) THAT I CAN APPRECIATE THEIR CLASS, AND ELEGANCE. ALL THE STORIES OF THE DISNEY PRINCESSES ARE PACKED WITH SECRETS TO BECOMING AN UPSTANDING YOUNG WOMAN. ♪
I'M GOING TO TRY HARD MYSELF, SO THAT I DON'T LOSE TO KILALA. ☆

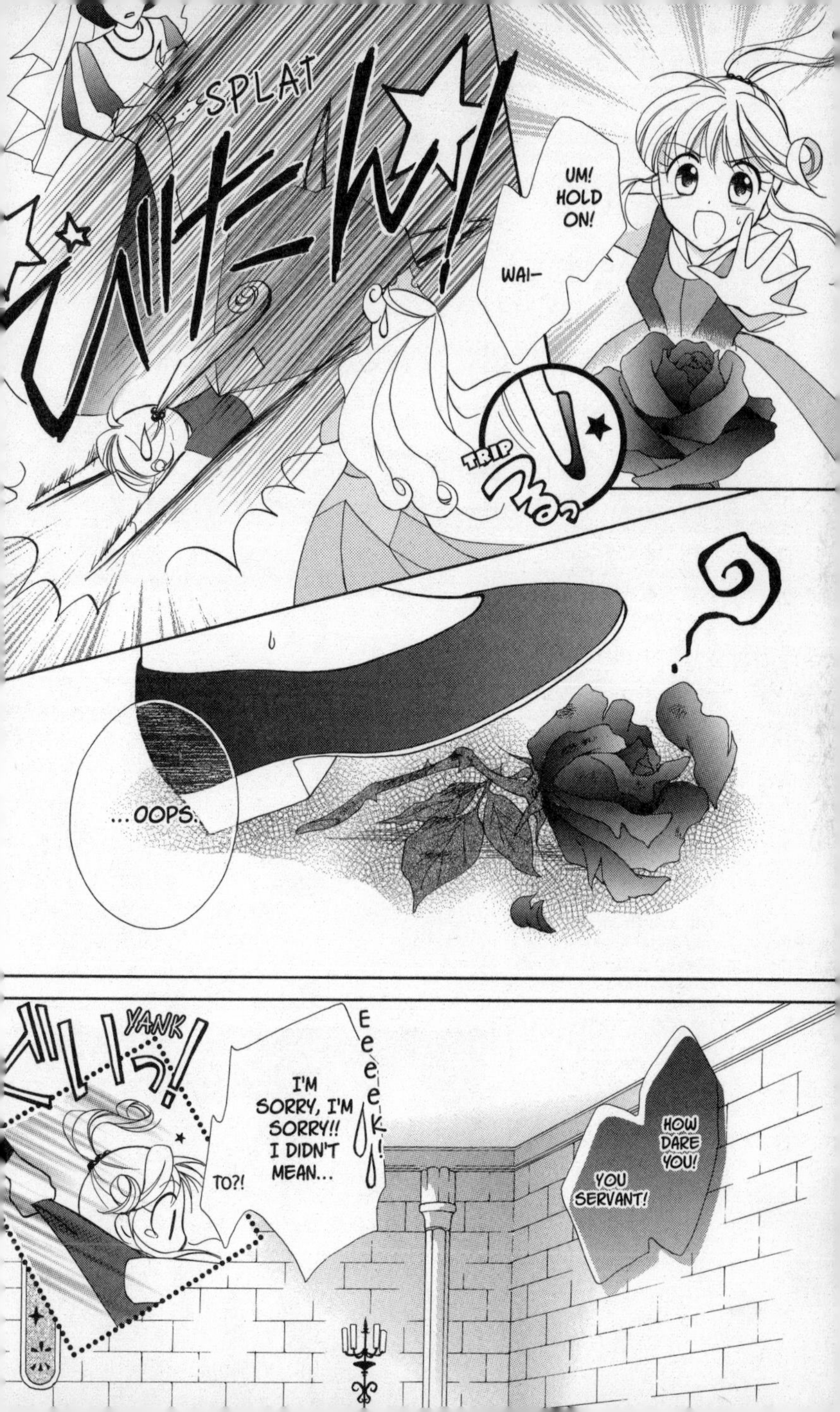
UM! HOLD ON!
WAI-
TRIP
SPLAT
...OOPS.
HOW DARE YOU!
YOU SERVANT!
I'M SORRY, I'M SORRY!! I DIDN'T MEAN...
TO?!
Eeeeek!
YANK

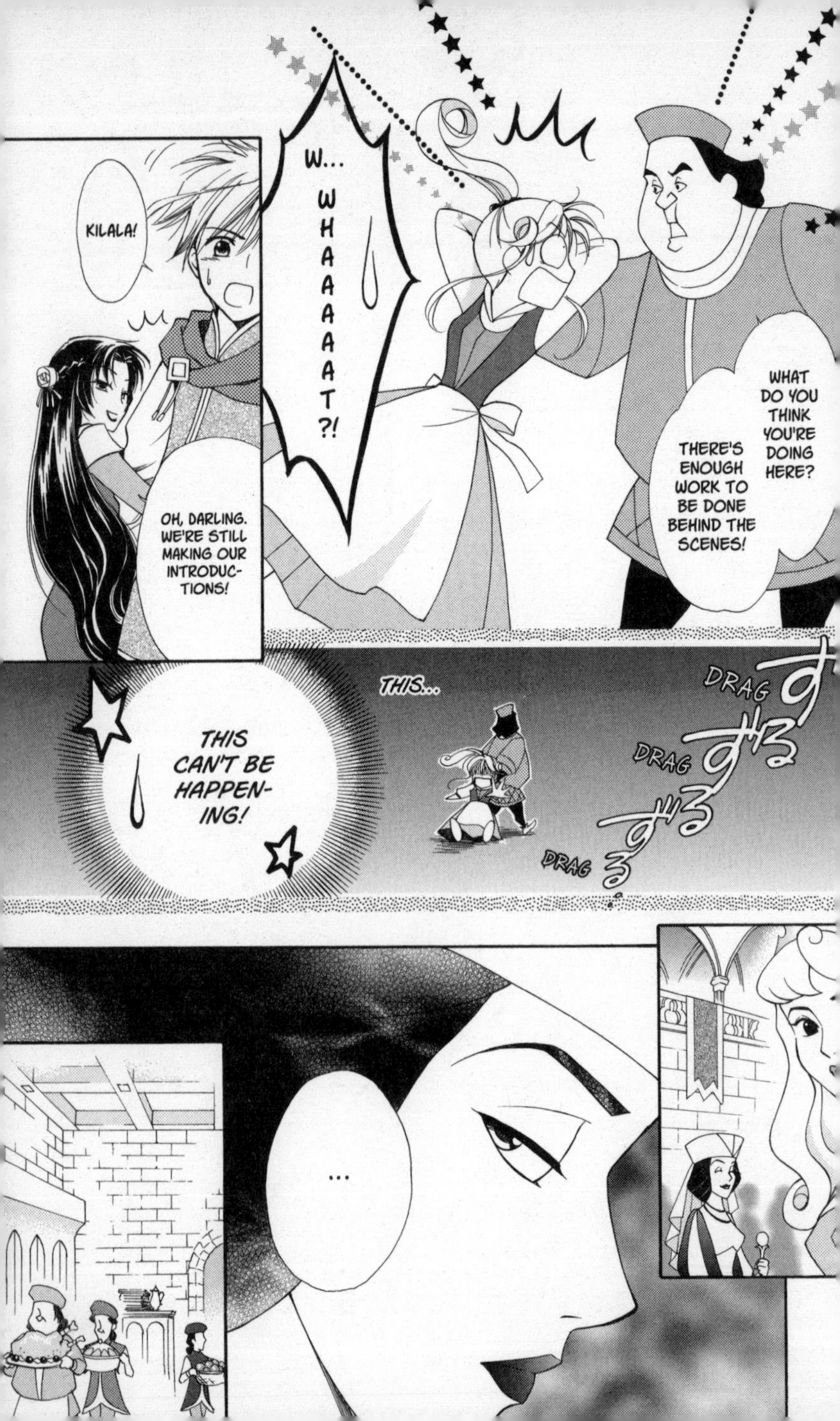
WHAT DO YOU THINK YOU'RE DOING HERE?
THERE'S ENOUGH WORK TO BE DONE BEHIND THE SCENES!
W... WHAAAAAAT?!
KILALA!
OH, DARLING. WE'RE STILL MAKING OUR INTRODUCTIONS!
DRAG
DRAG
DRAG
THIS...
THIS CAN'T BE HAPPENING!
...

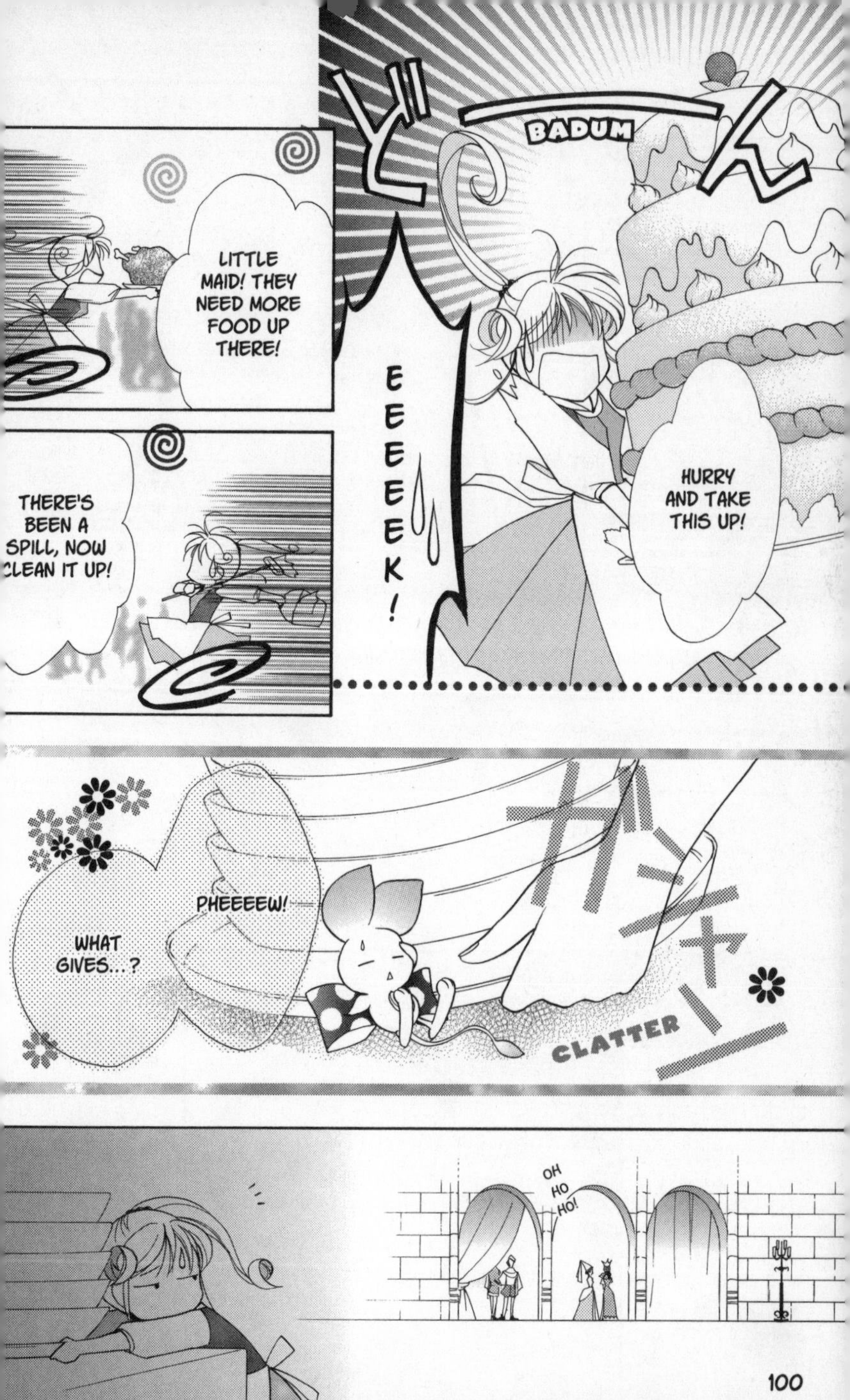

BADUM
HURRY AND TAKE THIS UP!
EEEEEK!
LITTLE MAID! THEY NEED MORE FOOD UP THERE!
THERE'S BEEN A SPILL, NOW CLEAN IT UP!
CLATTER
PHEEEEW!
WHAT GIVES...?
OH HO HO!

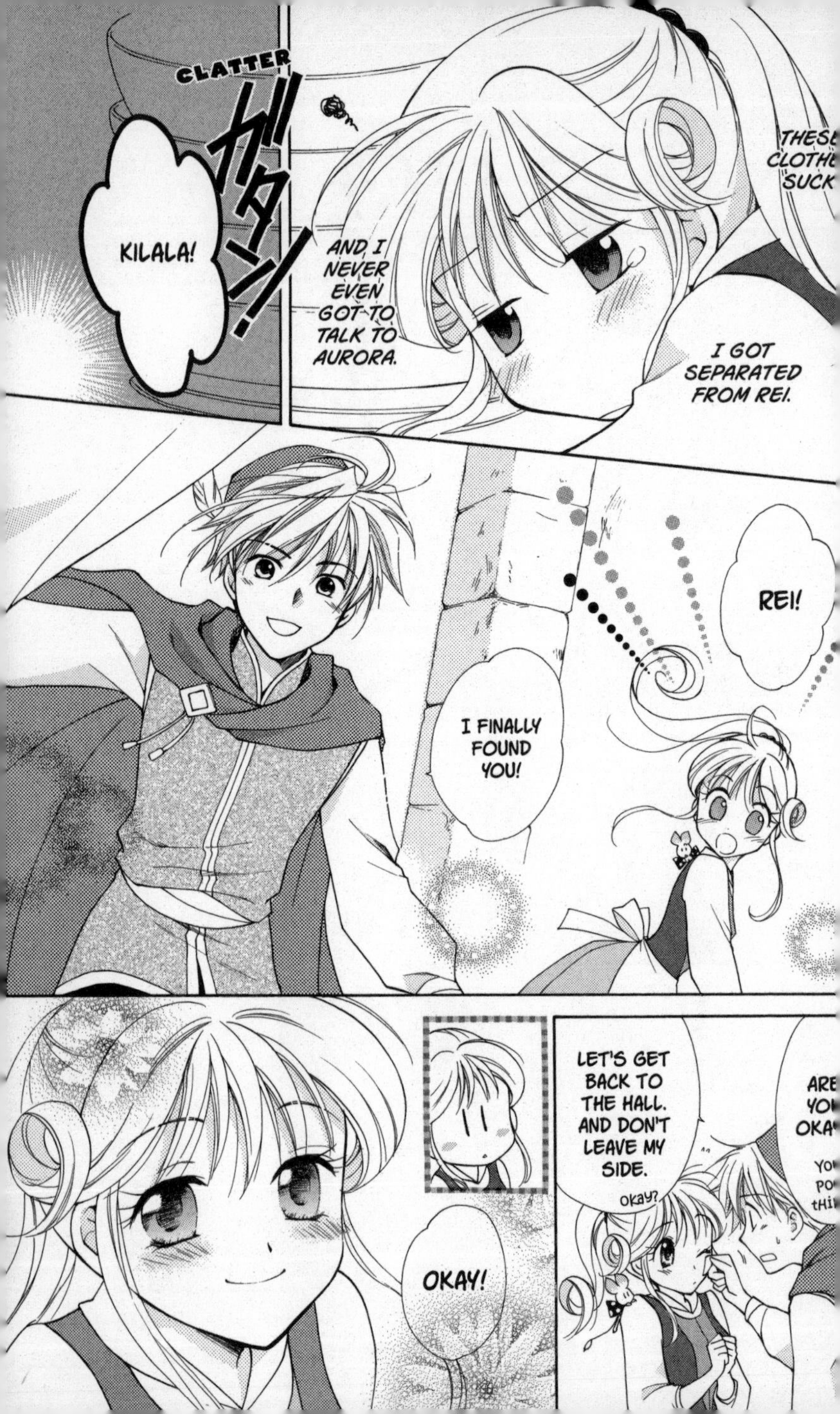
THESE CLOTHE SUCK
I GOT SEPARATED FROM REI.
AND I NEVER EVEN GOT TO TALK TO AURORA.
CLATTER
ガタン!
KILALA!
REI!
I FINALLY FOUND YOU!
ARE YO OKA
YO PO THI
LET'S GET BACK TO THE HALL. AND DON'T LEAVE MY SIDE.
Okay?
OKAY!

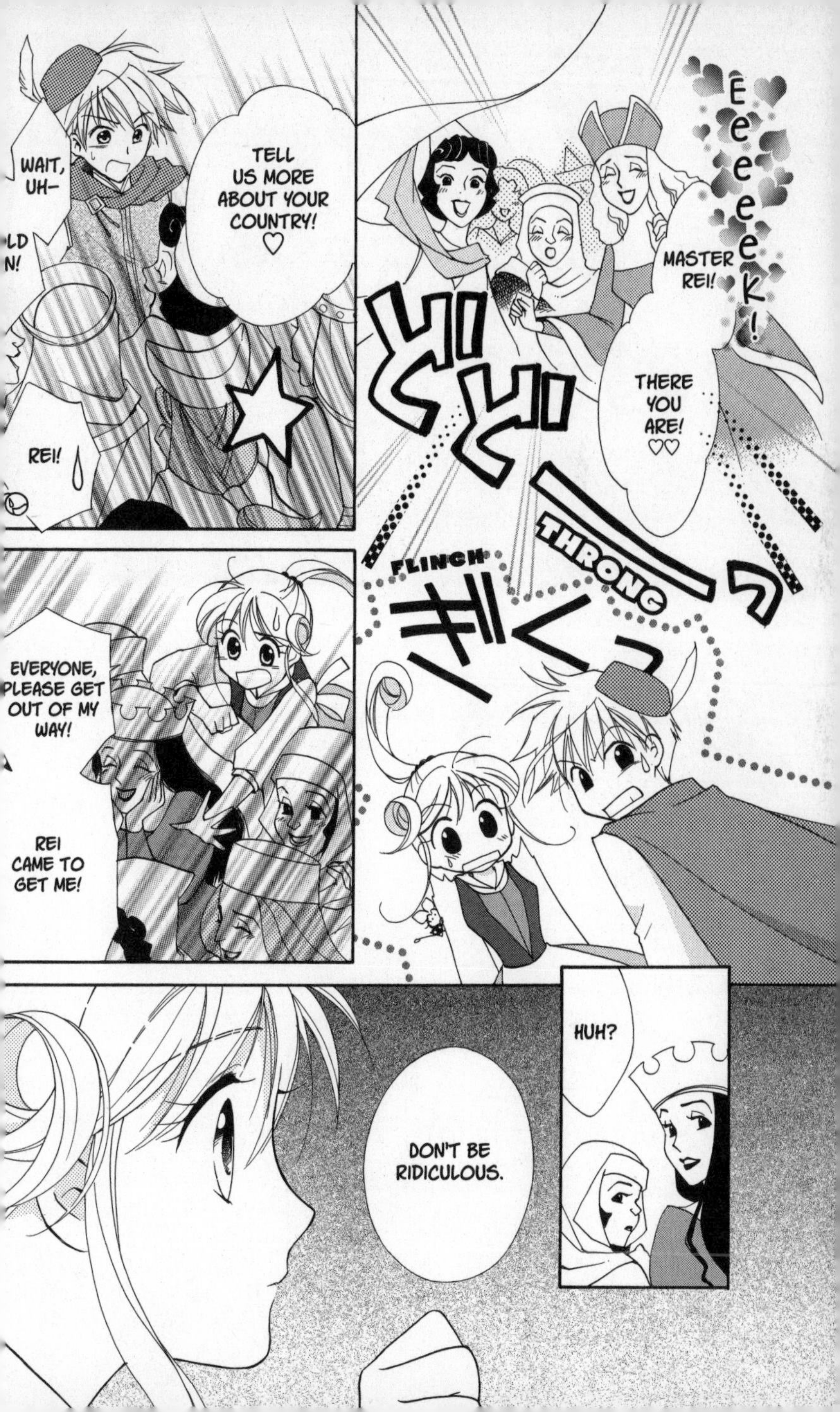
Eeeeek!
MASTER REI!
THERE YOU ARE! ♡♡
THRONG
FLINCH
TELL US MORE ABOUT YOUR COUNTRY! ♡
WAIT, UH–
REI!
EVERYONE, PLEASE GET OUT OF MY WAY!
REI CAME TO GET ME!
HUH?
DON'T BE RIDICULOUS.

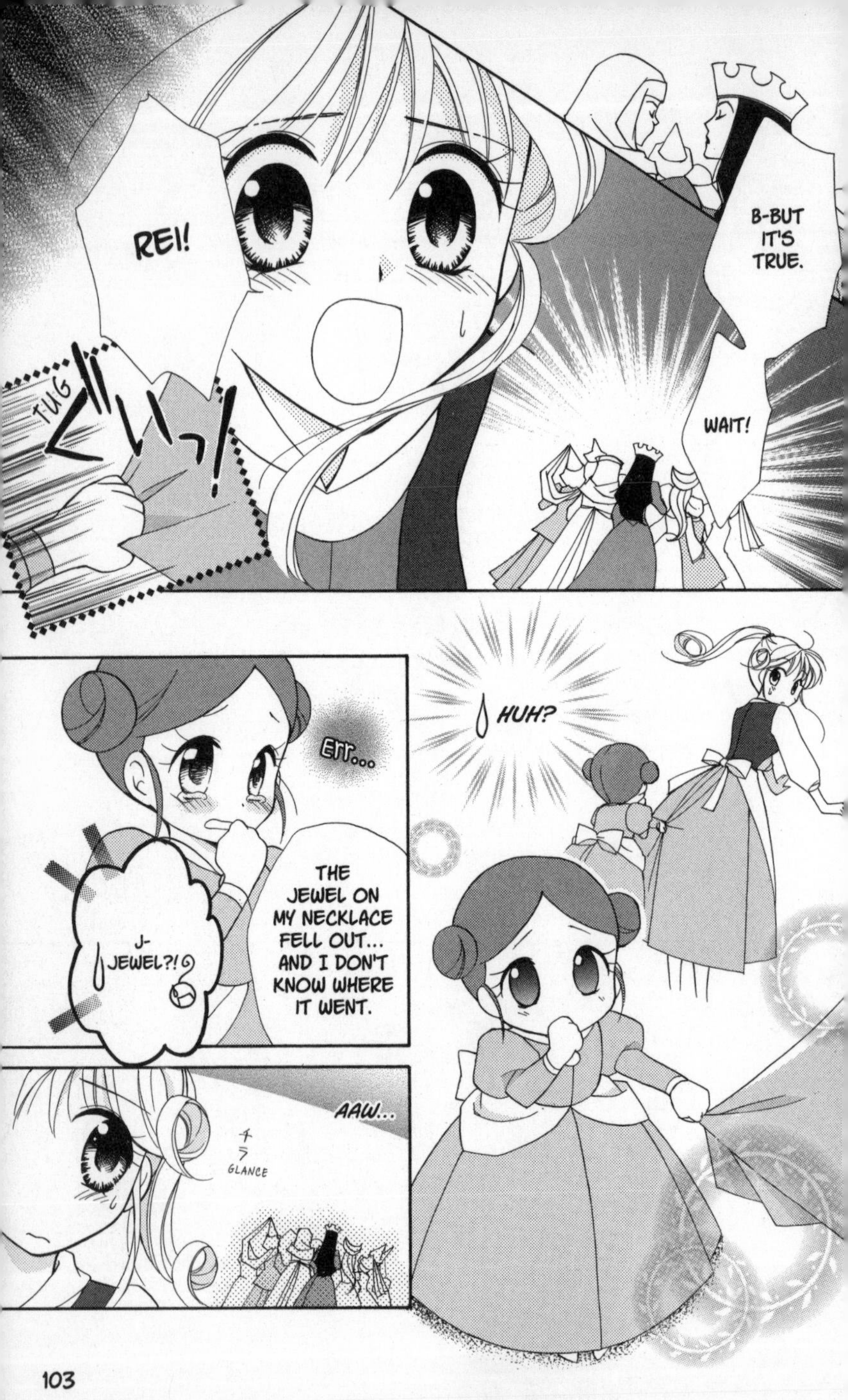
B-BUT IT'S TRUE.
WAIT!
REI!
ぐいっ!
TUG
HUH?
Err...
THE JEWEL ON MY NECKLACE FELL OUT... AND I DON'T KNOW WHERE IT WENT.
J-JEWEL?!
AAW...
チラ
GLANCE

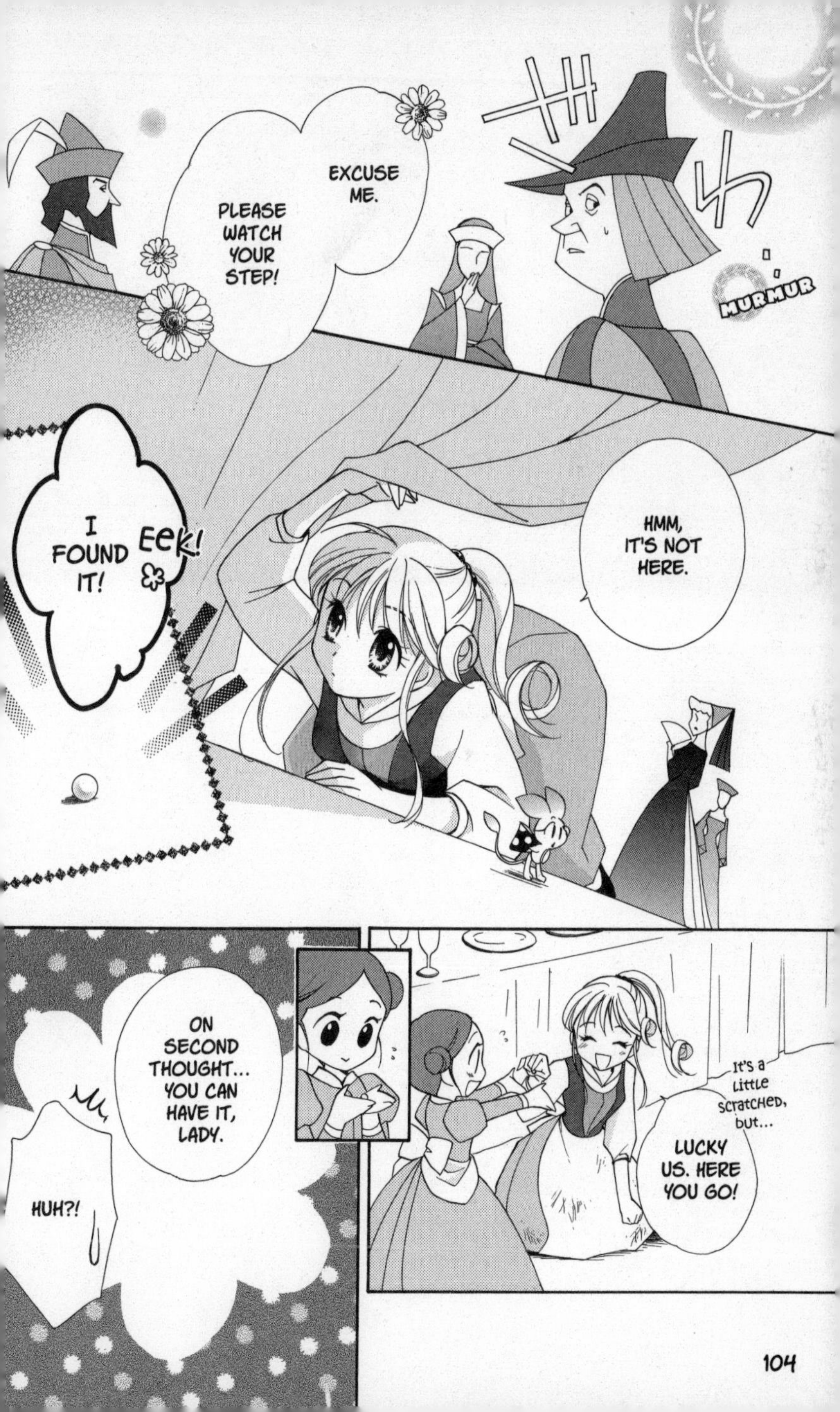
MURMUR
EXCUSE ME.
PLEASE WATCH YOUR STEP!
HMM, IT'S NOT HERE.
EEK!
I FOUND IT!
It's a little scratched, but...
LUCKY US. HERE YOU GO!
ON SECOND THOUGHT... YOU CAN HAVE IT, LADY.
HUH?!

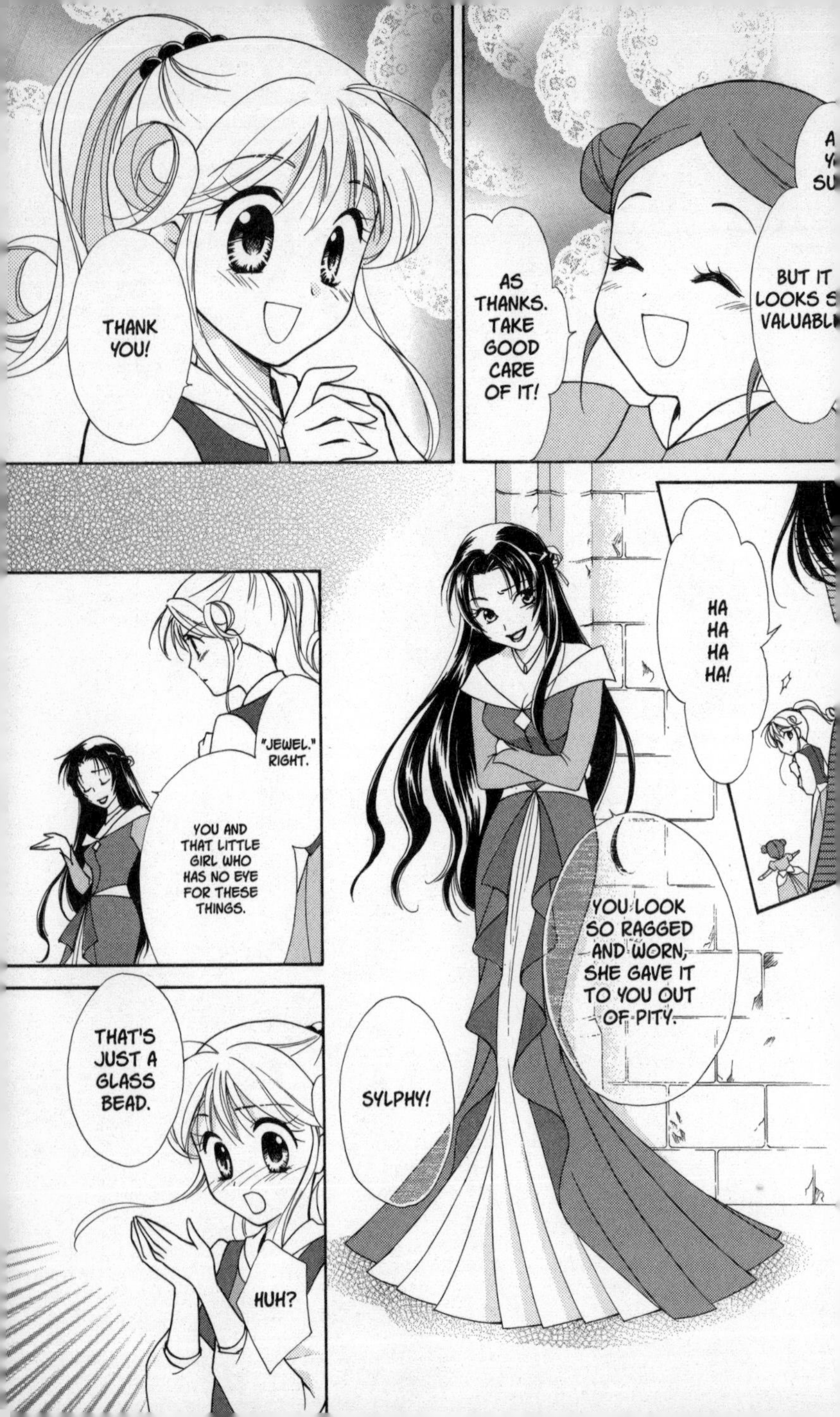
BUT IT LOOKS
AS THANKS. TAKE GOOD CARE OF IT!
THANK YOU!
HA HA HA HA!
YOU LOOK SO RAGGED AND WORN, SHE GAVE IT TO YOU OUT OF PITY.
SYLPHY!
"JEWEL." RIGHT.
YOU AND THAT LITTLE GIRL WHO HAS NO EYE FOR THESE THINGS.
THAT'S JUST A GLASS BEAD.
HUH?

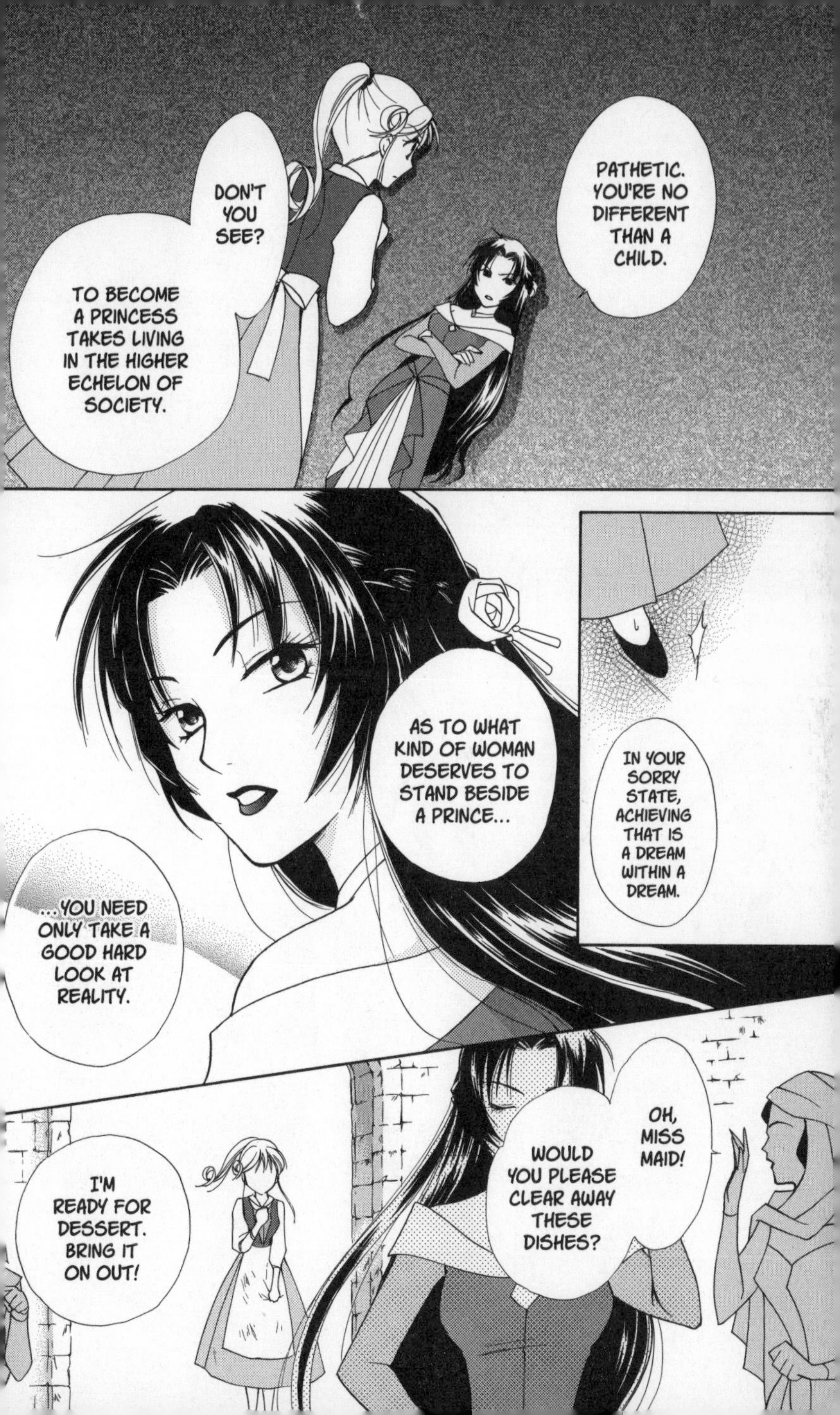
PATHETIC. YOU'RE NO DIFFERENT THAN A CHILD.
DON'T YOU SEE?
TO BECOME A PRINCESS TAKES LIVING IN THE HIGHER ECHELON OF SOCIETY.
IN YOUR SORRY STATE, ACHIEVING THAT IS A DREAM WITHIN A DREAM.
AS TO WHAT KIND OF WOMAN DESERVES TO STAND BESIDE A PRINCE...
...YOU NEED ONLY TAKE A GOOD HARD LOOK AT REALITY.
OH, MISS MAID!
WOULD YOU PLEASE CLEAR AWAY THESE DISHES?
I'M READY FOR DESSERT. BRING IT ON OUT!

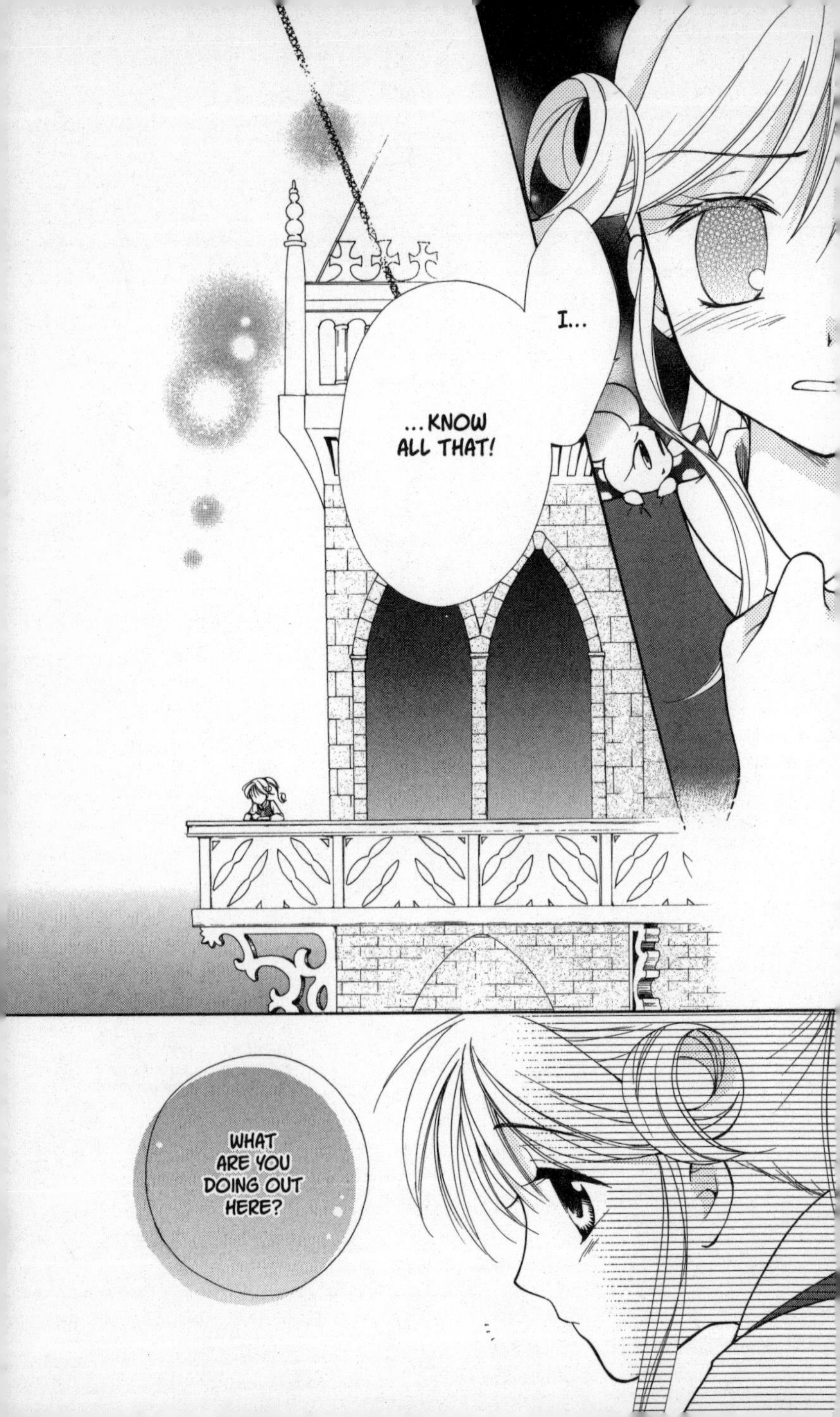
I...
...KNOW ALL THAT!
WHAT ARE YOU DOING OUT HERE?

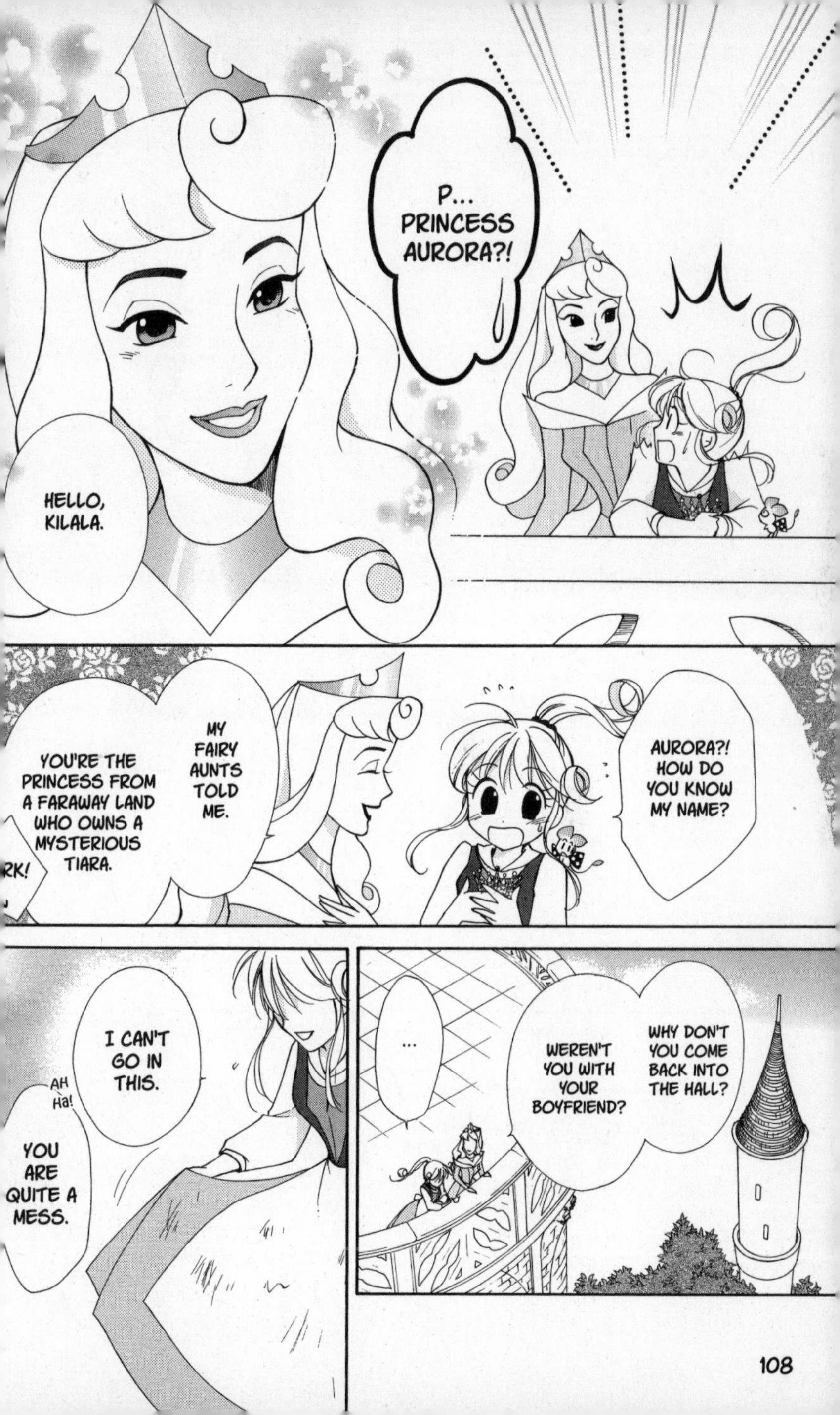
P... PRINCESS AURORA?!
HELLO, KILALA.
AURORA?! HOW DO YOU KNOW MY NAME?
MY FAIRY AUNTS TOLD ME.
YOU'RE THE PRINCESS FROM A FARAWAY LAND WHO OWNS A MYSTERIOUS TIARA.
WHY DON'T YOU COME BACK INTO THE HALL?
WEREN'T YOU WITH YOUR BOYFRIEND?
...
I CAN'T GO IN THIS.
AH Ha!
YOU ARE QUITE A MESS.

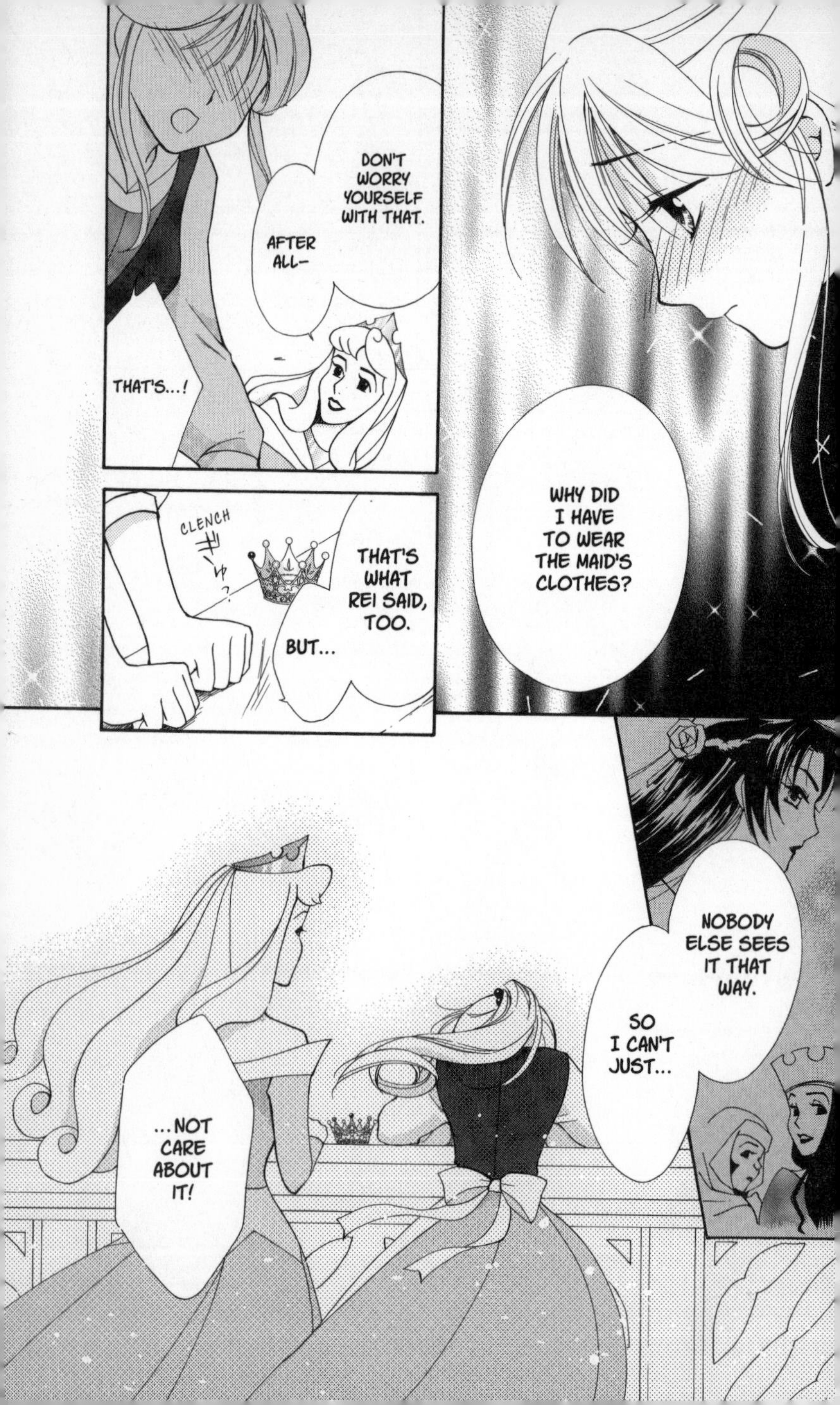
WHY DID I HAVE TO WEAR THE MAID'S CLOTHES?
DON'T WORRY YOURSELF WITH THAT.
AFTER ALL—
THAT'S...!
CLENCH
THAT'S WHAT REI SAID, TOO.
BUT...
NOBODY ELSE SEES IT THAT WAY.
SO I CAN'T JUST...
...NOT CARE ABOUT IT!

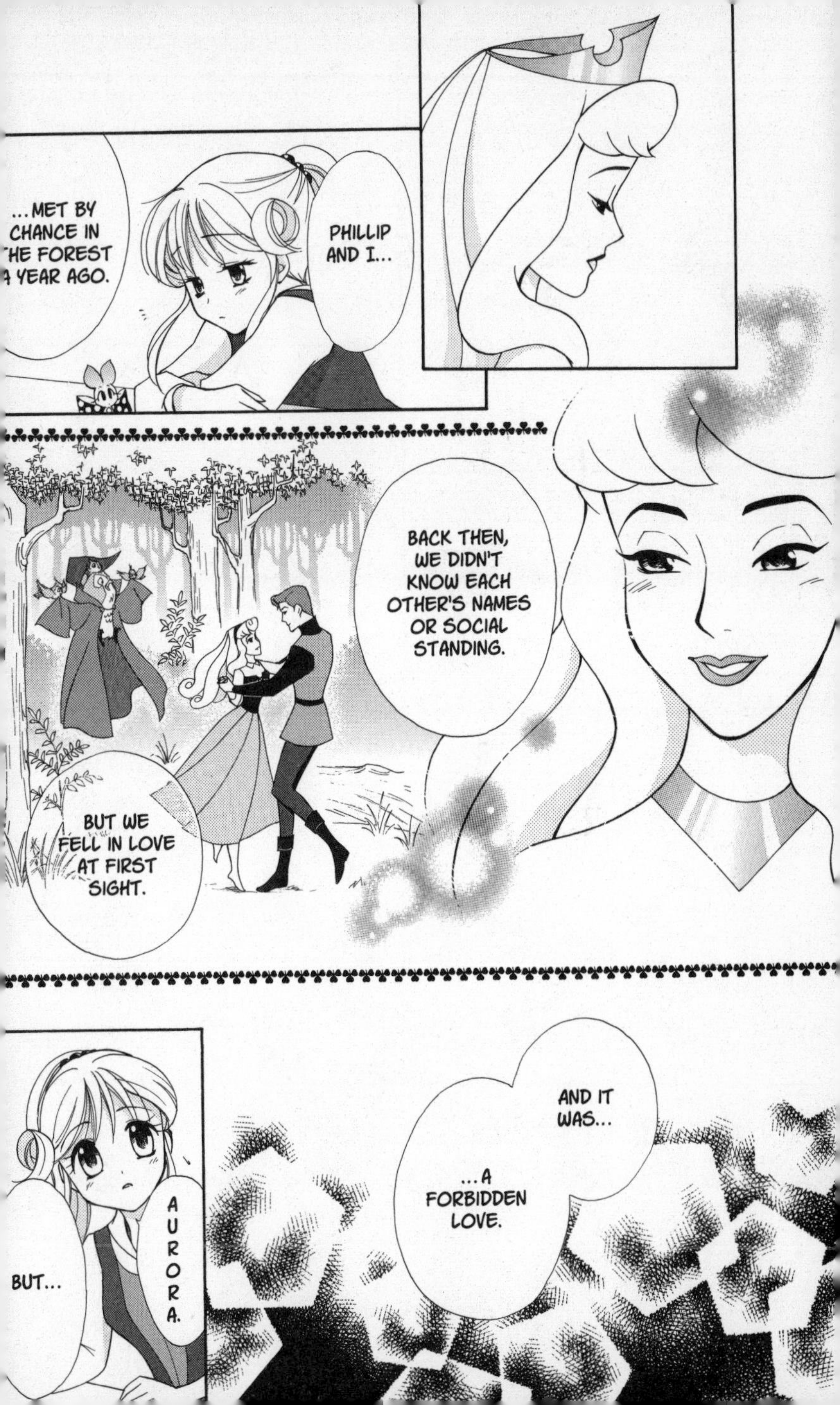
PHILLIP AND I...
...MET BY CHANCE IN THE FOREST A YEAR AGO.
BACK THEN, WE DIDN'T KNOW EACH OTHER'S NAMES OR SOCIAL STANDING.
BUT WE FELL IN LOVE AT FIRST SIGHT.
AND IT WAS...
...A FORBIDDEN LOVE.
AURORA.
BUT...

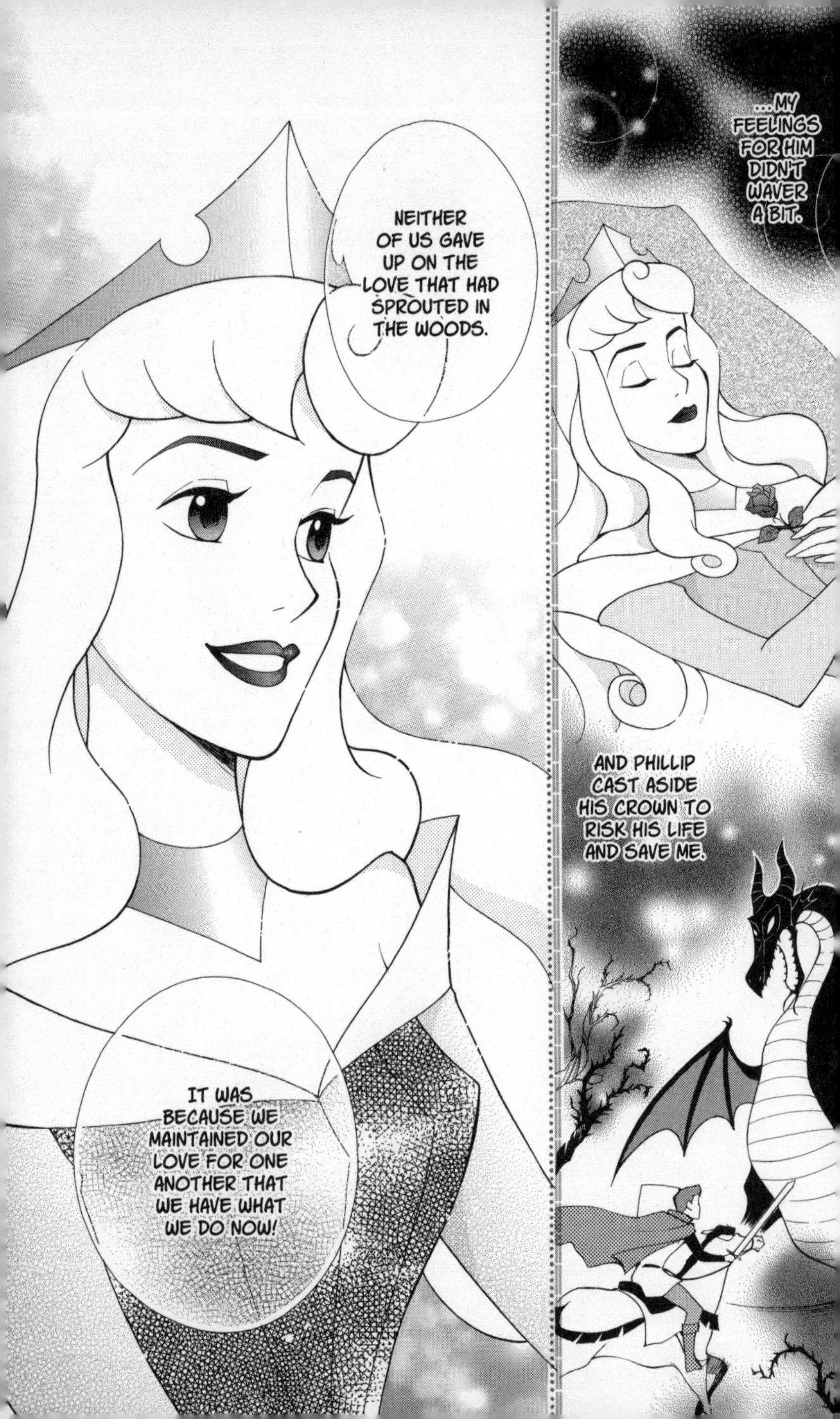
...MY FEELINGS FOR HIM DIDN'T WAVER A BIT.
AND PHILLIP CAST ASIDE HIS CROWN TO RISK HIS LIFE AND SAVE ME.
NEITHER OF US GAVE UP ON THE LOVE THAT HAD SPROUTED IN THE WOODS.
IT WAS BECAUSE WE MAINTAINED OUR LOVE FOR ONE ANOTHER THAT WE HAVE WHAT WE DO NOW!

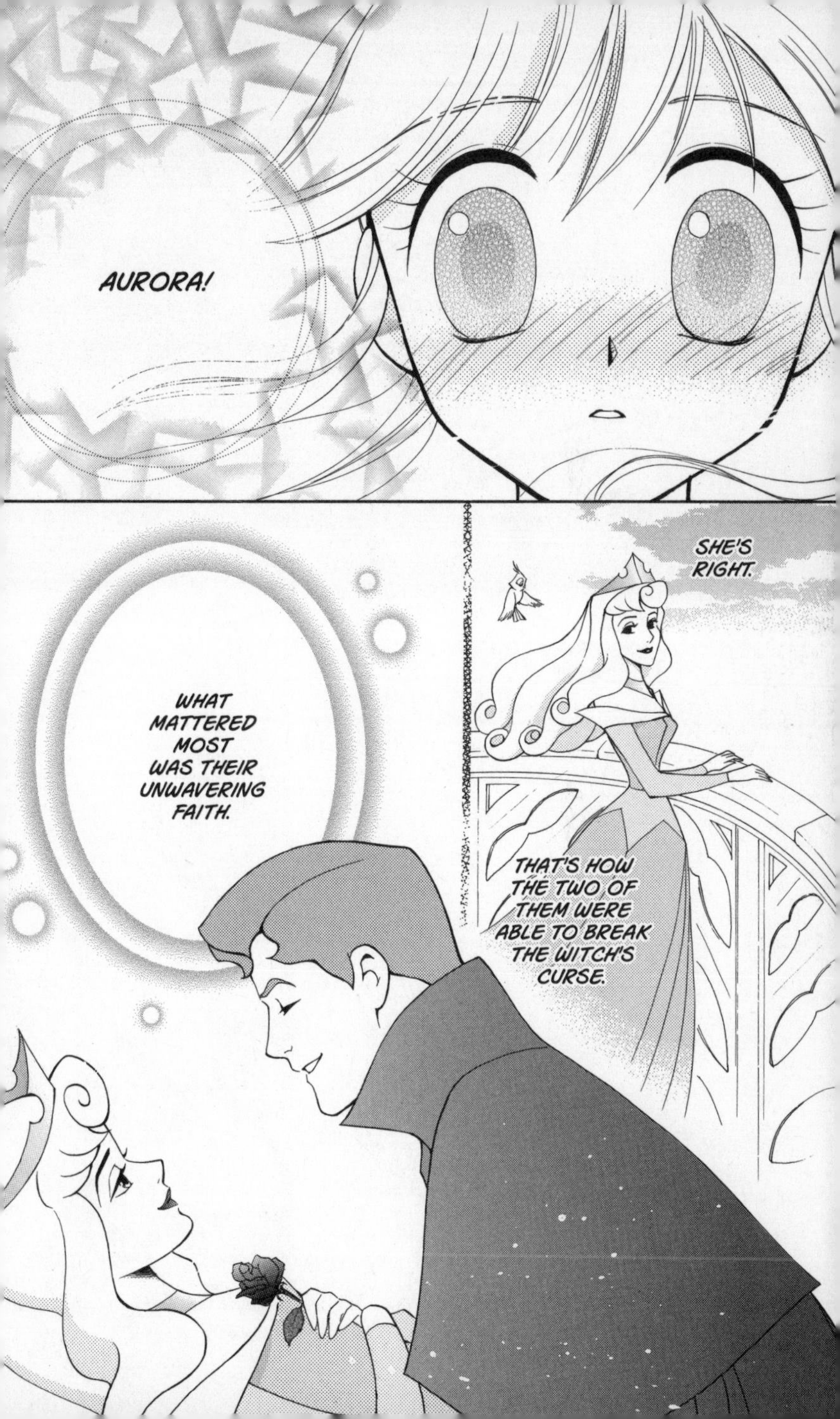
AURORA!
SHE'S RIGHT.
THAT'S HOW THE TWO OF THEM WERE ABLE TO BREAK THE WITCH'S CURSE.
WHAT MATTERED MOST WAS THEIR UNWAVERING FAITH.

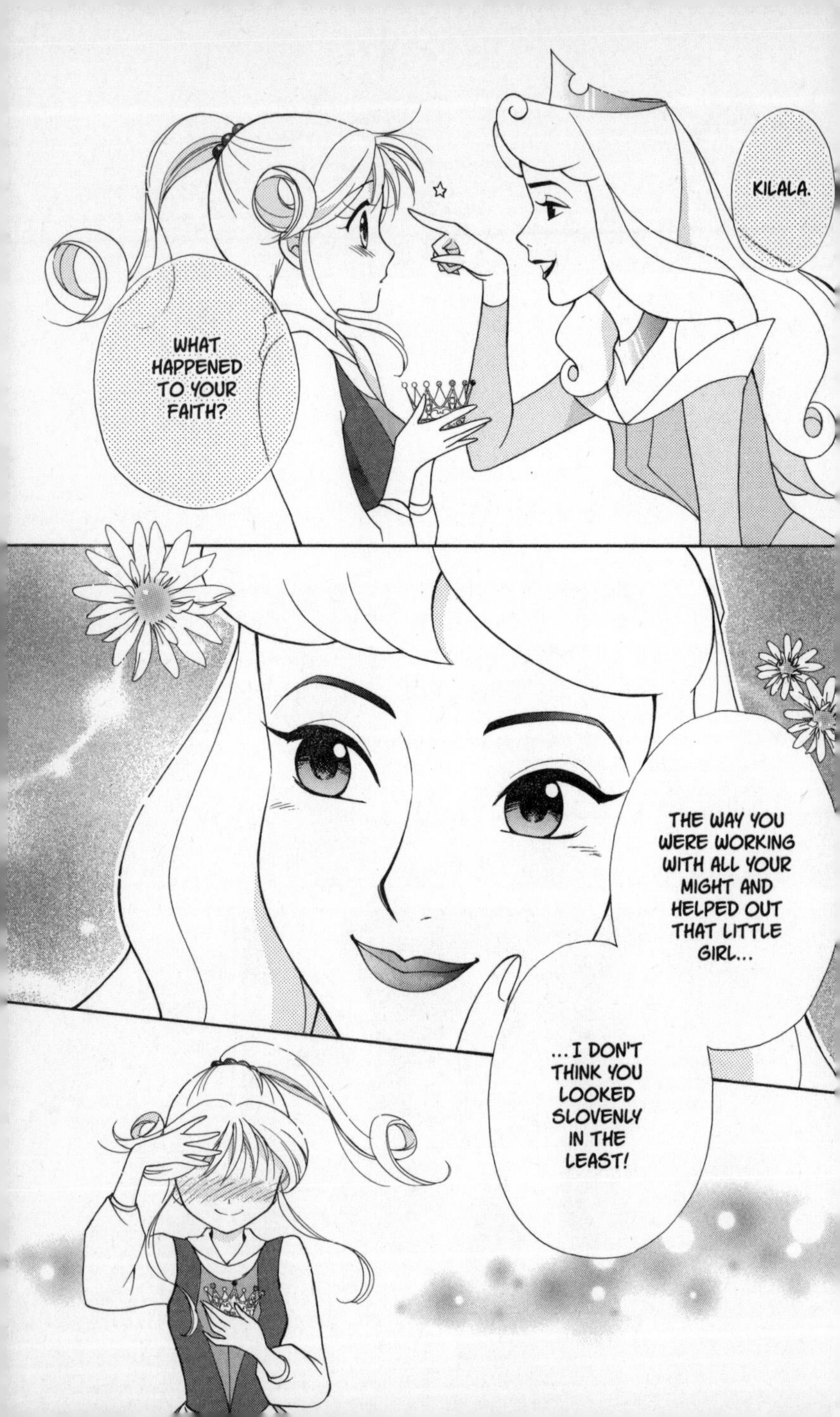
KILALA.
WHAT HAPPENED TO YOUR FAITH?
THE WAY YOU WERE WORKING WITH ALL YOUR MIGHT AND HELPED OUT THAT LITTLE GIRL...
...I DON'T THINK YOU LOOKED SLOVENLY IN THE LEAST!

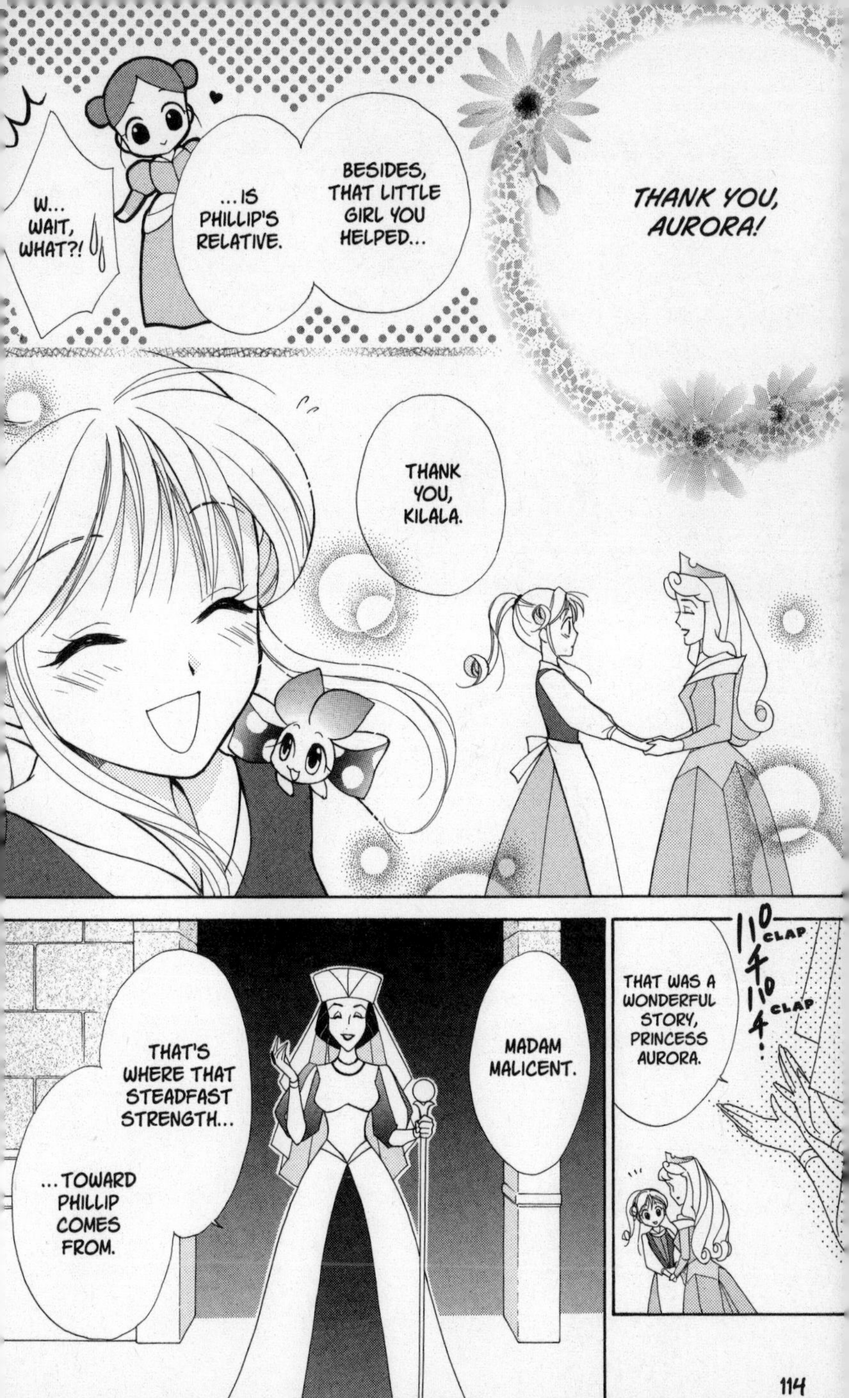
THANK YOU, AURORA!
BESIDES, THAT LITTLE GIRL YOU HELPED...
...IS PHILLIP'S RELATIVE.
W... WAIT, WHAT?!
THANK YOU, KILALA.
CLAP CLAP
THAT WAS A WONDERFUL STORY, PRINCESS AURORA.
MADAM MALICENT.
THAT'S WHERE THAT STEADFAST STRENGTH...
...TOWARD PHILLIP COMES FROM.

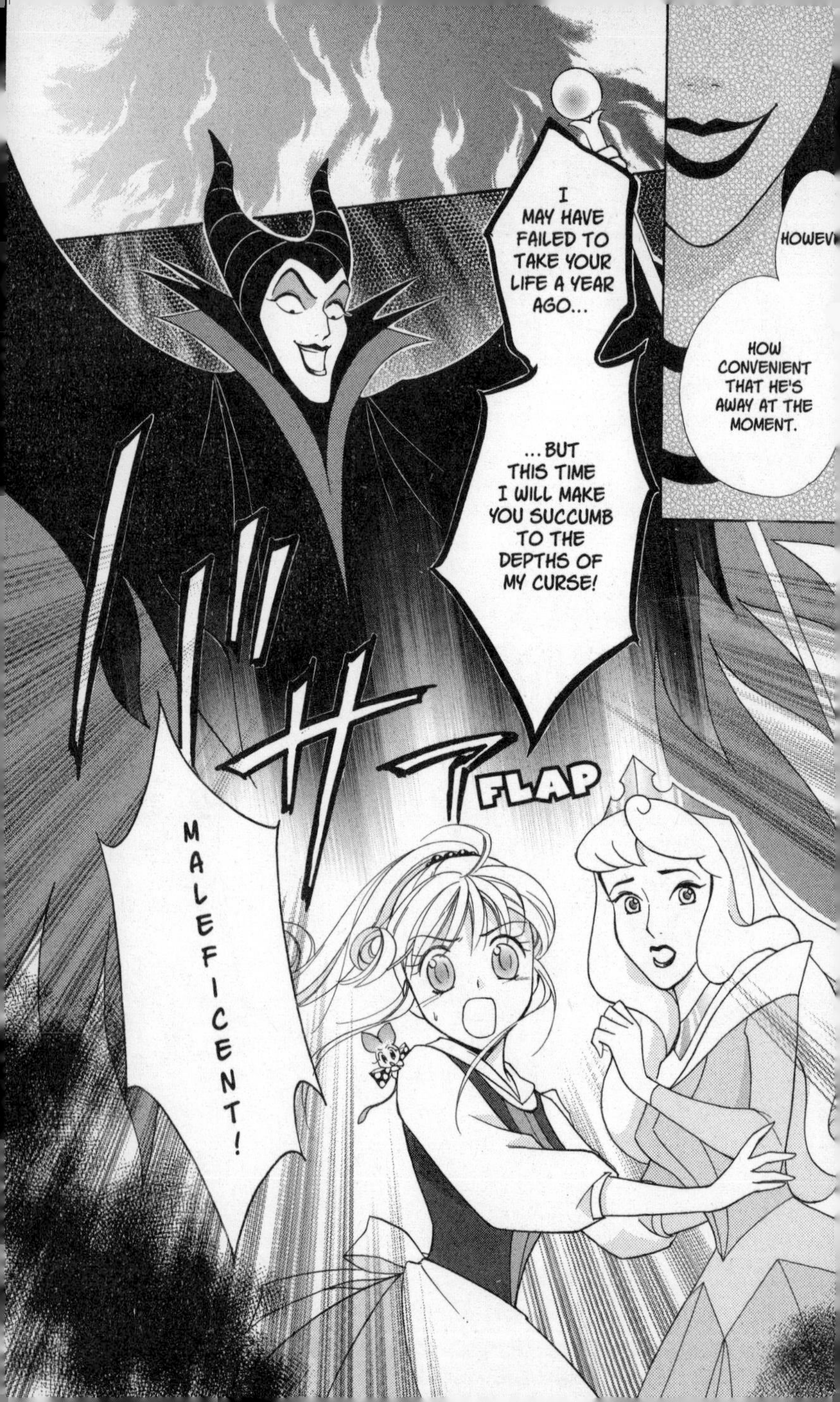
HOWEV
HOW CONVENIENT THAT HE'S AWAY AT THE MOMENT.
I MAY HAVE FAILED TO TAKE YOUR LIFE A YEAR AGO...
...BUT THIS TIME I WILL MAKE YOU SUCCUMB TO THE DEPTHS OF MY CURSE!
FLAP
MALEFICENT!

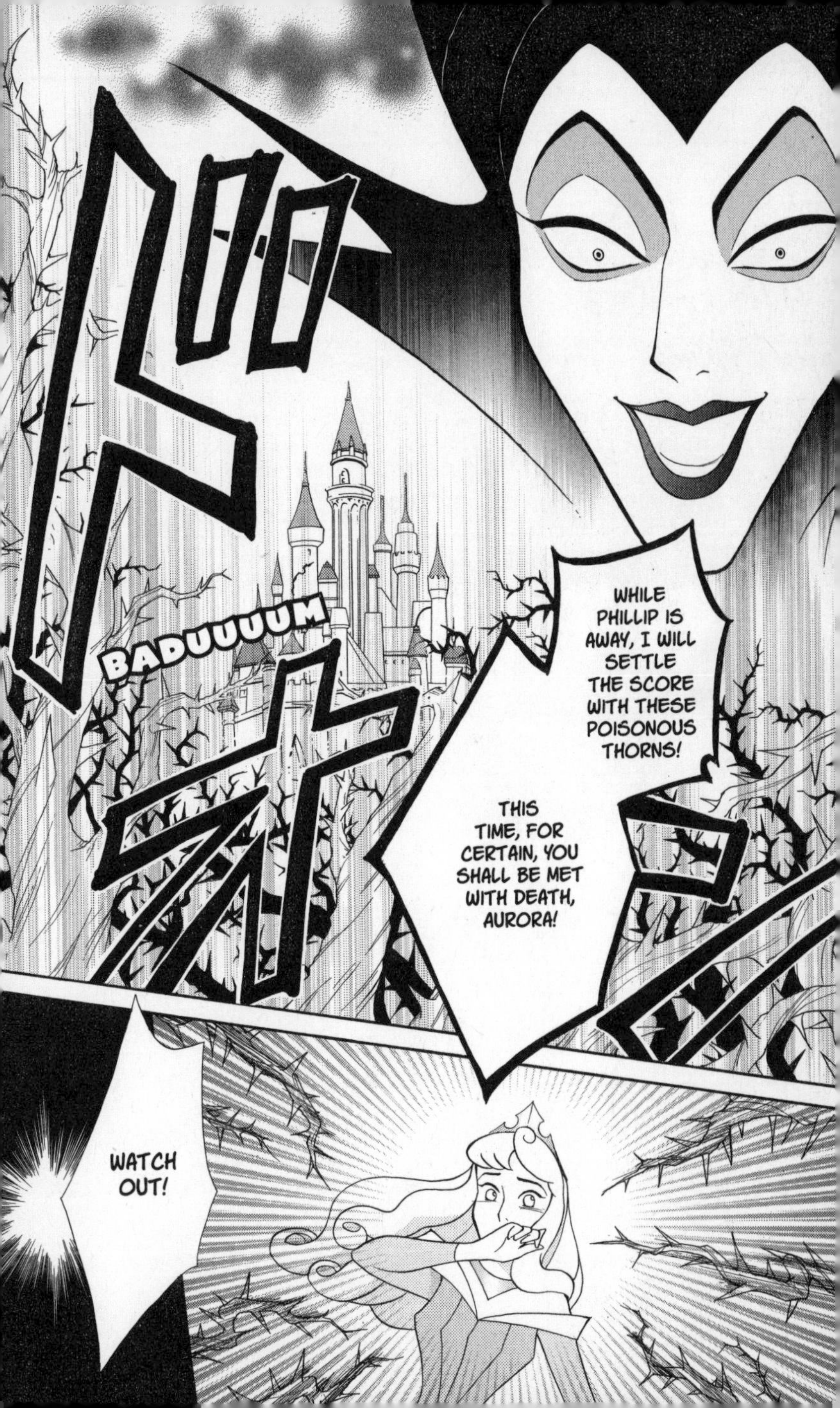
BADUUUUM
WHILE PHILLIP IS AWAY, I WILL SETTLE THE SCORE WITH THESE POISONOUS THORNS!
THIS TIME, FOR CERTAIN, YOU SHALL BE MET WITH DEATH, AURORA!
WATCH OUT!

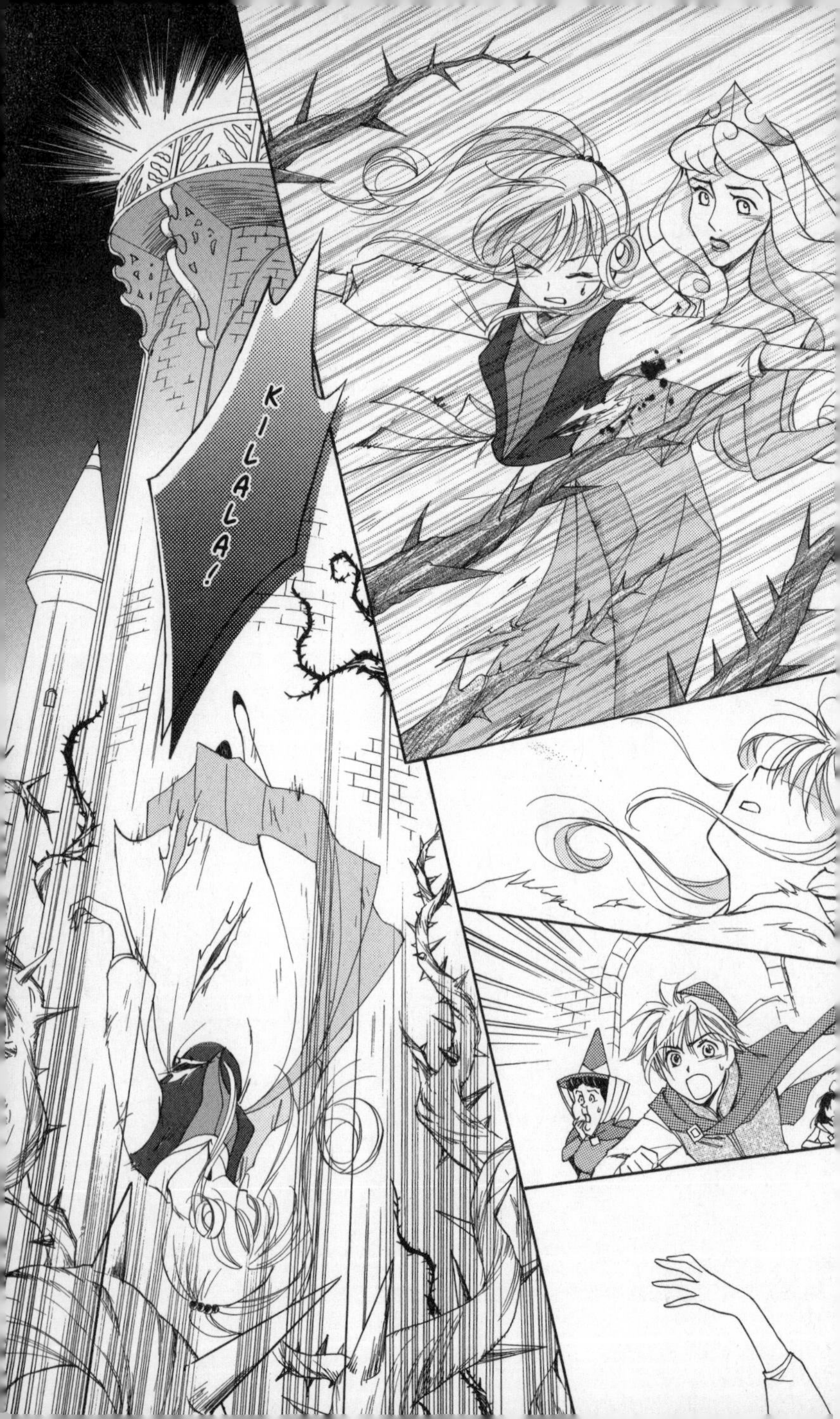
KILALA!

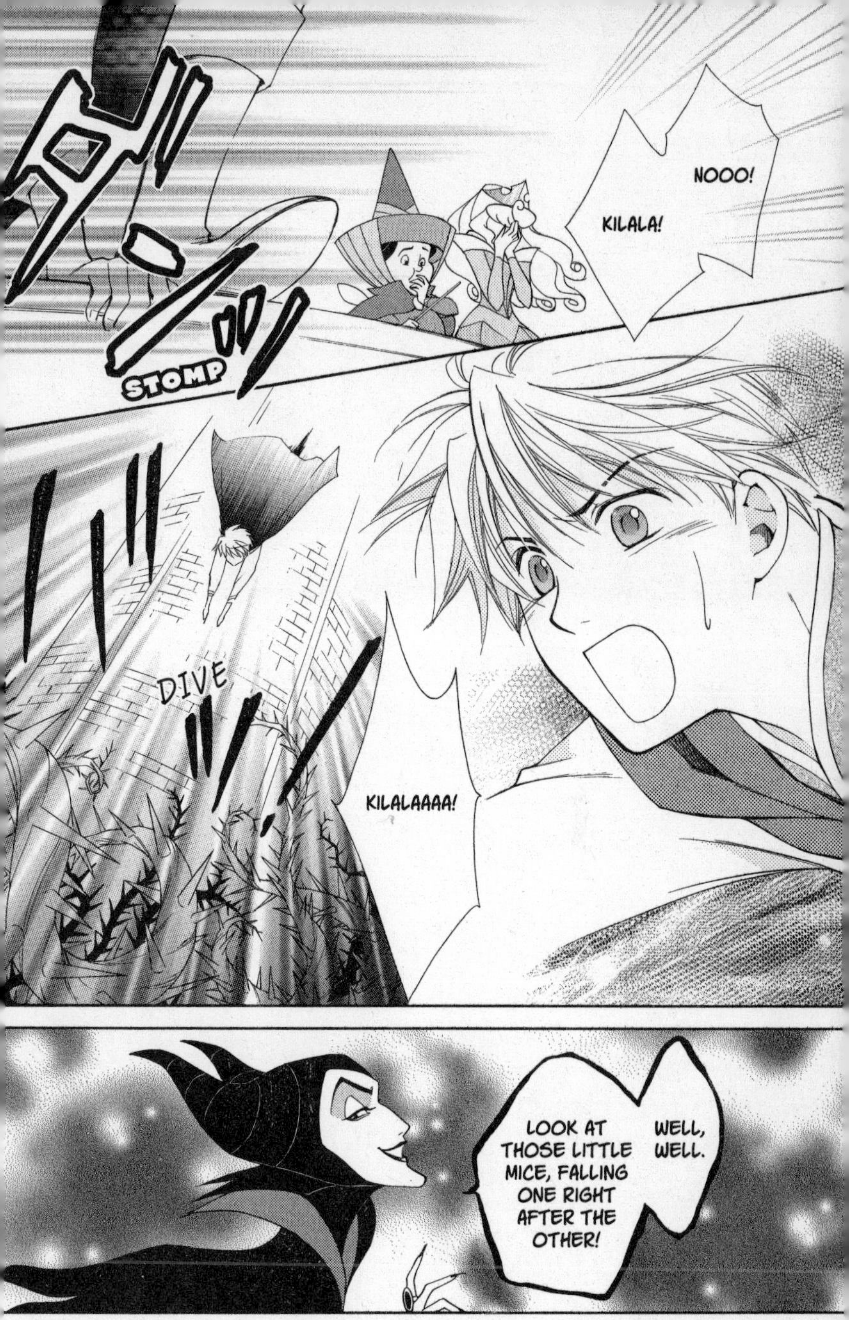
NOOO!
KILALA!
STOMP
KILALAAAA!
DIVE
WELL, WELL.
LOOK AT THOSE LITTLE MICE, FALLING ONE RIGHT AFTER THE OTHER!

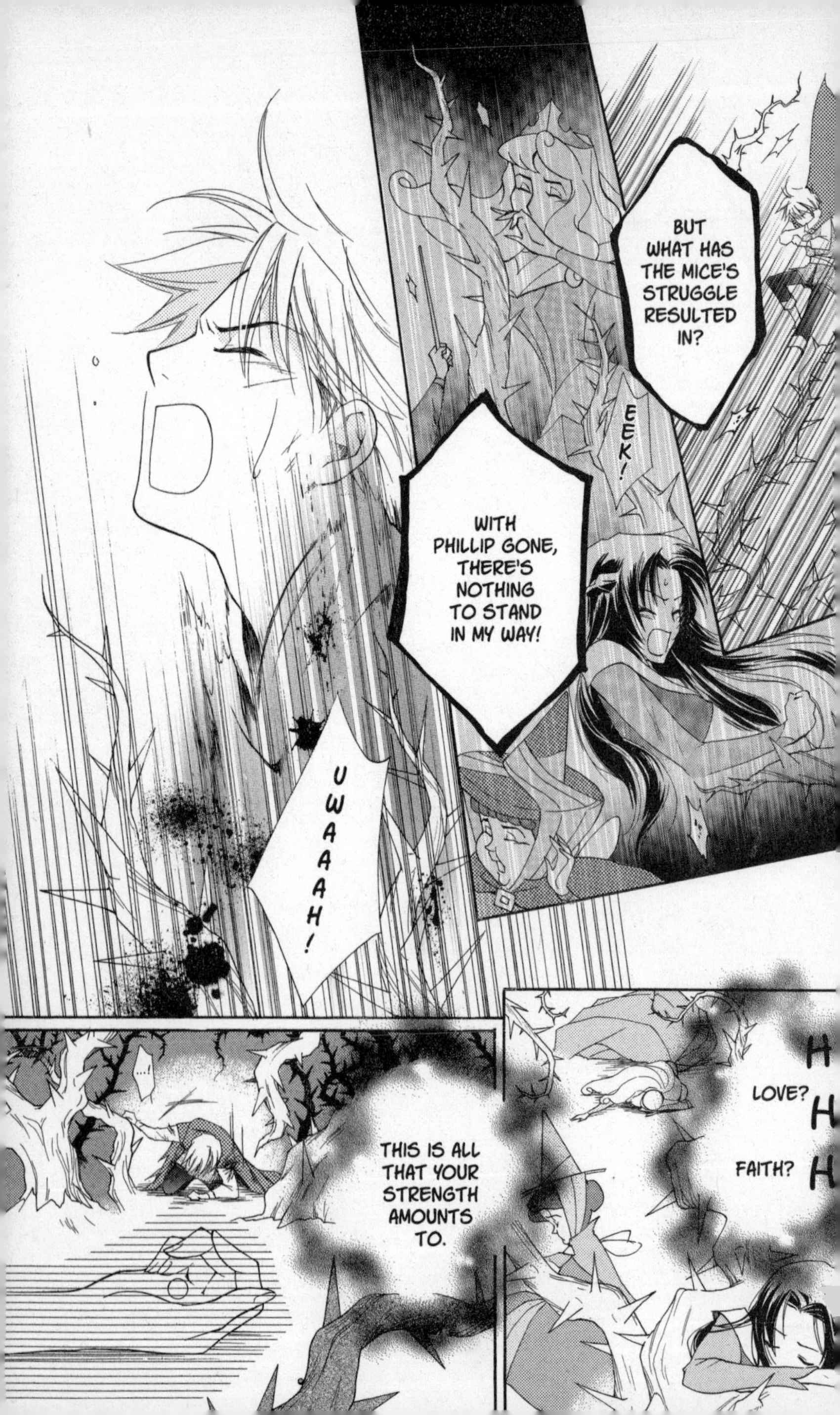
BUT WHAT HAS THE MICE'S STRUGGLE RESULTED IN?
EEK!
WITH PHILLIP GONE, THERE'S NOTHING TO STAND IN MY WAY!
UWAAAAH!
HHH
LOVE?
FAITH?
...!
THIS IS ALL THAT YOUR STRENGTH AMOUNTS TO.

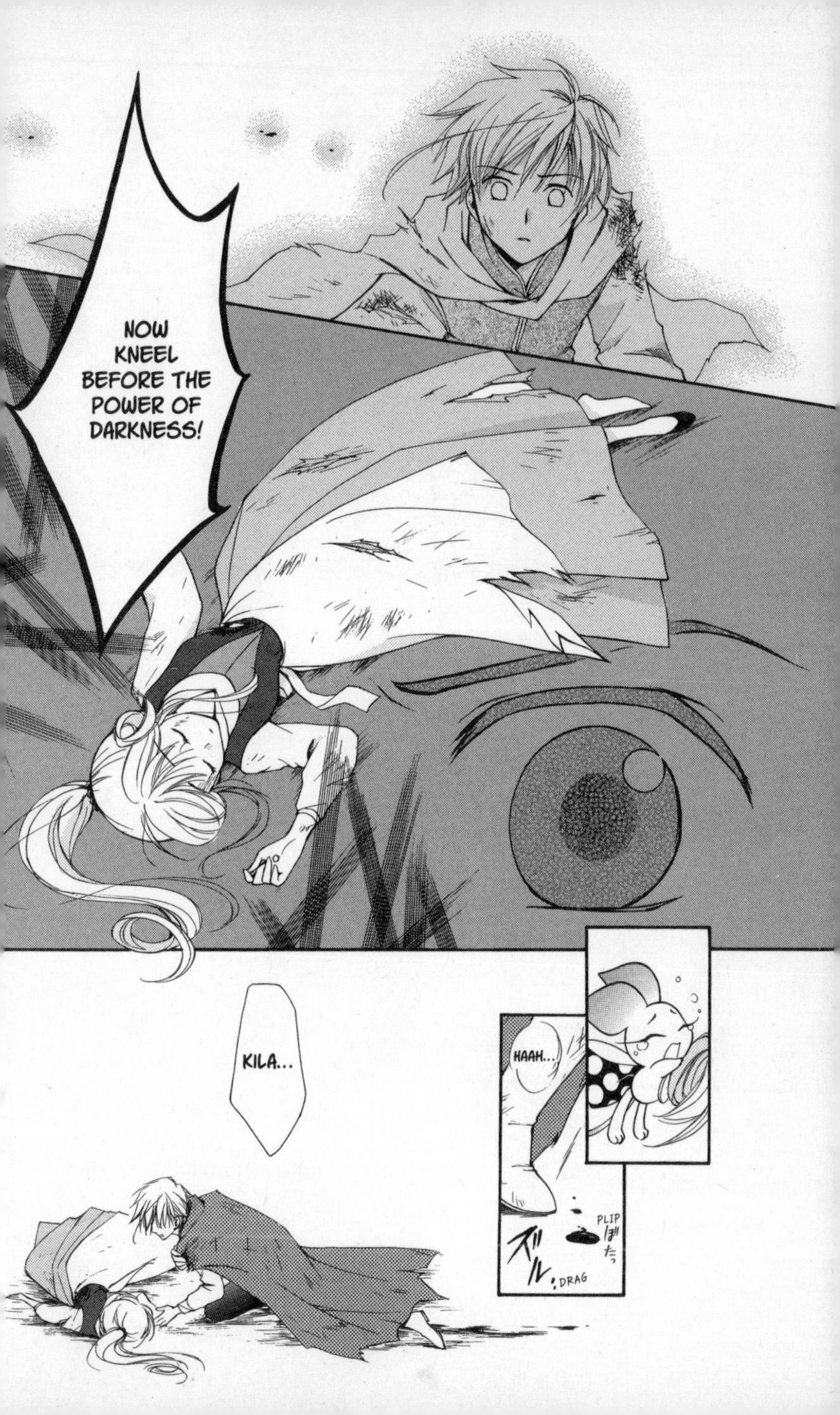
NOW KNEEL BEFORE THE POWER OF DARKNESS!
HAAH...
ぽたっ
PLIP
ズル
DRAG
KILA...

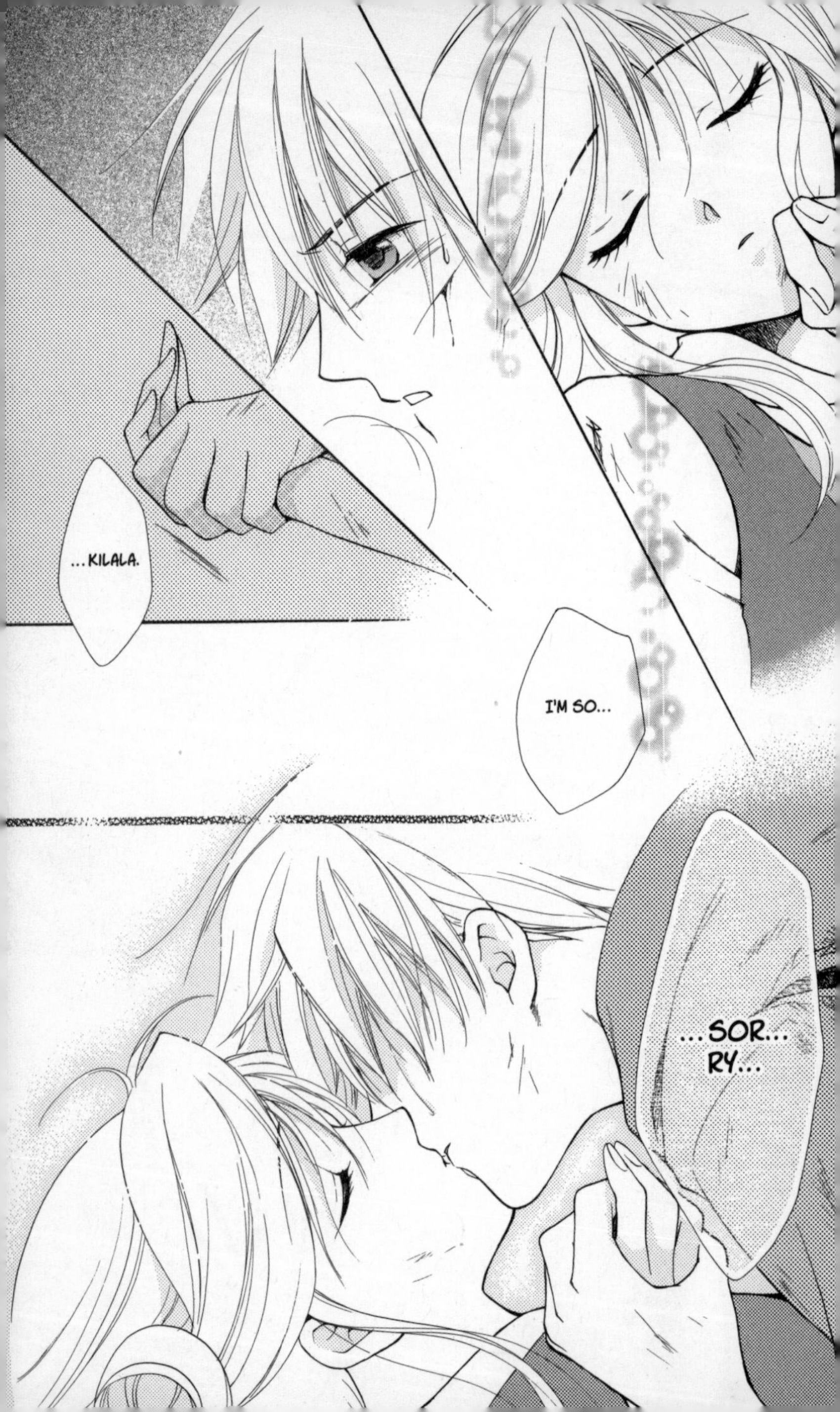
...KILALA.
I'M SO...
...SOR...
RY...

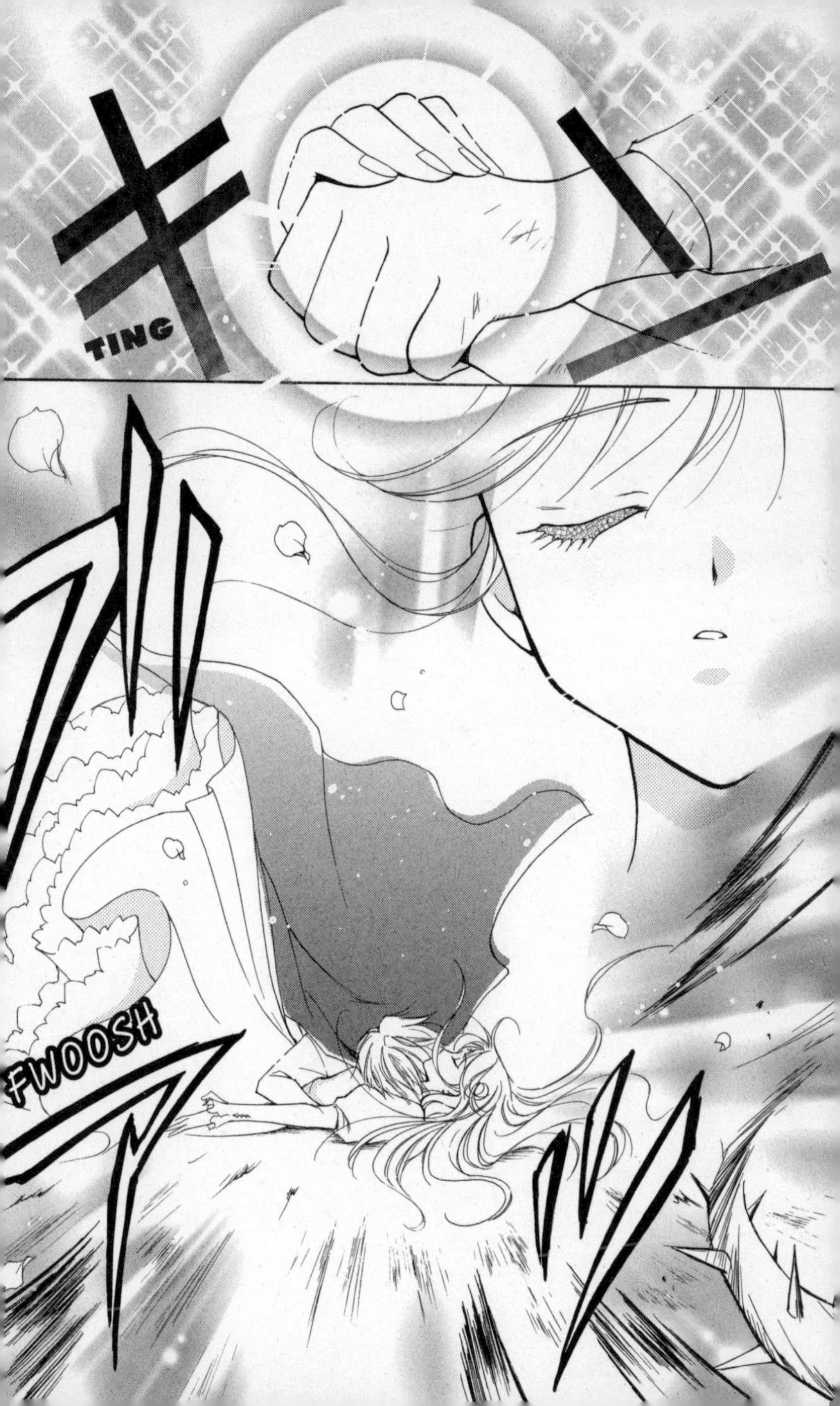
TING
FWOOSH

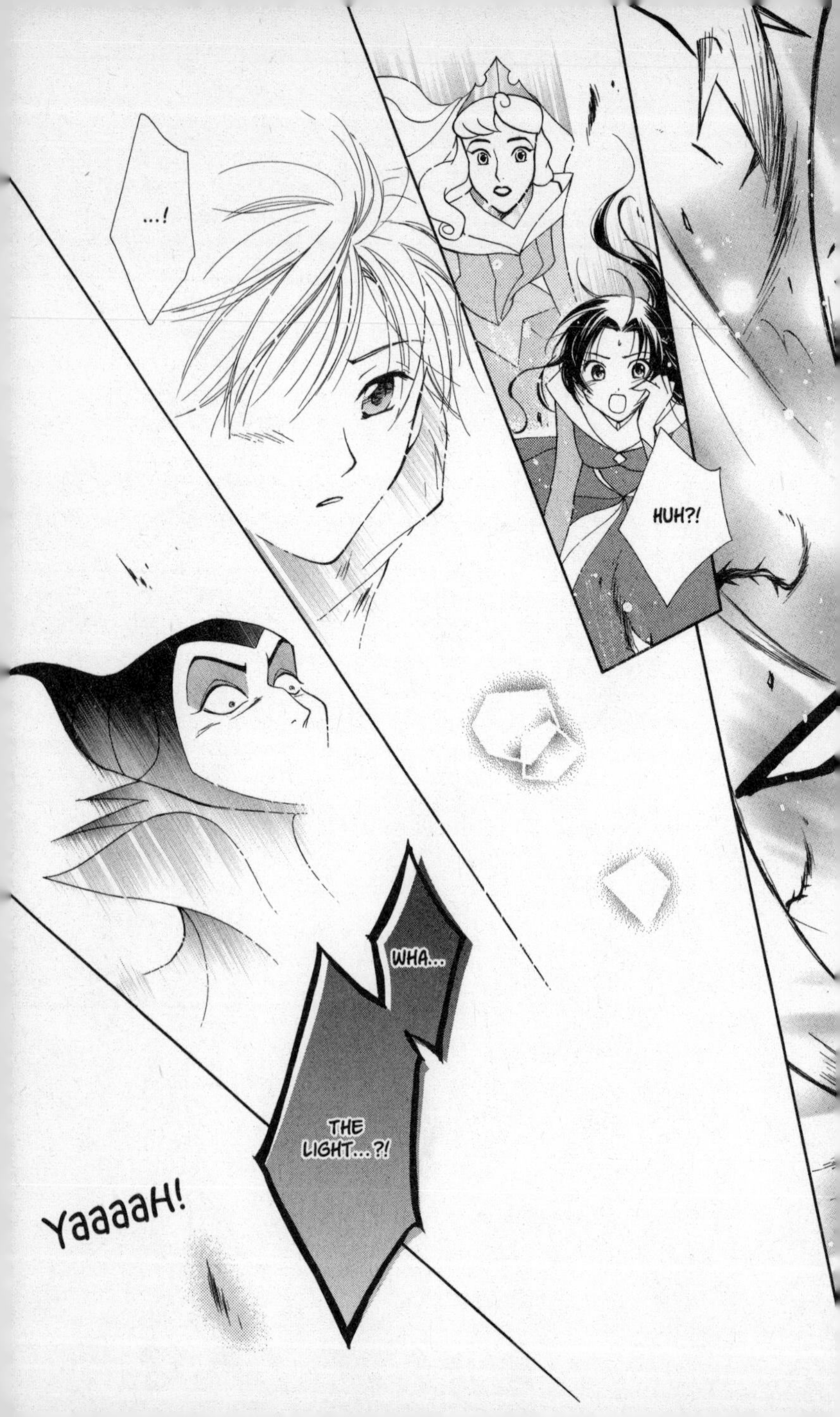
HUH?!
...!
WHA...
THE LIGHT...?!
YaaaaH!

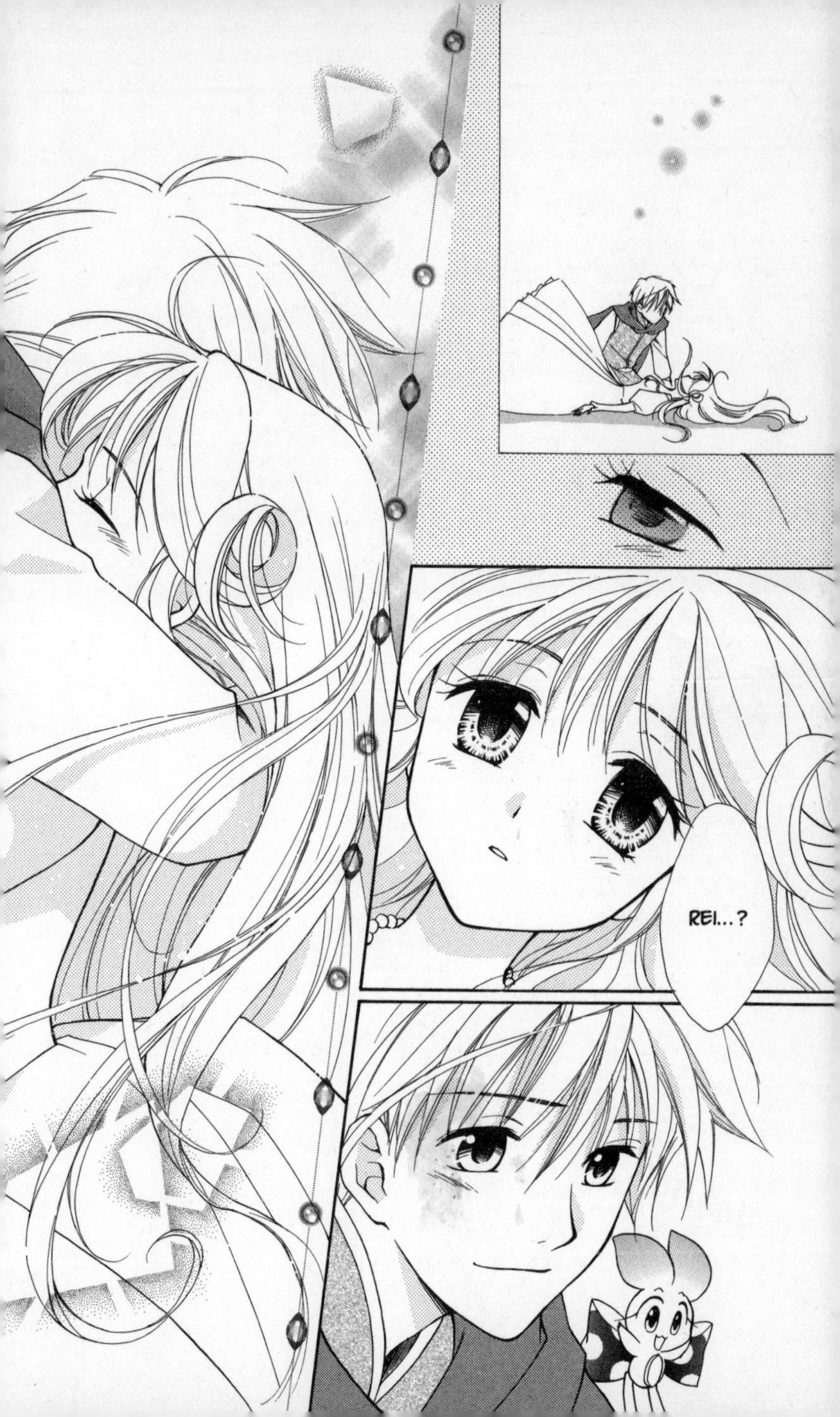
REI...?

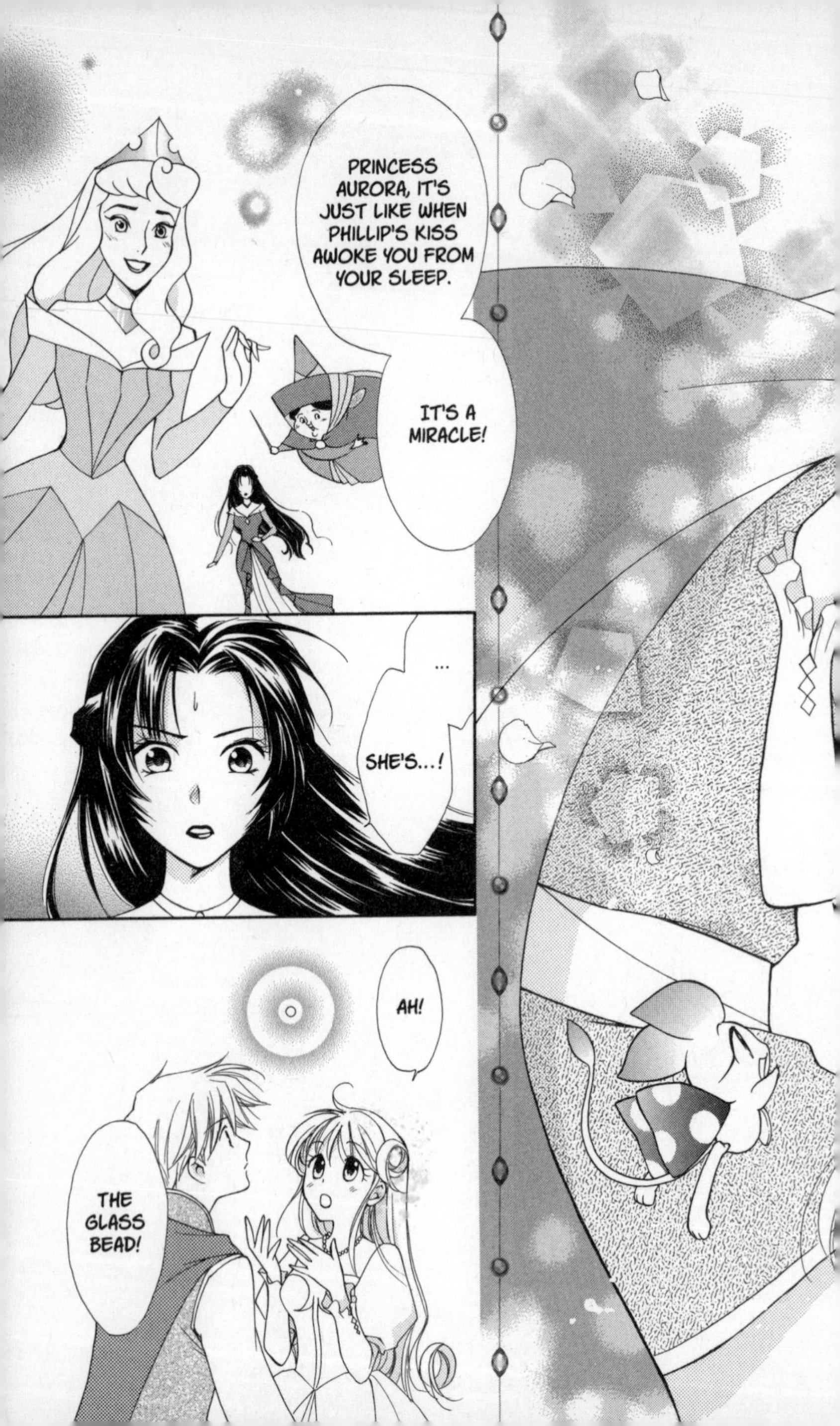
PRINCESS AURORA, IT'S JUST LIKE WHEN PHILLIP'S KISS AWOKE YOU FROM YOUR SLEEP.
IT'S A MIRACLE!
...
SHE'S...!
AH!
THE GLASS BEAD!

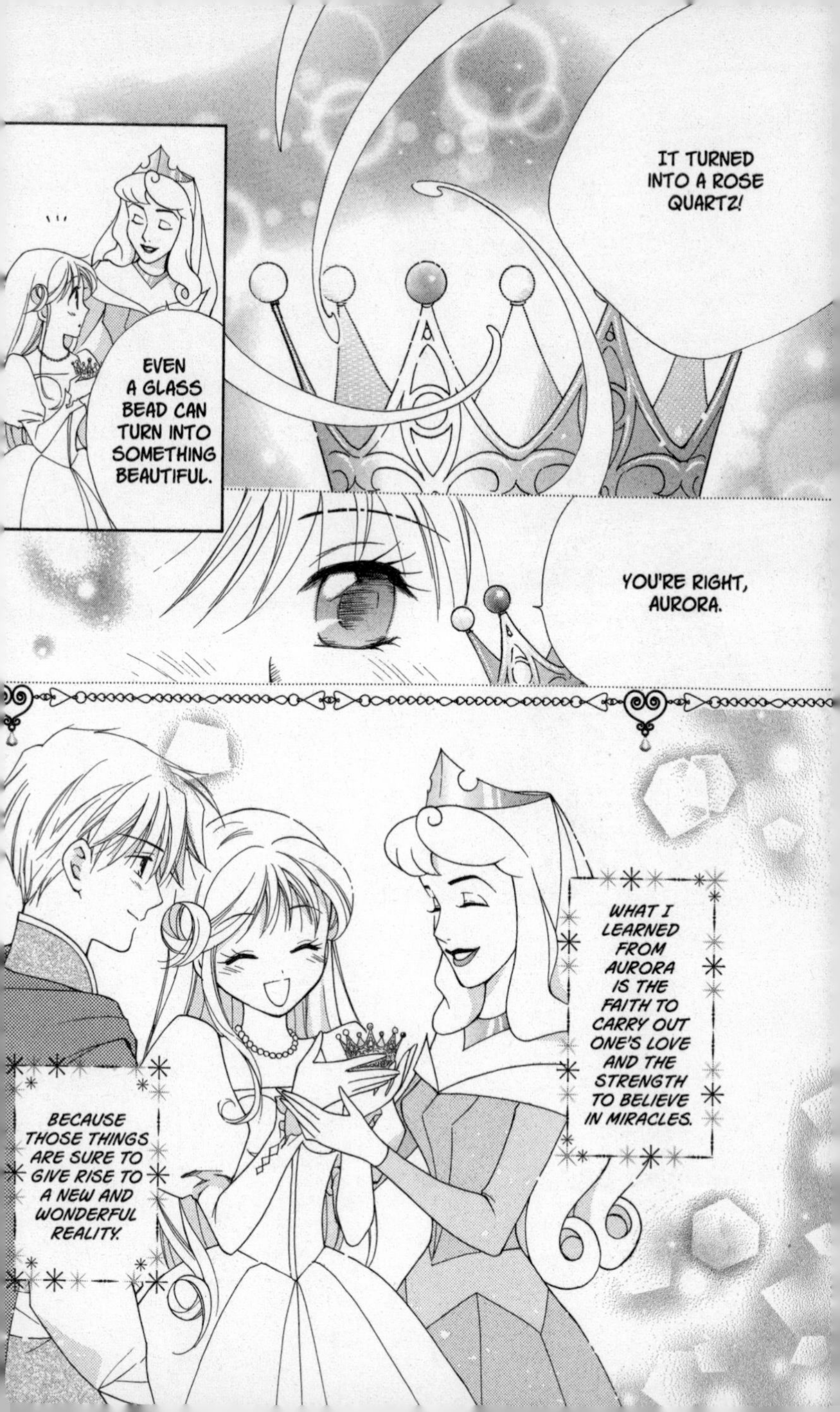
IT TURNED INTO A ROSE QUARTZ!
EVEN A GLASS BEAD CAN TURN INTO SOMETHING BEAUTIFUL.
YOU'RE RIGHT, AURORA.
WHAT I LEARNED FROM AURORA IS THE FAITH TO CARRY OUT ONE'S LOVE AND THE STRENGTH TO BELIEVE IN MIRACLES.
BECAUSE THOSE THINGS ARE SURE TO GIVE RISE TO A NEW AND WONDERFUL REALITY.

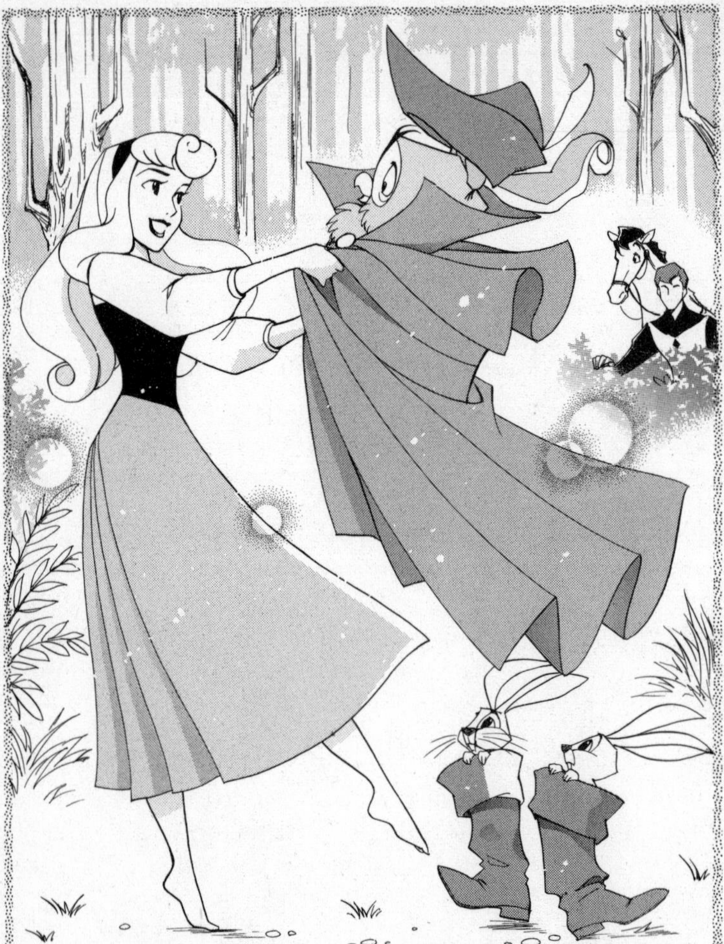

AURORA FELL IN LOVE WITH A YOUNG MAN SHE MET IN THE WOODS WHOSE NAME SHE DIDN'T KNOW. EVEN THOUGH SHE WAS TOLD NEVER TO SEE HIM AGAIN, SHE NEVER STOPPED LOVING HIM, AND KEPT THINKING ABOUT HIM UNTIL SHE AWOKE FROM HER SLEEP. SHE KEPT A FIRM GRASP ON HER WILL AND HER LOVE (WHICH RESULTED IN A MIRACLE HAPPENING). SHE'S A GIRL WITH A STRONG HEART.

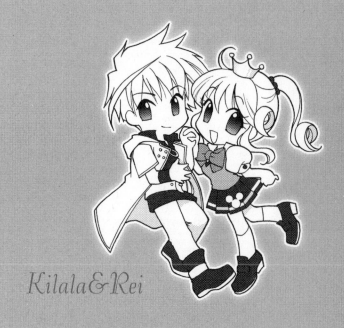

Kilala&Rei

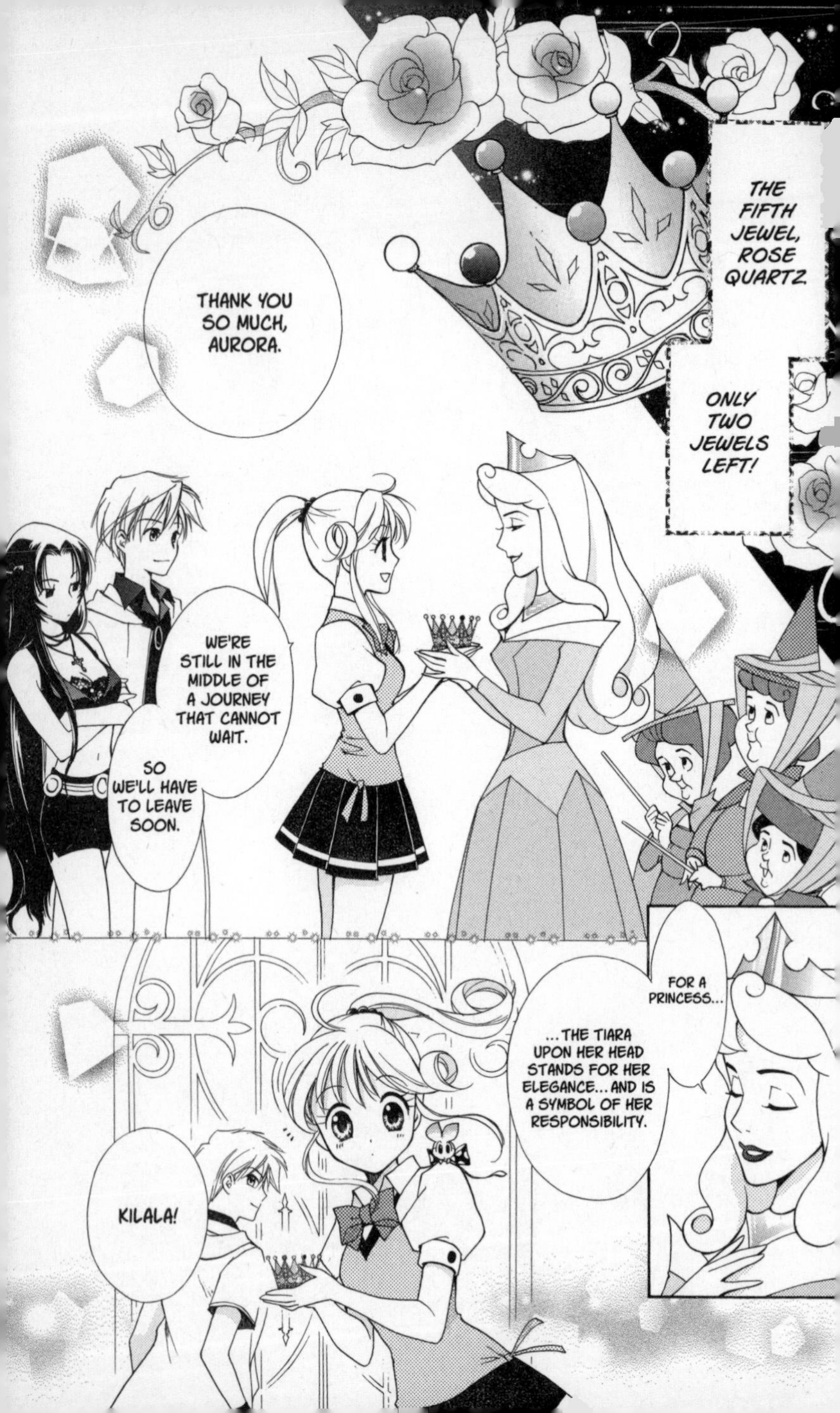
THE FIFTH JEWEL, ROSE QUARTZ.
ONLY TWO JEWELS LEFT!
THANK YOU SO MUCH, AURORA.
WE'RE STILL IN THE MIDDLE OF A JOURNEY THAT CANNOT WAIT.
SO WE'LL HAVE TO LEAVE SOON.
FOR A PRINCESS...
...THE TIARA UPON HER HEAD STANDS FOR HER ELEGANCE... AND IS A SYMBOL OF HER RESPONSIBILITY.
KILALA!

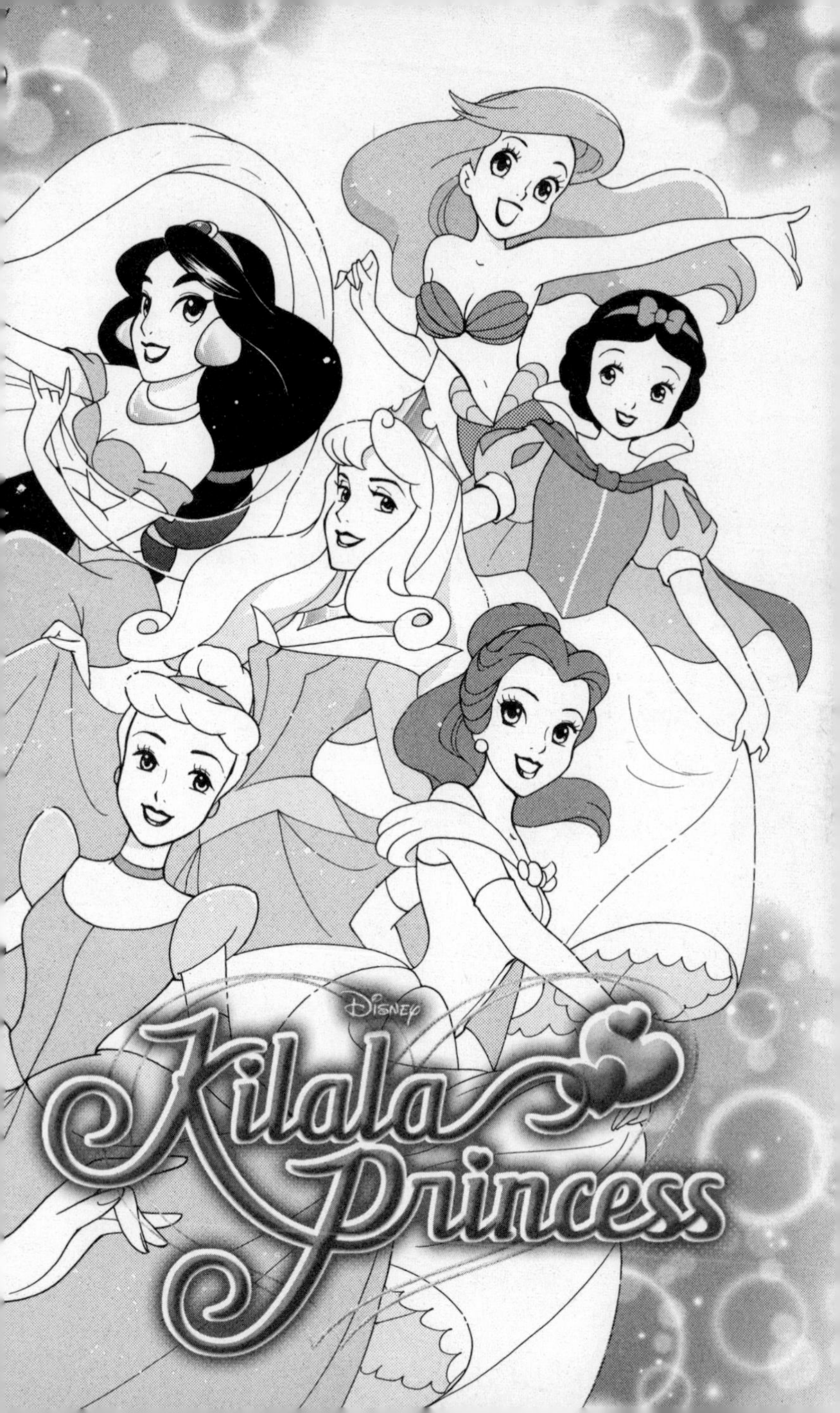
Disney
Kilala Princess

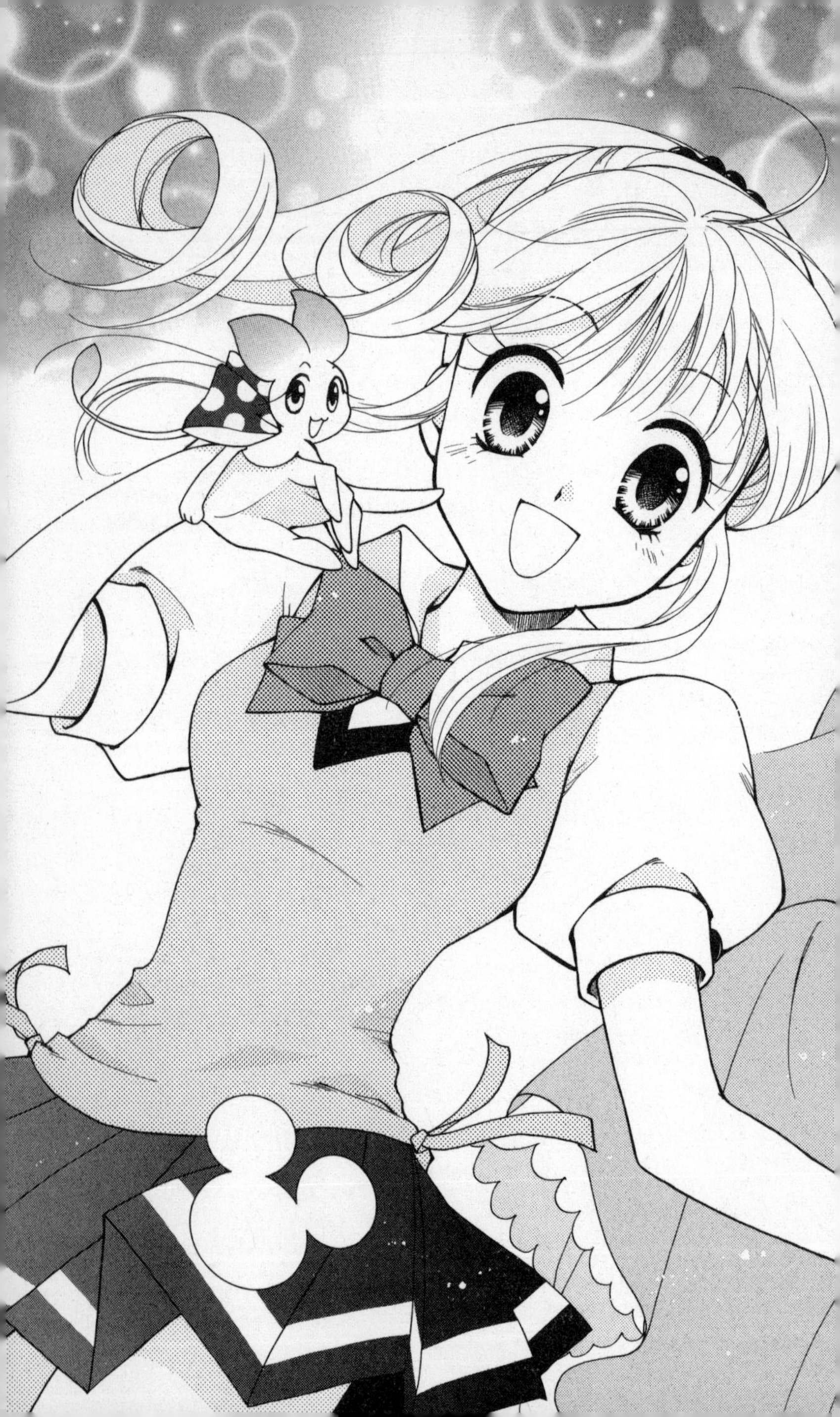

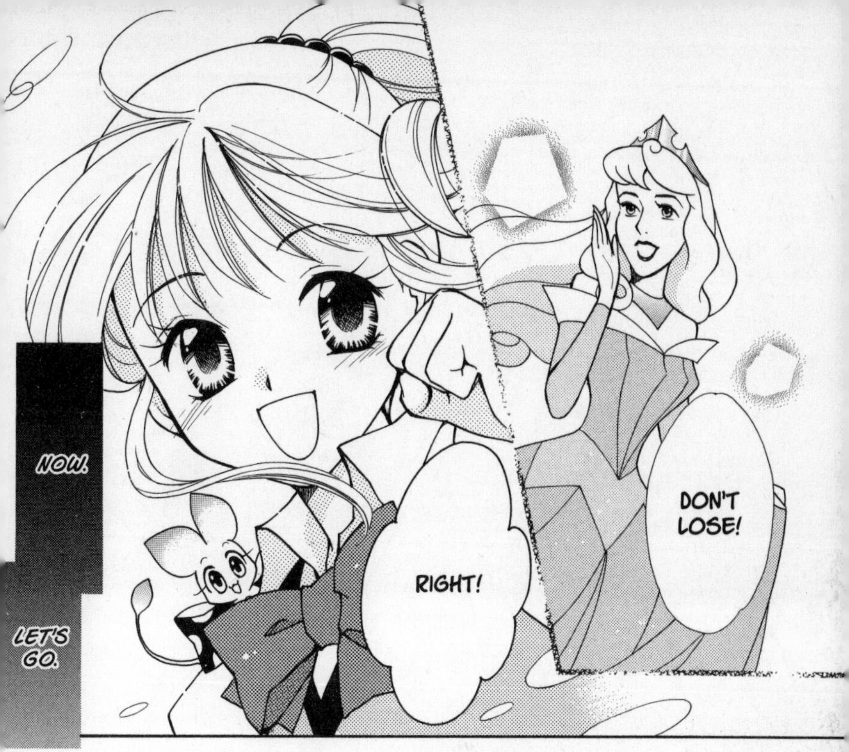
DON'T LOSE!
RIGHT!
NOW.
LET'S GO.

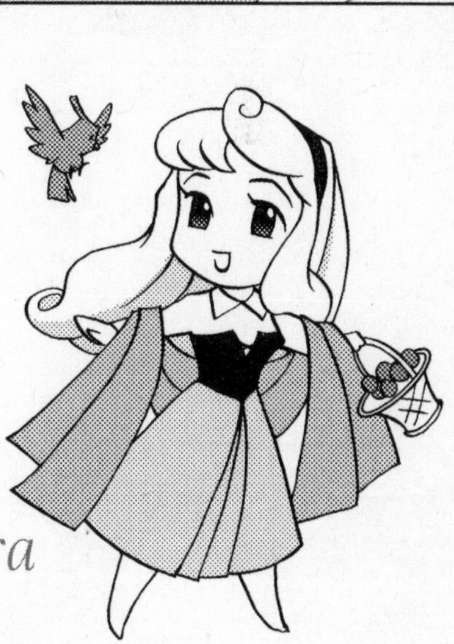

Aurora

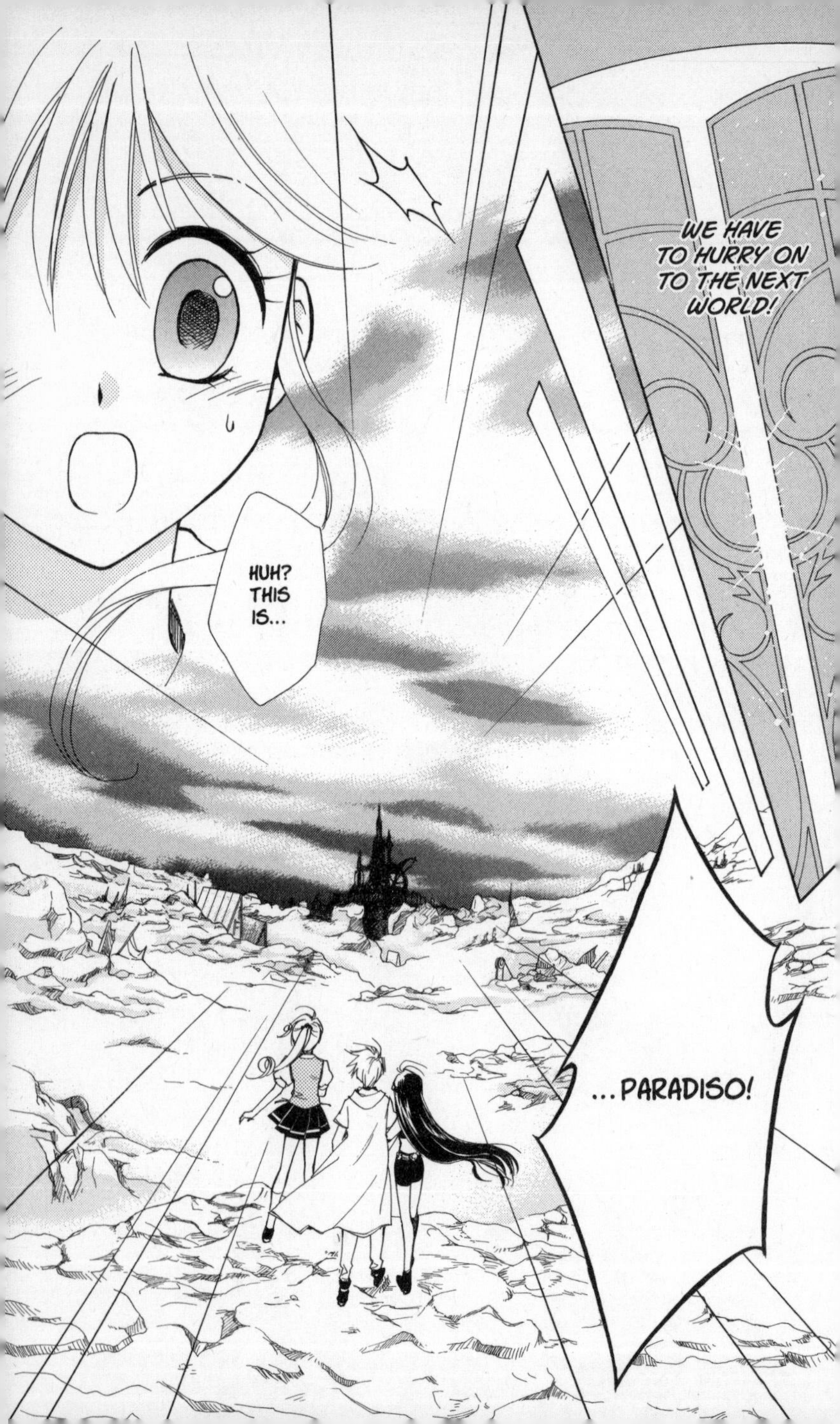
WE HAVE TO HURRY ON TO THE NEXT WORLD!
HUH? THIS IS...
...PARADISO!

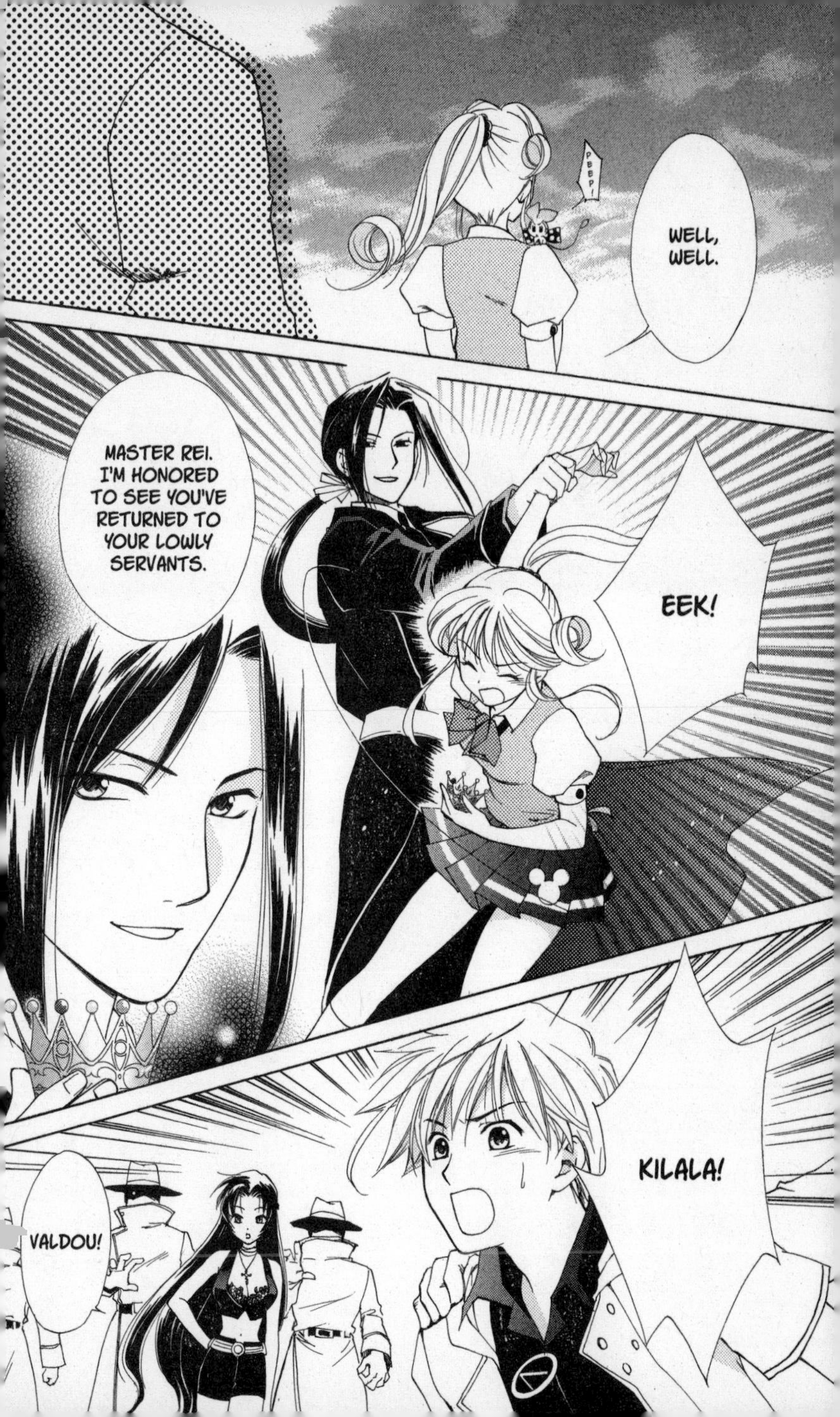
WELL, WELL.
PEEP!
EEK!
MASTER REI. I'M HONORED TO SEE YOU'VE RETURNED TO YOUR LOWLY SERVANTS.
KILALA!
VALDOU!

READ THIS WAY

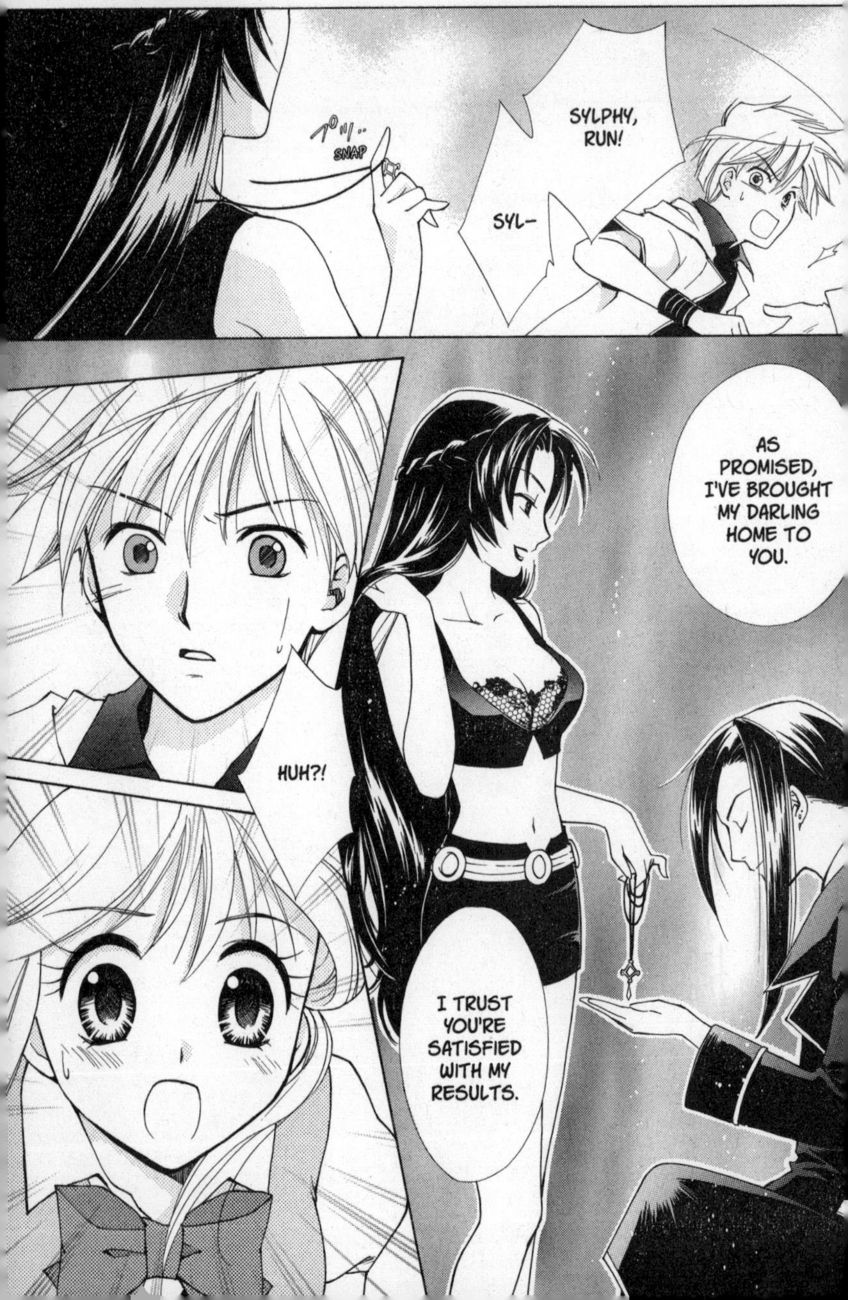
SYLPHY, RUN!
SYL–
SNAP
AS PROMISED, I'VE BROUGHT MY DARLING HOME TO YOU.
I TRUST YOU'RE SATISFIED WITH MY RESULTS.
HUH?!

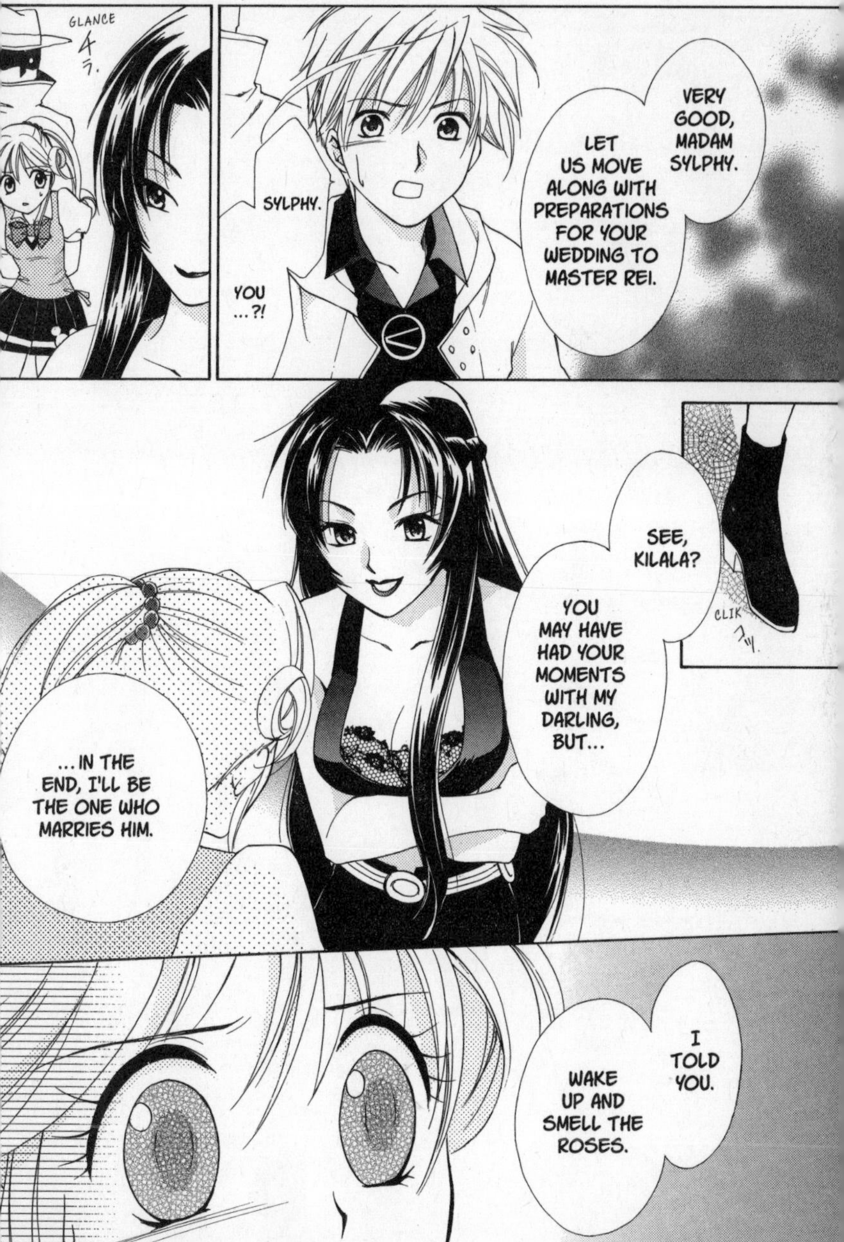

VERY GOOD, MADAM SYLPHY.
LET US MOVE ALONG WITH PREPARATIONS FOR YOUR WEDDING TO MASTER REI.
SYLPHY.
YOU ...?!
GLANCE
CLIK
SEE, KILALA?
YOU MAY HAVE HAD YOUR MOMENTS WITH MY DARLING, BUT...
...IN THE END, I'LL BE THE ONE WHO MARRIES HIM.
I TOLD YOU.
WAKE UP AND SMELL THE ROSES.

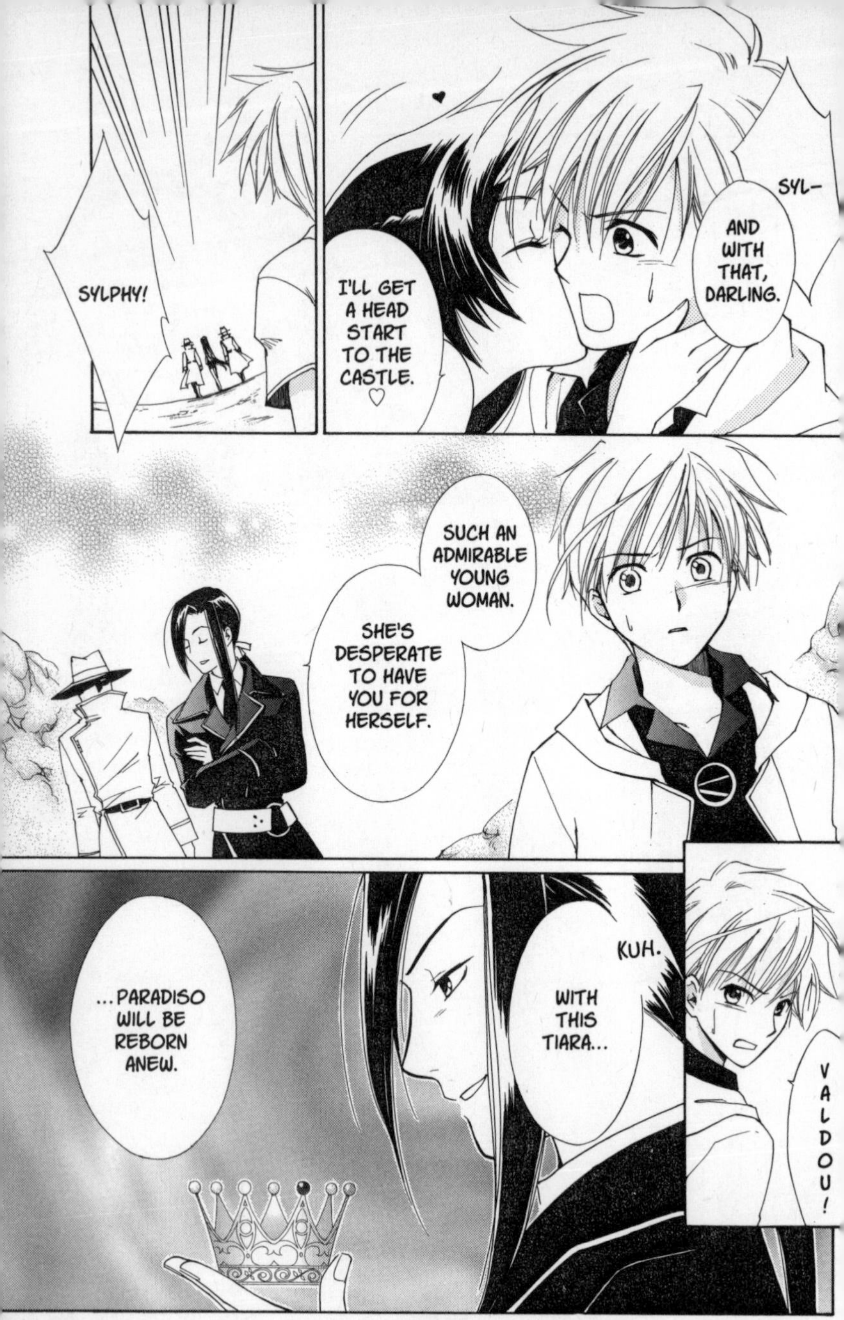
SYL—
AND WITH THAT, DARLING.
I'LL GET A HEAD START TO THE CASTLE. ♡
SYLPHY!
SUCH AN ADMIRABLE YOUNG WOMAN.
SHE'S DESPERATE TO HAVE YOU FOR HERSELF.
VALDOU!
KUH.
WITH THIS TIARA...
...PARADISO WILL BE REBORN ANEW.

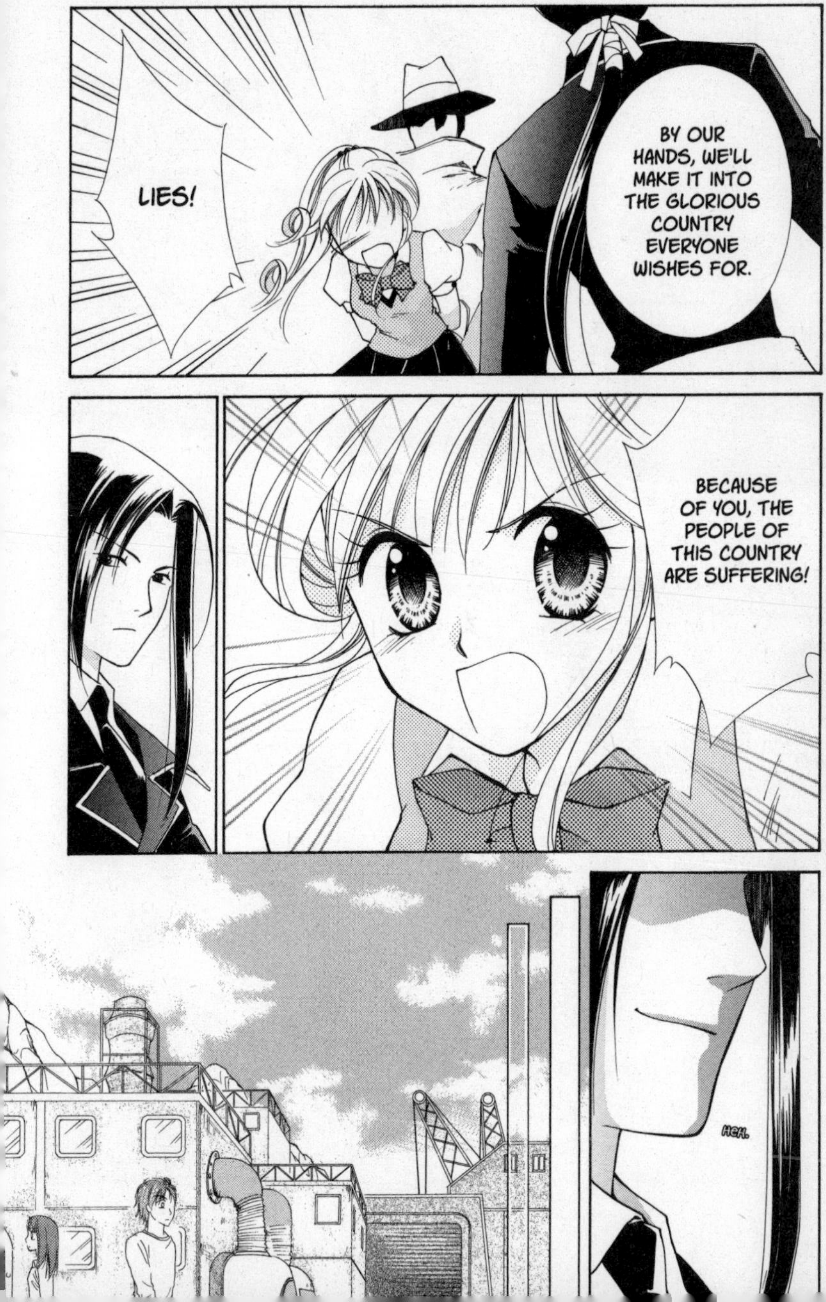
BY OUR HANDS, WE'LL MAKE IT INTO THE GLORIOUS COUNTRY EVERYONE WISHES FOR.
LIES!
BECAUSE OF YOU, THE PEOPLE OF THIS COUNTRY ARE SUFFERING!
HEH.

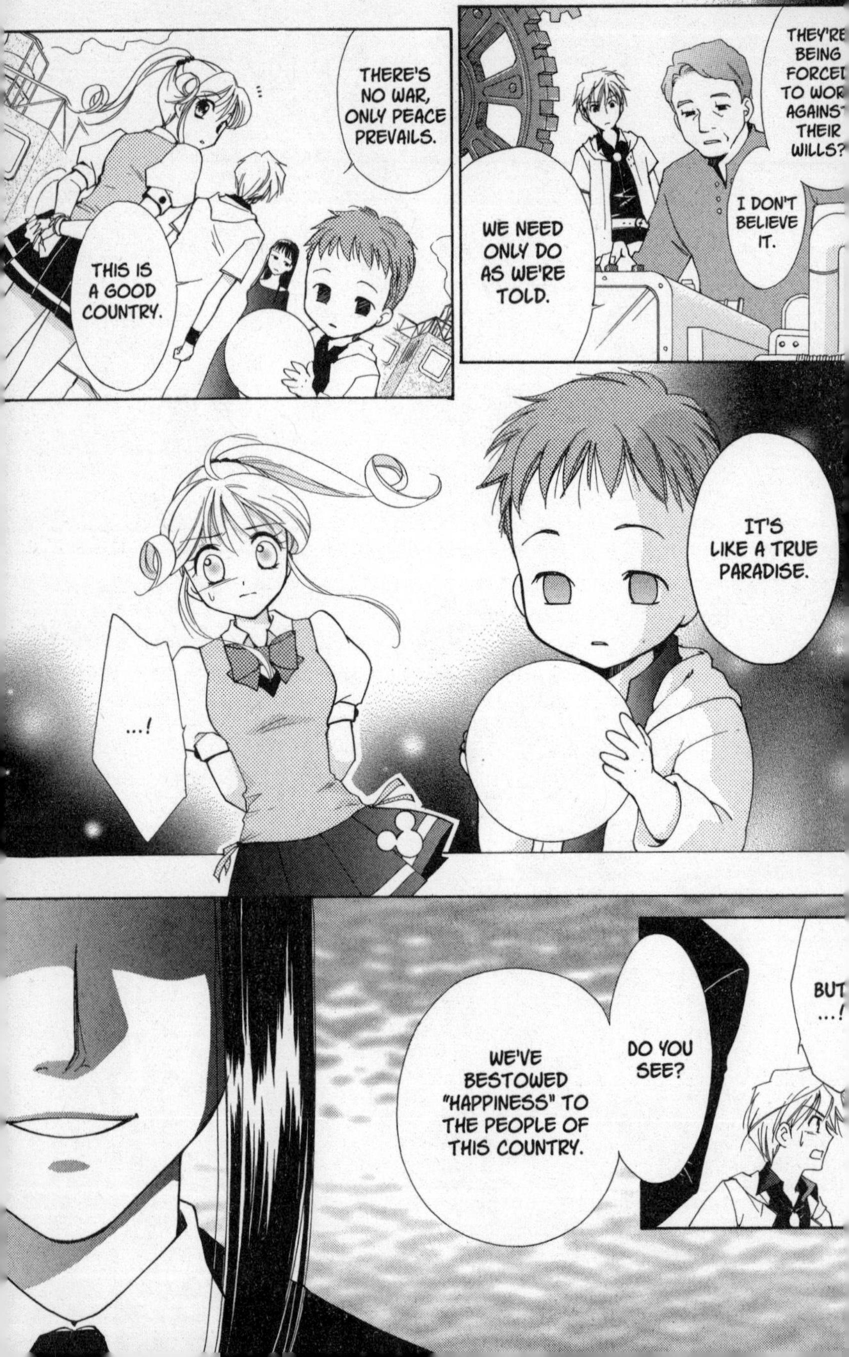

THEY'RE BEING FORCED TO WOR AGAINST THEIR WILLS?
I DON'T BELIEVE IT.
WE NEED ONLY DO AS WE'RE TOLD.
THERE'S NO WAR, ONLY PEACE PREVAILS.
THIS IS A GOOD COUNTRY.
IT'S LIKE A TRUE PARADISE.
...!
BUT ...!
DO YOU SEE?
WE'VE BESTOWED "HAPPINESS" TO THE PEOPLE OF THIS COUNTRY.

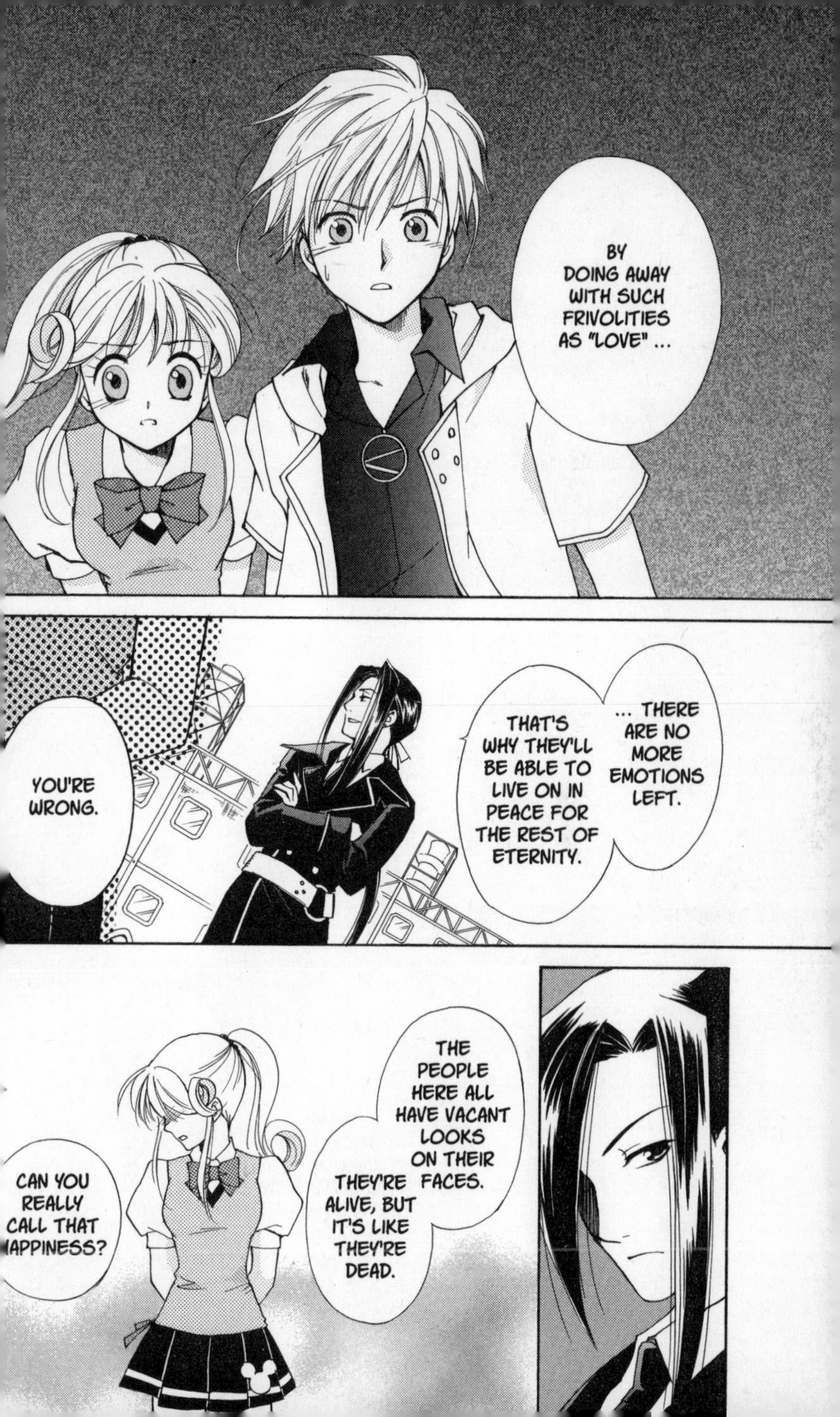
BY DOING AWAY WITH SUCH FRIVOLITIES AS "LOVE" ...
... THERE ARE NO MORE EMOTIONS LEFT.
THAT'S WHY THEY'LL BE ABLE TO LIVE ON IN PEACE FOR THE REST OF ETERNITY.
YOU'RE WRONG.
THE PEOPLE HERE ALL HAVE VACANT LOOKS ON THEIR FACES.
THEY'RE ALIVE, BUT IT'S LIKE THEY'RE DEAD.
CAN YOU REALLY CALL THAT APPINESS?

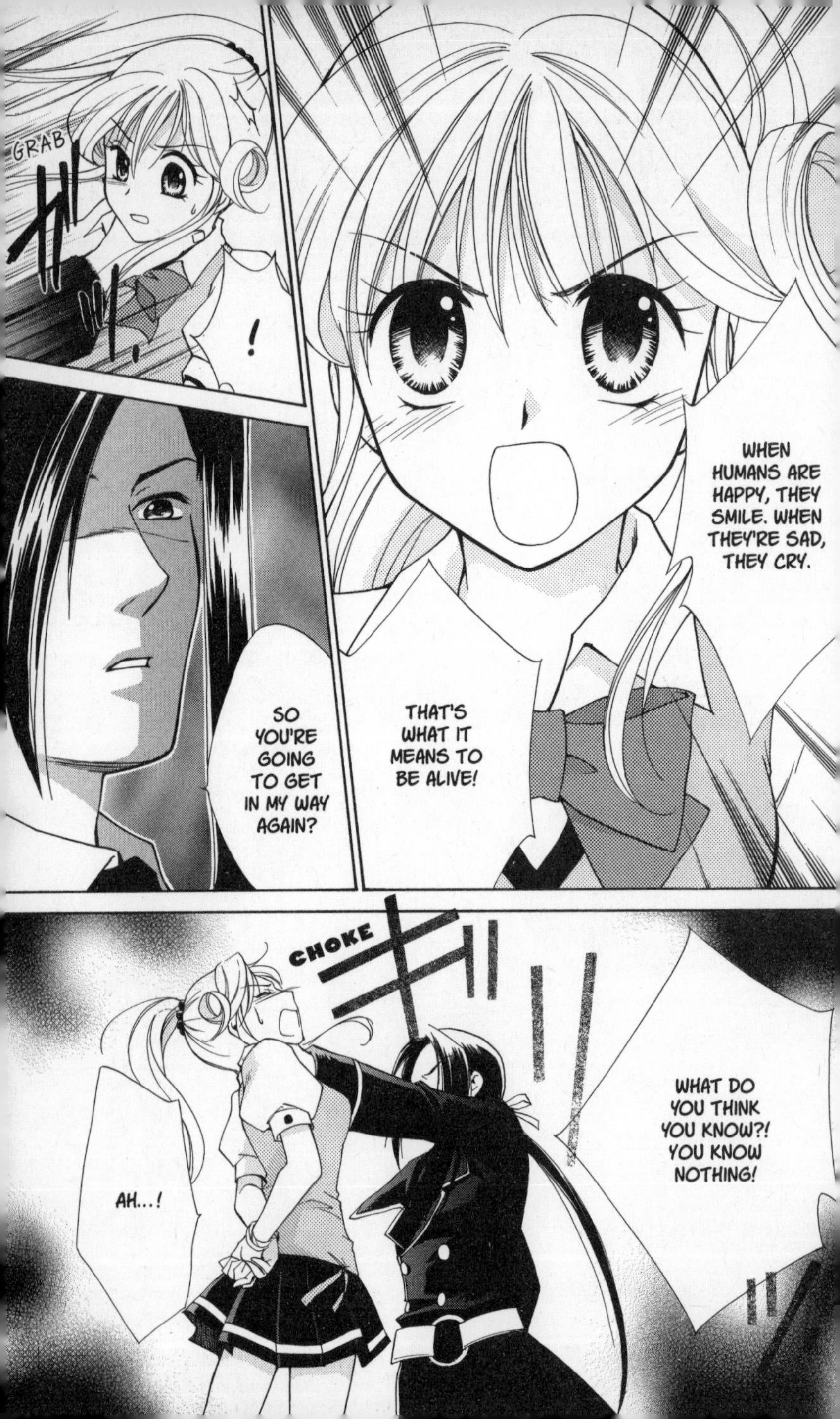
WHEN HUMANS ARE HAPPY, THEY SMILE. WHEN THEY'RE SAD, THEY CRY.
THAT'S WHAT IT MEANS TO BE ALIVE!
GRAB
!
SO YOU'RE GOING TO GET IN MY WAY AGAIN?
CHOKE
WHAT DO YOU THINK YOU KNOW?! YOU KNOW NOTHING!
AH...!

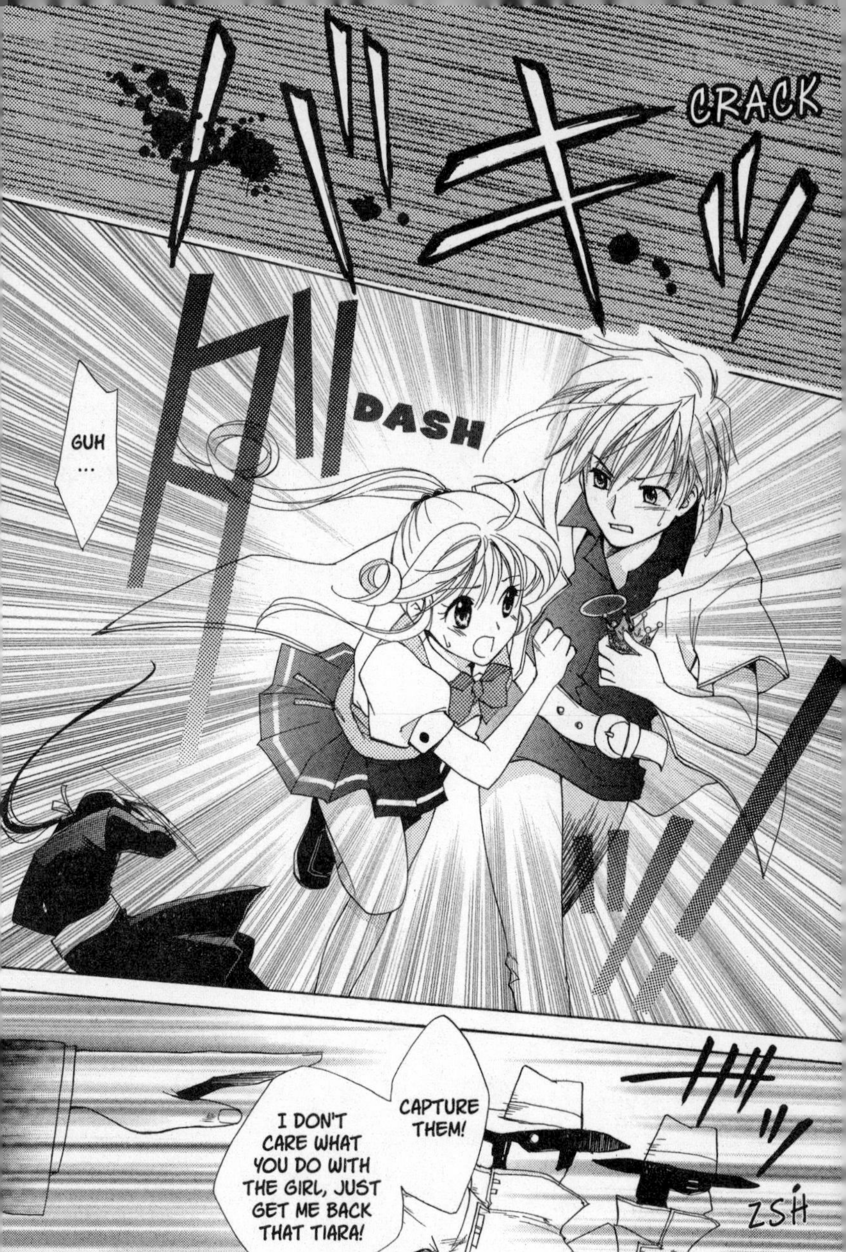
CRACK
DASH
GUH ...
CAPTURE THEM!
I DON'T CARE WHAT YOU DO WITH THE GIRL, JUST GET ME BACK THAT TIARA!
ZSH

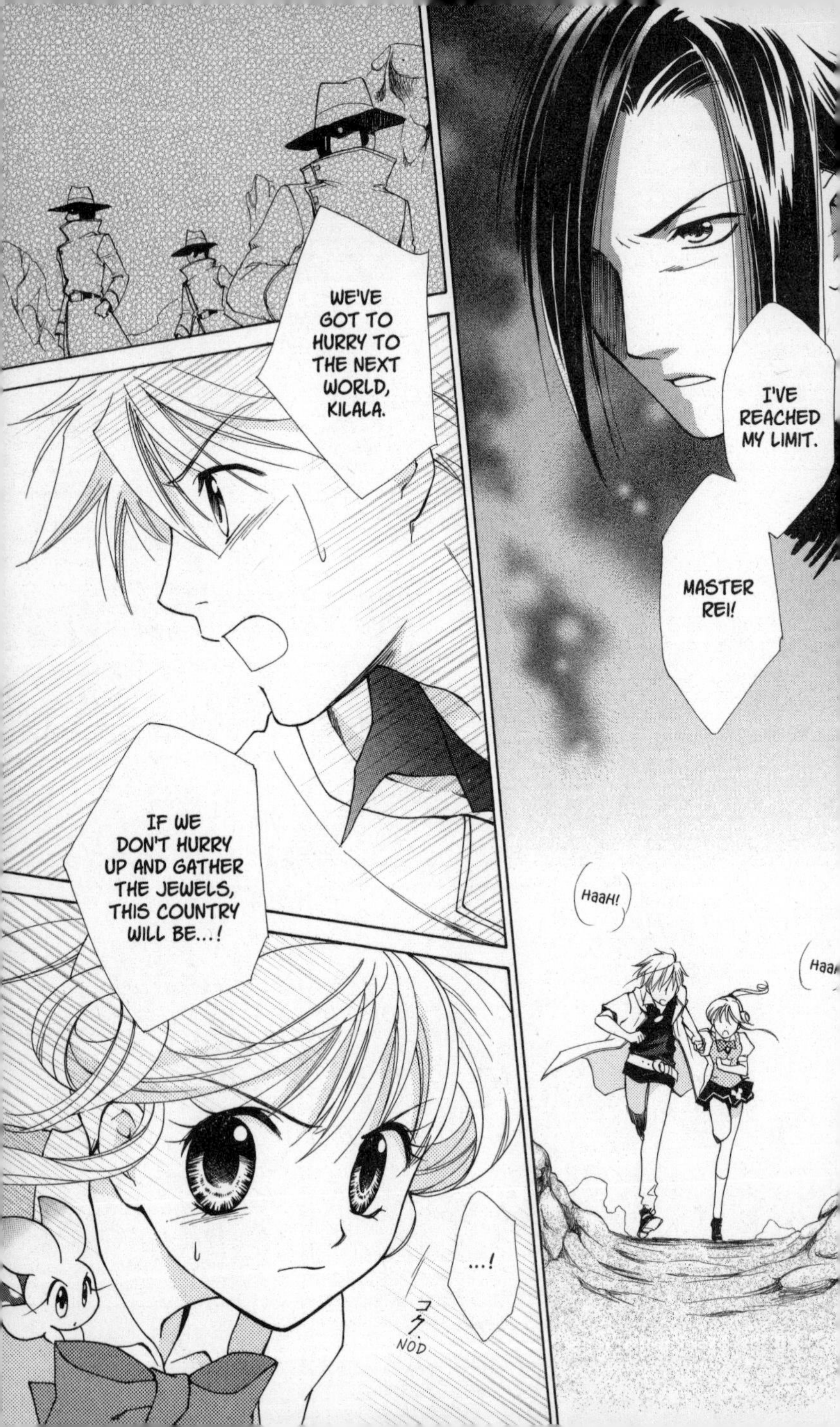

I'VE REACHED MY LIMIT.
MASTER REI!
HaaH!
Haa
WE'VE GOT TO HURRY TO THE NEXT WORLD, KILALA.
IF WE DON'T HURRY UP AND GATHER THE JEWELS, THIS COUNTRY WILL BE...!
...!
コク
NOD

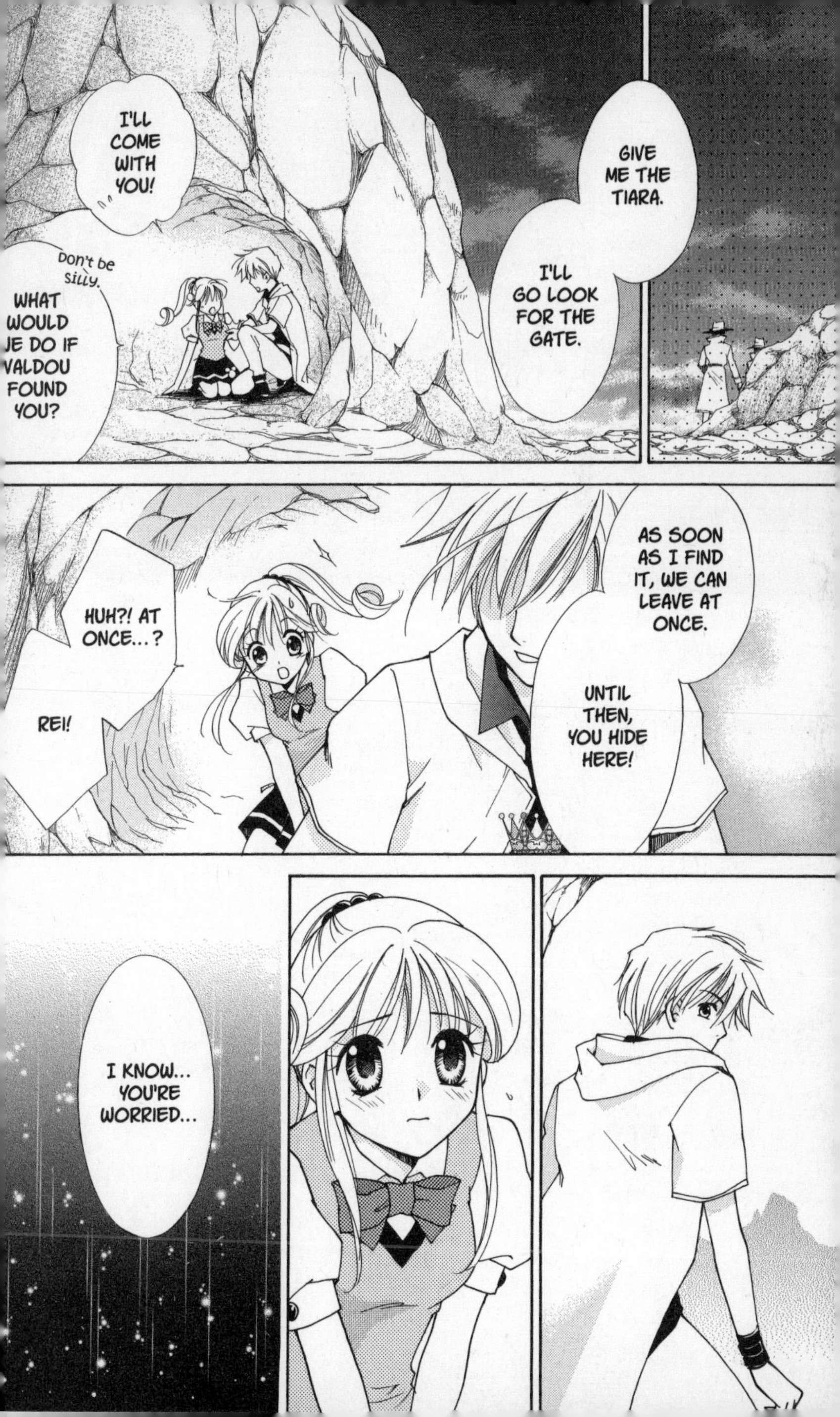
GIVE ME THE TIARA.
I'LL GO LOOK FOR THE GATE.
I'LL COME WITH YOU!
Don't be silly.
WHAT WOULD E DO IF VALDOU FOUND YOU?
AS SOON AS I FIND IT, WE CAN LEAVE AT ONCE.
UNTIL THEN, YOU HIDE HERE!
HUH?! AT ONCE...?
REI!
I KNOW... YOU'RE WORRIED...

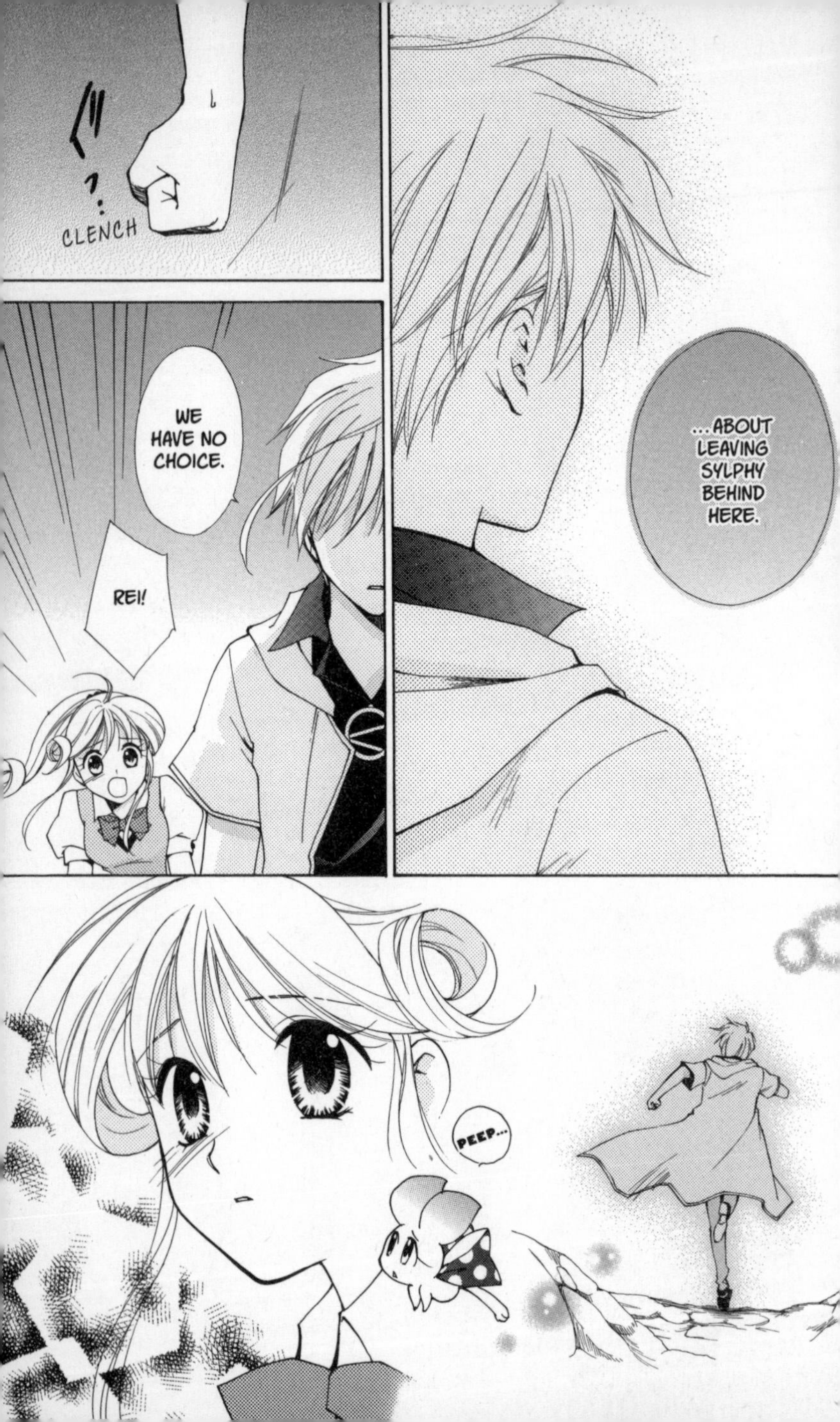
...ABOUT LEAVING SYLPHY BEHIND HERE.
CLENCH
WE HAVE NO CHOICE.
REI!
PEEP...

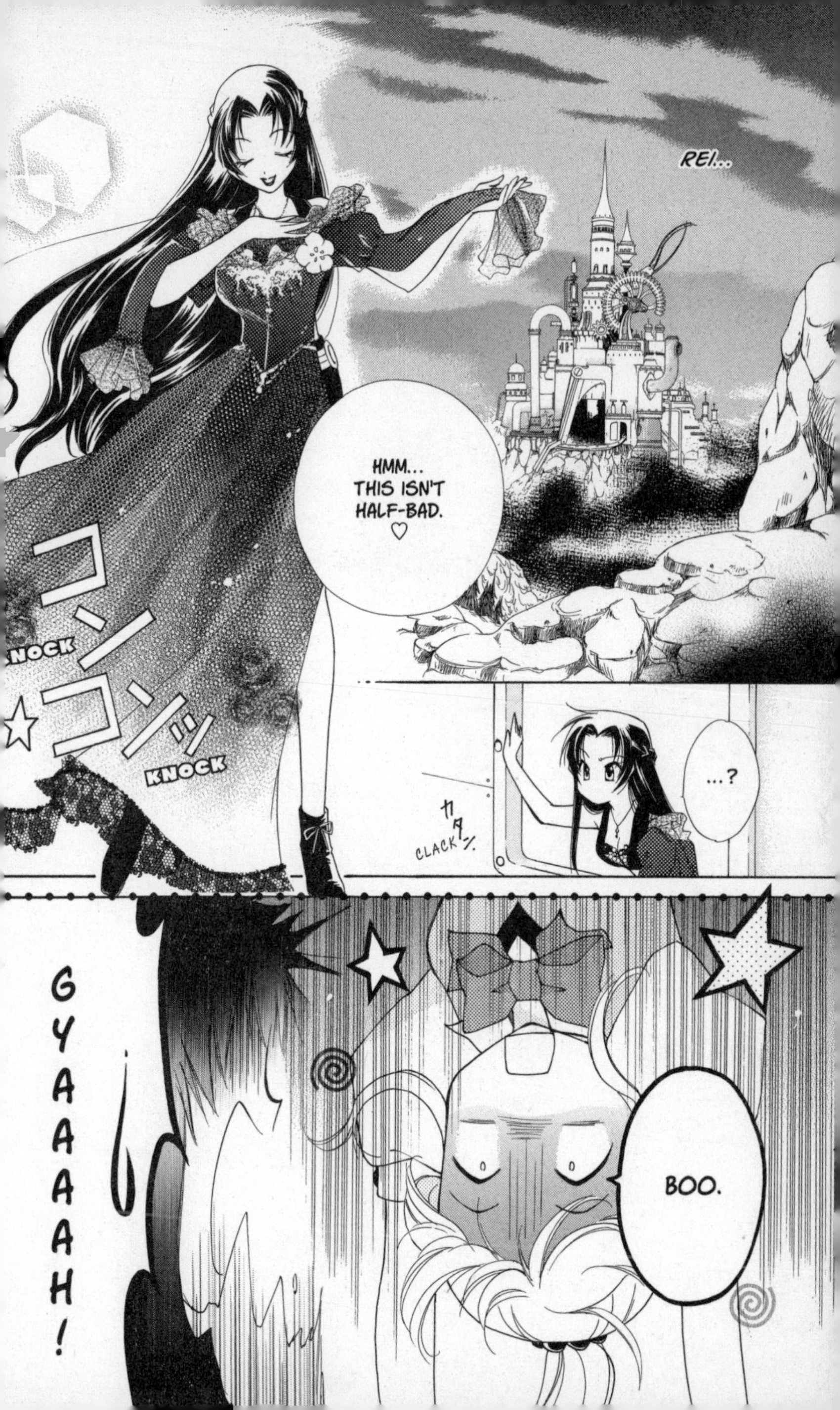
REI...
HMM... THIS ISN'T HALF-BAD. ♡
コンコンッ
KNOCK
KNOCK
...?
カタッ
CLACK
BOO.
GYAAAAAH!

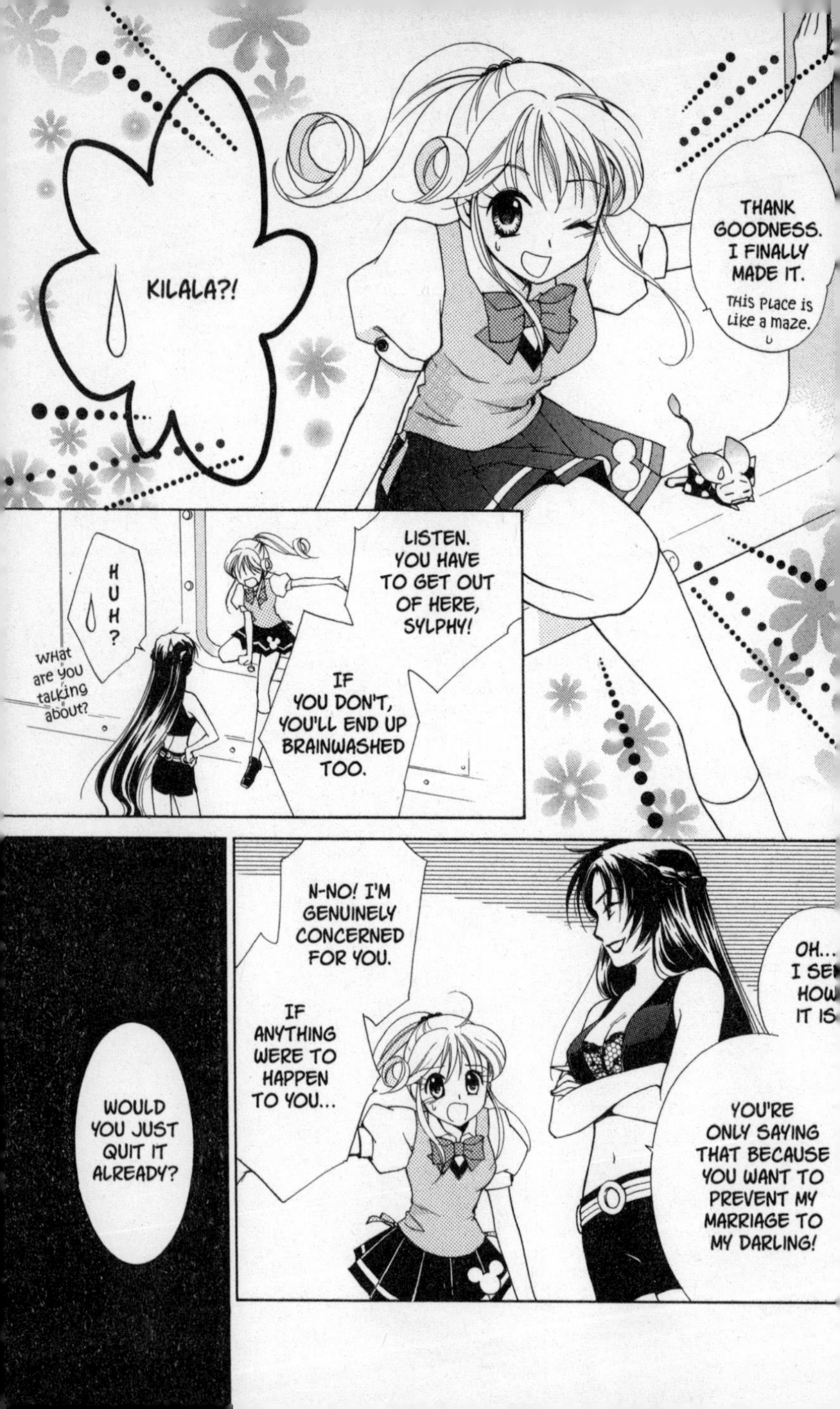
THANK GOODNESS. I FINALLY MADE IT.
THIS Place is like a maze.
KILALA?!
LISTEN. YOU HAVE TO GET OUT OF HERE, SYLPHY!
IF YOU DON'T, YOU'LL END UP BRAINWASHED TOO.
HUH?
WHAT are you talking about?
OH... I SE HOW IT IS
YOU'RE ONLY SAYING THAT BECAUSE YOU WANT TO PREVENT MY MARRIAGE TO MY DARLING!
N-NO! I'M GENUINELY CONCERNED FOR YOU.
IF ANYTHING WERE TO HAPPEN TO YOU...
WOULD YOU JUST QUIT IT ALREADY?

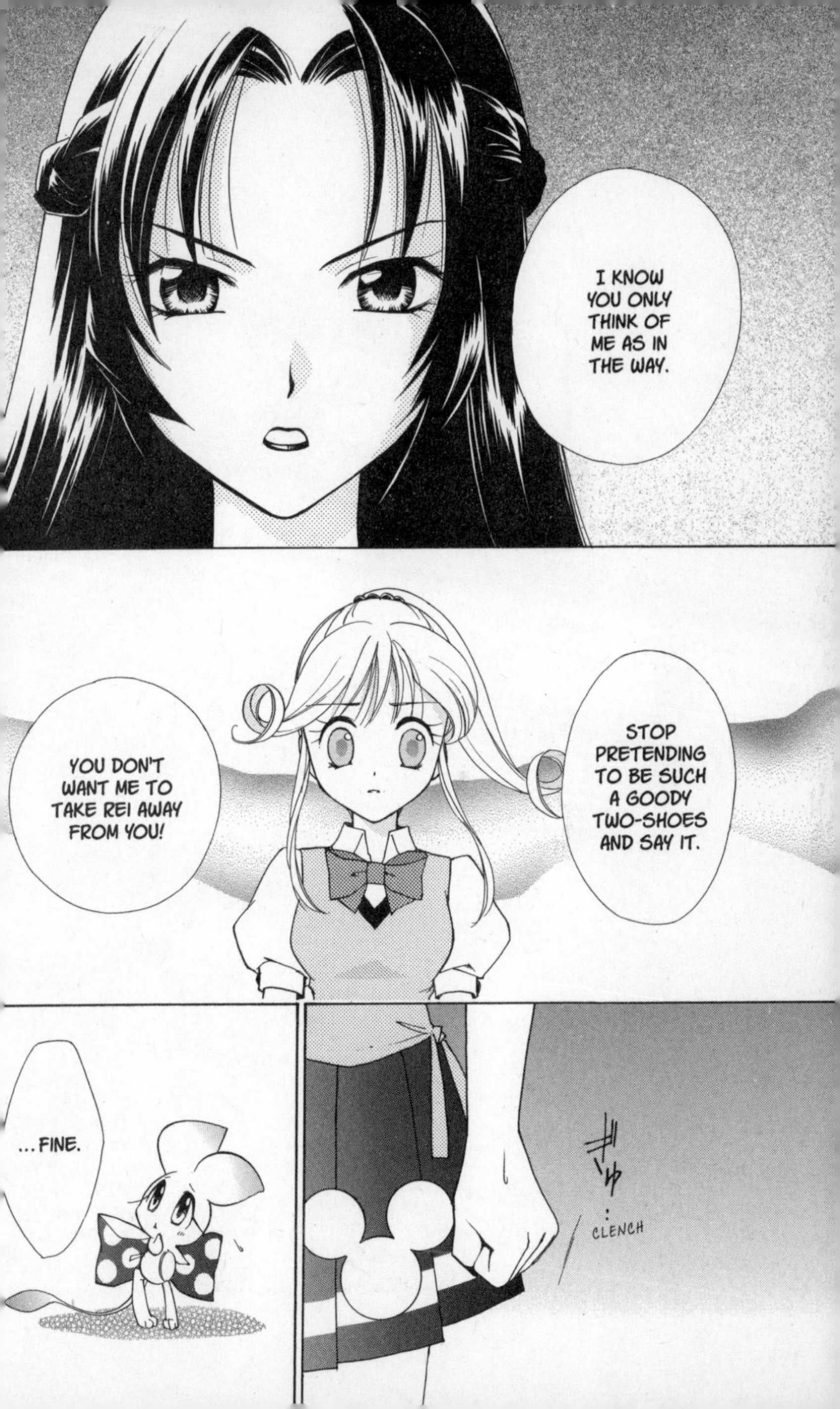
I KNOW YOU ONLY THINK OF ME AS IN THE WAY.
STOP PRETENDING TO BE SUCH A GOODY TWO-SHOES AND SAY IT.
YOU DON'T WANT ME TO TAKE REI AWAY FROM YOU!
CLENCH
...FINE.

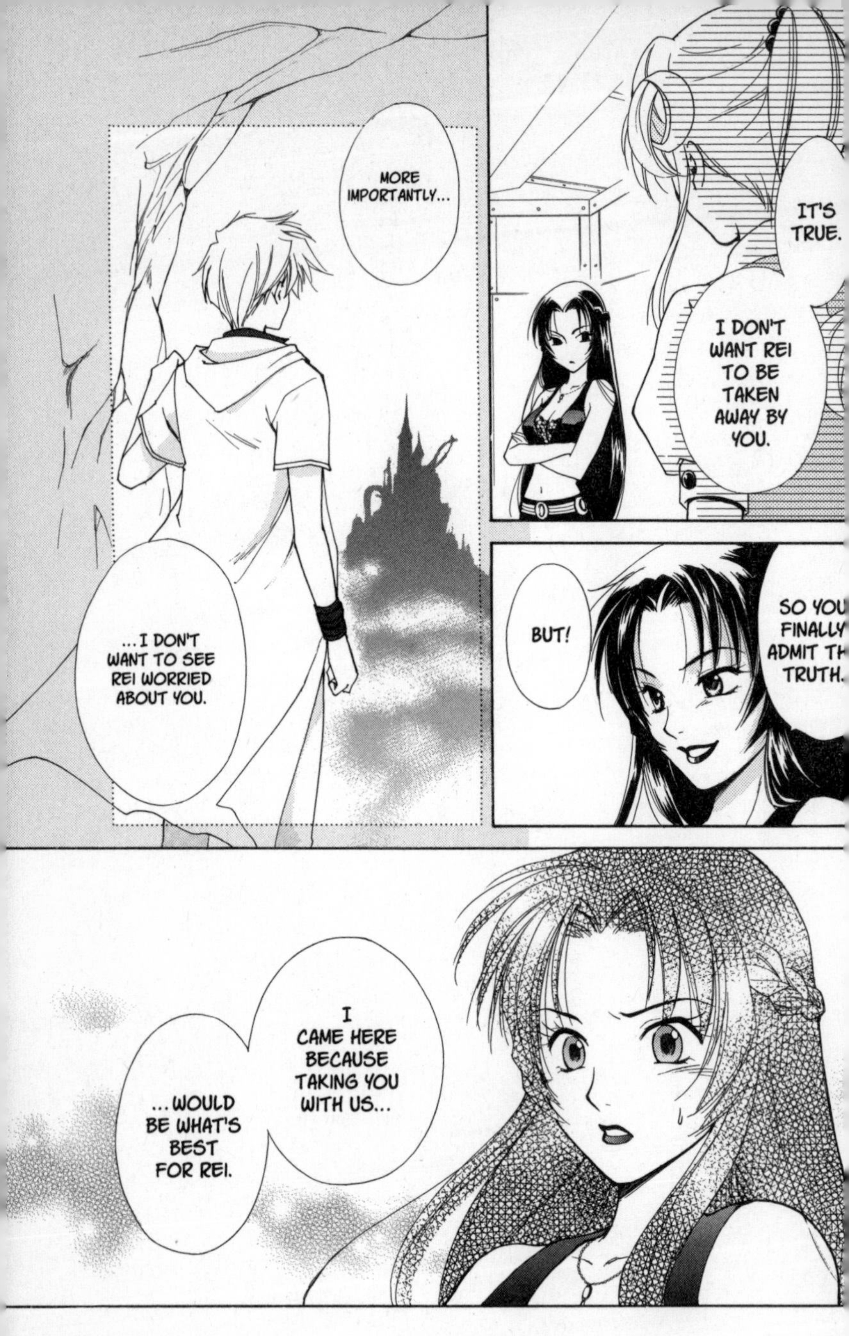
IT'S TRUE.
I DON'T WANT REI TO BE TAKEN AWAY BY YOU.
SO YOU FINALLY ADMIT TH TRUTH.
BUT!
MORE IMPORTANTLY...
...I DON'T WANT TO SEE REI WORRIED ABOUT YOU.
I CAME HERE BECAUSE TAKING YOU WITH US...
...WOULD BE WHAT'S BEST FOR REI.

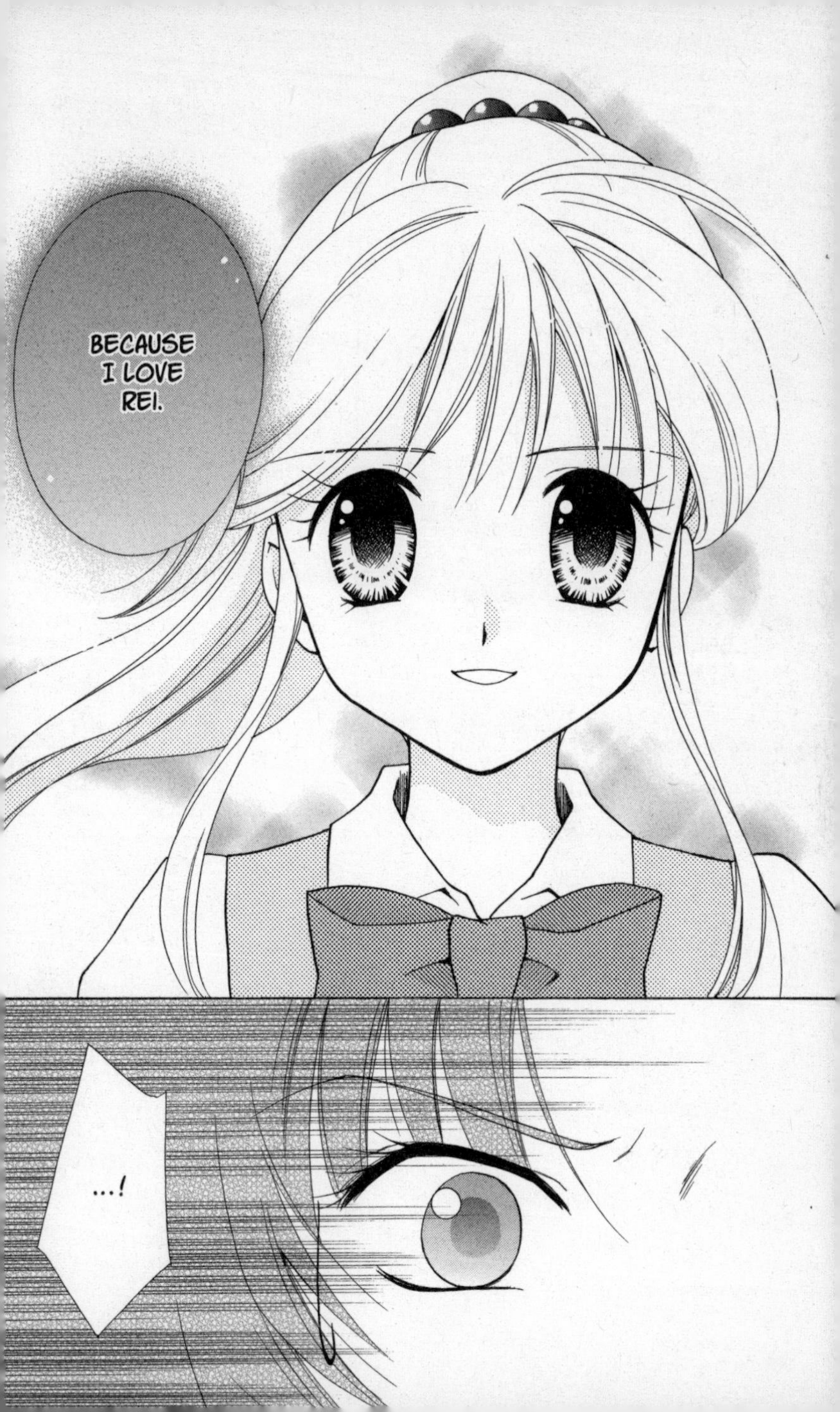
BECAUSE I LOVE REI.
...!

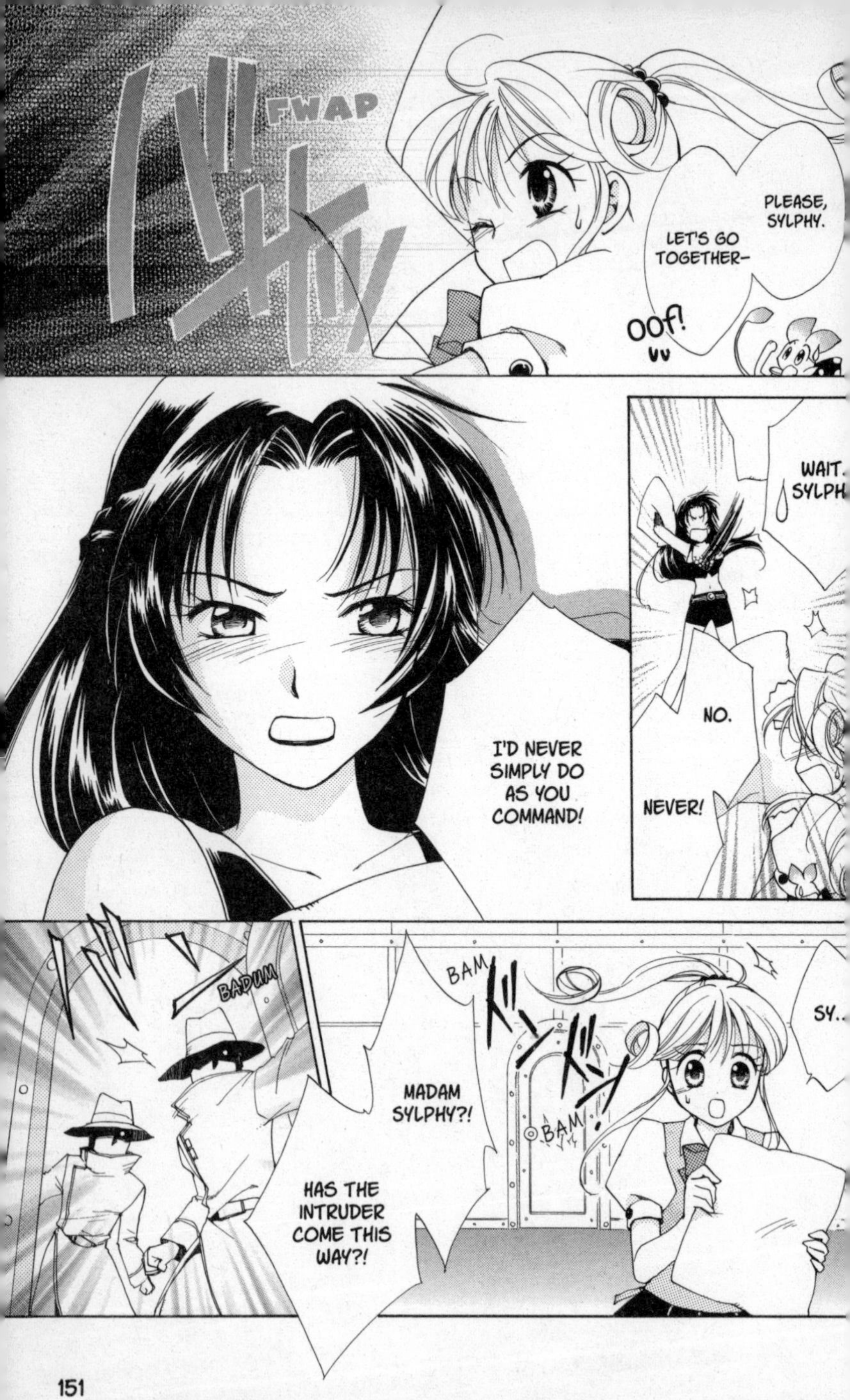
FWAP
PLEASE, SYLPHY.
LET'S GO TOGETHER–
OOF!
WAIT. SYLPH
NO.
NEVER!
I'D NEVER SIMPLY DO AS YOU COMMAND!
SY...
BAM
BAM
MADAM SYLPHY?!
HAS THE INTRUDER COME THIS WAY?!
BADUM

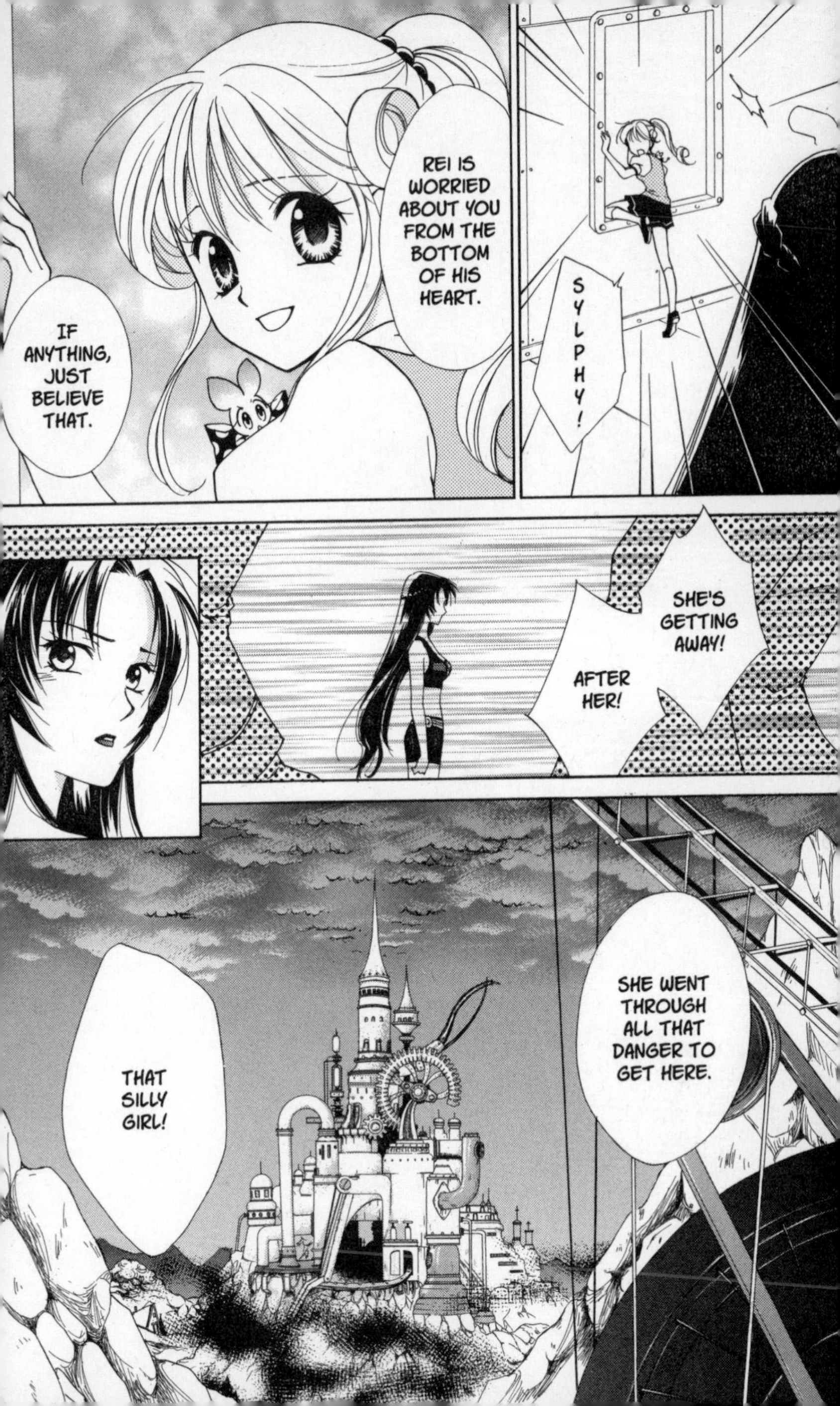
SYLPHY!
REI IS WORRIED ABOUT YOU FROM THE BOTTOM OF HIS HEART.
IF ANYTHING, JUST BELIEVE THAT.
SHE'S GETTING AWAY!
AFTER HER!
SHE WENT THROUGH ALL THAT DANGER TO GET HERE.
THAT SILLY GIRL!

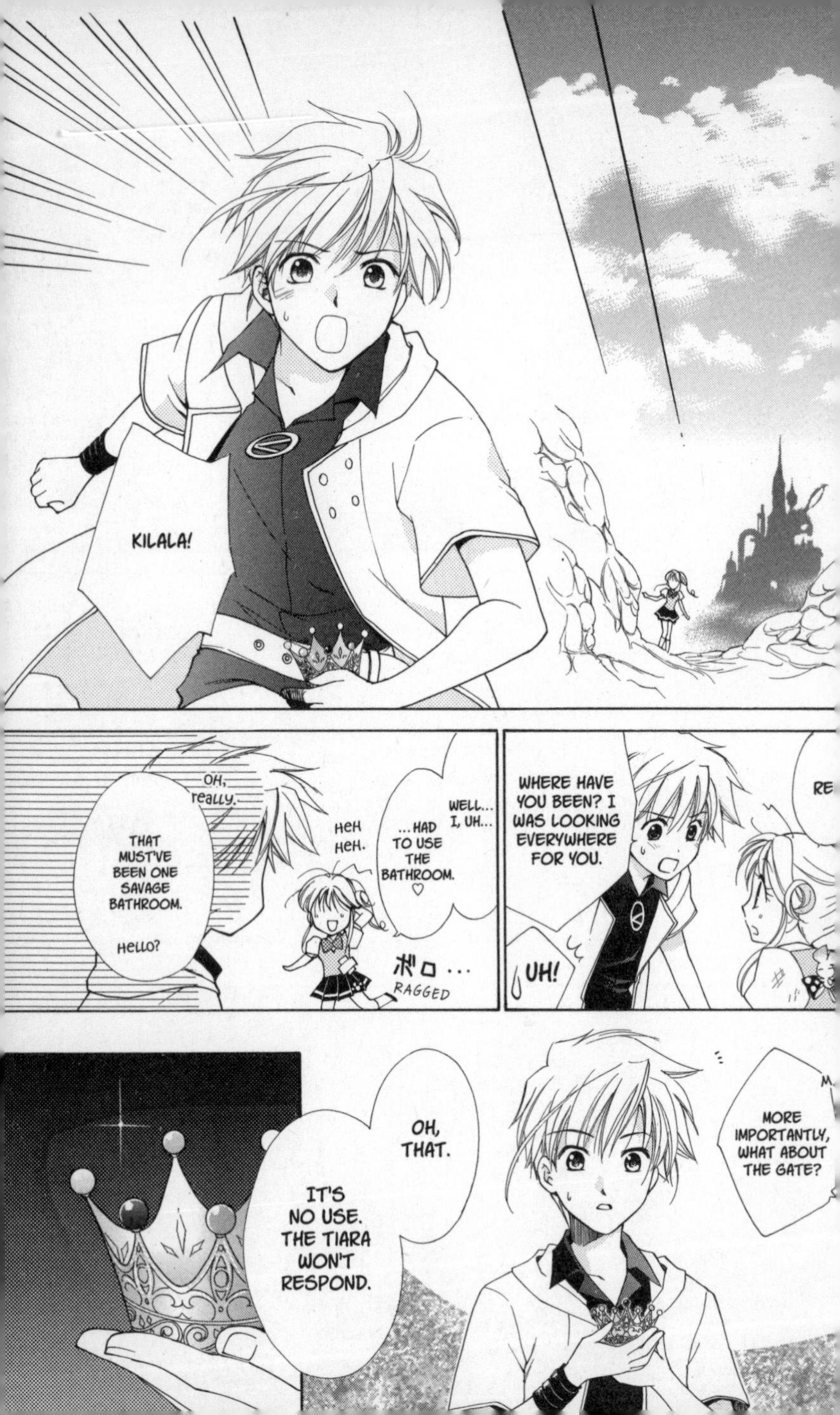
KILALA!
WHERE HAVE YOU BEEN? I WAS LOOKING EVERYWHERE FOR YOU.
UH!
WELL... I, UH...
...HAD TO USE THE BATHROOM. ♡
HEH HEH.
ボロ... RAGGED
OH, really.
THAT MUST'VE BEEN ONE SAVAGE BATHROOM.
HELLO?
MORE IMPORTANTLY, WHAT ABOUT THE GATE?
OH, THAT.
IT'S NO USE. THE TIARA WON'T RESPOND.

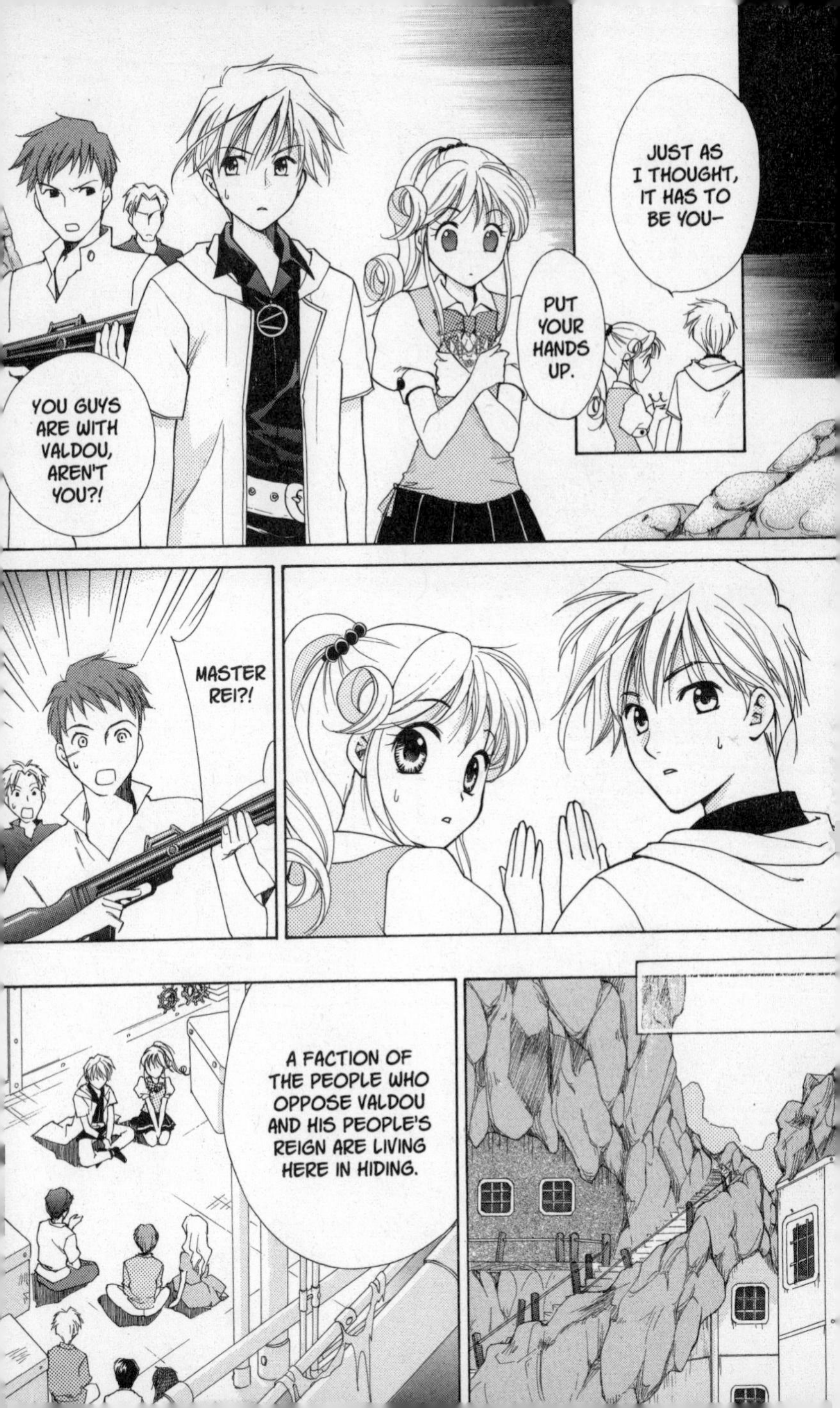
JUST AS I THOUGHT, IT HAS TO BE YOU–
PUT YOUR HANDS UP.
YOU GUYS ARE WITH VALDOU, AREN'T YOU?!
MASTER REI?!
A FACTION OF THE PEOPLE WHO OPPOSE VALDOU AND HIS PEOPLE'S REIGN ARE LIVING HERE IN HIDING.

READ THIS WAY

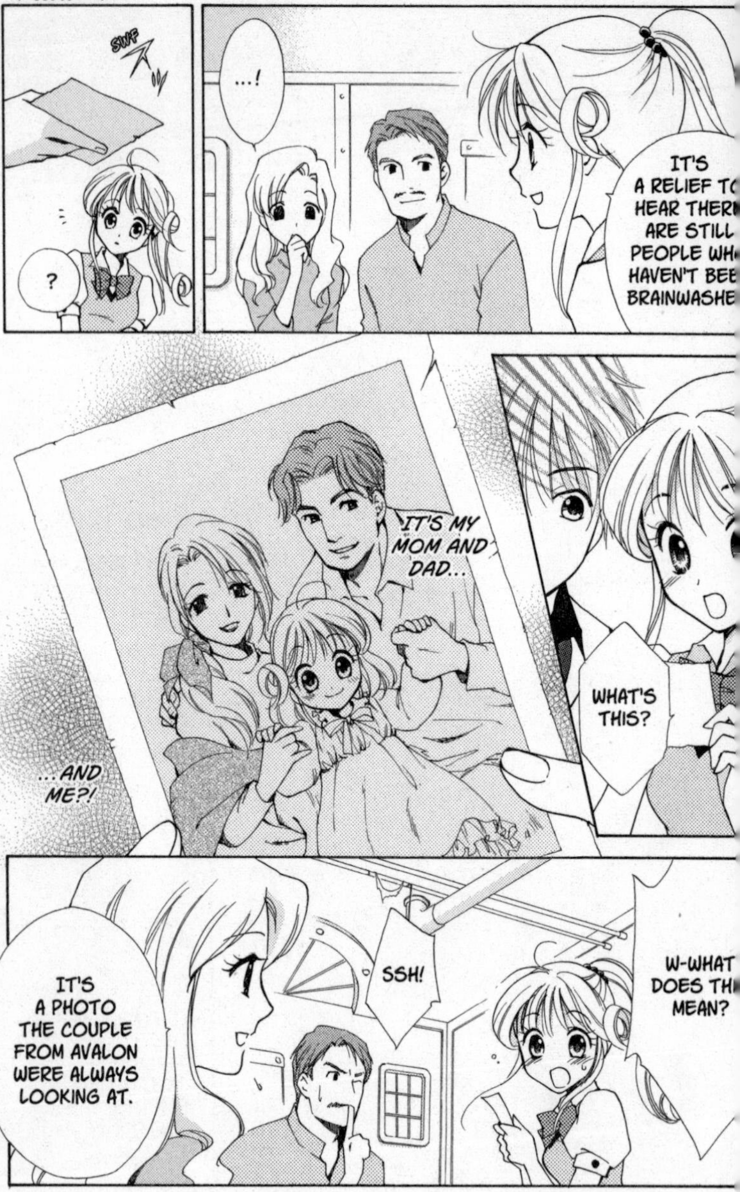

IT'S A RELIEF TO HEAR THERE ARE STILL PEOPLE WHO HAVEN'T BEEN BRAINWASHED
...!
SWF
?
WHAT'S THIS?
IT'S MY MOM AND DAD...
...AND ME?!
W-WHAT DOES THIS MEAN?
SSH!
IT'S A PHOTO THE COUPLE FROM AVALON WERE ALWAYS LOOKING AT.

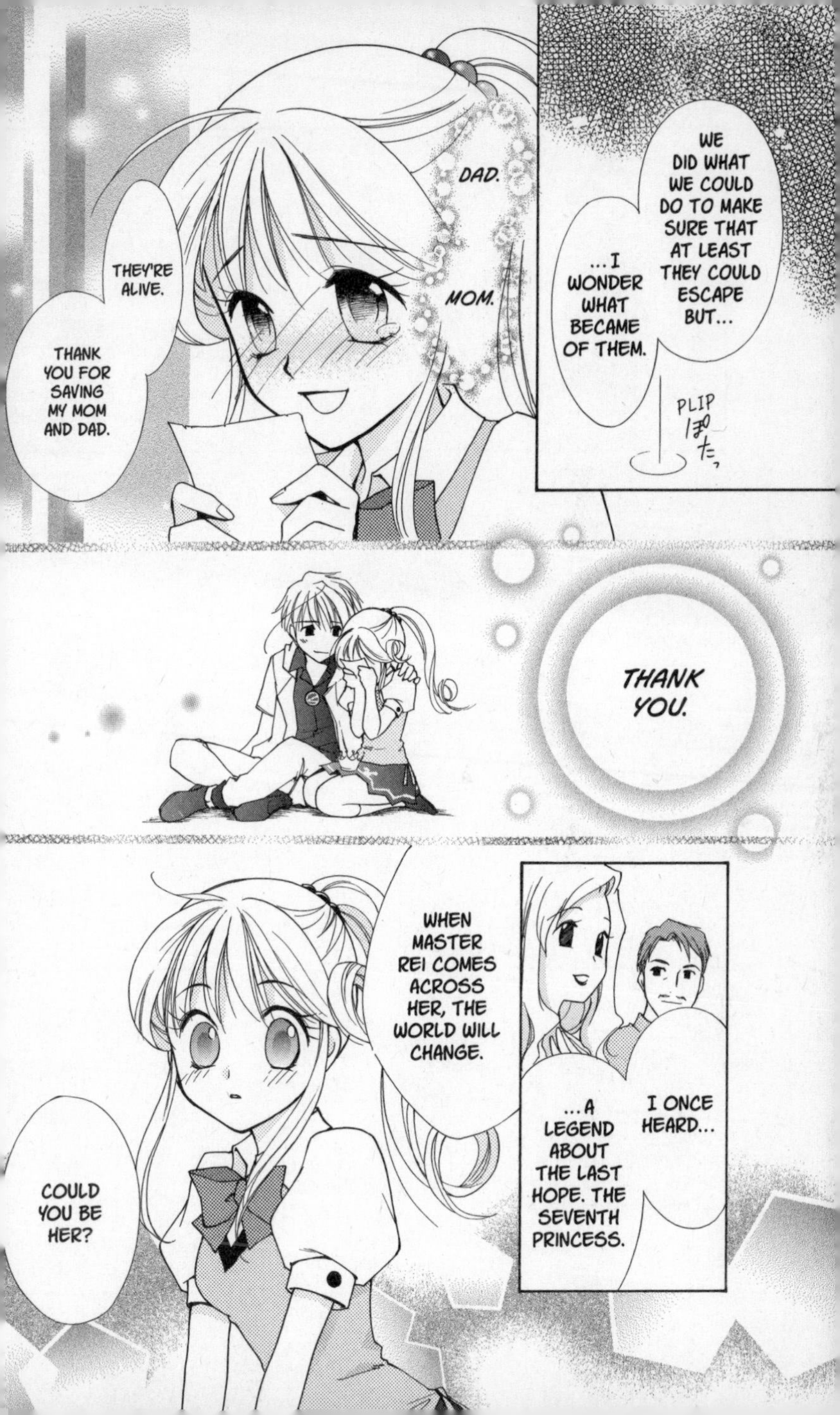
WE DID WHAT WE COULD DO TO MAKE SURE THAT AT LEAST THEY COULD ESCAPE BUT...
...I WONDER WHAT BECAME OF THEM.
PLIP
ぽたっ
DAD.
MOM.
THEY'RE ALIVE.
THANK YOU FOR SAVING MY MOM AND DAD.
THANK YOU.
I ONCE HEARD...
...A LEGEND ABOUT THE LAST HOPE. THE SEVENTH PRINCESS.
WHEN MASTER REI COMES ACROSS HER, THE WORLD WILL CHANGE.
COULD YOU BE HER?

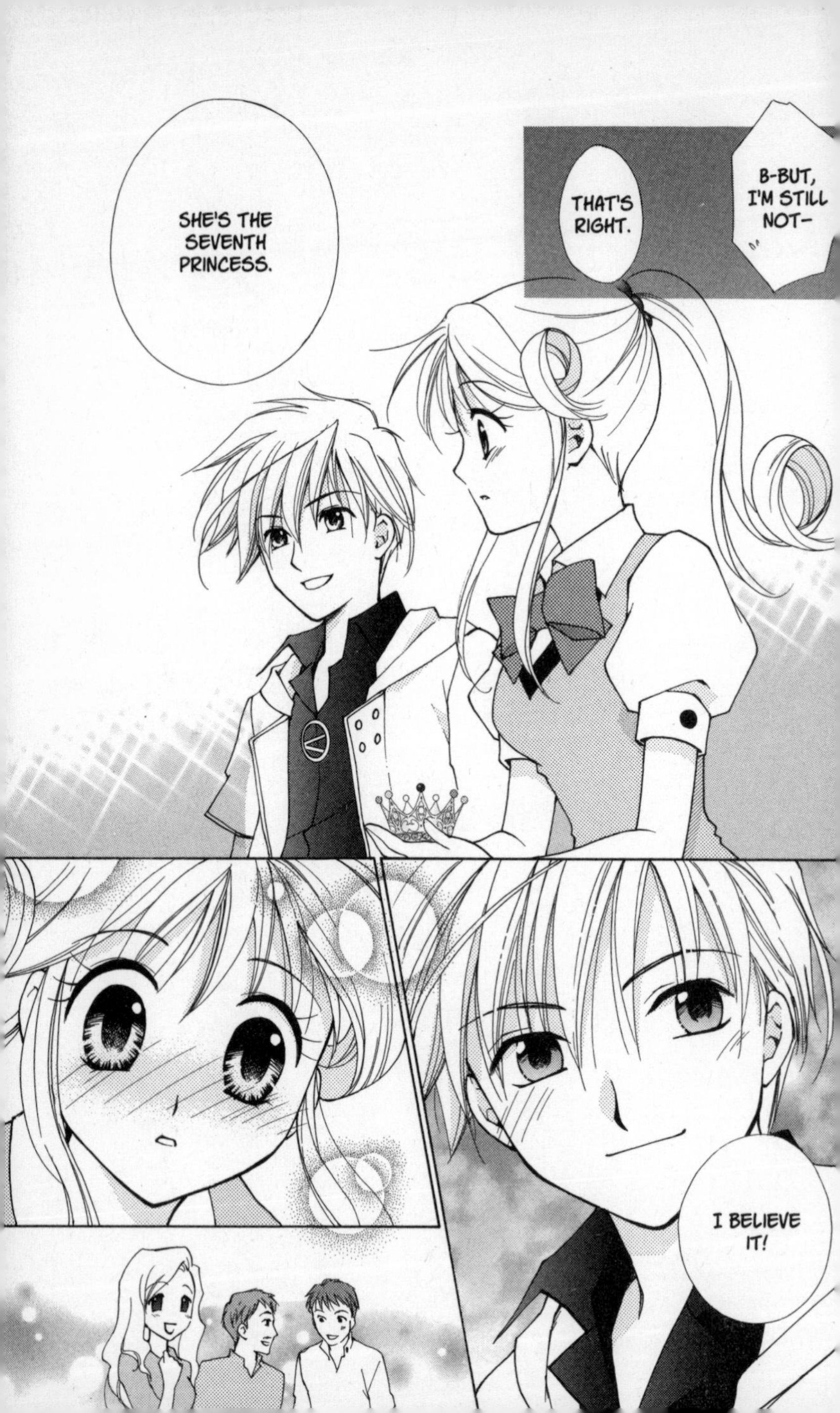
B-BUT, I'M STILL NOT-
THAT'S RIGHT.
SHE'S THE SEVENTH PRINCESS.
I BELIEVE IT!

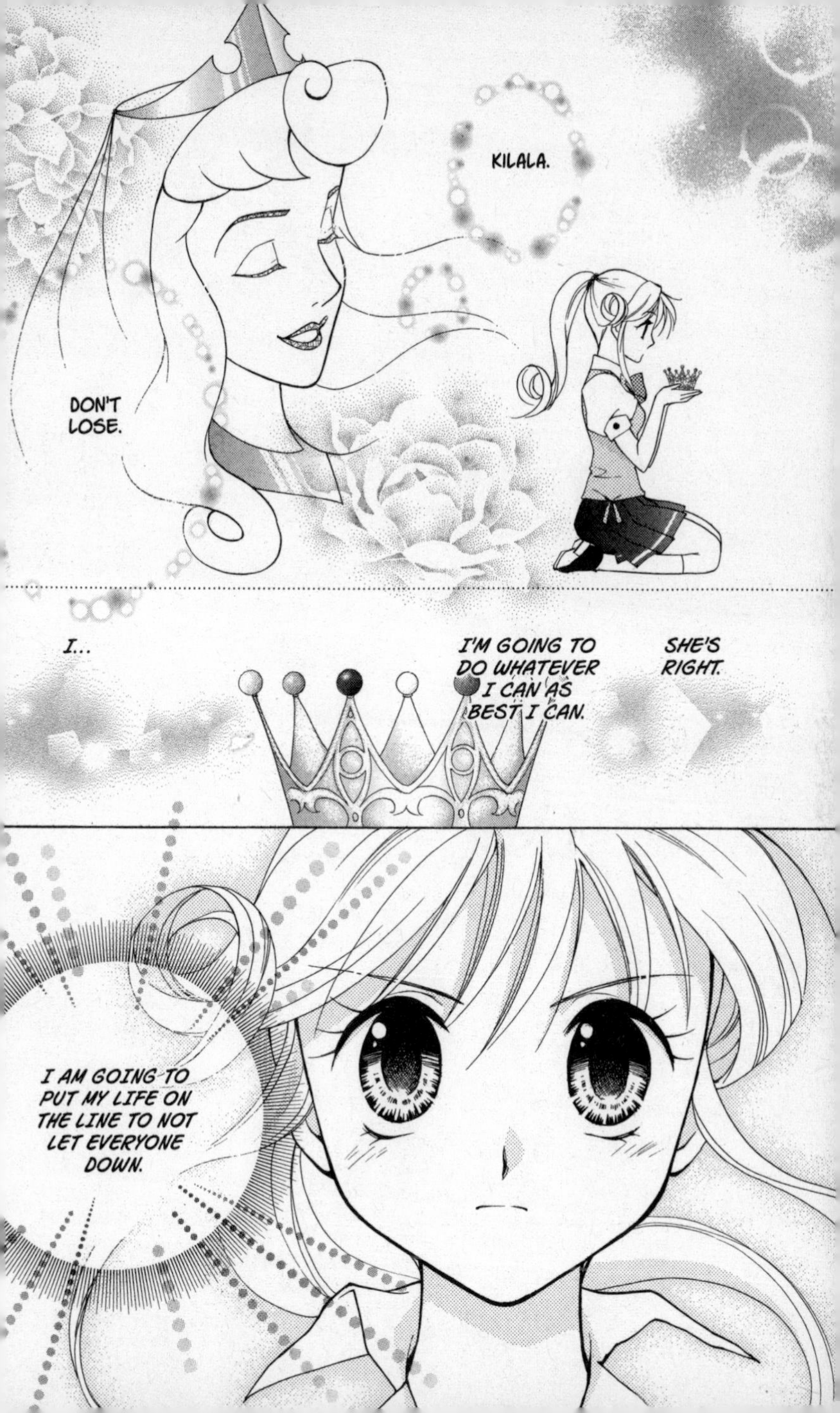
KILALA.
DON'T LOSE.
SHE'S RIGHT.
I'M GOING TO DO WHATEVER I CAN AS BEST I CAN.
I...
I AM GOING TO PUT MY LIFE ON THE LINE TO NOT LET EVERYONE DOWN.

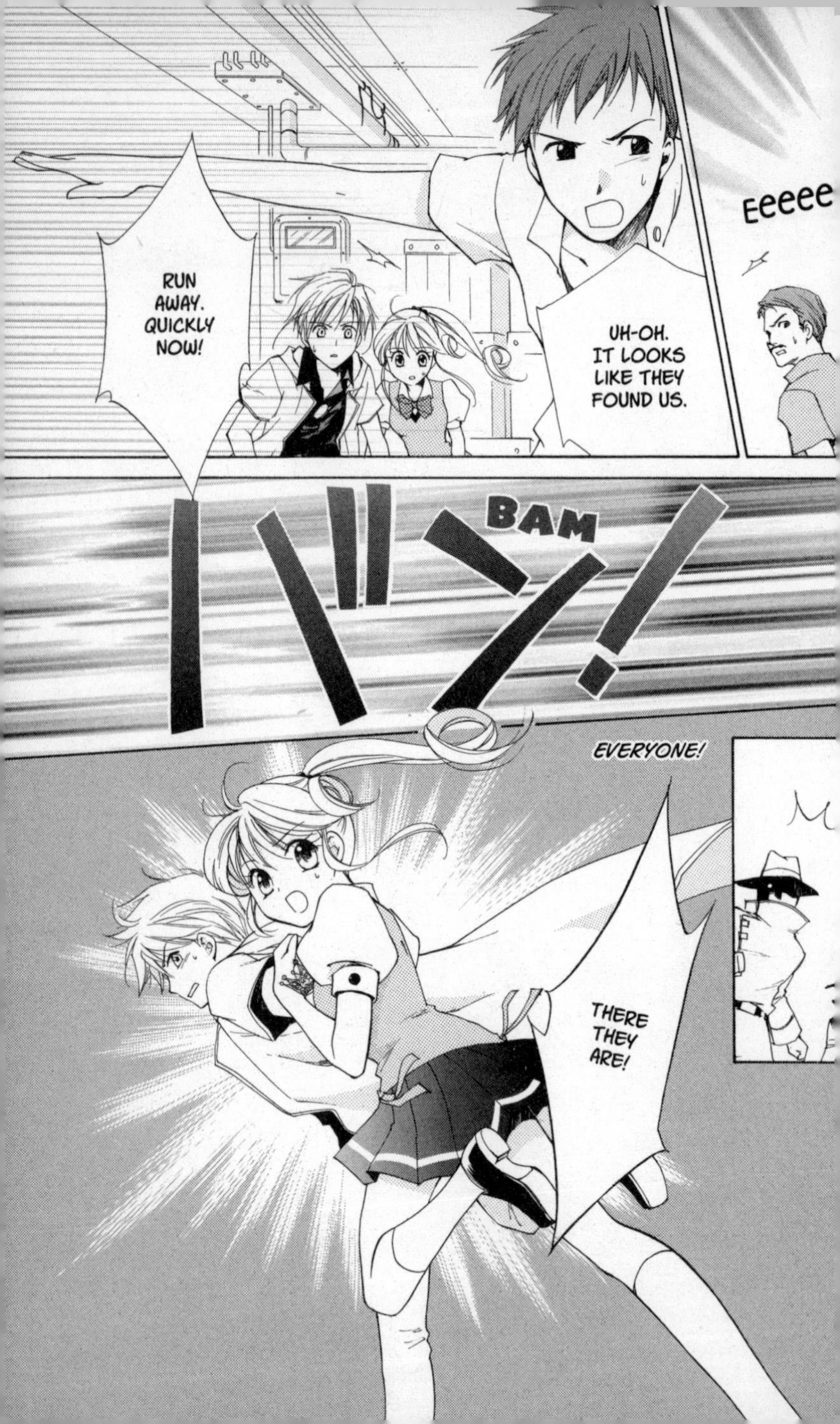
Eeeee
UH-OH. IT LOOKS LIKE THEY FOUND US.
RUN AWAY. QUICKLY NOW!
BAM
EVERYONE!
THERE THEY ARE!

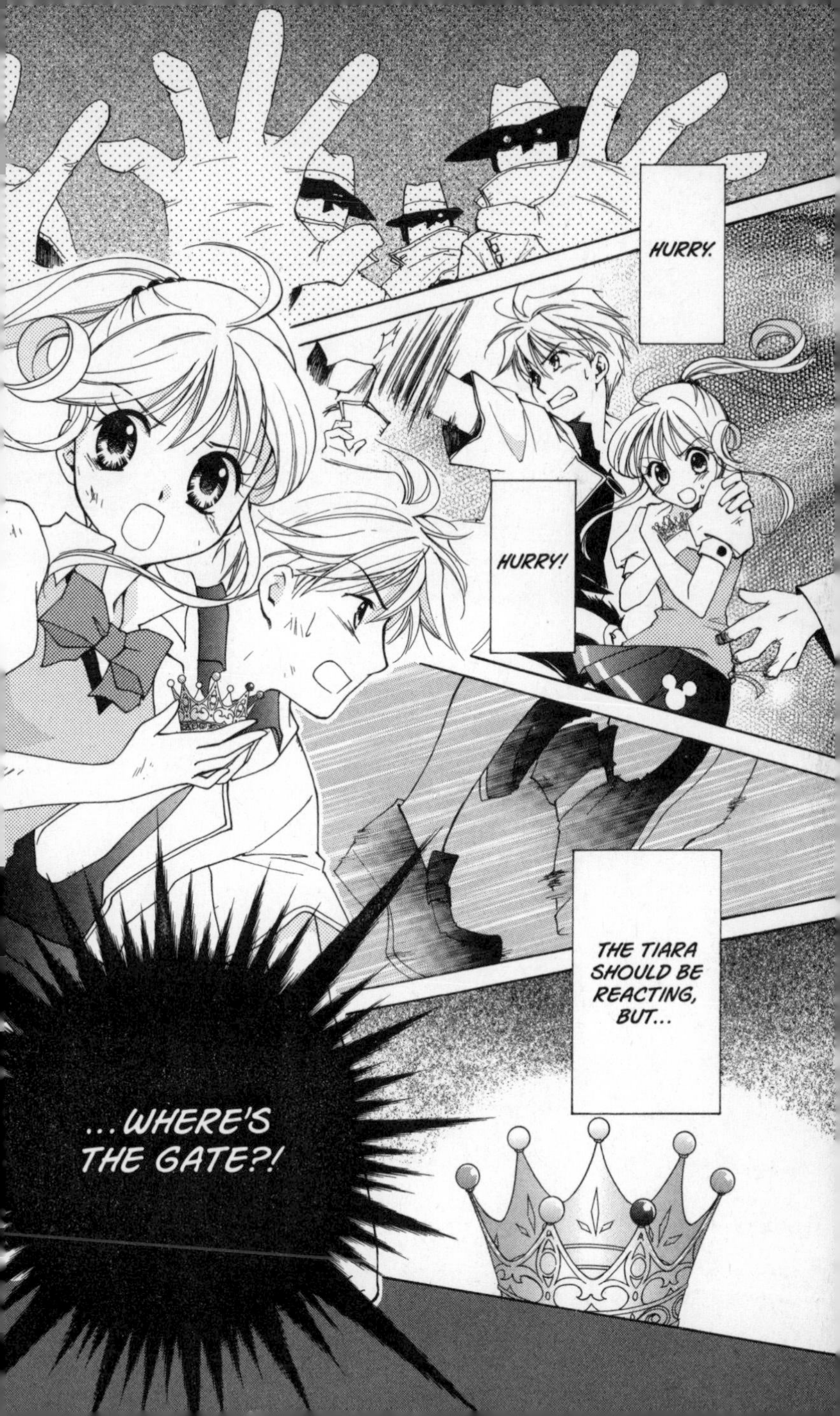
HURRY.
HURRY!
THE TIARA SHOULD BE REACTING, BUT...
...WHERE'S THE GATE?!

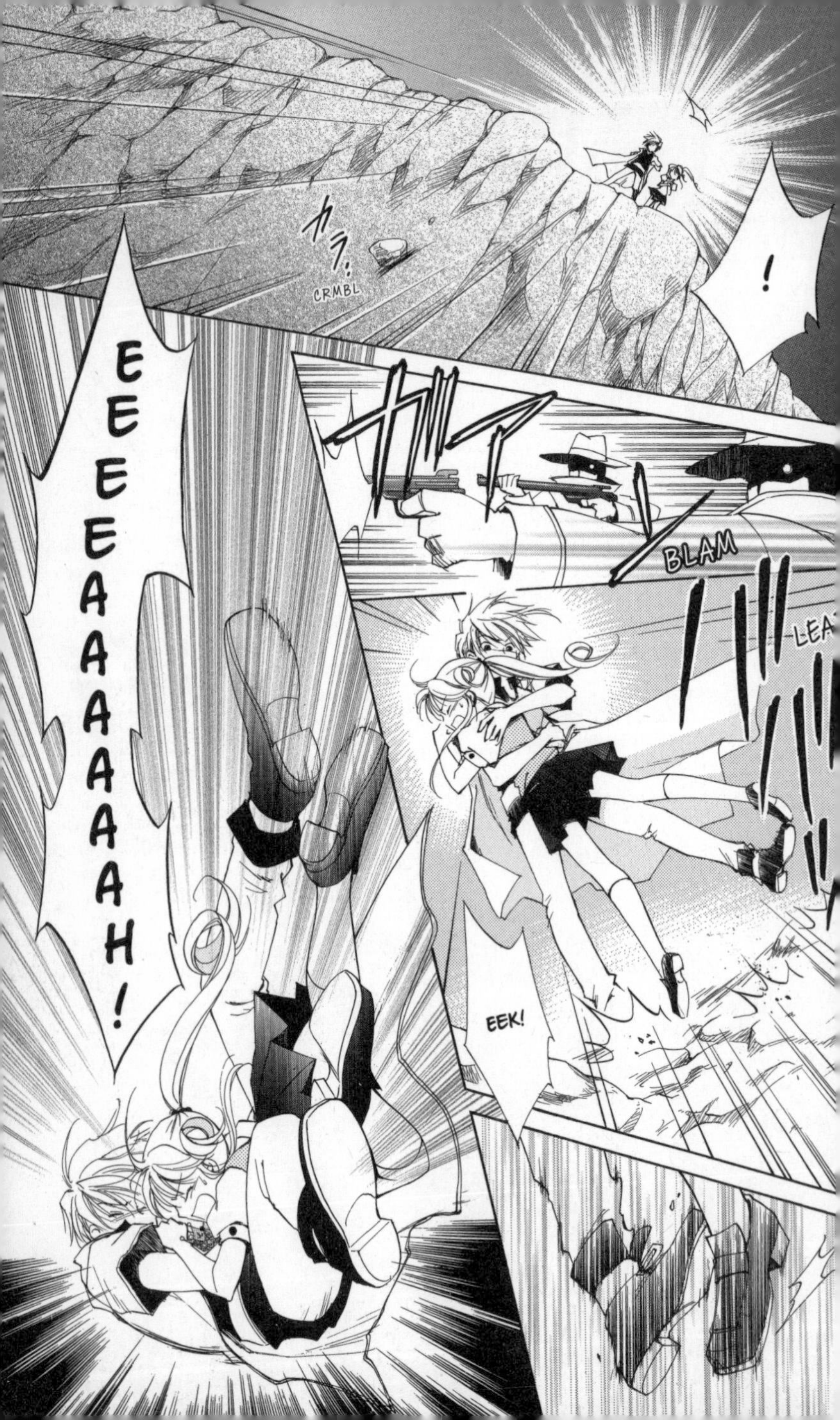
!
CRMBL
BLAM
LEA
EEK!
EEEEAAAAAAH!

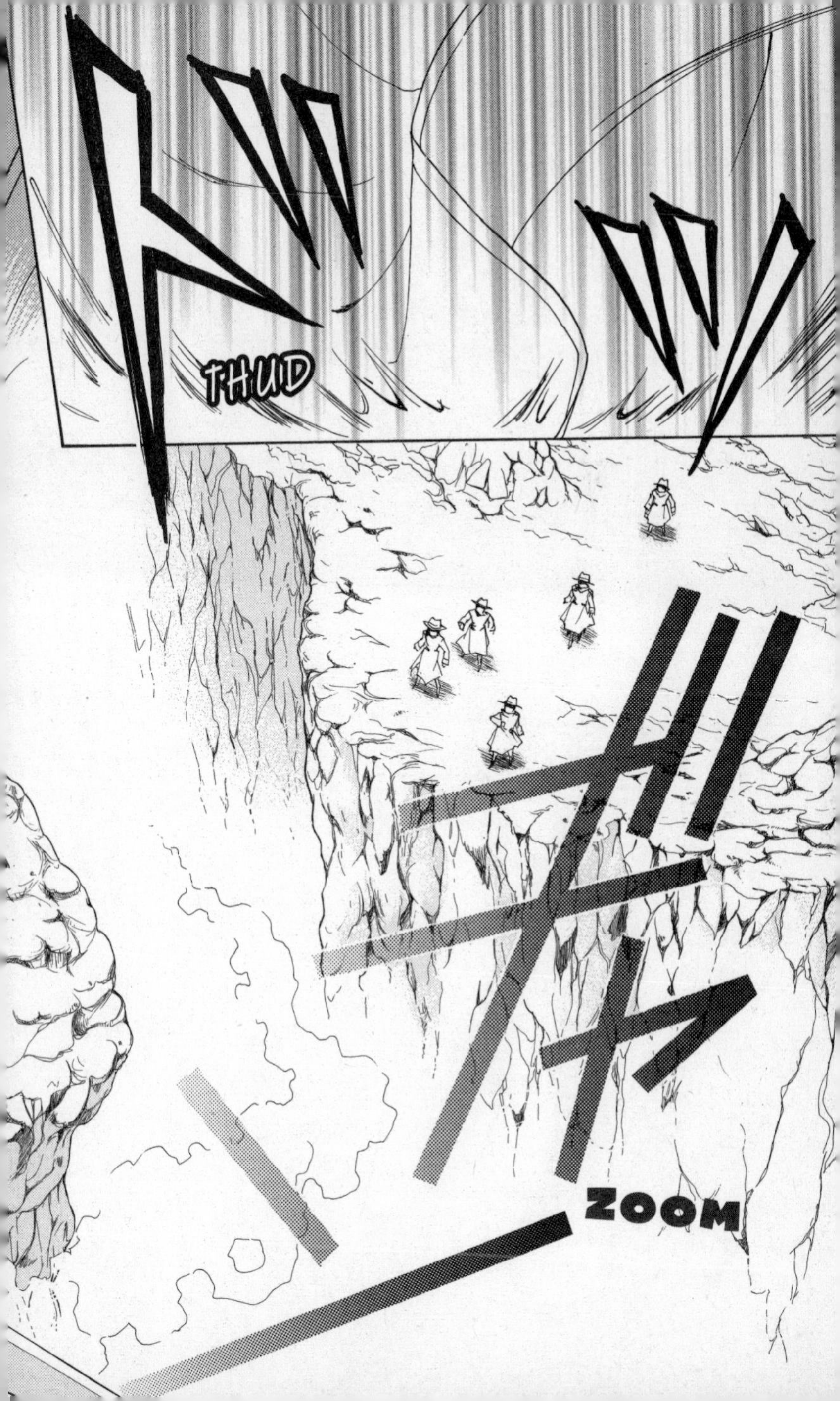
THUD
ZOOM

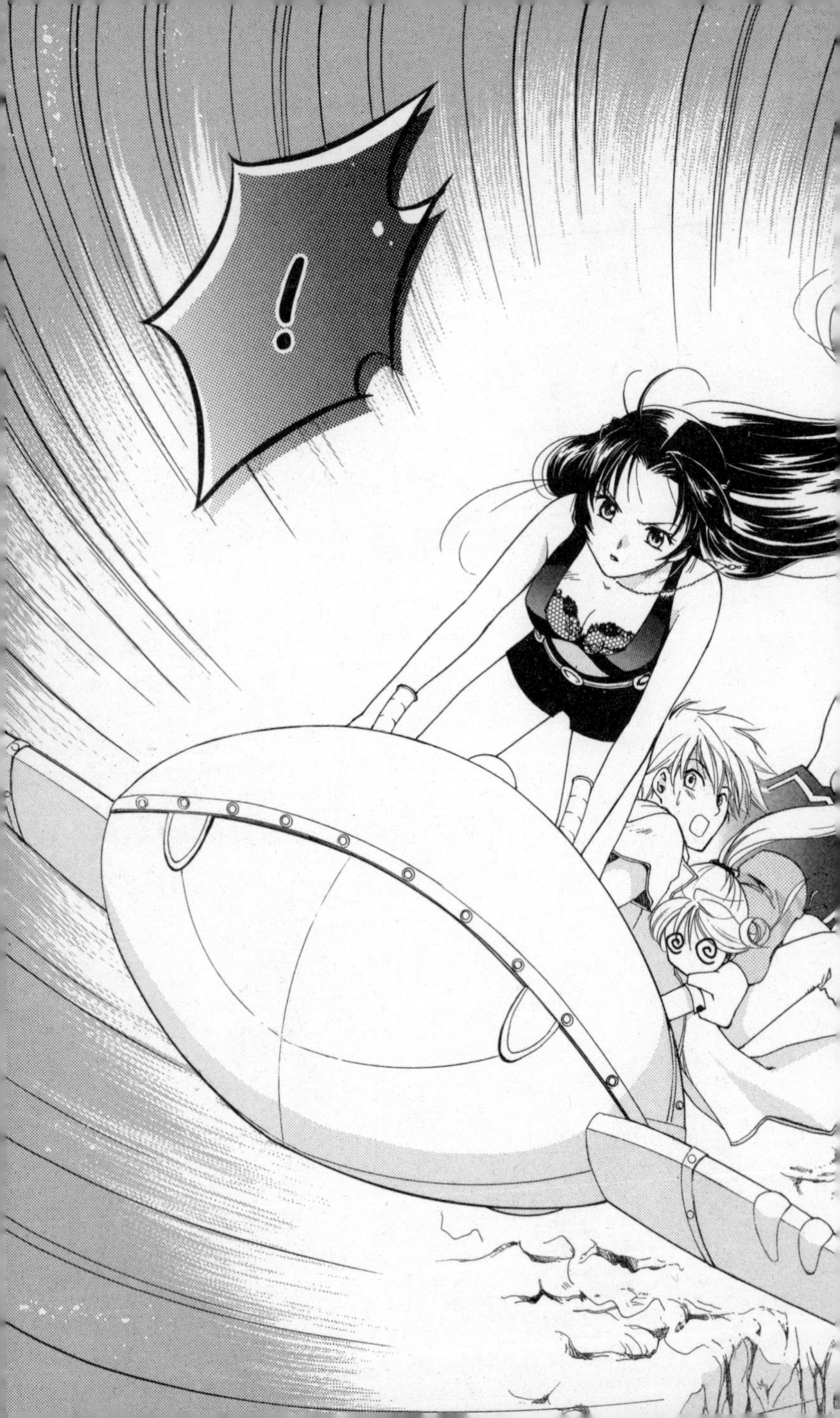
!

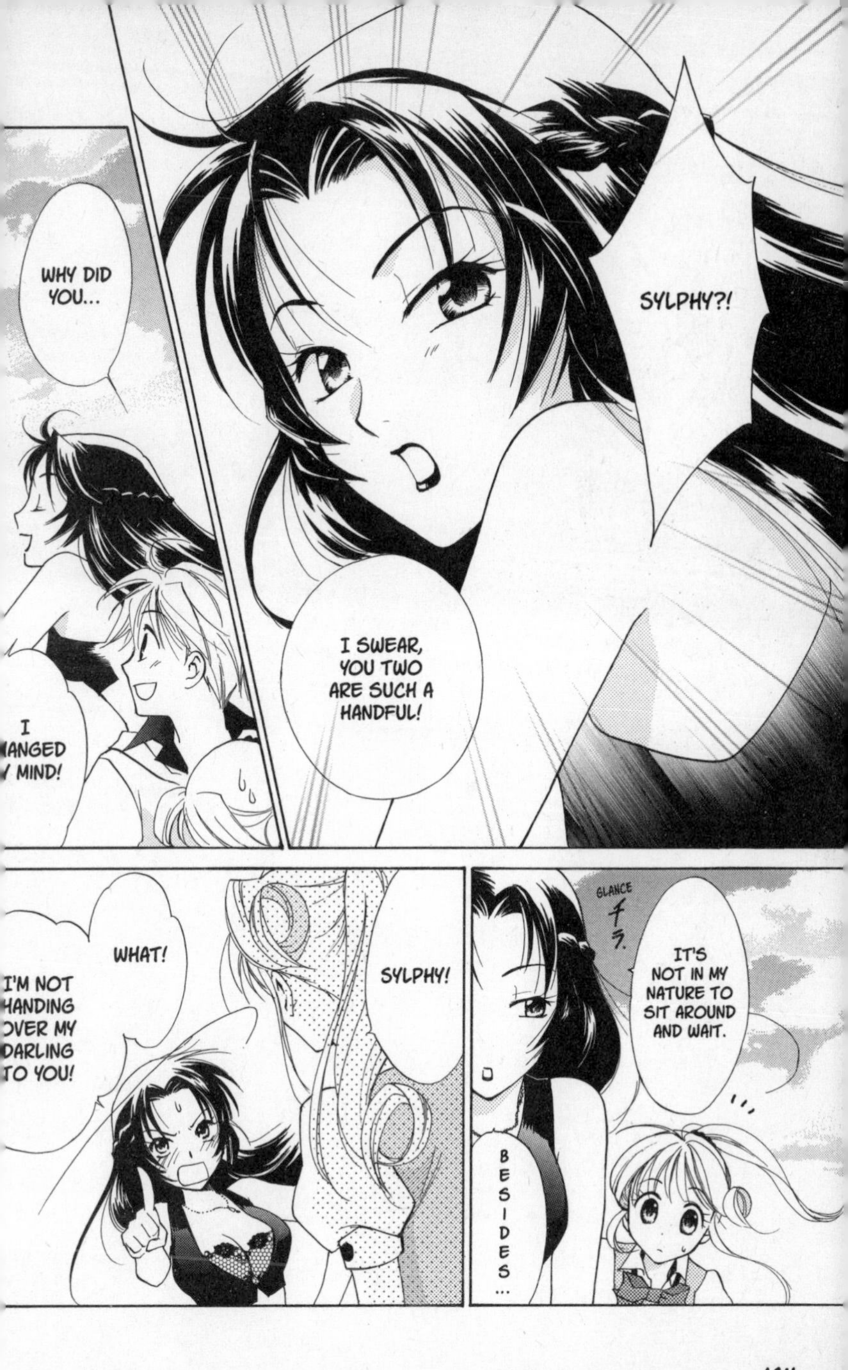
SYLPHY?!
I SWEAR, YOU TWO ARE SUCH A HANDFUL!
WHY DID YOU...
I ANGED MIND!
GLANCE
チラ
IT'S NOT IN MY NATURE TO SIT AROUND AND WAIT.
BESIDES...
SYLPHY!
WHAT!
I'M NOT HANDING OVER MY DARLING TO YOU!

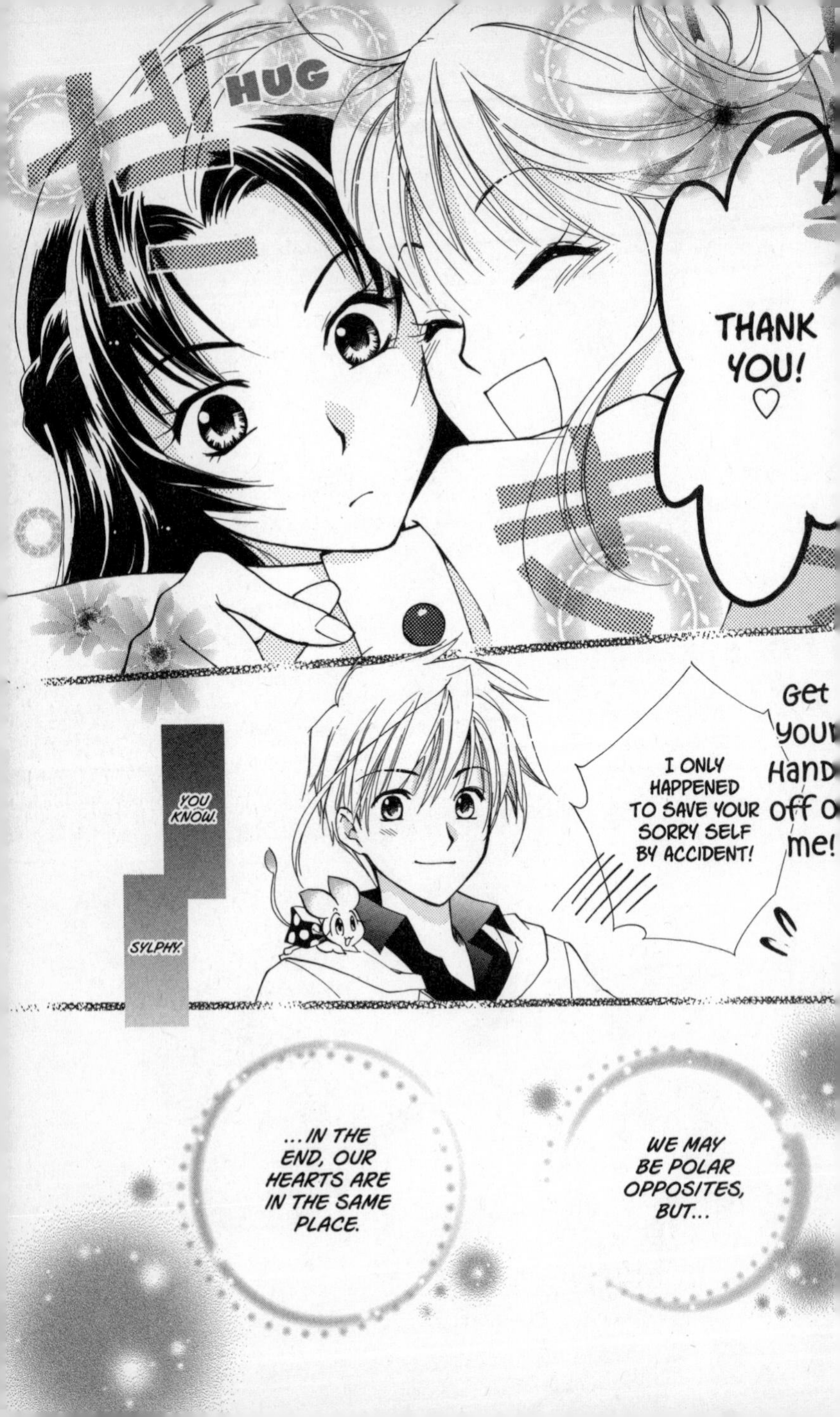
HUG
THANK YOU! ♡
Get your Hand off o me!
I ONLY HAPPENED TO SAVE YOUR SORRY SELF BY ACCIDENT!
YOU KNOW.
SYLPHY.
WE MAY BE POLAR OPPOSITES, BUT...
...IN THE END, OUR HEARTS ARE IN THE SAME PLACE.

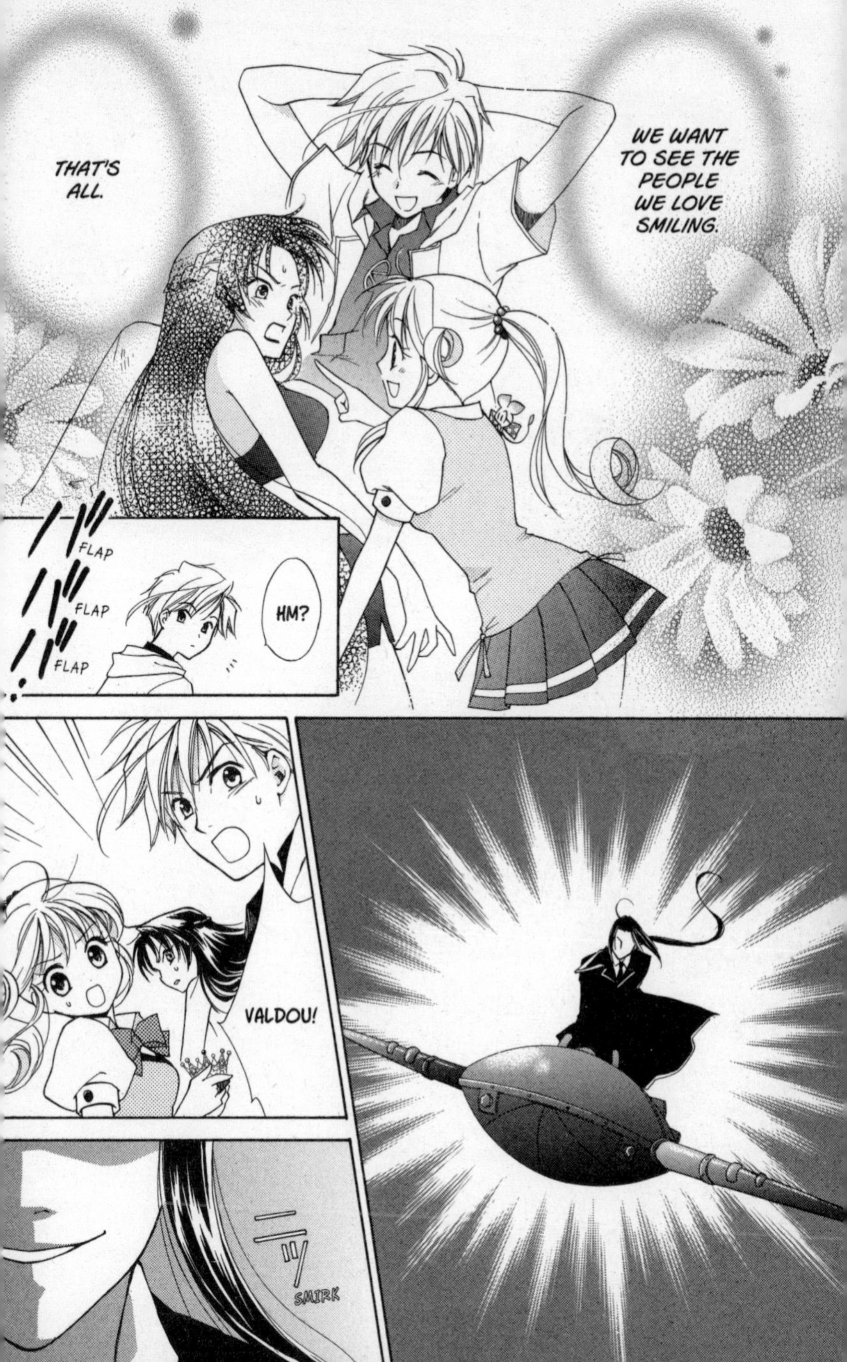
WE WANT TO SEE THE PEOPLE WE LOVE SMILING.
THAT'S ALL.
HM?
FLAP
FLAP
FLAP
VALDOU!
SMIRK

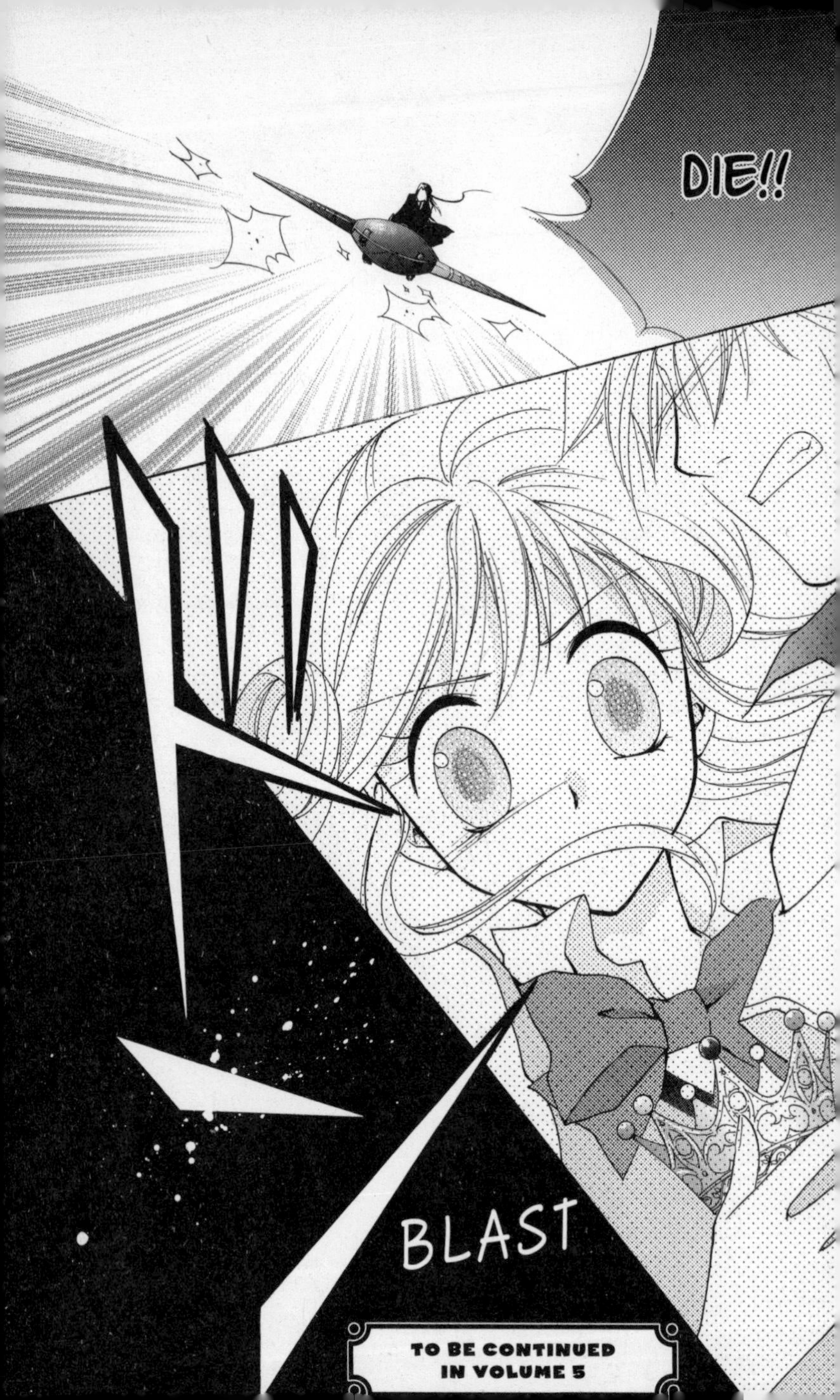
DIE!!
BLAST
TO BE CONTINUED IN VOLUME 5

IN THE NEXT VOLUME OF

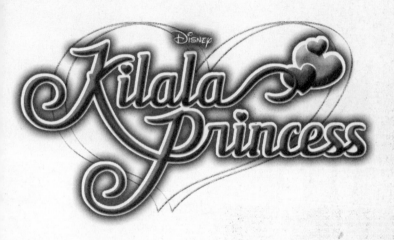

Kilala and Rei take a magic carpet ride into the world of Aladdin and Princess Jasmine to locate the sixth gem of the tiara. They're soon captured by guards and must plot their escape. Then the Genie's lamp falls into the wrong hands, and another woman tries to put Rei under her spell. Meanwhile, the search for the gem intensifies. Will Kilala be able to rescue Paradiso and live happily ever after?

**JOIN KILALA AND THE DISNEY
PRINCESSES FOR MORE
ADVENTURES IN VOLUME 5.**

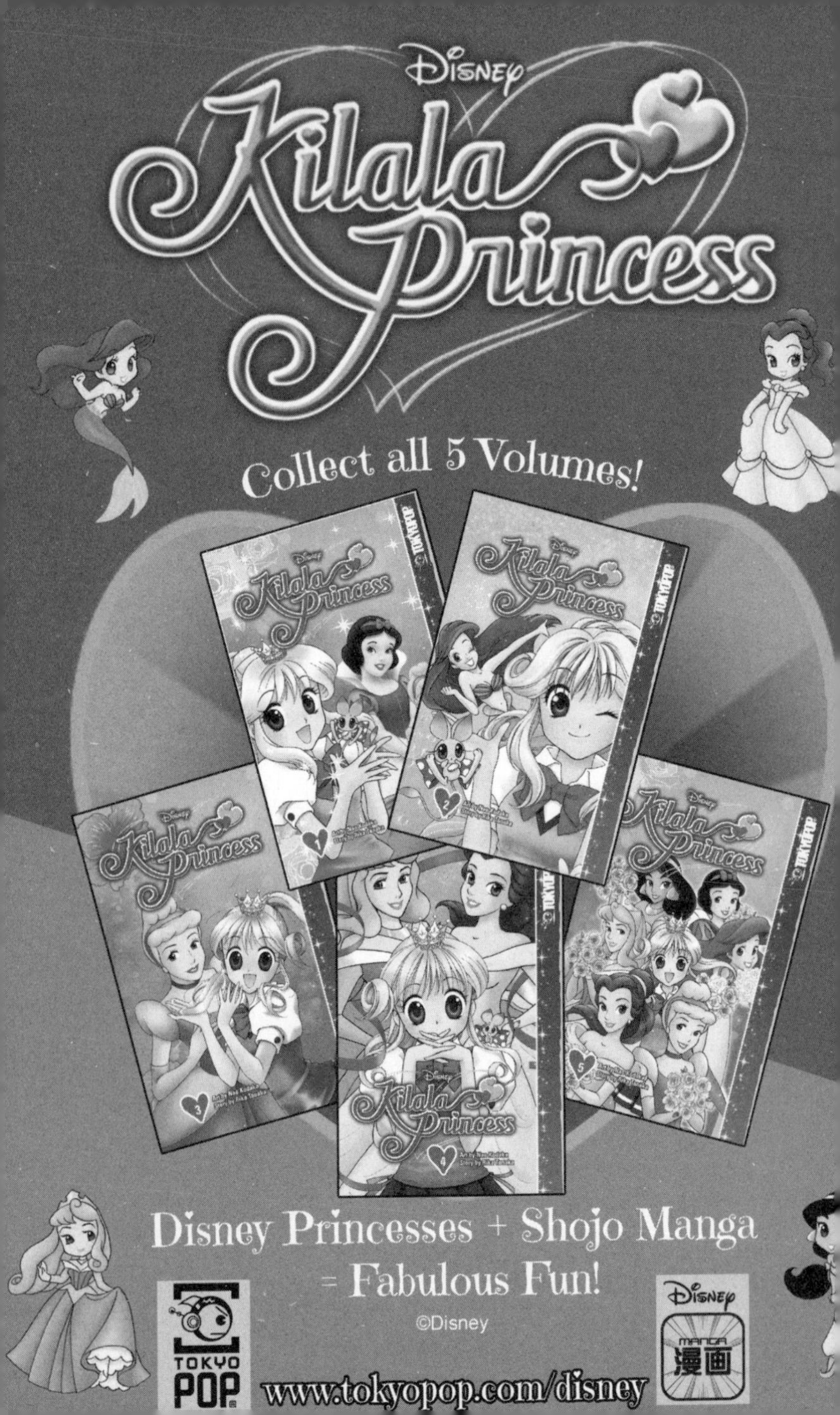
Disney
Kilala Princess
Collect all 5 Volumes!
Disney Princesses + Shojo Manga
= Fabulous Fun!
©Disney
TOKYO POP
www.tokyopop.com/disney
Disney
MANGA
漫画

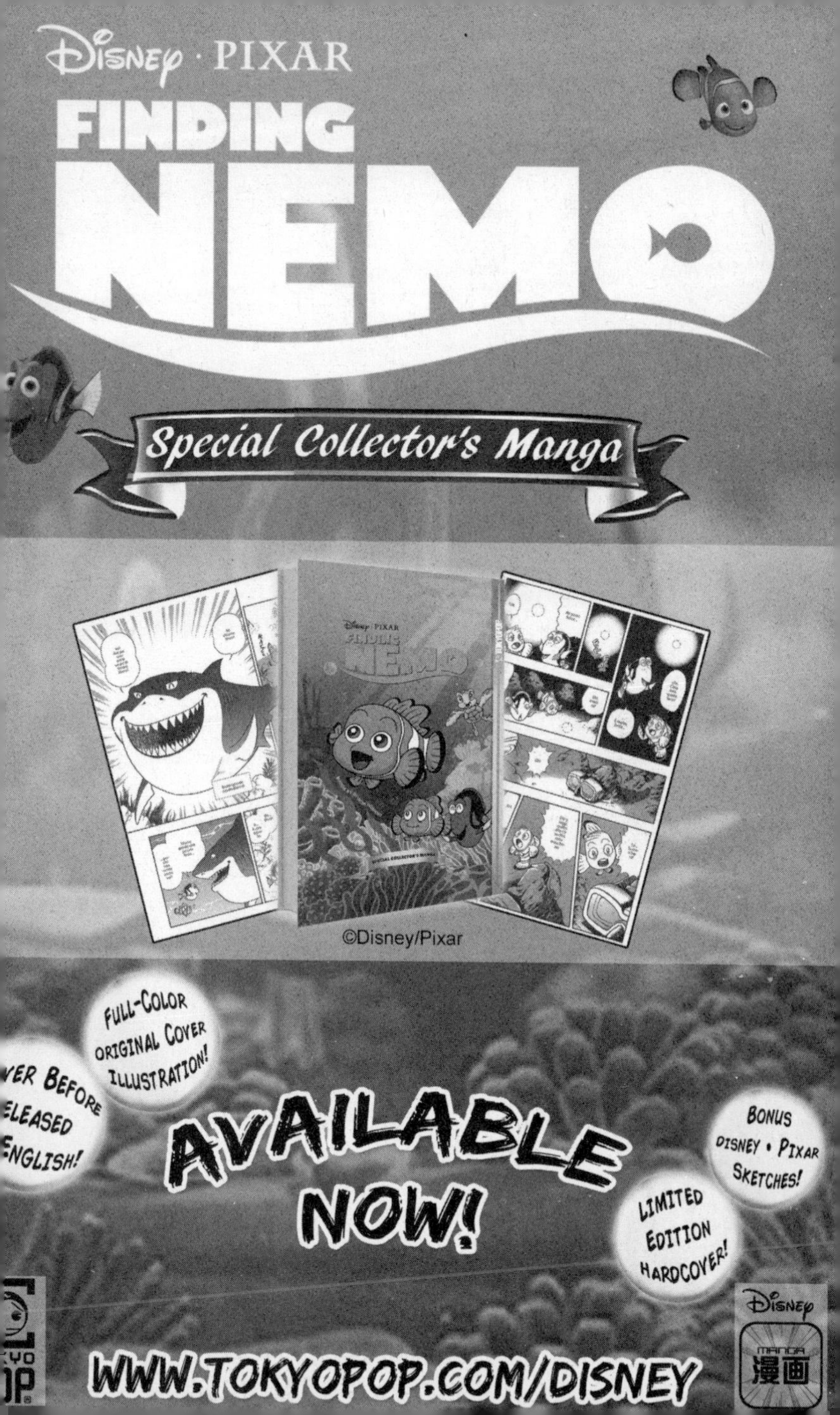
Disney · PIXAR
FINDING NEMO
Special Collector's Manga
©Disney/Pixar
FULL-COLOR ORIGINAL COVER ILLUSTRATION!
VER BEFORE ELEASED NGLISH!
AVAILABLE NOW!
BONUS DISNEY • PIXAR SKETCHES!
LIMITED EDITION HARDCOVER!
WWW.TOKYOPOP.COM/DISNEY
Disney
MANGA 漫画

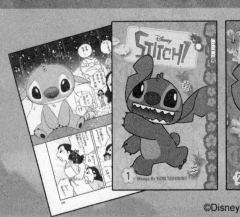
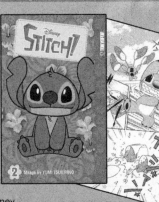
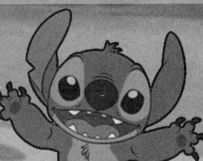

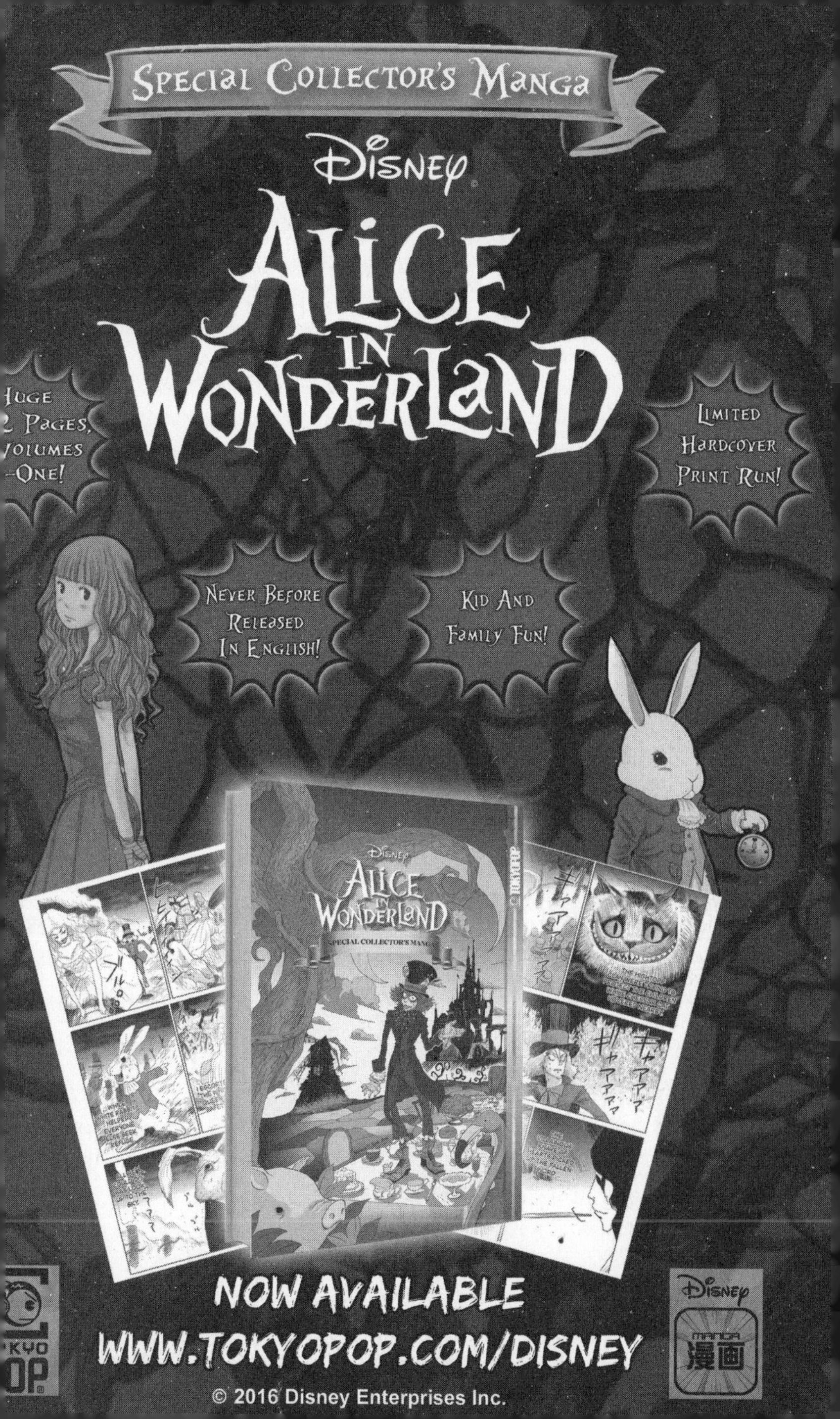
Special Collector's Manga
Disney
Alice in Wonderland
uge
2 Pages,
olumes
-One!
Limited Hardcover Print Run!
Never Before Released In English!
Kid And Family Fun!
Now Available
www.tokyopop.com/disney
© 2016 Disney Enterprises Inc.

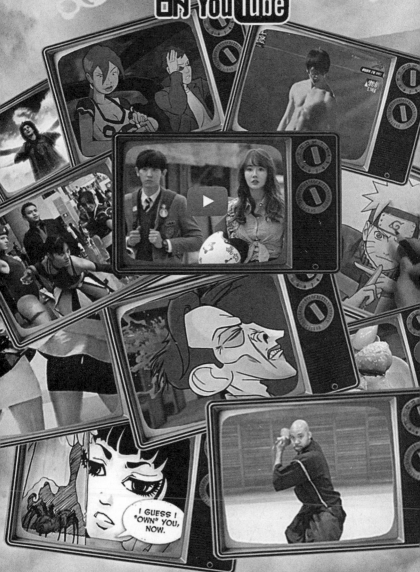

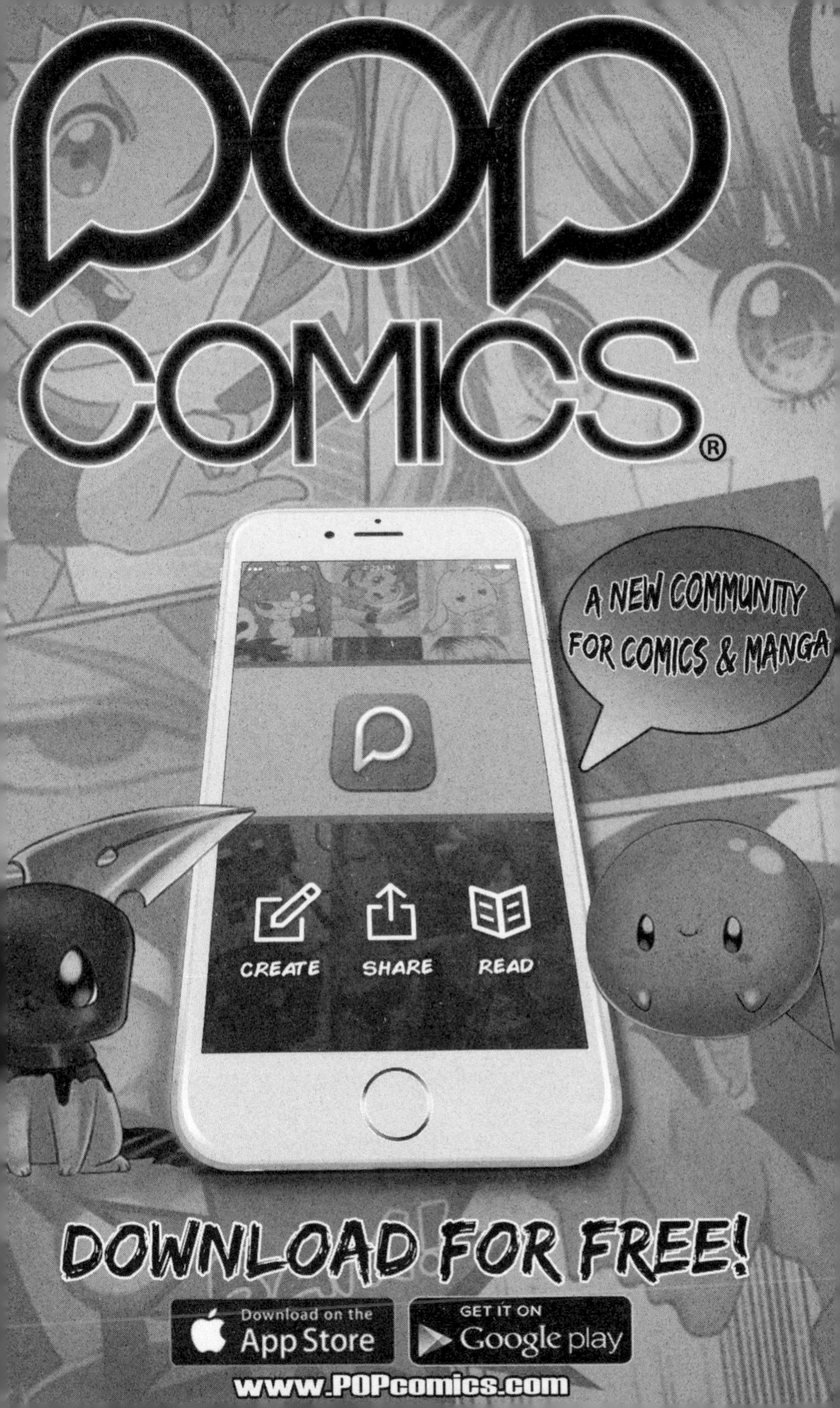
POP COMICS®
A NEW COMMUNITY FOR COMICS & MANGA
CREATE
SHARE
READ
DOWNLOAD FOR FREE!
Download on the App Store
GET IT ON Google play
www.POPcomics.com

Disney Kilala Princess
Story by Rika Tanaka
Art by Nao Kodaka

Publishing Assistant - Janae Young
Marketing Assistant - Kae Winters
Technology and Digital Media Assistant - Phillip Hong
Retouching and Lettering - Vibrraant Publishing Studio
English Adaptation - Christine Dashiell
Graphic Designer - Al-insan Lashley
Editor - Julie Taylor
Editor-in-Chief & Publisher - Stu Levy

A 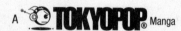 Manga

TOKYOPOP and ⓒ are trademarks or registered trademarks of TOKYOPOP Inc.

TOKYOPOP inc.
5200 W Century Blvd
Suite 705
Los Angeles, CA 90045 USA

E-mail: info@TOKYOPOP.com
Come visit us online at www.TOKYOPOP.com

f www.facebook.com/TOKYOPOP
🐦 www.twitter.com/TOKYOPOP
▶ www.youtube.com/TOKYOPOPTV
📌 www.pinterest.com/TOKYOPOP
📷 www.instagram.com/TOKYOPOP
t. TOKYOPOP.tumblr.com

ISBN: 978-1-4278-5667-8

First TOKYOPOP Printing February 2017
10 9 8 7 6 5 4 3 2 1
Printed in the USA

STO

THIS IS THE BACK OF THE BOOK!

How do you read manga-style? It's simple! To learn,
just start in the top right panel and follow the numbers:

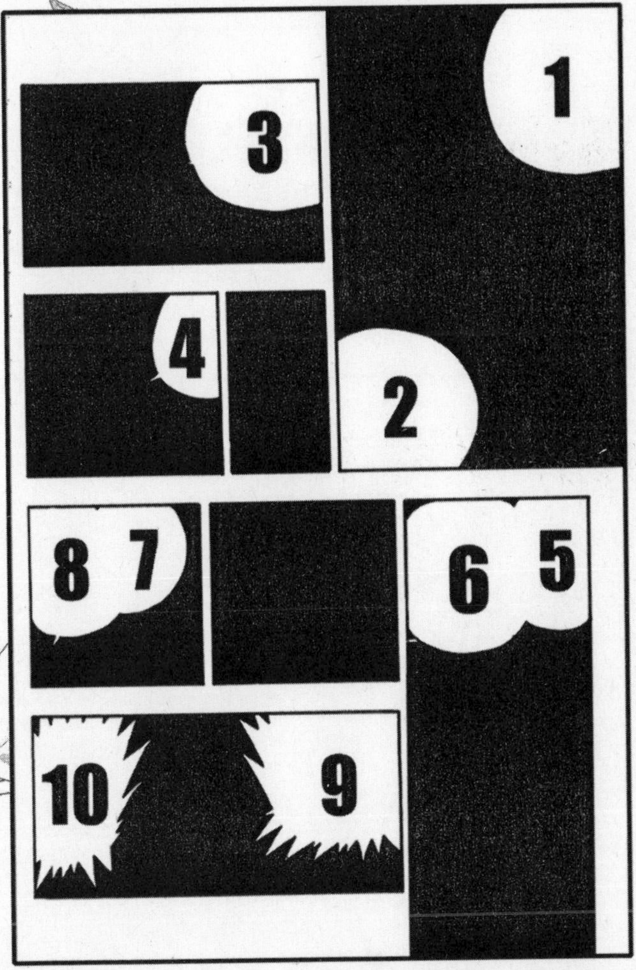
1
2
3
4
5
6
7
8
9
10